The Biggest Bounty

Päm,
Grab some
milk and
strap in
for a
thrill
ride!

The Biggest Bounty
A Zeus and the Pink Flower Novel
by
Brian Koscienski and Chris Pisano

© 2017

This is a work of fiction. All the characters and events portrayed in this book are either fictitious or are used fictitiously.

In-house editor: Ian Randal Strock

Fantastic Books
1380 East 17 Street, Suite 2233
Brooklyn, New York 11230
www.FantasticBooks.biz

ISBN 10: 1-5154-1015-3
ISBN 13: 978-1-5154-1015-7

First Edition

Chris wants to thank his friends and family, teachers and doubters. In one way or another, you provide the impetus for accomplishment.

Brian wants to thank his friends, family, and supporters, especially his father. You taught me the best way to reach the stars is through the written word.

Chapter 1

Bounty hunting was a lifestyle that could be overly romanticized. Exaggerated stories of bravery in the face of danger and overcoming insurmountable odds while tracking down the worst criminals in the galaxy stoked the imaginations of anyone listening to the tales. Every morning began a new adventure that ended with a big payday. Excitement and thrills awaited those stalwart enough to seize the opportunity. That was how Zeus viewed the profession, and why he became a bounty hunter himself. However, the one aspect of bounty hunting that he failed to take into consideration was the amount of boredom that came with waiting while staking out a bounty.

Relegated to standing in an alleyway, Zeus fought with himself to stay focused on the bar across the street, waiting for his prey to exit. Every time his mind started to drift, he reminded himself of the bounty, the overly romanticized stories about it, and the big payday. That focused him. Now, if there was only a way to get his partner to do the same.

"I hate this," Fiore grumbled, leaning against the cool stone wall of the alleyway.

Zeus, leaning against the opposite wall, regarded his partner with steel blue eyes. A monster of a human being, Fiore was seven feet tall and 400 pounds of solid muscle. He proudly displayed his physique by wearing black boots, pants, and a leather vest that showed off the tattoo on his right shoulder—a Grim Reaper holding a flame thrower standing on a bed of skulls laced together by one pink rose along with the calligraphic inscription, *Il Fiore Dentellare*. A bandoleer with dozens of pouches ran the diagonal of his hairy chest. Goggles rested on top of his head, partially pulling back his long, black hair that flowed over his shoulders. His mustache, thick enough to be mistaken for a beard, ran the entire length of his chin and neck. To finish off the menacing façade, Fiore scowled, but Zeus knew well enough that was just for show.

"We got a lead that our target is in the bar across the street," Zeus replied.

Fiore crossed his arms over his chest and tapped his foot. "Exactly! That's where we should be!"

Rolling his eyes, Zeus went back to watching the people enter and exit the building across the street. "We are bounty hunters, not some mad militia. The price on this guy's head is so high, I'm sure every hunter in the galaxy is looking for him. With your size, we walk into that bar and we'll tip him off, or cause one of the many other hunters to make a move. We need stealth. We stay here until he leaves, and then we follow him."

Squinting, Fiore turned to his partner. Zeus was human as well, though considerably smaller, shorter by sixteen inches and lighter by 240 pounds. The smaller man hid his blond curls and pale skin under a thick green, hooded cloak. Fiore grunted his distaste for the plan, and went back to watching the bar as well. "Waiting is stupid."

"Don't you have anything in that chemical vending machine of yours to calm yourself down?"

Fiore looked at what Zeus referenced—a sheath containing six chambers wrapped around his left forearm. Wires and tubes sprouted from it, infusing themselves at different points along his arm, shoulder, and chest. In theory, it was conceivable to use it to give him a sense of calm, but he knew that such a concoction was not among the "ingredients" within the pouches of his bandoleer. He grunted again and went back to watching the bar.

From the shadows of the alley, Zeus tried to ignore his fidgeting partner by focusing on the bar, waiting for his target to exit, but the bustle of the city lured his attention. Vehicles of all shapes and sizes crawled along the congested streets. Beings of various heights and colors and appendages and fashion styles flowed along the sidewalks. Streams of hover-vehicles followed the same traffic flow twenty feet above the ground. In typical cities, there would be more layers. However, on the planet Tarsim, the architecture prevented more than one layer. Buildings stretched from five stories to fifty stories, a dense web-work of walkways among the buildings choked the skies. Adding to the potential hazards were decorative, yet often random, jagged juts from many of the façades, no matter how high in the sky they might be.

"Fulson is a beautiful city," Zeus muttered to himself.

"Yeah. Beautiful," Fiore mumbled back.

Thinking his partner's response an affirmation, Zeus continued, "Since this planet is so mountainous, the indigenous peoples used a lot of bridges to traverse the peaks and valleys during their primitive years."

"Peaks and valleys."

"Even though they evolved like so many other species in the galaxy, and can easily shape their environment, the homage to their ancestors can be seen in their architecture. All those walkways aren't needed. Neither are the jut-outs on all the buildings. But to the people of Tarsim, they serve as reminders of the jagged mountain terrain they had to overcome millennia ago."

"Jagged mountains."

A faint smile crept across Zeus's lips as he pointed to a building in the distance. "As you can see on that building there, they—" but he cut himself short when he looked at his partner. "What are you doing?"

Fiore had his goggles over his eyes and used his right hand to control their magnify function, zooming into the cleavage of two prostitutes standing across the street. He quickly let go once Zeus snapped at him. Hiding both hands behind his back, he stood straight and blurted, "Nothing!"

Frowning, Zeus looked across the street. "You were looking at hookers? You were probably using the magnify function of your goggles, too, weren't you?"

"No!"

"Fiore!"

"Oh, come on! Look at them! The saurian girl is spilling out of her bra, and the orange girl with tentacles is so top heavy I don't know how she doesn't fall over!"

Zeus squeezed his eyes shut and pinched the bridge of his nose. "Look. If we can collect this bounty, we'll be able to get you as many hookers as you can handle."

Fiore blushed. "Me? Get a… get a… hooker…? I would… I would… never… I would… never—"

"—even a six breasted Korvan woman. But we need to collect—"

"—never… wait… the women on the planet Korva have six breasts?"

"—the bounty first, and we need to… yes, the women on the planet Korva have… are you not even listening to me?"

"How can I concentrate with all this breast talk going on?"

"What? You're the one who started it by choosing to gawk at hookers instead of focusing on our mission! If we miss our target, I blame you!"

"Me? You were the one getting misty-eyed over a bunch of buildings!"

Zeus scowled and inhaled. Before he could unleash the scathing retort he had prepared, a man walked into the alleyway, and froze, startled by the pair before him. Thinner than Zeus and just as tall, his skin had a lime green hue. Black eyes punctuated a hairless, noseless, and earless face. Having no discernable lips either, his mouth rippled as it opened and closed. "Oh! I apologize. I didn't mean to disturb."

As abruptly as he appeared, he turned and left the alleyway.

Zeus and Fiore looked at each other in silence. Zeus pulled out his handheld computer from a pocket while Fiore tapped away at the touch screen on his arm sheath. They each accessed an image of their target, Dryn Tammeryn, the man who had just left the alley where they had been standing for the past three hours.

"Damn it!" Zeus yelled, as he and Fiore jumped onto the crowded sidewalk. "Where is he?"

"Over there!" Fiore pointed to a thin spot in the crowd. They both saw the back of a small green head popping up between the uneven gaits of random crowd members. "You keep an eye on him, I'll get the bike."

Fiore ran back into the alley while Zeus focused on their target. However, he was not the only one looking at Dryn Tammeryn.

Zooming down the street and weaving through the idle traffic zipped two emerald-scaled saurians who Zeus immediately recognized as two of the Zaurn brothers. Zarn drove a traditional two-wheeled motorcycle, his long, forked tongue flopping free from his mouth as he shifted from the street to the sidewalk, pedestrians screaming and diving out of the way. Zossa piloted a hovercycle, staying close to the ground; occasionally skimming across the roofs of the stopped, land-bound vehicles.

Bringing his motorcycle to the edge of the alleyway, Fiore saw the commotion on the street and heard the cacophony of people yelling and horns blaring. "What's going on?"

"The Zaurn brothers," Zeus replied as he jumped on the back of the motorcycle and gripped Fiore's vest.

Engine revving, Fiore and Zeus burst from the alleyway, dodging screaming pedestrians. "Which ones?"

Fiore's hair flopped and flipped in Zeus's face as they wove through the traffic. "Zarn and Zossa."

"I hate Zarn! He's a psycho!" Fiore yelled as he accelerated. "Where are the other two Zaurn brothers?"

"I don't know! I can't see a thing with your hair in my face!" Zeus adjusted himself, trying to move his head without getting it hit by any of the vehicles Fiore zoomed past. He repositioned himself just in time to see Zarn motor next to Dryn, scoop him up, and sling him over his shoulder. Dryn struggled, unable to affect his dire predicament.

As soon as the saurian apprehended the target, gunfire erupted. Lasers, bullets, energy bolts, and controlled arcs of lightning shot from building windows and vehicles, both on land and in the air. Vehicles on the ground and in the air swerved as pedestrians ran for any form of shelter they could find. A ball of crackling white light whizzed past Zeus's head, charring the hood of an adjacent vehicle. "See! I told you every bounty hunter in the galaxy is after this guy! This is what would have happened if we tried to apprehend him in the bar!"

"At least we'd have him!" Fiore yelled back. Avoiding the crossfire and panicked bystanders, he guided the motorcycle onto the sidewalk, getting closer to Zarn, getting closer to the bounty. His success was short lived.

Whooping and hollering, Zarn lifted Dryn over his head with one arm and passed him to his brother, Zossa. As soon as Zossa had the squirming bounty, he tried to maneuver his hovercycle through the nonstop barrage of weapons being discharged to the now frenzied layer of traffic above him. The firing weapons proved to be too daunting, preventing him from hovering any higher than ten feet.

"We're losing him!" Zeus yelled.

"Not yet!" Fiore sped up, gaining on Zossa, who was still unable to guide his hovercycle up to the layer of floating traffic. Fiore jumped from his motorcycle and grabbed the bottom left side of Zossa's hovercycle. Almost as an afterthought, Fiore yelled down to Zeus, "Take the motorcycle!"

Profanities spewed from Zeus' mouth as he fought to control the metal beast. Fiore ignored his partner as he adjusted his grip, his bulk causing the hovercycle to list to the left. Avoiding beams and bullets from unseen shooters, Zossa fought to keep his vehicle from crashing. He screamed at Fiore, "Let go! It can't handle your weight! We'll crash!"

"Let me have Tammeryn!"

Hanging on as best he could, Dryn Tammeryn was draped across the cycle seat behind Zossa like recently bagged game. The saurian looked back at Tammeryn, his prize, then at the webwork of beams and smoke trails that he guided his wobbling vehicle through. His thick lizard lips curled into a snarl as he drew his own gun and used it as a reply to Fiore's request.

Twisting to avoid getting shot, Fiore inadvertently jerked the hover-cycle into the path of an oncoming wheeled-transport. He lifted his legs just in time to run along the side of the transport. Once past it, he used the momentum to swing to the right, releasing his right hand so he could grab the other side of the air cycle. Still keeping the hovercycle from gaining any altitude, Fiore ran across the rooftops of the land-bound vehicles.

"Fiore!" Zeus yelled, struggling to guide the large motorcycle around the other vehicles on the road. "Fiore!"

"Little busy right now, Zeus!" Fiore yelled back, trying not to get pulverized by oncoming traffic.

"The other brothers!"

Fiore twisted himself to look around the bottom of Zossa's hovercycle. He caught glimpses of an open-topped hovercar, containing the other two Zaurn brothers, Zyf and Bahb. Still running across the roofs of wheeled vehicles, he watched Bahb lean over and grab Tammeryn. Taking advantage of an oncoming high-roofed vehicle, Fiore kept his feet churning and pulled his chest toward the bottom of the hovercycle. He then kicked his feet out toward the hovercar. He wrapped his legs around Bahb's torso and released his grip from the hovercycle.

Bahb was the largest of the four brothers, bigger than the other three combined. Face resembling an alligator's, he had nubbed ridges running along his head, back, arms, and legs. Even though his chest and arms were muscled enough to lift all of his brothers at once, his waist was gelatinous enough to flop over the top of any pair of pants that he wore. As a whole, he was large enough to support Fiore dangling from him. "Zyf! Zyf! Help! Fiore's got me!"

Using one hand to control the hovercar, Zyf, barely the size of Bahb's leg, reached out with his free hand to grab Bahb's shirt. "I gotcha!"

Bahb braced himself with both hands against the closed doors of the hovercar. "I don't think that's helping! He's pulling me over!"

"Pull him in! You're bigger than he is!"

Doing as his brother suggested, Bahb grabbed a hold of Fiore's legs and leaned backward. With one final twist and yank, the large saurian pulled Fiore aboard, both men flopping to the floor. Bahb jumped to his feet, fists clenched and ready for Fiore to attack, ready to engage in fisticuffs with a rival bounty hunter trying to steal his bounty. However, he wasn't prepared for Fiore's style of fighting.

As soon as Fiore hit the floor, he started swinging his fists and kicking his feet. He rolled around and spun twice. Eyes closed, he thrashed about, flailing his arms and legs. Bahb simply stood there and watched.

Even though the hovercar was large enough to support the weight, Fiore's frenzied convulsing caused Zyf to struggle with the controls. Turning from the main street, Zyf flew down a random alley, removing them from the chaos of the crowds, traffic, and gunfire from other bounty hunters. "Fiore, stop! You're going to singlehandedly knock us out of the sky!"

Slowing, but not stopping, Fiore opened one eye and noticed that Bahb stood over him with his arms crossed. Taking advantage of his enemy's lackadaisical approach, Fiore jumped to his feet with his fists at the ready. Then fell down. Then jumped to his feet again, fists still at the ready. Feeling confident, he threw a jab with his right. Completely missing Bahb's face, Fiore's knuckles grazed Bahb's shoulder. Bahb unfolded his arms just long enough to punch Fiore in the gut.

The air vacated his lungs in a fraction of a second. Fiore doubled over, arms wrapped around his waist. Wheezing, he tried to inhale and fought hard to keep from vomiting. His goggles hid the tears welling in his eyes. Since the other three passengers watched him, he was the only one to see the pulse burst coming right at them. He made an attempt to point and announce the impending danger, but all that came out of his mouth was a desperate squeak.

The blast shredded the bottom of the vehicle, pitching the whole thing to one side. Disabled, the vehicle plummeted. Bahb grabbed his brother with one arm and jumped, using his free arm to brace both of them as they landed on the confines of a nearby balcony.

Still unable to stand upright, let alone jump from the falling craft, Fiore dove toward Dryn Tammeryn and collapsed on him, preparing for impact. The crash was not as devastating as Fiore expected. The impact jolted him, and the screeching noises of the hovercar skidding to a halt hurt his ears, but he barely felt the bumps as it bounced between the alley's walls. He crinkled his nose at the smells of the hovercar's leaking fluids mixing with the spilled contents of all the trash receptacles that the crashing vehicle destroyed. But he lived. So did his target. He was happy with that.

A bit woozy, Fiore made it to his knees, as did Dryn Tammeryn. They smiled at each other and started to laugh. The laughter stopped when a voracious shadow swallowed the alleyway in front of them. Smiles fading, they looked up to see who had shot them down: The Legend, a bounty hunter so feared that other hunters simply gave their prey to him whenever he arrived. This time was no different.

Unable to will himself to move, Fiore stared slack-jawed at the other bounty hunter. Almost equal to Fiore in height and mass, The Legend wore black boots and a long black duster that concealed an arsenal—one that stories had deemed endless and without equal. A wide-brimmed hat and a shimmering silver ventilator hid most of his face, leaving just enough space for his eyes—one glowing red with cybernetic optics, the other a primal black and holding the memories of many hard years. The minimally exposed skin was tan, etched with mahogany scars. The Legend stepped forward and reached for Dryn Tammeryn.

The smaller, green creature grabbed Fiore by the vest and pleaded, "Please! Help! Help me!"

Frozen, Fiore could only watch as The Legend grabbed the bounty and extricated him with one yank....

Chapter 2

"I can't believe you let him go!" Zeus yelled, wringing his hands together. These were the first words he had spoken to Fiore since leaving Tarsim. He had watched The Legend snatch the bounty from Fiore. Right from his hands! Zeus couldn't believe that Fiore had allowed that to happen without even a struggle. Too furious, he couldn't acknowledge Fiore during the entire trip to the planet Estrassus, to their shared apartment that Fiore referred to as their "headquarters."

The outburst did very little to relieve the frustration that continued to build in Zeus. He paced about the room, large enough for two plush couches and a square table with four chairs. A small bar accompanied by four stools separated the living area from the small kitchen, composed of a sink, cabinets, counters, and a large refrigeration unit. On the floor of one corner of the room were two bowls—one for food, one for water, but both empty—that belonged to Hydrynx, Zeus's pet who was following its master in an attempt to get him to rectify the empty bowl situation.

"Like I said before—it was *The Legend*. I am *not* gonna try to take a bounty from The Legend," Fiore replied. Sitting on the one couch large enough to accommodate his bulk, he tapped away on the screen embedded in his wrist sheath. Taking up more than half of the wall in front of him, a monitor displayed the results of his actions. Graphic depictions of two hands holding seven cards—each with various flashing shapes and colors—placed three face down on the video rendition of a table and slid them to the left. The videographic hand then picked up the three cards that came from the right of the viewing area and added them to the four they still held.

Zeus paused in his pacing to glare at the back of Fiore's head. Hydrynx stopped pacing as well, looked up to its master, and offered a raspy mew. It fluttered its wings, covered in malachite scales, and bristled its emerald fur for attention, but the effect garnered none. Serpentine tail twitching, it tried a guttural purr while exposing and retracting its claws. Still nothing. Sitting on its haunches, all Hydrynx could do was watch its master fret. And fret he did.

Finding Fiore's excuse unacceptable, Zeus yelled, "So? He's still just a hunter. And you're bigger than he is!"

"Are you kidding me? He's the best there is. That's why his name is 'The Legend'! Plus, it doesn't matter how big I am—I'm bigger than Zyf and Bahb and they kicked my ass."

"That's because you suck at hand-to-hand combat! I'm going to sign you up for a class or something."

"Hey! I didn't see you rushing in to fight The Legend."

"That's because I was too busy trying not to wreck after you stuck me with the task of operating a motorcycle built for someone three times my size!"

"I was chasing our bounty!"

Zeus threw his hands to the sky in disgust and continued his pacing, Hydrynx in tow. Not knowing what else to say, he went behind the bar and opened the refrigerator. Bottles and jars and containers and cartons of spiced milks dominated the entire space. Milks from different animals from different planets infused with different spices lined the shelves. "Why do we have so much spiced milk?"

"I like spiced milks. Don't you like spiced milks?"

"Certain kinds, I do, but I'm in the mood for something stronger."

"You mean alcohol? But every time we go on assignment, you only drink milk."

"That's when we're *on assignment.* I want to make sure I remain as focused as possible. When hunting a bounty, the last thing I want is to be dulled by alcohol."

"Ummm… that's the same reason why I drink only spiced milk—to stay focused."

"But we're not on assignment right now… because you let our bounty go… and now I'm frustrated and angry and need something stronger."

"Sorry. I didn't know you drank alcohol. When I was decorating our headquarters and stocking our supplies, I knew you liked milk."

Zeus looked around the headquarters and wondered about Fiore's taste in décor. The façades of the table and bar were made of sheet metal ribbed with treading and lined with chrome. Animal furs lined the backs of the black leather chairs and stools. The wall opposite the giant monitor had a mural of a large hand crushing a skull, while the other two walls were black with gaudy flames painted on them, reds flowing into yellows. They had moved into this place two weeks ago, and he regretted not being a part of the decorating process. "About that. Despite the décor being cheap and gauche... where did you get the money for all of this? We've collected five bounties together, and three of them have been people's pets. I know you never got a bounty before you met me, so...?"

"So...?" Fiore asked, his tone indicating that he wasn't sure what Zeus was asking.

"So?" Zeus threw his hands in the air again. "So, where did you get the money to pay for all this?"

"Terrellian poker tournaments."

"You mean like the one you're losing right now?"

"Well, you're distracting me."

"You've lost two hundred creds in ten minutes. That's half of your share of our last bounty!"

Fiore tapped away on his touchscreen. On the monitor, he placed his cards on the table face up, ending the hand. He lost another fifty creds. "Damn it!"

"You are *terrible* at this game."

"I'd do a lot better if you weren't always yelling at me."

Zeus slapped his hands on the bar top and walked to the door, donning his cloak along the way. "Fine! You don't want me yelling at you, then I'm more than happy to leave!"

After slamming the door shut and storming down the hallway of the building—a warehouse divided into four individual apartments where three of them were vacant—Zeus found himself outside. All alone.

Still seething, he put his hood up, shoved his hands into his pockets, and trudged along the nighttime city streets in anonymity, lost among people of all shapes, sizes, and species. He just couldn't let go of the anger, couldn't accept that he had lost a bounty worth ten billion creds. Ten billion. The largest bounty to his knowledge had been one million creds. He reasoned that he shouldn't be so mad about not getting it since he and his partner were such novices to the profession. Then again, they were *so close* to getting it! Fiore had had his hands on Dryn Tammeryn! However, Fiore was right—Zeus did little to assist, and that bothered him.

Aimless, Zeus strolled along the sidewalks. Streetlights and the bright flashing colors of garish marquees lit the way. Being back on his home planet of Estrassus comforted him, having walked these streets many times in his twenty-four years of existence. Blending in and fading away helped focus him, comfort him. Being alone in a crowd afforded him time with his thoughts. Every time he had jumped from a different trade or job or new study in school, he would weigh the consequences and set new goals while bustling along unnoticed with the city's denizens. It was just last year he came up with a detailed plan for beginning his career as a bounty hunter. A slight smirk tugged at the corners of his mouth as he recalled that day. He had grown bored with his time at university, finding the experience inadequate since he knew more than the professors about almost everything from technology to biology to business theories. He had been milling about while eating a fried Puzal Grouse leg when he decided that bounty hunting would be a worthwhile pursuit. His parents were unhappy that he quit university. They were *always* unhappy when he quit a trade or job or school, but he needed to find an adequate challenge, one he wouldn't get bored with when he started to excel at it. But now, more than a year later, his heart sank, realizing that he was nowhere near the stage he thought he should be. Frustrated, he decided that he needed to find a fried Puzal Grouse leg vendor before he could analyze the situation. Luckily, one of the best was nearby.

Seeing a break in the crowd, Zeus hastened his pace, lest he miss the opportunity to change direction. After scooting through the opening, he slowed his step to keep pace with this new bustling crowd. As he did, he noticed a reflection in a store window—a figure in a dull red cloak behind him made the same maneuver.

Trying not to be conspicuous, Zeus changed direction again and watched the reflections in the windows from the corner of his eye. The figure changed direction as well, staying five paces behind Zeus. Heartbeat quickening, he forced himself to act casual. He tried to keep from looking too long at the reflections, his eyes darting to the side. Mind racing, he tried to formulate a plan. Too late—the figure pressed forward.

Breaking into an immediate sprint, Zeus ran down the nearest alley. Being a short alley, Zeus found himself on a parallel street and continued to run. He glanced down every alleyway as he ran past, his mystery pursuer visible at the other end, keeping pace. Zeus weighed his options as he ran, but found it difficult to concentrate while avoiding others sharing the same sidewalk as he sprinted along. Glancing down the alleyway he ran past, he noticed the pursuer was no longer mirroring him on the other side. Scenarios and possibilities bounced through his mind, wondering who chased him and why. Too many questions distracted him—he narrowly escaped capture as his pursuer shot out from the next alleyway.

Fire raging through his legs, burning all the way down to his bones, Zeus envied Fiore's forearm mechanism. All he had to do was insert a couple cartridges and push a button to give his body more energy and a burst of speed. Zeus pushed that idea from his mind; a stray thought that did no good for the situation at hand, one becoming more dire as his energy waned.

Disgruntled faces in the crowd sneered at Zeus as he ran through. Too dense, the crowd didn't dissipate, but it shifted, moved. The option to flee was no longer available. Zeus prided himself on hand-to-hand combat, needing to rely on it to get himself and Fiore out of bad situations on more than one occasion. He needed it now, and looked around for any kind of strategic advantage. His pursuer was almost equal in size, and right behind him. He needed to act... now!

Grabbing a signpost, he used his momentum to spin around. He shifted his body and extended his right leg, turning himself into a missile. He had hoped that the quick misdirection would be enough to catch his pursuer off guard. Much to his chagrin, it did not.

The pursuer leapt over Zeus with ease, did a midair flip, and landed feet first. Zeus, thrown off by not connecting with his kick, landed at an awkward angle on the sidewalk and tucked into a somersault to avoid any injury from his mistimed attack. Jumping to his feet, he stood with clenched fists in front of him, ready to strike or defend. Leg muscles thankful for any form of respite, Zeus cautiously approached the other cloaked figure. The crowd mutated, forming a semicircle of onlookers; the other boundary of the makeshift arena being a building's façade.

The cloaked figure approached, arms outstretched. Zeus struck, slapping away the attacker's arms with his left hand and swinging at his opponent's head with his right. This attack was just as ineffective as his last one—his punch connecting with air. His opponent spun and threw a kick, boot sole slamming Zeus squarely in the chest.

Zeus's vision became overwhelmed by pinprick bursts of light as he stumbled backward and fell. Wind knocked out of him, every muscle in his torso combined to help him inhale. Scrabbling to his feet, he grabbed the shirt of a biped creature with tusks and a moist snout. The tusked man took exception to this and pushed Zeus away. Landing hard on the sidewalk, an explosion of pain erupted through his hip.

Sucking in large gulps of air, his body desperate for oxygen, he stood. His joints felt as sharp as broken glass. His assailant came at him again. Heart beating at the base of his throat, Zeus looked around for escape possibilities. Thoughts of trying to muscle his way through the thick crowd manifested, but lacked any substance due to his less-than-imposing size. The slight whirs from the building behind him caught his attention, and he thanked all the gods he could think of.

Using fear to motivate a burst of speed, Zeus ran toward the crowd and leapt. Planting his feet on the shoulders of the tusked and snouted man, Zeus leapt again, toward the building. His timing perfect, he gripped the top of one of the building's washing units. The hovering device was thin, but wide, and strong enough to support Zeus as he pulled himself up. Standing on the flat surface, he watched the dozen other units move rhythmically up and down as they sprayed thin mists of cleaning chemicals. The building was only ten stories tall, so Zeus estimated each unit would only need four to six passes before retiring into their cubbyholes for the remainder of the night. He planned on riding the unit to the roof, until he watched his pursuer mimic the same maneuver that he had used.

With one pull, the cloaked figure deftly jumped up and climb to the top of a washing unit, three removed from Zeus. Balancing himself, Zeus stood, observing the vertical pattern of the washing unit next to him. He jumped as his pursuer jumped. However, he needed more time to right himself, and his pursuer leapt to the next washing unit, now only two away. Zeus cursed as the unit behind him lined up for his pursuer, while the unit in front of him remained elusive. His pursuer jumped, landing on the washing unit next to him. The unit in front of him was below the one he was on, but ascended faster. Seeing no other choice, he jumped just as his pursuer did.

Zeus landed well, as he had hoped, giving him enough time to lie down and grab one of the washing turrets that sprayed the chemicals. The gears and servos fought him, but he managed to turn it just as his unit floated past the one his pursuer was on. As planned, he sprayed his pursuer in the face with the cleaning chemicals.

Arms waving and grasping at air, the pursuer lost balance and fell. Zeus heaved a sigh of relief. Panting, he relaxed his aching muscles for the remainder of the four-story ride, needing little effort to make it to the roof of the building. Unfortunately for Zeus, he only made it a few steps before something slammed into him.

The hit came from behind. Forceful, strong enough to jolt his spine and snap his head back, the blow sent Zeus tumbling across the rooftop. Dazed and grimacing, every bit of his body throbbed or burned; he flopped over to his back. He made an attempt to sit up, but stopped half way once he found himself looking down the barrel of a gun. Holding the gun was a very angry looking woman. "You killed my sister! Now, I'm going to kill you!"

Chapter 3

Fiore lost again.

"Damn it!"

Using his right index finger to glide across the touch screen of the mechanized sheath around his left forearm, he called up another game. Still sitting on the plush couch, feet on the metal table decorated with rivets along the edges and flame painted on the top, he looked up to the wall in front of him. The scene was a first-person view of sitting at a Terrellian poker table in a virtual casino, including beautiful women and handsome men flaunting their expensive tastes with exotic drinks and the latest in clothing fashion. He knew the world being presented to him was fake, but he enjoyed the spectacle nonetheless.

"Okay, Fiore," he said as he repositioned himself in the couch, hunkering down. "Pay attention. Focus."

The game started and he liked his cards. He wagered twenty.

He played the round perfectly. His bet was now up to fifty.

The next round was even better. He wagered another twenty.

The computer generated blonde seated across from him at the virtual table with the low-cut dress bent over.

Fiore played the wrong cards.

He lost again.

"Damn it!"

Having lost almost one thousand creds, Fiore sighed. "That ten billion cred bounty is looking better and better. Speaking of bounty, where is that partner of mine?"

Fiore turned and noticed Hydrynx sitting on the couch next to him. The emerald hued cat's wings were flat to mimic the expression of disgust on its face. It offered a low, guttural growl.

"Why are you looking at me like that?" Fiore asked. "He left on his own free will!"

Hydrynx opened its mouth, forked tongue squirming like a two headed serpent, and produced a swirl of fire in the back of its throat. Smoke wafted from its nostrils.

Fiore stumbled down the path of memory to the last time he saw the creature assume such a stance. Two weeks ago, Fiore failed to notice Hydrynx sitting in the nearby alleyway as he pulled in. His motorcycle hit a puddle and splashed the dragon-cat hybrid. Before Fiore could make amends, the soaking wet beast bounded up Fiore's motorcycle and belched a plume of fire big enough to cover Fiore's face, causing painful burns and the flash removal of all the hair from his head. Still smoldering, Fiore had inserted the proper ingredients into his arm sheath. Within seconds, the chemicals entered his body. Nature, aided mightily by science, took its course. In less than two minutes, Fiore's skin was healed and his thick hair had grown back. But the process was far from painless.

Remembering that experience, Fiore jumped from the couch and yelled, "Why? Why do you always have to burn my face off? It's not my fault he left!"

Stance unchanged, Hydrynx still glared at Fiore.

Frustrated, Fiore exited from the poker tournament and stormed over to the refrigerator. Pondering his choices, he decided on Mulluvian mule milk. Pricey, but the decadence was worth it. Closing his eyes, he took a sip and let the concoction soothe his nerves and infuse his very soul with liquid happiness. Opening his eyes, he saw Hydrynx by his feet, its reptilian tail curled around its feline body. With every panting growl, flame flittered from the corners of its mouth, an inferno engine ready to combust.

"Oh, fine!" Fiore barked, defeated. He poured the rest of the container into Hydrynx's bowl on the floor.

Scampering over to the bowl, Hydrynx lapped away and purred. Fiore moaned, "You're welcome," Hydrynx looked up and replied with a hiss, the expensive milk dripping from its chin.

"Ugh! I can't win!" Fiore shouted. No longer feeling welcome in his own home, he stormed out of the headquarters.

As he walked down the crowded streets, jostling among all sorts of different sized and colored and attired creatures, Fiore felt badly for Zeus. Maybe Zeus was right? Maybe Fiore screwed up? Fiore certainly had size, but self-admittedly lacked skill. There was no way he could have taken on The Legend! *It's not like I can take bounty hunting classes*, he thought. He just needed more experience, more practice. Fiore sighed, knowing that Zeus was right—he needed to start taking this more seriously and working harder. He decided he should apologize and ask for help. First, he needed to find Zeus.

Being taller than most of the others on the sidewalk, Fiore had no problems looking over their heads at the storefronts and business signs, reading each one and analyzing the odds of Zeus being there. He found nothing of interest, and wasn't sure if Zeus would lose himself in any of the many bars available.

As Fiore looked around, he began to recognize some of the establishments and realized that he had been to this part of town before. He remembered that Zeus would get excited anytime they were here. Something about food. Yes, definitely food. Meat. Bird meat. A leg, in fact. That was it! A Puzal grouse leg! Zeus would go on and on and on about how good they were and how they always made him feel better. Fiore remembered that the vendor was nearby.

He moved as fast as the flowing crowds allowed him, trying not to use his massive size to bully through. Sometimes it just couldn't be helped, jostling others on the sidewalk as he turned a corner into a mass of stagnant bodies. Confused as to why the crowd density increased, he pushed onward until he burst free into an opening. Finding it odd, he looked back to the tightly packed semicircle and noticed everyone was looking up. Curious, he looked up too. Just in time to catch a falling girl.

The crowd released a collective gasp. But murmurs of it being an elaborate publicity stunt quickly spread. The citizens became callous and despondent, and seamlessly returned to their apathetic lives as if not having witnessed anything of interest. Fiore, however, knew very well that it wasn't a stunt of any kind and stared, mouth agape, at the girl wearing a red cloak. "Are… are you… okay?"

The girl removed her hood, and Fiore's heart dropped. In his arms was a girl with deep pink rose petal skin and lush hair, seemingly random locks of every hue available between the colors of white and crimson flowed from her head. Her eyes started with ocean blue in the center and softly diffused through shades of blue ending with azure at the edges. Fiore hoped for a "thank you" or some other conversation starter. However, she squirmed herself free, landing deftly on her feet, and said, "Come on! We have to hurry."

"We…? What? Why?"

By the time Fiore blurted out his questions, the cloaked girl had already run around the corner of the building, down an alleyway. She glanced back just long enough to gesture for him to follow and say, "It's Zeus! He's in trouble!"

Fiore tried to process that one moment he was looking for Zeus and then the next he caught a beautiful girl falling from the sky who knew where Zeus was. His head started to hurt, so he decided just to follow her instead thinking about it any longer.

Once he caught up with her, she finished overriding the locking system on one of the building's back doors and opened it to expose a stairwell. Impressed, but still confused, Fiore asked, "Who are you? How do you know Zeus? How... how did you get through the lock so quickly?"

Hood still down, she turned, her face tucked in her thick, multihued locks, the perfect painting bordered by the perfect frame. So mesmerized by her eyes, Fiore forgot that he had even asked questions until she answered, "My name is Valla. My sister and I are bounty hunters, like you and Zeus. I used a reader to replicate the necessary data needed to make the locking mechanism 'think' I have authorized access. I made it myself." Her voice held a youthful innocence and she spoke quickly, her words like notes from a love song. Every word a melody, every syllable a tune that sent tingles down Fiore's spine.

Valla bounded up the stairs, floating like a feather upon a strong breeze. Chasing after her, Fiore found it difficult to keep up. "*You're* a bounty hunter? You're way too..." *Cute. Beautiful. Gorgeous.* All words he was thinking, but what came out his mouth instead was, "...small."

Two full flights ahead of him, Valla paused and watched as Fiore struggled with his mountainous body to catch up. "Just because I am smaller than you doesn't mean I'm incapable or ineffective in our chosen profession. For example, I am much faster than you."

By the time Fiore reached where she had been standing, she was already gone, sprinting the rest of the way to the roof. He debated about infusing himself with a concoction that would boost the muscles in his legs as well as give him a hyper burst of energy. He decided against it, thinking back to his earlier epiphany about needing more experience. Logic dictated that if he did take a chemical infusion, he would speed up the stairs, burst through the door like a bullet, and propel himself off the roof. As he pushed away the images of himself splattered on the streets below, he reached the roof access, rendering his internal debate moot.

Fiore charged from the stairwell and onto the roof just in time to see Valla run to a large woman pointing a gun at Zeus. Waving her hands, Valla yelled, "Huva! Huva! Don't shoot him! I'm okay."

Heart fluttering for a different reason than running up ten flights of stairs, Fiore instantly became enraptured with Huva's beauty, a different kind of beauty than her sister's. Standing a mere six inches shorter than Fiore, Huva had skin an identical shade of pink as Valla's and taut from straining to contain the muscle within. Sides of her head shaved, a strip of hair containing just as many colors between white and red as Valla's flowed along the middle of her scalp and long enough to touch the center of her back. Huva had similar facial features to her sister, just more chiseled. Even though they possessed far more anger, her eyes also started with the same dark blue and lightened away from the center. However, the colors seemed to swirl, a vortex of ire. Huva barked at her sister, "He threw you off the building!"

Barely coming up to her sternum, Valla had to crane her neck to look up to Huva. "It was a misunderstanding."

Still flat on his back, Zeus looked at Valla and said, "*You* were the one chasing me?"

"Yeah," Fiore said, looking at Valla, completely forgetting that her sister had a gun trained on Zeus. "It's hard to believe that she's a bounty hunter because she's so… small."

Confused, Zeus scrunched his face. "What? What does her size have to do with anything? And how are you involved with her, anyway?"

"I caught her after you threw her off the building."

Upon hearing Fiore's words, Huva went rigid, regaining her resolve to shoot Zeus for his violent transgressions against her sister.

Squirming in an attempt to get away, Zeus hollered, "I didn't throw her off the building! She fell as she was chasing me!"

Valla stepped in front of Huva, putting her hand on her sister's arm. "Huva, listen. This was my fault. We wanted to meet them, and I was surprised at how easy it was to find him, so I started to follow him. I forgot that I had my hood up. I startled him and he ran."

Zeus asked, "You chased me to meet me?"

"Well… I wanted to catch you."

"Even by following me up moving window washing units?"

Her gaze fell to the rooftop as her pink cheeks reddened to a blush. "I… thought it would be fun.…"

Huva lowered her gun and yelled at her sister, "Are you serious?"

With little effort, Fiore grabbed Zeus by the arm and hoisted him to his feet. As Fiore dusted off Zeus, he looked at the sisters, his attention drawn to the taller one. First, he noticed her cleavage, then the tight black top trying to contain her cleavage. Clearly, the top wasn't designed to contain much other than the scattered pouches and pockets, because its sleeves had been removed to make way for her bulging arms. The top tapered from her abundant cleavage, over her muscular waist to the flare in her hips. Just like her cleavage; her legs, shaped from striated and corded muscle, were squeezed into tight black pants, also covered with pouches and pockets. Knife handles poked out from Huva's thick black boots. Seeing all he needed to, his gaze went back to her cleavage, a soft canyon created by two mounds of.… His attention quickly changed to the gun barrel pointed at his face. Huva growled, "I'd show them to you, but they'd be the last things you'd ever see."

Fiore stood in frozen silence, wondering about the validity of her offer and contemplating if it would be worth it.

"Idiot," Zeus hissed to his partner as he yanked his arm away. He then turned to Valla and said, "We've established that you thought endangering our lives by chasing me through crowds of people and up the side of a building via window cleaning units just to meet me would be fun. So, the question remains—why did you want to meet me?"

"You were the closest to Dryn Tammeryn."

"But The Legend got him," Fiore said.

"True," Valla replied. "But you got the closest."

"How do you know that?"

"Crazed vehicle chase through the capital city of one of the most populated planets in the system? You made not only planetary news, but intergalactic as well."

"Really?" Fiore said, unable to stop an ear-to-ear grin from forming. "We made the big time? That's so cool!"

"No!" Zeus shouted at his partner. "Not cool! Now everyone will know who we are."

"Actually," Valla said. "They won't. The media had no idea who you were. They focused more on the fact that The Legend was involved. You two barely had any screen time."

"Well, you and your sister found us."

"Because of my skills," Valla said, her voice brimming with pride. "I created a program that tapped into all kinds of public cameras to collect images of you and ran them through a facial recognition program, also one that I created, and then I used *another* piece of software I created to calculate the probability of.…"

"Still doesn't explain why you wanted to contact us," Zeus cut her off.

"Well, it was you or the Zaurn brothers," Huva said, holstering her gun. "But there is *no way* we want to work with them."

"Work with…?" Zeus looked from one sister to the other. "You want to *work* with us?"

"It's logical," Valla said, approaching Zeus. "Finding The Legend will require a considerable amount of resources and skills. Some, we have. Some, you have. I think I've proven what skills we can offer by tracking you down and subduing you."

Fiore puffed out his chest and said, "We were *not* subdued."

Offering a wan expression, Valla glanced at Fiore and said, "You were subdued."

"No! Not even close!"

Huva shifted her stance just enough to accentuate her ample cleavage. Fiore's eyes went right to the luscious valley of… Huva drew her gun, and again pointed it right between Fiore's eyes. "Consider yourself subdued."

"Damn it!"

Ignoring his partner's antics, Zeus asked, "Why us?"

"Because you almost had him. You almost had your target. That means you knew what you were doing, that you knew more about the target than many, many other bounty hunters out there. You were even closer to him than we were," Valla said, words rapid-firing from her mouth.

Fiore looked at Zeus and shrugged his shoulders. "She does have a point. The four of us could make a good team."

"The Legend has him," Zeus protested. "The bounty is as good as lost."

"He can't collect yet," Valla countered. "Don't forget the terms of the bounty. He needs to be alive and he can't be delivered any sooner than three days from now. That gives us plenty of time to find The Legend and liberate the bounty."

"You and Valla have the brains, Fiore and I have the muscle. It's a 'can't lose' situation," Huva said, again holstering her gun.

"The four of us work together?" Zeus asked. He turned to Fiore, who wore an expression of desire more pitiful than the one Hydrynx used to beg for a treat. Huva stood with her arms crossed, impatience etched on her face. Valla looked at him with a wide smile, arms straight and fingers folded together. Zeus sighed.

"No."

Chapter 4

Fiore pouted. Slumped shoulders, stunted gait, his enormous frame looked as if it fought to keep from collapsing in upon itself. In his left hand, a sealed onyx carafe of Unnatyx Goat milk, the container tinted just perfectly to let in precisely the proper amount of light to balance the flavor and richness. The fingers of his right hand curled around a foot-long glass tube, loose as if they had lost the will to hold anything ever again. A stopper in the center divided the tube into two halves, either end flaring into a bulb, each filled with orange tinted milk. Due to the unique nature of the planet Yrthed, the native bovines developed a need to divide their nutrients into two separate udders, making a rare delicacy to be enjoyed only immediately after the liquids combined. "I can't believe we said no."

Zeus rubbed his temples, trying to dull the thrumming in his head. Fiore had been repeating that very statement for the entire walk between the gourmet milk shop and their headquarters. As he did each time after Fiore's lament, Zeus replied, "I'm sorry to have disappointed you so, but I think it's the best choice."

"I was just so excited to go back after the bounty. Ten billion creds would set us for good."

Stopping once they got to the main door of the building that housed their headquarters, Zeus stood in front of the security sensor for the lock and turned to his partner. "You seem to be doing pretty well financially, considering the price you paid for those two containers of milk."

"Hey, after you threw your tantrum and left, I started winning at Terrellian Poker. Made a good profit," Fiore lied.

The security system finished its scan and accepted Zeus. The door's mechanisms clicked and whirred away as it unlocked. "Uh-huh. Anyway, we are still going to go after the target. We're not giving up on the ten billion."

"We'd have a better chance with their help."

The door opened with a whoosh, and the two men entered. A simple hallway leading all the way to the other end of the building greeted them.

There were only two doors on either side of the hallway, and theirs was the second on the right. Fiore trudged the whole way, his shoulders almost touching the walls due to his exaggerated gait. Zeus led the way, ignoring the spectacle behind him. "We don't need their help. That's the point, Fiore. We're partners. We. Us. No one else."

"But this one time...."

"But this one time turns into another time and another. We've collected five... *five*... bounties together. Don't you want to establish a reputation? Don't you want to make people think of us first when they need hunters? We can't do that if we're always working with other people."

"Well, yeah. But..."

"But nothing, Fiore. *We* can track down The Legend and steal back our bounty ourselves."

Even though Fiore agreed with Zeus in principle, he still liked the idea of working with Valla and Huva. Valla was so pretty that every time Fiore blinked he could see her thick, colorful hair flowing around her face. But Huva had amazing cleavage. But Valla was smart, and since she talked so fast it made Fiore think she was even smarter. But Huva had great cleavage. But Valla displayed ambition by tracking down Fiore and Zeus, she being the one to suggest that the four of them work together. But Huva had wonderful cleavage. It slowly dawned on Fiore that maybe his desire to work with them wasn't based purely on the need to track down The Legend.

Zeus interrupted Fiore's epiphany with, "Plus, we don't even know them. Who knows who they are? They could be scam artists who make us do all the work and then they'll kill us and collect...."

"Do you think we should meet them for dinner?" Fiore blurted.

Zeus stopped in the middle of the hallway and looked up at his partner. His face twisted with confusion and disgust as he spat, "*What*? Haven't you heard a single thing I said? I say that they may want to murder us, and now you want to date them?"

As if splashed by ice water, Fiore stood straight, eyes wide with alarm. Sweat formed around the perimeter of his hairline. "What? I didn't mean... date... them! I meant... I meant... meeting them somewhere getting to know them better!"

"So... *a date*!"

"No! You said you didn't know anything about them. This is how we get to know them."

Souring his face, Zeus reeled back and said, "It's Huva's cleavage, isn't it?"

"It's not just that!"

"Not *just* that? So, you *do* like her!"

"And Valla too!"

Now Zeus stood straight. His face went slack as he processed Fiore's words. With a bit of timidity that Fiore had never seen before, Zeus asked, "You like... you like... Valla?"

Still frenzied from being swept up in a conversation he had little control over, Fiore shouted, "I don't know! Maybe? I don't know! We can't find out unless we meet them again!"

Turning and continuing to their door, Zeus snapped, "Well, we're never going to see them again, so it doesn't matter."

"Oh, come on! Why can't we at least...?" Fiore stopped himself when Zeus went to the door and clicked the latch. But it shouldn't have unlatched, since Fiore remembered locking the door on his way out.

Lacking the time to articulate his thoughts, Fiore dropped his newly purchased exotic milks, containers shattering, and slammed into Zeus as soon as he opened the door. Adjusting his angle, he drove both of them behind the counter of the kitchen area. Angered, Zeus started to shout, "What the—?" but the flurry of projectiles cut him off.

Zeus stayed on his belly and scurried on his elbows to peer around the edge of the counter. Three humanoid figures clad in black, each with a gun, jumped around the room to defensive positions as well. Two ducked behind the couch; one flipped the table over and hid behind that. Zeus craned his neck a bit more to see Hydrynx. The emerald-hued dragon-cat hybrid lay as a heap of fur and scale next to a burn mark on the floor. A tiny dart stuck in its left hindquarter. A lump formed in the back of Zeus's throat until he saw its chest rise and fall, the soft rhythm of sleep.

Pulling his head back, Zeus looked at the wall behind them, where the projectiles had hit. A straight line of a dozen identical darts. Moving next to Fiore, he whispered, "They don't want to kill us."

"What should we do?" Fiore asked, whispering as well.

"We don't have much time before they realize that we're unarmed. But I have an idea." Zeus twisted and reached up for the refrigerator door.

No sooner had he opened it than a barrage of darts rang against the metal door. Shrapnel rained to the floor, tips bent, housings shattered. Satisfied with the result, Zeus hopped to his feet and used the door as a shield. However, he was very unsatisfied with the complete lack of anything that could be used as a weapon. "Seriously? All we have in here are milks."

"Because we like milk," Fiore replied, his whisper harsh and angry.

"We like other things, too!" Zeus replied with a harsh and angry whisper of his own. "Is any of this at least flammable?"

"What? No! It's milk!"

Zeus weighed his options and chose the containers small enough to throw, but heavy enough to do some damage. Much to Fiore's chagrin, they just happened to be the more rare and expensive ones among the selection. Zeus peeked around the door and threw containers at the couch. The intruders returned fire, but their projectiles shattered against the metal refrigerator door. Three well-placed throws connected with the gunmen. Two containers shattered, liquid splashing and slopping against the gunmen's visors.

Wasting no time, Zeus threw two more containers at the gunman behind the table and yelled to Fiore, "Get him!"

Staying low, Fiore launched himself from behind the counter. His shoulder connected with the left side of the table as his knees and feet continued to drive him forward. However, instead of pushing it backward as he had hoped, the center of the sideways table created a pivot point, causing Fiore to spin the table. Even though the intruder had milk dripping from his visor, he was deft enough to follow Fiore's lead and push on the opposite side of the table. Frustrated that his plan wasn't working, Fiore pushed harder, causing the table to rotate faster. One full revolution. Two revolutions. Three. Four. He so hoped that Zeus was faring better.

When Fiore rushed the assailant hiding behind the table, Zeus charged forth toward the two behind the couch. Hopping over the back of the couch, he flung one last fist-sized container of milk at the one attacker's head while jamming his knee into the chest of the other, knocking him over. As the gunman hit the ground, Zeus somersaulted to his feet. Before the other interloper could wipe the splashed milk from his visor, Zeus lunged forward with a leaping kick to the man's chest. Grunting in pain, the gunman flew backward and dropped his gun. But Zeus wasn't fast enough.

As he turned to continue his assault on the first gunman, a dart struck his chest. He yanked it free as fast as reflex would allow, but the drug that the dart administered began working immediately. Through labored breathing, Zeus tried to advance upon the gunman, but his vision spiraled, swirling his world around him. Within two steps, he slumped to the floor, unconscious.

Fiore lost count of how many times he went in a circle after ten. He knew he was getting nowhere, and when Zeus went down, his outlook became much more grim. As he spun toward his original starting point, he leapt, aiming for the protection of the kitchen counter and the open refrigerator door. However, as he dove, he felt a pinch in his right ass cheek.

Fiore landed hard, slapping the floor with his face and chest. He quickly removed the dart and started to fumble with the chemical cases of his bandoleer. Blinking hard and opening his eyes wide, he tried to maintain focus, tried to fight the spinning of the room. He inserted one cartridge into his forearm unit, the contents designed to accelerate his heart. Breathing was hard, but he inserted a second cartridge that would dilate his blood vessels. A third cartridge to… a third to… he couldn't remember, couldn't focus, couldn't stop the spinning room. He prayed that whatever was in the third cartridge would directly counteract the toxins commanding him to sleep. As his eyes shut to sweet oblivion, his thumb pressed the go button, injecting the ingredients.

Snapping open, Fiore's bloodshot eyes bulged from their sockets. His body shook, tremors rippling up his arms and down his legs. He clenched his fists in an attempt to control his squirming fingers. Sweat rolled from the ridges of his protruding veins. Lips curling back, he couldn't stop from gritting his teeth. His insides burned as his hammering heart pounded blood through his body. Standing, he released a roar normally reserved for braying beasts.

Only two of the attackers had guns, but all three reeled back when Fiore bellowed at them. The two that were armed quickly aimed and fired. Too late. So electrified by his concoction, Fiore couldn't formulate a plan more complex than what instinct dictated, and that was to use the refrigerator door for protection. He tore it from its hinges.

The projectiles bounced off the makeshift shield and fell impotently to the floor. With wide-eyed mania, Fiore threw the door at the attackers and thundered with rage. The door missed the men and slammed into the wall behind them. The metal bent and clanged to the floor, leaving behind a spider web of cracks in the wall. The three intruders looked at each other, then at the devastation, then at the panting and shaking hulk in front of them. Without even trying to communicate with each other, all three men sprinted out of the headquarters, escaping down the hallway.

Still quaking violently, Fiore's mind raced, ideas evaporating as quickly as they formed. But two things were apparent even in his frenzied state: the threat was gone, and he needed to stop the lightning racing through his body. Between shaking too hard and being unable to focus long enough, he couldn't pull ingredients from his bandoleer to reverse the process.

He turned to the darts in the wall.

Fiore yanked one of the darts from the wall, but it quickly bounced from his tremulous hand. Using his other hand to grab his wrist for support, he snatched another dart. Before he could lose it, he jammed it into his thigh. He felt the effects immediately; his body no longer shook with quite the same vigor. It wasn't enough, so he used another dart. Then another.

Finally calm enough to think, he went to the sink and splashed cold water on his face. Feeling more in control of his faculties, he looked around the apartment. Sideways table, nicked and scuffed. Bent refrigerator door against a mangled wall. Couch full of rips and tears. Floor burnt where Hydrynx slept. In the middle of it lay his unconscious partner. Fiore's blood chilled when he thought of how irate, and downright unbearable, Zeus would be once he awoke. Before he could entertain any ideas of running away before that happened, Fiore noticed something that might provide some answers. One of the assailants had left a gun....

Chapter 5

Zeus sat at the table. He had just woken up from the tranquilizer dart minutes ago, and swore that every joint in his body had atrophied. His head felt like cotton—eyes dry, mind fuzzed, tongue puffy. Elbows on the table, he rested his chin and cheeks in his hands, a laborious task. Every time he moved or shifted in the slightest, a new stabbing pain or infernal throbbing emerged. Moving only his eyes, he looked at the glass of Mutakkan medicinal milk that Fiore had poured for him, and even that act hurt.

Curled on the table in front of Zeus was Hydrynx, paws drawn tight and tail wrapped around its body, wings pulled high and close like blankets covering its face, only its nose and right eye visible. It attempted a mew, but that turned into an exhausted groan of pain. In a small saucer next to it lay a pool of Mutakkan medicinal milk.

Between the two of them, in the center of the table, lay the gun that had been used to tranquilize them. Fighting the pain, Zeus reached out to turn the gun, looking for any distinct markings that would give him a clue about its origins. It hurt to spin the gun, then it hurt to think about the gun. He rode the wave of pain as long as he could, but finally decided to give Fiore's stupid idea a try, and took a sip of the milk. To his surprise, the effects were immediate, muting the pain from "nauseating" to "unbearable".

Sighing, he sat straight up and then turned to the kitchenette, where Fiore busied himself with cleaning. "How is it that you were shot, but have no issues?"

Standing, Fiore wrung out a towel full of spilled milk into the sink. He nodded toward his bandoleer, now resting on the counter, and said, "Told you. Right when I got shot, I pulled the right chemical combo and burned it through my system."

"No pain for you, huh?" Zeus grunted his reply as Fiore knelt back to the floor to soak up more spilled milk.

"Other than being sad and angry about how much milk we lost, no." Fiore stood and wrung the contents of the towel into the sink again. "Keep drinking the Mutakkan medicinal milk. It'll help."

Zeus turned back to the gun on the table and took another sip of the milk. Again, it shooed away some of the pain. A strange curiosity popped into his mind about what kind of animal on the planet Mutakk could produce milk with medicinal properties, but he quickly shoved it aside, fearful of the answer. "Okay. We come home and are ambushed by three gunmen. They were using tranq darts, so they clearly wanted us alive. What could they want from us?"

On the floor, Fiore poked his head over the counter, "Do you think it has something to do with Dryn Tammeryn? Or The Legend? Or both?"

Zeus sighed. Even though the milk helped dull the pounding in his head, his thoughts still remained muddled. "Possibly? I don't know. Now we have two issues—finding The Legend so we can get Dryn Tammeryn back from him, and finding out who is after us."

"Three things." Fiore stood and dropped the saturated towel into the sink. As gentle as touching a newborn, Fiore ran his fingers over the scuff marks on the doorless refrigerator. "We need to fix up our headquarters."

"Actually, we'll need to leave the headquarters for a while."

Spinning around, Fiore snapped, "What? Why?"

"Because whoever they are, they know where we live. If they come back, I'm sure it will be with more than three gunmen."

"But I don't wanna leave," Fiore whined.

"Hey, if you want to face heavily armed men who will probably want some form of payback because you kicked their collective asses all by yourself, there's nothing stopping you. I am not going to stay here."

"Fine!" Fiore stormed from the kitchen and down the small hallway.

"What are you doing?"

"Packing a bag!" Fiore shouted from his bedroom.

Zeus took another swig of milk. Feeling much better, he lifted the gun off the table. Lightweight. Two feet long. Dull black. Sturdy polymer. He removed the clip of darts and thoroughly examined the gun. Nothing. No markings that he could see. Just as he admitted defeat, Fiore returned with a rucksack in his hand and plopped it on the floor. As he put his bandoleer on over his vest, he said, "We need to figure out who they were and what they wanted."

Feeling better, but far from good enough to tolerate Fiore's inanities, Zeus's reply was thick with sarcasm, "What an amazing idea. So, how are we going to start?"

"First of all, we need to learn more about that gun. Like, who made it."

"Again, brilliant. How do you propose we do that?"

"Just contact one of your contacts. Set up a meeting for them to look at it."

Zeus grimaced. "Contacts? What contacts?"

Confused, Fiore said, "Don't you have contacts? I thought you had contacts?"

"Why would…? How would…? We work together, moron! Whatever contacts you have, I have! Since you have no contacts, that means *we* have no contacts!"

Face reddening, Fiore yelled, "I didn't know! I thought you had contacts!"

"Well, I don't, genius!"

"We would have contacts if we teamed up with the sisters!"

"They're not contacts, they're competition. If you bring them up again today, I'm going to use the rest of the darts in this clip on *you*. In fact, for all we know they were the ones behind the attack."

Fiore stopped yelling and slouched, obviously affected by Zeus's last statement. "Do you… do you *really* think they were behind the attack?"

Knowing that he somehow hurt his partner's feelings, though he was *never* quite sure how, Zeus softened his tone. "I doubt it. I really do. However, we can't assume they're not involved just because we don't want to believe they are."

Fiore's mood brightened as his eyes widened. "I got an idea. Grab the gun. Let's go."

"Where are we going?" Zeus asked as he stood. He lowered his shoulder for Hydrynx, licking the fur around its mouth from having just finished its saucer of milk. Still lethargic, Hydrynx climbed Zeus's arm and nestled on his right shoulder. Once settled, Zeus donned his cloak, the form of Hydrynx under it giving him a hunchbacked appearance. Before leaving, he then tucked the gun underneath his cloak.

Slipping his goggles over his head, Fiore beamed as they left their headquarters. "Trust me! You'll love this idea."

Zeus most certainly did not. He never enjoyed surprises. He always wanted to know where he was going. More importantly, he never understood the logic behind many of Fiore's plans. Grousing as he blindly followed Fiore out of the building and through the crowded streets, Zeus weighed the odds of starting a solo bounty-hunting career. Much to his chagrin, he needed Fiore, even when his ideas led them to pawn shops.

"You can't be serious," Zeus moaned as they stood outside of the establishment.

"Very." Fiore said, pride dripping from his word.

"You can't be serious."

"Pawnshop owners know everything about everything," Fiore said as he opened the door and strode in.

"You can't be serious," Zeus mumbled as he followed.

As soon as they walked in, Zeus wondered how Fiore hadn't knocked over everything in the shop. Ceiling-high metal shelves struggling to contain their contents created tight aisles. Different parts of various pieces of clothing flopped over edges. Wires and tubes from electronic equipment and vehicle parts and appliances and computers reached for Zeus, desperate prisoners begging for escape. Boxes of trinkets rattled with every step Fiore took. There were items spilling from the shelves that Zeus couldn't even fathom what they were, let alone their purpose.

When they finally freed themselves from the alleyway of shelves and reached the back of the store, the feelings of claustrophobia didn't cease. The wall hangings were clustered so close together that Zeus questioned if there were actually any walls or if all the junk kept the roof from collapsing. Signs and drapes and tapestries and more electronics dangled from the ceiling, Fiore creating waves as his head passed through them.

Even the see-through counter threatened to burst from being stuffed with merchandise, mostly weapons. On the counter were displays lined with jewelry and ornaments. Behind the counter was one lone individual whose content expression led Zeus to believe that if he sold nothing all day, he'd still be happy ruling his solitary kingdom of borderline garbage. "How can I help you?"

Despite being purple with a skin complexion that made him seem spongy, Zeus could tell the shop owner was young, maybe around his own age. The shop owner was a cyborg, his right arm and leg made of gleaming silver metals, colorful wires, and black servos. The upper right quarter of his face had a metal casing as well; a crimson light emanating from an ocular implant where his eye should be. Moppy green hair covered the top of his head as well as part of his cybernetic implant in the same way his shirt, swirled with colors, and his black pants covered most of his robotic arm and leg.

Zeus wondered if Fiore forgot that he was an intergalactic bounty hunter, or that he was seven feet tall and four hundred pounds of pure muscle, or that one snarl from his hair-covered face could send rabid animals running for cover. With that frightening combination, all Fiore had to do was utter a command and anyone would trip over themselves to follow it. Instead, Fiore stuck out his hand and offered an ear-to-ear smile. "Hi! I'm Fiore. This is Zeus. We were wondering if you would be willing to give us any kind of background on... an item... we found."

The purple creature behind the counter smiled as well as it could with a thin slit of a mouth. His smooth, oval face held no lips, a subtle ripple with two small holes for a nose, similar ripples with holes on the sides of his head for ears, one beady black eye, all atop an elongated neck. Shoulder to shoulder, Zeus would have been equal to his height. However, the shop owner had an elongated and thin neck, making him three inches taller than Zeus. Using his metal hand, the purple fellow shook Fiore's and said, "Hi! I'm Billix. I'd love to take a look at this item of yours. Is it an antique? What planet did you find it on? Do you recognize the culture of it?"

"Ummm, hold on," was Fiore's answer to all three questions as he extended his hand to Zeus.

Frowning, Zeus mumbled, "This is a bad idea."

Trying his best to whisper, Fiore said, "He wants to look at it."

"He's a pawn shop dealer. I doubt he'll be able to help us."

"He has weapons in the display case and on the wall behind him. He'll know what it is."

"It's a weapon?" Billix asked, rubbing his hands together in excitement. "What kind? What planet? What era? New? Used? Who else have you—"

"Oh, damn it! Here!" Zeus snapped, and threw the gun at Billix just to shut him up. "Do you know what it is?"

Billix's natural eye widened, or at least Zeus thought it did, an obsidian marble imbedded in purple foam. As if clutching an egg, Billix lifted the gun with reverence. "Ooh. Nice. Very nice indeed."

"Do you know who made it? Who it belongs to?"

"I have an idea," Billix said. As he rummaged through various drawers, Zeus shot looks of anger at Fiore, while Fiore replied with looks of confusion and then confidence that his plan was working.

Billix found what he was looking for—a canister no larger than his thumb. A blue light beamed when he squeezed it. Shining the light on the base of the handle, he turned the gun so Zeus and Fiore could see as well. A sigil appeared, circular with angled lines crisscrossing inside of it. "Just as I thought. The gun was manufactured by Sivka Corp. A high-end one, too. I know they keep their logo hidden on their high-end products."

"See?" Fiore said to Zeus. "I knew he'd know."

"Okay, smart guy, ask him who would own such a gun?"

"That I can't tell you," Billix said. "I do know a guy who can, though. He's a bit eccentric and lives on the planet Jajlava. Here." Billix started tapping away at his robotic arm, his purple fingers dancing across the touch screen. Before either Fiore or Zeus could ask what he was doing, Fiore's wrist sheath beeped.

"What's this?" he asked as he accessed his computer.

"I downloaded the coordinates to your computer. I had mine scan yours. It was a friendly enough protocol, so I had no issues sending them to you."

"Awesome," Fiore said, smiling.

"Not awesome!" Zeus snapped. "If he was able to do that so easily, imagine what else could be done to that thing. Maybe that's how they tracked us?"

"So, what are you guys? Cops? Special Forces? Or are you gunrunners? Smugglers? Dealers?"

"Bounty hunters," Fiore said, still focusing on the new information contained in his computer.

"Awesome!" Billix said.

"Seriously?" Zeus shouted. "What is wrong with you?"

"What?" Fiore asked.

"You don't go around telling everyone we meet that we're bounty hunters."

"Why not? We're new at this, and need to make a name for ourselves, so it's not like we should be hiding."

"We live in this neighborhood! Our neighbors shouldn't know that we're bounty hunters."

"Actually," Billix interjected. "I didn't assume you two were my neighbors until you just said that you were."

"See?" Fiore yelled back. "Plus, now we have a contact."

"I'm a contact?" Billix asked, the excitement in his voice obvious.

"Yes!" Fiore said.

"No!" Zeus yelled at the same time.

"Sure he is. We need contacts, and he provided us with valuable information. He's a contact. In fact," Fiore paused to regard Billix. "Let's say a rival bounty hunter stole a bounty from us, but we still have time to get it back. What should we do?"

"I'm assuming you neither know where he can be found nor how to contact him?" Billix asked.

"That is correct," Fiore replied.

"Hmm. Interesting. Interesting, indeed." Billix stroked his face with his natural hand while the fingers of his metal hand drummed on the counter.

Zeus rolled his eyes.

"I got it. Just post another bounty."

"What do you mean?"

"Just put a name out there and attach a bounty to it. That will lure out your rival."

"What if it has to be a really large amount of money?"

"That doesn't matter if you make the bounty a friend of yours and keep him close to you at all times. Your rival will come after you, since you already have the bounty, and then you steal back the bounty he stole from you. You collect on the real bounty, and everyone will think that you also got the fake bounty."

"I like it!" Fiore shouted.

"I can't believe I have to agree with you, but I can't think of a better idea," Zeus moaned.

"Whose name do we put out there as a bounty?" Fiore asked.

"I don't know. That seems to be the inherent problem with this…" Zeus trailed off as he looked at Billix. He then looked at Fiore and smirked. He then looked back at Billix. "I think I solved that problem."

Billix stopped smiling. "No!"

Fiore looked at Billix as well and said, "You did say to use a friend."

"No!" Billix said again.

"Or, better yet, someone we just met and don't care about," Zeus said.

"No!" Billix yelled louder.

Fiore and Zeus strolled around the counter to discuss their plan with their new contact.…

Chapter 6

"I can't believe I'm doing this," Billix said. He glided the hovercar forward one spot closer to the jump-port.

"Quit whining," Zeus replied from the passenger seat. Even though he frequently used jump-ports to get from planet to planet, they still made him anxious. The occasional news report about jump-port malfunctions sending vehicles careening into a star or into the endless abyss of space always caught his eye and made the hairs on the back of his neck stand on end. He double-checked all the windows and doors to make sure they were closed and secured. "You always wanted adventure."

From the driver seat, Billix regarded Zeus and frowned, tiny ridges forming along his spongy, purple forehead. "When did I say that? I never said that! I was more than happy to stay in my pawnshop. Now I have a bounty on my head."

"Hey, it was your idea."

"I didn't mean I wanted to be the bounty! A ten *billion* creds bounty! That's enough for every bounty hunter in the galaxy to come looking for me!"

"Relax. We'll be with you the whole time. We just need to lure The Legend out long enough for us to steal back the bounty that he stole from us."

"So, this makes us partners then, right? Do I get any money out of this?"

"Sure!" Fiore jumped into the conversation from the back seat. Even though the back of Billix's hovercar was designed to transport merchandise, it was still too small for Fiore. Shifting so he could see out the front window as well, he sat behind Billix and Zeus, head hunched down as his shoulders pressed against the ceiling, arms wrapped around his legs as his knees dug into his armpits.

"No! Why do you want to make everyone we meet a partner?" Zeus yelled.

"Not that!" Fiore yelled back. "I meant paying him. He should get a little something."

"He's a contact. Contacts pay each other in favors."

"I can only *imagine* what favors I could get from you," Billix moaned.

"We're getting you out of that stuffy store and into the real world. You should consider that a favor."

Billix rolled his natural eye. "So, there are others you're thinking about making partners?"

"Yes," Fiore said.

"No!" Zeus snapped. "They're other bounty hunters."

"That's why they'd make great partners."

"They're competition. And you want to 'partner' with them for more reasons than hunting bounties."

Fiore blushed and stammered, "I… I think… they'd be… umm… great…"

Confused, Billix asked, "So, what's so special about these bounty hunters?"

"They're really pretty sisters," Fiore blurted it so fast that he turned his whole statement into one word.

"Really?" Billix laughed. "You think your competition is pretty?"

"No," Zeus answered.

"No?" Fiore asked, a smirk sliding across his face. "Not even Valla?"

"No! What kind of stupid question is that?"

"No? So you wouldn't mind if I asked her on a date when we get back?"

Crunching his smooth face into a grimace, Billix turned to the two and said, "How is it possible that you are bounty hunters? You're acting like children! And I have my life in your hands? How are you two possibly going to steal back the bounty that you lost? How are you going to keep me safe?"

Crossing his arms over his chest, Zeus slouched in his seat and looked out the front window. More than happy to change the subject, he mumbled, "We're up next."

Billix glided the vehicle close to the jump-port. "Computer. Billix 98723489 to jump-port. Destination, planet Jajlava. City, Momonol."

"Confirmed," came the voice from Billix's console. "Scanning vehicle for travel integrity."

Anger and frustration constricted Zeus's throat as he and the other two sat in Billix's hovercar before the jump-port. The ring, three stories in diameter, had various warnings and instructions labeled all along the exterior. A dozen such rings could be found in this particular port, two rows of six rings. Other vehicles floated above and beside them, all properly adhering to their respective lanes. However, one ring was closed for repairs. Zeus couldn't stop looking at that one. He wondered what problems existed, and if they were found before or after the malfunction propelled the unwitting travelers to a horrible demise. So focused on the nonworking one, he didn't notice the scan had been completed and the intergalactic doorway had opened to their requested destination. And through they went.

Normally a seamless process, Zeus felt unprepared. Once they passed through to the other side, at the jump-port in the city Momonol, Zeus felt disoriented and nauseated for the second time in one day. He jerked his legs close to his chest, preparing for a crash that never happened.

"What is wrong with you? Are you *sure* you're a bounty hunter? You're very jumpy. I should be the jumpy one, with a bounty of ten billion creds on my head," Billix said.

"I'm fine," Zeus lied. "Just get us to this gun expert of yours."

"It's not that simple. He doesn't live in the city, and where he lives isn't accessible by hovercar."

"What? You waited until *now* to tell us?"

"Sorry, I was too busy being kidnapped by bounty hunters! You didn't give me a chance to talk. You *never* give me a chance to talk."

"So, where is he?"

"About ten miles away, into the jungle. The hovercar can get us about three miles closer, to the edge of the jungle. We'll have to walk from there. I know a place in the city to get supplies before we go."

As Billix guided the hovercar through the small city, Zeus felt a headache brewing, and hoped that whatever store they were going to get supplies from carried Mutakkan medicinal milk. No such luck. Zeus knew of this planet, Jajlava, a massive jungle that flirted with both poles. Geological surveys had determined that what little resources the planet had to offer were hardly enough to justify the costs of trying to mine them. The planet remained relatively untouched, other than a few dozen cities like this one, mostly inhabited by scientists studying the indigenous life and those who chose to give up the hustle and bustle of other population centers for the tranquility of communing with nature. Like all cities, though, there was commerce, plenty of traders finding a profit from importing their wares to Momonol. Unfortunately, the law of scarcity also applied all too well.

Knowing there were no other vendors for certain supplies, Zeus had little room to haggle, spending far more than the products were worth, mostly containers of food and water, chemicals to repel insects, first aid kits, and other survival necessities. Between Fiore trying to be friendly and Billix trying to assert his opinion, Zeus asked himself if the ten billion cred bounty was enough to make the pain worthwhile. It was, and he knew it. He just wished it could be done without so much chatter. All three ended up with full rucksacks; Fiore had two since he was bigger, and the trio crammed back into the hovercar and departed.

The city was composed of mostly one- or two-story buildings. Zeus assumed many of them to be laboratories or apartments for the denizens of the city, mostly scientists and researchers. However, the city was so small that after obtaining their supplies, they glided beyond the border before Zeus could absorb the ambiance, though he did enjoy the new scenery.

Zeus noted the majesty of the mountain range behind them, extending from horizon to horizon and tall enough that the peaks seemed to break free from the atmosphere. The three mile trip from the city to the edge of the jungle was filled with a lush field of grass and batches of multi-colored flora, an emerald sea with a multitude of chromatic islands. The jungle was ominous, lush-leafed trees reaching for the heavens. Zeus found this planet to be quite cathartic, and resolved himself to do more research after collecting the bounty for Dryn Tammeryn. Maybe even spend a research vacation here with the scientists in Momonol.

The trip was short; the flora of the fields thickened and hindered the progress of the hovercar. Billix found a small clearing close to the edge of the jungle and stopped there. The first thing that Zeus noticed after exiting the hovercar, that could change his mind about ever revisiting this part of the planet, was the humidity.

Like a slap in the face, the oppressive air instantly caused him to sweat. His cloak caught the sun's heat, baking him. He hated to go on a mission without it, but it was meant to provide stealth in urban situations. It did offer some protection, the material difficult to pierce, but the detriment it caused at the moment outweighed any potential benefit. It had to go.

Zeus removed his cloak, and Hydrynx winced from the sunlight as he awoke from his nap. Billix looked over and screamed, "Aah! What is *that?*"

Confused, Zeus looked at Billix and said, "What? You thought I had a hump on my back?"

"Umm, yes! A growth. Or a mutation. Or a backpack. Or bionics. Certainly not... *that.*"

Offended, Hydrynx arched its back and fluttered its wings as it let out a low growl. Zeus reached up to scratch behind its ear, and said, "Easy, easy. It's okay, Billix. Its name is Hydrynx. I created it by splicing together genes from a cat and a dragon."

"Splicing...? Why? Why would you *do* that? What is *wrong* with you? Where did you even *find* dragon genes? Who does that?"

Lowering his goggles from the top of his head to his eyes, Fiore adjusted the shading settings to combat the sun. "Now you feel my pain, don't you? This is what I have to live with."

"Living with you is no picnic, either," Zeus replied. To side with its owner, Hydrynx arched its back and growled at Fiore.

Fiore sneered as he pulled three small canisters from his bandoleer. He inserted them into his wrist gauntlet and started the process. The chemicals flowed from the canisters into his body, followed by a few jerky dances, as if someone had splashed him with ice water.

Spraying himself with insect repellent and sunscreen, Billix asked, "What was that?"

"Same thing you're doing, but internally," Fiore answered. He extended his arms from his sides, examining them. "Look. No sweating!"

"That's so awesome!" Billix said, running over to study Fiore's sweat-free arms. "I so need to upgrade my cybernetics to do that! If I can even do that. I'll have to do some research later."

Zeus wiped sweat from his brow, a few of his blond curls already matting to his forehead. "If you're done with your love fest, maybe we could get started? Do you know where you're going?"

Billix tapped away at his robotic arm. On the screen, two blinking dots appeared—one representing his location, the other his destination—as well as numbers informing him of distance, elevation, and other potentially useful data. After a few more taps, the screen on Fiore's forearm computer came to life, displaying the same information. "I've visited my contact only once before."

"So, you've done this before? You know the way?" Zeus asked.

"If you're asking if I remember the way, I don't. It's a jungle, so it all pretty much looks the same. Plus, I was with a larger party consisting of scientists, researchers, students, traders, merchants, missionaries, mercenaries, so there was plenty of conversation and storytelling. I have the coordinates to where he lives, and I just gave them to Fiore."

Fiore tapped away at the screen. "That is amazing."

"What is wrong with you?" Zeus asked. "He keeps hacking into your computer and you act like it's the greatest thing that's ever happened to you."

"Actually it's not as easy as I make it look," Billix said. "He does have one of the most sophisticated security systems I've ever seen. Probably in the galaxy."

Fiore smirked at Zeus. Zeus frowned in reply. "So, how is it that you can bypass his security so easily?"

"Because that's what I do."

Fiore's smirk grew as he elbowed Zeus. "See? I told you it was a good idea going to the pawnshop. Billix is a *great* contact."

Zeus shook his head and pulled a container of water from his rucksack. After taking a swig and offering a sip to Hydrynx, he said, "Shall we begin?"

The trio double-checked their provisions and ventured into the jungle. As soon as they started, Zeus couldn't stop himself from checking over his shoulders, feeling as if they were being followed.

Chapter 7

"Are we there yet?" Fiore whined.

"No!" Zeus yelled.

"Seriously?" Billix asked. "Look at your computer display. The red number is the distance between our destination and us. Right there. In front of you this whole time was your answer."

Frowning, Fiore lifted his arm and looked. "Oh. Why didn't you tell me before?"

"I didn't think I had to. The number decreases with every step we take. I thought you'd be able to figure it out. It's not that complicated. We move forward, the number goes down."

"Three miles to go. What's his name again?"

"Connit. For the fourth time, Connit. Do I have to send it to your computer? I can. I will if you need me to."

"Why are you so grumpy?"

Clearing a path through the jungle, Billix swung his Zytherd saber, a knife as long as his arm with a curved blade. A thin, high-powered laser beam ran the length of the sharpened blade, assisting in the cut with every swing. Leg sized branches and leaf bundles as thick as a chest fell away with ease. As he conversed with Fiore, his ire-fueled swings became more forceful. "Why? Well, unlike you, I can't control my biology with chemicals, so I'm hot, sweaty, and getting rashes in places I didn't know I had. I swear even my robotic leg itches."

Wincing, Fiore said, "It's not my fault you don't have the technology that I do."

"It's your fault that I'm *here*! Hiking through a jungle. With a bounty on my head. Ten billion creds, by the way, just in case you forgot."

Irritable from the humidity and the inane conversation, Hydrynx mewled at Zeus, then jumped from his shoulder.

"Don't go too far," Zeus said to his pet.

Hydrynx meowed a reply, then quickly busied itself chasing a yellow bug with large green wings laced with and glowing red veins. Despite its wobbly, uneven flight path, it deftly avoided Hydrynx's every pounce. Hydrynx bounded after the flying insect, growling after every miss. Determined to catch the elusive bug, Hydrynx growled once more, this one accompanied by a plume of flame. The bug roasted, wings shriveling and body blackening, and fell to the ground. Hydrynx enjoyed a nice, crunchy snack. Running its tongue across its face to collect any stray morsels, Hydrynx spied another one of those yummy bugs and gave chase.

This bug eluded Hydrynx's attacks just like the last one, finally landing on the side of a tree. Hydrynx made it to the base of the tree and stood on its hind legs, its front paws on the smooth bark. The bug scurried higher, always out of reach. Hydrynx could stretch no more and extended its claws, sinking them into the bark. Hydrynx was rewarded with a strike to the stomach, knocking it away from the tree. Confused, the cat-dragon hybrid approached the tree, wings curved forward like a shield, a fireball brewing at the back of its throat. Warm vapors wafted over the base of the tree as Hydrynx sniffed. A flap of bark twitched, slapping Hydrynx. The emerald-furred cat sprayed fire at the offending tree.

The moving patch of bark peeled itself from the tree; Hydrynx arched its back and hissed, creeping away as the size of the moving bark kept getting bigger. When finished, a humanoid shaped creature, the same shade of brown as the trees, stood in front of Hydrynx. The creature reached to the tree and removed a straight branch, a rudimentary spear. Hydrynx arched its back and hissed again, ready to stand its ground, until it saw more of these creatures peel themselves from other nearby trees.

Spear-tips pierced the ground behind and beside Hydrynx as it fled. Startling its trio of bipedal companions, Hydrynx burst from the flora and ran to Zeus and cowered at his feet. Concerned, Zeus stopped walking and looked down at his quaking pet. "Hydrynx? What has you so scared?"

"I didn't think anything could scare that little demon," Fiore mumbled, hoping beyond all hope that Hydrynx didn't understand him.

Within seconds, the pursuing creatures burst through the foliage as well. They were almost as tall as Fiore and just as wide, but thinner, their chests no more than a few inches thick. As before, each of the creatures plucked a branch-like spear from the nearby trees. They all tilted their heads—rectangular, with no discernable facial features—toward Hydrynx, now crouching between Zeus's feet. The creatures threw their spears.

With its feline reflexes, Hydrynx easily avoided the projectiles. Zeus dodged them as well, but with far less grace. As the primitive spears flew toward his feet, he leapt backward, stumbling on the uneven jungle floor. His back struck a tree. At first he figured the soreness from the impact was far better than having his legs run through with spears, but he couldn't move. He was pinned against the tree. Strips of the bark looking exactly like the arms and legs of the attacking creatures wrapped around him, pinning him to the tree. "They blend in with the trees! Stay away from the trees!"

Pulling cartridges from his bandoleer, Fiore yelled to Billix, "I'll take care of these guys, you free Zeus!"

"Got it!" Billix replied. He held his robotic arm in front of him, aiming at Zeus, and pressed buttons with his other hand.

"What are you doing?" Zeus hollered.

"My arm might not be as advanced as Fiore's cybernetic enhancements, but I do have a weapons system. I'm going to try an energy beam first. Okay, don't move."

"Don't move?" Zeus yelled. "I *can't* move! Careful! Careful!"

"Quit yelling! I need to concentrate...." Billix activated the beam. From the tip of his finger he unleashed a green beam, crackling with spirals of yellow. Zeus closed his eyes and jerked his head to the right, the beam charring the tree mere inches from his face. Surprised by the intensity of the beam, Billix jerked as well, trying to control the angry green light as it scalded a black path up the tree. Billix turned off his energy beam to assess the damage. Other than a burn mark across the tree, his attack had been rather ineffectual. So, much to Zeus's loud and vocal chagrin, he tried again.

Unaware of the calamity behind him, Fiore focused on the five creatures in front of him. Six, now that another one peeled itself from a nearby tree. All six had spears. They stayed in front of him, clicking communicatively to each other. Fiore assumed that they were strategizing, so he needed to come up with his own. He reached into his bandoleer.

Being outnumbered, Fiore knew he wouldn't be able to leave the fight without sustaining injury. One canister for skin, muscle, and organs. Once canister for bone. And one canister to promote rapid healing. If he got pierced by a spear, the wound would fully heal within an hour. A broken bone would return to its strong state in less than half a day. With the push of the button and a full body quake later, Fiore was ready for phase two. He wondered if Zeus would have complimented him for thinking ahead.

Too busy trying to dodge erratic energy beams, Zeus couldn't see what Fiore was concocting let alone offer any form of encouragement. Instead, he yelled to Billix, "Stop shooting at me!"

"I got it this time! I have six mini-missiles in here that launch from my index finger!"

"What good will that do? The creature is reaching around the tree from *behind* me! Go to the other side of the tree and use the Zytherd saber!"

"I'm not good at hand-to-hand combat. Just stay calm. I have everything calibrated."

"If you have a sharp, pointy weapon, it's *not* hand-to-hand combat!"

"Hold still!" With one last button press, Billix released a mini missile. It shrieked through the air, the noise lasting a split second. A billowing white tail of smoke bridged from Billix's metal finger to the tree, slamming into it six feet above Zeus. A brief conflagration accompanied a booming explosion, large enough to shake the jungle floor.

While Zeus had been begging Billix to find an alternate solution to his problem, Fiore dodged tree creature attacks. They were nothing more than cautious spear pokes meant to ferret out Fiore's ability. While he parried them with ease, Fiore inserted three more cartridges into his forearm sheath. Dodging another few strikes, he reached into another pouch to retrieve a thick, brown energy bar. Despite its density, Fiore wolfed it down with ease, needing the condensed nutrients in the compact bar. Satisfied that he was ready to fight, he pressed the start button.

Muscles bulged and expanded underneath his reddening skin; veins throbbed and squirmed from the increased blood flow. Fiore roared. Fingers curled, ready to rend anything he could clutch, Fiore charged toward the spear-wielding creatures. Screams and spittle spewed uncontrollably from his mouth as he ran. The creatures simply moved out of the way.

Despite being twice as strong as normal, Fiore couldn't stop his momentum. Smashing face first into a tree didn't hinder his rage, though. Under the rain of leaves and twigs shaken loose from the impact, he turned to recalibrate his attack. Again he bellowed and frothed, and then charged toward his targets—until a tree fell on him.

Billix stood stunned, unaware of the power that his mini-missiles possessed until now. The explosion sheared off the top of the tree, dropping it on Fiore.

"The saber!" Zeus yelled, still pinned to the tree. "Use the Zytherd saber!"

Finally listening to Zeus, Billix did as suggested and wielded the jungle tool as a weapon.

"Don't let them surround you," Zeus shouted.

"I got it under control! I'm using my ocular implant to target them. I know where they are at all times," Billix shouted back.

"Wait. You have an ocular targeting system? Why didn't you use *that* when you were shooting at me?"

"Shut up! Quit distracting me! I need to focus if I'm going to defeat the natives."

Billix raised the saber over his head and ran toward the closest native. The native used its spear as a staff and smacked Billix in the ribs. The purple-skinned cyborg dropped the saber and howled in pain. Another native ran by and hit him in the knees. It took only two more strikes to reduce Billix to a sniveling ball as he lay in a fetal position on the jungle floor.

Zeus sighed. He then looked at the prone figure of Fiore under the foliage of the fallen treetop, and hoped that he wasn't injured.

Fiore suffered six fractured bones, two torn ligaments, a puncture in his right arm and leg, a collapsed lung, and various lacerations about his body. Having been unconsciousness for the last two hours, he would never know about most of his injuries. Injecting his body beforehand with the necessary ingredients of vitamins, minerals, and chemicals, he healed as he slept. The functionality of his lung had returned fifty minutes ago. Many of the cuts disappeared, not even a scar to remember them by. Major puncture wounds shrunk to thumb-sized scabs. The fractures and ligament tears were in their final stages of healing, nothing more than dull aches when Fiore awoke.

Groggy and sore, consciousness came to him slowly. He felt the sensation of movement first, then the feeling of lying on something firm, but pliable. He tried to move his arms, but couldn't. Frustrated, his eyes snapped open to see small pieces of the sky through the dense treetops. On his back, he lifted his head to look down his bound chest to his tied feet. His eyes widened as he moved his feet apart to look between them. Voice hoarse from dryness, he asked, "Am I on a snake?"

Hands tied together with thick vines, Zeus trudged along beside Fiore and said, "Yes. Yes you are. It was the only thing large enough to carry you."

The snake, wide enough to fit Fiore comfortably down its gullet if it so chose, slithered with its head eight feet above the ground. Perched at the base of its head was one of the native tree creatures, holding reins attached to a bit in the snake's mouth. Head lolling from side to side, Fiore's body shifted with every wriggle of the snake's movement.

Looking at Zeus, Fiore asked, "What happened? The last thing I remember, I infused myself with my 'battle mixture' and went on the offensive."

"Oh, it was offensive all right," Zeus moaned. "You attacked. You ran into a tree. You attacked again. A tree ran into you."

Fiore sighed. "Yeah. That sounds about right. Where are they taking us?"

"I don't know. Their language consists mostly of clicking noises. It's rather fascinating, actually. I'm assuming they're taking us back to their village or city or wherever they live."

"I'm picking up a lot of signatures resembling these creatures up ahead with my ocular implant," Billix said. "I think we're getting closer. It seems like we're getting closer."

"A lot of good your cybernetic eye did," Zeus moaned.

"My targeting system is new!"

"You couldn't target a *tree*! A large, immobile tree!"

"He couldn't target a tree?" Fiore asked. He turned his head at an awkward angle to look at Billix, walking on the other side of the snake. "You couldn't target a tree?"

"I'm sorry I'm not a seasoned veteran in the art of skirmish like you two highly lethal bounty hunters. And if you remember, I *did* hit the tree. Half of it fell on Fiore. And…" Billix cut himself short when the party crossed from the thick jungle into the natives' village.

Sparser than the dense jungle, trees were the foundation of the natives' habitation. Some twisted together to form a framework for crude huts, the branches of others grew together in an eternal embrace as the foundation for shelters above the jungle floor. The ground itself sloped upward on the east side of the village, housing many small, inhabitable caves. A slight downward slope to the west led to an expansive swamp where natives rode upon snakes through the waters, collecting fruits and fish.

The natives stopped their activities and watched as the small party of their fellow denizens led their captives through the middle of the village, toward the largest structure—an open-faced hut constructed from strategically placed fallen trees and thatched from bundles of the large leaves. In the center was a throne of rudimentary carved wood. On the throne sat what Fiore assumed to be their leader.

However, he didn't look like them. He was a completely different species. He looked vaguely familiar to Fiore, but he couldn't figure out why. Billix solved the mystery when he said, "Hi, Uncle Connit."

Chapter 8

The natives cut the ropes binding Fiore, and he flopped to the ground. Standing, he wobbled a bit, his body still shaky from being crushed by a tree top and sore from the accelerated healing process. As he stretched, he watched the two purple creatures engage in a handshake.

Since Connit was Billix's relative, he had a similar shape to his nephew's, with an upside-down teardrop head atop an elongated neck and purple skin, although his was a deeper shade of violet. Connit had cybernetic implants as well, but different than his nephew's; a silvery metallic cup where his mouth and chin should be, and two black metal feet stuck out from his pants, which were tan and frayed at the cuffs. Even though his shirt, similar in color to his pants, hid his doughy body, Connit's age could be seen by the numerous wrinkles in his skin and the white hair growing around the whole circumference of his head. His beard and mustache created a gossamer perimeter around the machine part embedded in his face.

When Connit spoke, his deep, smooth voice held only a hint of electronic reverberation. "Good to see you, Billix! I'm sorry my people were so rough on you."

"No, Uncle Connit, it's my fault for dropping in unannounced. But I don't remember you being… a king?… of a tribe."

"Meh. More like a 'god'. I had set up a residence not too far from here, and lived off the land. Foraged for fruits and trapped animals. One of these aboriginals got caught in a trap. I released it and patched it back up. One thing led to another, and now I'm their god."

"They seem pretty dangerous."

"No more than any other primitive tribe. They thought you three were threats. I'm just happy that no one got hurt."

"Ha!" Fiore exclaimed as he twisted his head, trying to get a crick out of his neck.

Connit glanced at Fiore, then did a double take when he saw the computerized forearm sheath. Excited, he ambled to Fiore. "Well, look as this beauty."

Fiore twitched as Connit ran his fingers along the tubes and wires that went from the unit into his skin. It tickled. Connit tapped the receptacles and said, "Let me guess: you place some ingredients into these, and the machine infuses them into your body, transforming biological functions from hours or days into mere seconds."

"Yep," Fiore giggled. It still tickled.

"That must take a considerable amount of energy. What's the fuel?"

Fiore reached into a pouch of his bandoleer and pulled out one of his dense nutrition bars. "These. They taste like dirt, but they get the job done."

Connit laughed. "I bet they do. I bet they do." He ambled back to his nephew, parts of his metal feet clicking, worn down from the rigors of time. "So, Billix, what brings you and your… friends?… here."

Billix reached into one of the rucksacks that Fiore had been carrying and pulled out the gun in question. "First of all, they're not friends. Well, not really friends. They're bounty hunters, and, apparently, I'm one of their contacts. Actually, only contact, from what I can figure out. Second, we were wondering if you can tell us about this gun."

Connit's eyes rounded as if smiling. "Bounty hunters? Well, as a retired one myself, I can certainly attest to the need for good contacts."

Fiore crossed his arms over his chest and gave Zeus a smug smile. Zeus could only roll his eyes. Atop Zeus's shoulder, Hydrynx glared at Fiore, its tail twitching. Fiore scowled at the cat creature, then went back to paying attention to what Connit had to say.

Examining the gun, Connit pulled a small light from his pants pocket, and shined it on the bottom of the grip. "Well, if you look at the symbol here, you'll see that's it's manufactured by Sivka Corp."

"I did see that. But they make different guns for different armies and agencies and police forces and commercial uses. Zeus and Fiore were wondering if you'd be able to narrow it down for them."

Slowly rotating the gun in his hands, he brought it closer to his face. "Where did they get this?"

Zeus answered, "Three men broke into our… headquarters. We fought them off and were able to take this from one of them."

"Interesting. This is a very top-of-the-line model. Great construction, high-quality material. A much higher quality product than the ones they sell to police or armies. And look at the chamber. It's adjustable, so it can shoot darts, capsules, bolts, or even old-fashioned bullets. Were the intruders wearing any kind of uniform?"

"All black. Not sure if they were uniforms or not, but it was all the same style visors and gear."

Connit's eyes went wide. He handed the gun back to Billix. "The gun belongs to Sivka Corp."

"We know that. We were hoping you could tell us who—"

"You don't understand. That is who came after you. It was Sivka Corp."

Fiore couldn't reconcile what Connit meant. He turned to Zeus, but realized he was just as confused. Even Billix looked confused. Eyebrows furrowed, Zeus turned back to Connit and asked, "What do you mean, 'it was Sivka Corp'?"

"They have their own private security force. Rumor has it that they dispatch them to commit some rather felonious dealings, but nothing to ever warrant an investigation from the intergalactic police."

That notion made Fiore's head hurt. "That… that… that…."

"Is absolutely ludicrous," Zeus articulated Fiore's thoughts.

Billix shrugged his shoulders. "It kinda makes sense to me."

"It what galaxy does that make sense?" Zeus asked. "There is no way Sivka Corp would circumvent authorities like that. They're so large that the intergalactic police would prioritize them over anyone else."

"Yeah!" Fiore snapped. "What he said."

Billix grimaced. "Seriously? They're the largest corporation in the galaxy, yet they rarely get into any kind of legal trouble. Every time they make the news for something bad, it's quickly cleaned up or hushed up or swept away. I could believe they have a secret goon squad taking care of things like that."

"What did you two do to garner such attention?" Connit asked.

"From them? No idea," Fiore replied. He looked at Zeus and asked, "Do you think this has anything to do with Dryn Tammeryn and The Legend?"

"I can't imagine how," Zeus replied.

"Did you say, 'The Legend'?" Connit asked.

Billix answered, "Yes. Apparently, The Legend stole a bounty from them and they're trying to track him down. So they put a bounty on me to lure him out. Ten billion creds."

Robotic feet squeaking, Connit trundled closer to his nephew and asked, "These two bounty hunters put a bounty of ten billion creds on *you*?"

Billix chuckled. "To lure out The Legend. It's a crazy idea, right?"

"Yeah… crazy.…" Connit mumbled, as he reached his right hand behind his back. In a flash, he jumped behind Billix and grabbed him, pinning the younger man's arms behind his back. In his right hand was a gun, pressed against Billix's head. "I claim him as bounty!"

"*What?*" Zeus yelled. "You can't be serious!"

"Is this some kind of weird family inside joke or something?" Fiore asked. "If it is, I don't get it."

"Did you two put a bounty for Billix on the wire?" Connit asked, grinding the gun muzzle against his nephew's head.

"Yes, but—" Zeus started.

"Then 'but' nothing. Pay up!"

"Uncle Connit!" Billix cried out. "I'm your nephew!"

"Not right now, bounty. You can be my nephew after these two pay up."

"We don't have ten billion creds, you old fool," Zeus yelled.

A series of clicks snapped from the cybernetic implant on Connit's face. In unison, two dozen natives sprang to attention, pointing their spears at Zeus and Fiore. For reinforcement, four snake riders positioned themselves behind the bounty hunters. With a dire tone, Connit said, "Then I suggest you think of a way to get it."

"Uncle Connit," Billix pleaded. "You can't do this. I'm family!"

"No bounty is ever family."

"You said you came to this planet to retire."

"Well, for ten billion creds, I unretired."

Billix sighed. He looked at Fiore and Zeus and said, "Get ready."

"For what?" everyone asked simultaneously.

"This!" With his hands still behind his back, Billix pressed the necessary button on his robotic arm to release the energy blast from his fingertip. He finally hit his target: his uncle's robotic ankles, severing his feet from his legs in metallic shreds.

Sparks crackled and liquids spewed from Connit's legs as he fell backward. Windmilling his arms, he fired his gun impotently at the jungle or into the air. The natives with the spears looked from their leader to their prisoners. The natives without spears ran around and shrieked with their clicking language. With a smack, Connit fell to the jungle floor. Trying to sit up, he clicked commands to his worshipers. A few dropped their spears and ran to his aid, while the others focused on the prisoners, now escaping among the confusion.

Wasting no time, Billix joined Zeus and Fiore as they sprinted to the nearest snake. Sitting at the base of its head, the rider commanded the snake to rear up, its head now ten feet off the ground. As he ran, Fiore scooped up the rucksacks with one hand and then grabbed Hydrynx from Zeus's shoulder. Before any harm could befall him, Fiore threw the cat-dragon hybrid at the snake's rider.

The yowling ball of fire and fur and wings collided with the rider. Having no chance of winning a fight with the twisting bundle of fury, the rider jumped from his perch. Much to his surprise, Zeus found himself following the same path as Hydrynx after Fiore picked him up and tossed him toward the snake's head.

Sliding about the smooth scales as the snake wriggled, with his irate pet digging its claws into his back, Zeus wrestled with the reins, swearing as he tried to slip his feet into the stirrups. Within a few seconds and a hundred foul words, Zeus gained control of both the serpent and his pet, using the straps to guide his mount and promising Hydrynx it could burn Fiore's face after they recaptured their bounty.

Zeus guided his serpent to Fiore and Billix, both now running in circles and dodging thrown spears. Quickly figuring out the rein system, Zeus commanded the snake to collide with one of the other serpents, knocking its rider free from the saddle. Fiore grabbed Billix by the back of his shirt and jumped onto the snake that Zeus controlled. Straddling the reptile as best he could, Fiore hugged it with his free arm. Knowing there was no way for Billix to find purchase on his own, he tightened his grip on the back of the cyborg's shirt.

Zeus guided the snake away from the flying spears of the natives and the shouts of Connit, but the villagers were not going to allow an easy escape. A serpent with rider caught up to the bounty hunters on the right side. The two snakes' heads were even, slithering in unison. A second snake with rider appeared on the left side, immediately snapping its jaws at the flailing Billix. The snake on the right side did the same thing, lunging in an attempt to bite at Zeus.

Avoiding another strike, Fiore dangled Billix over the side, jungle floor rushing by beneath his kicking feet. Shaking Billix, Fiore yelled, "Shoot! Shoot! How do you make this thing shoot?"

Grabbing his robotic arm with his flesh-and-bone hand, stinging from the whipping lashes of branches and leaves, Billix cried, "Stop shaking me! Why are you even doing that? That's not how you work the gun! I work the... *tree*!"

The snake with the native rider avoided the oncoming tree, but lost some ground in the process. Fiore yanked Billix out of the way of the tree, but couldn't stop the momentum, and slammed him against the right side of the snake. Upon impact, a green energy beam discharged from his finger, frying a small burn mark into the adjacent snake's skin. The snake hissed and winced, but continued to race alongside the bounty hunters.

Finding success in his last action, Fiore tried it again, lifting and slapping Billix against the snake's side. Again, a green energy beam zapped the adjacent snake. Despite Billix's vigorous protesting, Fiore continued to shoot in such a fashion until the pursuing snake slowed.

Whipping and winding through the trees and brush, both native-mounted snakes maintained pursuit. Whenever one got close enough, the rider commanded the snake to bite at the tail of the bounty hunters' snake, prompting Fiore to use his newly acquired weapon.

Doing his best to clutch the serpent, Fiore twisted and held Billix toward the pursuers and shook him again. "Fire the missiles! Fire the missiles!"

"Stop shaking me! Stop shaking me!" Billix yelled back, trying to fumble with his weapon system while flopping about. Due to all the shaking, he accidentally released all of his mini-missiles. Launching one at a time, five mini-missiles shrieked through the air. Having no preordained target, they corkscrewed wildly until striking the nearest objects—four trees and one of the snakes.

The struck trees exploded to splinters, while plumes of flame and smoke quickly engulfed the chunks of flying snake meat. The conflagration caused the pursuing snake to give up and retreat, slithering back whence it came. All three riders of the remaining snake watched in wide-eyed awe as the patch of billowing fire shrunk from their view. They still looked back, even after the smoky scene disappeared. Zeus was aware enough to snap his head around to guide their snake in the right direction.

After a few minutes of no repercussion and no signs of further pursuit from the natives, Fiore started to chuckle. Then Billix. Fiore's joy grew to laughter, and Billix quickly joined in. Even Zeus couldn't contain his glee, laughter pouring uncontrollably from him. They had escaped! They had come out of a perilous situation unscathed using a blend of Zeus' wits and Fiore's brawn. Zeus felt good about his partnership with Fiore.

Even though the jungle was dense, Zeus remembered the direction they took to get to the village, so backtracking was easy. The snake's speed made the return trip faster. No sooner did they squirm their way out of the jungle, into the field where they had left Billix's air-car, then they were greeted by the gun-wielding Zaurn brothers....

Chapter 9

Zeus yanked the reins. By the time the snake came to a slithering stop, all four Zaurn brothers had their guns trained on the new arrivals.

"Well, isn't that mighty nice of Zeus and Fiore," Zossa said, standing by Billix's car. "They hand-delivered the bounty right to us."

"Shoot them! Shoot them!" Zarn hissed, forked tongue twitching with every word. He and his diminutive brother Zyf stood by their vehicle. Floating a foot above the ground, it was twice as big as Billix's car and had no top. Zyf jumped up and slapped the back of Zarn's head. "No. No shooting them. We need the bounty alive, remember?"

"Didn't say nothin' about needing the delivery boys alive," Bahb said, bringing his rifle up to eye level. He braced the butt of his gun against his shoulder, and watched through the scope as Fiore slid off the snake, keeping Billix in his grasp.

"Careful, Bahb," Zyf said. "We don't want to accidentally vaporize ten billion creds. Plus, Fiore and Zeus are smart enough to know that they're outnumbered."

Frustrated, Fiore looked at Zossa and said, "How did you even find us? Before today, I never even heard of this planet."

Zossa and Zyf laughed like they understood the punch line of a joke no one else could comprehend. Zarn laughed too, but everyone knew that he did so because he was insane. Bahb remained silent as he continued to track Fiore through the scope of his rifle. "Simple," Zossa shared the secret. "You used the bounty's car for the jump port—and his personal access code. All jump-port records are accessible to the public."

"Why didn't you think of that?" Fiore yelled at Billix.

"What?" Billix yelled back. "Why didn't I think of that? Well, it may have had something to do with the duress I was under from getting kidnapped by two bounty hunters that put a ten-billion-cred bounty on me!"

"You were the one who gave us the idea!" Zeus yelled from atop the snake. "You need to take at least some responsibility for screwing up the plan."

"Screwing up the plan? It was a dumb plan! And you're dumb for following a plan made by a complete stranger! So, I didn't screw up the plan!"

"Really? How about the fact that we barely escaped from *your uncle* trying to kill us?"

"I didn't know he'd try to do that. How was I supposed to know that?"

"He's a retired bounty hunter!"

"I didn't know that either! Growing up, he was always just eccentric Uncle Connit who told crazy stories."

Zossa laughed again. "Did you just say that your own uncle tried to kill you? Even the Zaurn brothers aren't that cold blooded."

"Shoot them! Kill them! Kill them dead!" Zarn blurted.

A chill ran down Fiore's spine as he looked at Zarn. The saurian's tongue refused to stay in his mouth while his eyes darted around, independent from each other. The tip of his tail twitched, as did half of his fingers holding the gun.

Zossa hissed at his brother. "I told you, Zarn. No!" He turned back to Fiore and said, "We don't need to shoot anyone, because Fiore is gonna hand us the bounty, just like he did for The Legend."

Fiore scowled as all four Zaurn brothers slowly advanced toward him. He hadn't been a bounty hunter for very long, but allowing The Legend to take his bounty was the low point of his career. Being reminded of that made him angry. If only he had thought of something, some way he could have stopped him. If only he... had... an idea....

Fiore held Billix up by the scruff of his shirt. "I have a gun!"

Squirming, Billix yelled, "Not again! Put me down! Stop picking me up!"

The Zaurn brothers stopped and passed furtive glances among themselves, confused by Fiore's statement. Bahb said, "Don't look like a gun. Looks like a purple guy."

"His robot arm is a gun," Fiore continued, shaking Billix for emphasis. Hoping Zeus would jump in, he glanced up at his partner.

Reins in his right hand, Zeus leaned forward on his left elbow. Still on his shoulder, Hydrynx fluttered its wings and hissed, swirling flames danced in its open mouth. Looking down at the Zaurn brothers, Zeus said, "My partner is right. He has a gun. I have a fire-breathing cat-dragon. And, most importantly, I'm on a twenty-foot snake that can move at the speed of lightning. So, I suggest you put all your weapons in our hovercar, step into the jungle, and let us drive away."

The Zaurn brothers' expression shifted from confusion to anger as they continued to glance at each other, calculating their options. Finally, Zossa spoke. "We don't believe you. Not many civilian cyborgs have weapons in their limbs."

"Oh yeah?" Fiore asked, happy to demonstrate the upper hand in these negotiations.

"No!" Billix yelled. "Don't shake me! Just put me down and I'll show them. I'll shoot a tree or something. Just don't shake me."

Fiore shook Billix; a flash of crackling green energy discharged. This time, however, it came from a different finger, and was larger. Much larger. Large enough to blow a fist-sized hole clean through the back of the snake's head.

The blast happened so fast and so clean, the snake's head stayed upright long enough for Zeus to comprehend what had just happened. Even Hydrynx seemed shocked, the hissing and swirling fire stopped, its expression frozen. As the serpent's head fell to the left, Zeus slid down its body and deftly landed next to Fiore. Mouth agape, Zeus stared at Fiore.

Staring at the still-smoking hole in the snake's head, Billix mumbled, "Speechless. I'm speechless. I am utterly speechless. I can't think of words to say right now."

Smirks and smiles, the Zaurn brothers raised their guns and stalked closer to their prey.

Still sticking with his original threat, Fiore waggled the now limp Billix. "Stop! Don't move any closer, or I'll shoot!"

Zossa laughed as he advanced. "Sorry, Fiore. Now that your nasty little snake is out of the way, we're no longer scared. You might be able to shoot one of us, but I'm pretty confident that the other three can take you and that green kitty of yours."

Fiore knew his fate and that of his friends rested in his hands. He had to think fast. He considered Zeus the strategist of the duo, but lately Fiore had been coming up with some stellar ideas. It was he who came up with the great idea of taking the Sivka Corp gun to a pawn shop to make a great connection with Billix, and then being smart enough to agree to Billix's idea of using him as a fake bounty. The thought of "using Billix" bounced around in his mind, until an idea struck him.

As gently as dealing with an egg, Fiore lowered Billix to the ground. He then quickly wrapped his left arm around Billix's torso and pulled him close. With his right hand, Fiore grabbed Billix's machine hand and held it against the young man's purple head. "I shake him and he shoots!"

"What are you doing?" Billix shrieked.

The Zaurn brothers all stopped, again looking at each other, trying to make sense of the nonsense they were witnessing. Gun at the ready, Zossa said, "Fiore, what are you doing?"

"I'll shake him. I swear I'll do it!"

"You're not going to shake him… shoot him… shake… whatever it is you think you're going to do, you ain't gonna do it."

"Sure I will. I shot my snake, didn't I? I'll shoot him!"

"You'd shoot your own friend?"

"He's not my friend," Fiore lied. "If I shake him, then it's ten billion creds vaporized. Is that what you want?"

Zossa stood straight and lowered his gun.

"You've gone insane!" Zeus yelled at his partner. "It's from all those chemicals you've been injecting. They liquefied your brain!"

Gesturing his head toward Billix's car, Fiore said, "Get in."

Zeus moved toward the waiting hovercar, but stopped as Zyf, Zarn, and Bahb trained their guns on him. Looking at Zossa, Fiore gave a little shake of Billix.

"Stop!" Zossa yelled. The thick upper lip of his scaled muzzle curled into a snarl as he growled to his brothers, "Lower your guns. He's right. I still don't think he'd shoot him, but he does have a gun pointed at ten billion creds."

"Get in the car, Zeus," Fiore growled.

"Fiore…" Zeus tried to reply, but his partner cut him off.

"Zeus, I got this! I got it all under control!"

"Fiore…"

"Come on, Zeus, move!"

Sighing and rolling his eyes, Zeus got into the car's passenger seat. Fiore released Billix into the driver's seat and then jumped in the back. Billix started the car as Fiore patted him on the back and said, "Sorry about that, buddy, but I needed to do that for my genius plan to work."

Arms crossed, Zeus nodded at the Zaurn brothers as they piled into their car. "Well, genius plan maker, what I was trying to tell you was that we should have taken their guns and disabled their car."

No sooner did the threesome and pet speed away, then red energy beams flashed by as the Zaurn brothers gave pursuit.

"Faster! Faster!" Fiore screamed, looking behind him.

"No more talking from you!" Billix yelled back, putting his full weight on the accelerator, swerving every time a flash of red streaked past the car. "I'm done with you! I don't want you talking. I don't want you coming up with any more ideas. I don't want you *touching* me. And by everything that is holy and unholy, I *never* want you picking me up and shaking me again. *Ever again*!"

Confused and a little saddened, Fiore looked at Billix and said, "I was just trying to help."

"Enough of your helping! When you help, I get hurt. Stop it! Stop helping!"

The car rocked, the back end sliding about as one of the energy beams clipped the corner. Putting a halt to his diatribe, Billix fought with the steering mechanism to regain control. Even though the car hovered over a majority of the wild grasses in the fields between the jungle and Momonol, taller plants and flowers splattered against the windshield. Billix shifted around in his seat and craned his neck to see past the ever-growing pulpy mess.

"Look out!" Zeus yelled as they crossed the border from the field to the city, almost hitting a pedestrian. The Zaurn brothers showed no signs of relenting, still shooting as they closed the gap between them and their targets. Billix continued to push the car as fast as it could go, despite the lack of visibility.

The sparse number of inhabitants on the streets screamed, but their cries went unheard by those in the cars, zipping by too fast. Billix avoided all of them, usually by skidding off other moving vehicles as well as parked ones, or careening off various street vending carts and signs.

Not having the same compunction for others' safety, the Zaurn brothers continued to shorten the distance between them and their prey. The front of their car tapped the back of Billix's. Fighting to control the bucking rear of the vehicle, Billix smashed through a drink vendor, the liquids washing away some of the field debris from the windshield. Zeus pointed and yelled, "There! Go there. The jump-gate."

Billix yelled back, "Your ideas are as bad as Fiore's. We don't have the luxury to sit through the pre-jump routine."

One lone car waited at the jump-gate, the lights flashing along the circular gateway as the computer processed. A slick smile slid across Zeus' face. "We're going to steal his jump."

A pair of lights turned solid green along the metallic ring of the gateway. Only a dozen more to go and then gateway would provide an opening to another city. Two more lights went green. Pointing as if his windshield wasn't opaque, Billix yelled, "It's one jump per car! Once he goes through, the jump closes."

Two more green lights. "Then we have to get through before he does."

As two more lights flicked to green, Billix accelerated. "If he goes through before us, the portal closes and we crash into the building behind the jump-port. At this speed, I doubt even the monstrous science experiment in the backseat will survive."

Two more lights. "Then go faster!"

Two more lights. Fiore watched as the Zaurn brothers halted their pursuit, slowing down and veering off the path that Billix had put them on.

The final two lights flipped to green, and the air within the perimeter of the gate rippled and changed to the destination. Fiore didn't even notice what the scene was; too busy screaming along with Zeus and Billix. Even Hydrynx sensed the impending doom, and tucked in a ball on the floor in between Zeus' feet.

The car that requested the jump, glided forward, aiming for its targeted location.

As they zoomed to catch up, Zeus twisted in his seat and braced from impact, "Faster! Faster!"

"We're not going to make it!" Billix hollered, muscles tensing with every word.

With the front of the other car ready to break the plane between Momonol and its destination, the threesome drew parallel. Fiore closed his eyes....

Chapter 10

Fiore squeezed his eyes closed even tighter, tucking his head between his knees as he jostled about. His shins bashed against the seats in front of him as his shoulders slammed the car's ceiling. Zeus's swearing and Billix's screaming were occasionally muted by the chaotic sounds of screeching and crashing. Metal shrieked against metal. Hydrynx howled. Fiore made mental lists of the ingredients he would need, depending on if the mayhem ended with lacerations and gouges, or if it ended in burned and charred limbs. But the madness ended in neither.

Feeling the momentum slow to a slight jolt from a sudden stop, Fiore opened one eye. No fire. No missing limbs. No running and screaming. He opened his other eye. Both Zeus and Billix were still in their respective seats, panting and covered in sweat. They looked at each other with fear-laced gazes of wonder. Then they laughed; the more they realized they were unharmed, the harder they laughed… until half a dozen gun barrels interrupted their moment, as did a voice saying, "You boys mind tellin' me who you are and why you're messin' up my town?"

Zeus and Billix exited the vehicle first. Fiore stretched as he followed, happy to escape the confines. The left side of the car nuzzled against a long, metal-sided building, big enough to be a warehouse. Behind the crumpled car, charred skid marks streaked the gray streets and sidewalks. Two lamp-posts lay broken, exposed wires belching sparks, while three more had car-shaped bends in them. The town consisted of one- and two-story buildings, simplistic in shape and style, mostly painted stone with glass windows. Right across the street from the crashed car was a building with the words "Constable's Office" in large letters over the main door.

"Ummmm," Fiore said with all the eloquence he could muster.

"Let me rephrase, then. I'm the Constable. You're under arrest for messin' up my town. And delaying my order of Thuthil whale milk."

The constable was tall, almost as tall as Fiore, but thinner. Taut muscles rippled under his uniform. His skin glistened as if smeared with a thin layer of oil, and shared the same shade of murky blue as the twilight sky. He had no hair, except for six finger-thick strands, three sprouting just above each corner of his lips. Fiore thought they looked like dark blue worms dangling from his face.

Since neither Zeus nor Billix seemed to have come up with an idea for how to get out of this, Fiore kept talking. "Thuthil whale milk? You have that here?"

"Clearly the leap in logic necessary is a bit too far for you to jump, huh? I do not have Thuthil whale milk here. That is the very reason why I need to have it *imported*. I have a contact who can supply me with Thuthil whale milk, and I was expecting a delivery to come through the jumpgate, but for some unexplained reason, you three came through instead."

Fiore couldn't resist taking a moment to lean close to Zeus and whisper, "See? It's always good to have contacts."

Zeus whispered back, "See? You're an idiot."

Fiore scowled at Zeus, but became all smiles when he turned back to the constable. "I'm quite the milk connoisseur myself. I certainly appreciate Thuthil whale milk."

"Well, if you can pay for all the damage you caused and tell me who you are, I might share a half-pint with you when my delivery arrives."

As the constable finished his sentence, a motorcycle pulled up. The driver, a man of the same race as the constable, got off and approached. "Sorry, Constable, but as these three came through, their car hit the jump gate causing a bit of damage. Looks easy enough to repair, but it'll take a couple of days."

Frowning, the constable turned back to the trio standing by the wrecked car. Gesturing with his gun, he said, "All right, you three. You're comin' with me."

The five other men—two the same species as the constable, the other three were different species far more monstrous and imposing—trained their guns on the interlopers. The trio had no other option than to do as they were instructed. Fiore looked back into the car to see Hydrynx crawl under the front seat.

As he stepped off the sidewalk, Zeus looked at the gray ground. "Is… is the ground… metal?"

"That it is," the constable replied. "We are on a diamond mining rig."

"*This* is a diamond mining rig?" Zeus asked, looking around at the buildings as if he had forgotten there were six guns leading him into the constable's office.

"You've heard of Ruukan diamonds?"

"Yes."

"Well, this is the planet Ruuka, and this is how we get them."

"But there are buildings and streets, and you have your own jump-port."

The constable and his men led the trio in through the door. The large room served as both his office and jail. The constable continued, "Well, we *had* a jump-port, then you three came along. But Ruuka is mostly swamp and inhospitable land. Excavation of the diamonds is an arduous process, so we decided to build a three-mile by three-mile platform around the excavating unit. There are a dozen more like this one, but the closest is a half a day away. The south and west parts of this platform are housing for the miners and their families. North is the excavating unit. We're standing on the east side, where we have shopping, and my office. Which also has the jail cell that I must now ask you to step inside."

The trio did as instructed. Head hanging low, Billix turned to the constable and asked, "Would it help me if I said I wasn't with these two?"

"No," the constable replied. "Since you were driving, I find that to be evidence contrary to your statement. Now, you three get comfortable. After I figure out a way to clean up your mess, I'll figure out what to do with you."

The small cell had three benches, one for each of the men. Fiore watched the constable as he dismissed the other five men, learning that he had no true staff or deputies, simply calling upon the rig's citizens to assist when necessary. The constable bemoaned his life choices as he sat at his desk and mumbled to himself about removing the car and fixing the damage, listing names of those who might be willing and able to help.

Fiore didn't stay seated for long, pacing from the bench to the front of the cell. He wanted to come up with a plan, but it didn't seem like either of his cellmates would be willing participants in that discussion. Zeus slouched against the wall. Billix sat hunched over, resting his arms on his lap, his moppy green hair covering his face. Plus, Fiore figured, whatever they discussed could easily be heard by the constable. He needed to figure out a plan on his own. Much to his surprise, he didn't have to think long until an opportunity arose.

Bursting through the door came three panic-stricken citizens: a man and a woman, Ruukan like the constable, clutching each other in fear, and a woman whose yellow skin was speckled with dark brown patterns. Her black hair grew in finger thick strands well past her shoulders. Scale covered ridges curled above her eyes and converged between them to form a pointed, yet flat, nose. Full breasts pushed against the confines of her thin shirt. Fiore lowered his eyes and admonished himself for looking at her chest when she was so clearly distraught. He took one last peek and then listened to the commotion.

"Constable," the blue skinned woman sobbed as her mate held her. "Our son... he's... he's..."

"No," the constable growled. "Not again!"

"It's true," the yellow skinned woman said. Even though tears streamed down her face, her voice held steady. "My daughter, too. They were both playing right outside. Right outside of our houses."

The blue skinned woman then noticed the three in the holding cell. She yelled, "Who are they? Are they involved? Are they a part of this?"

Jerking from the verbal attack, both Zeus and Billix sprung up to attention. They joined Fiore at the bars, close to the ruckus. Zeus asked, "A part of what?"

The constable put his hand on the woman's shoulder and said, "No, ma'am. They're not a part of this. I don't know much about them, but I do not believe they are involved."

"They look like they could be!" the woman snapped. Her mate wrapped an arm around her shoulders and guided her away while offering comforting words.

"What's she talking about?" Billix asked Fiore and Zeus. "Did I miss something? Why was she yelling at us? What did she accuse us of doing?"

"Our children are disappearing," the yellow skinned woman said. "My name is Weelah. I'm the captain of one of the cargo ships on this mining facility. And my daughter was... was just..." This time, she couldn't contain her emotions. The constable put his arm around her shoulders. She rested her head against his shoulder, an awkward gesture, since she was as tall as him, but much more substantial. She whimpered, "Help me."

"I will," he replied. "I'll get some volunteers for a search party and we'll...."

"We'll help!" Fiore exclaimed. All eyes shifted to him; Weelah looked confused, but appreciative, the constable looked angry, the indigo-skinned couple looked dubious.

Zeus and Billix glared at Fiore. Billix whispered, "What is *wrong* with you?"

"Think about it," Fiore turned his back to everyone in the office and whispered to Zeus and Billix. "First of all, it gets us out of this jail cell. Second, if they run Billix's car through the system, there's a good chance they'll see the wire about his bounty. If that happens, we'll have a whole island of people wanting to collect ten billion creds. Third, she's a cargo ship pilot. If we can help her find her daughter, I'm sure she'd be willing to take us wherever we need to go next. And it doesn't hurt to have an interstellar cargo pilot as a contact."

Zeus and Billix stared, mouths agape. Zeus recovered just enough to mutter, "That's... that's... a really good idea."

Billix shook his head. "How is it you were able to come up with amazing logic like that less than an hour after you accidentally shot our snake?"

"Hey, we escaped didn't we?" Fiore asked.

"Yes. Did you happen to notice that we escaped *to jail*?"

Brows furrowed, the constable strolled over to the cell. His mustache worms wiggled with every word as he asked, "Did you say you want to help look for the kids?"

"Yes, sir," Zeus said.

Squinting, the constable asked, "Why?"

"We're bounty hunters. Finding people is what we do. If we help find the kids, then all we ask is a lift off this planet when possible."

The constable looked back to Weelah. She crossed her arms and regarded the three men in the jail cell. Wiping away silent tears, she grimaced, but nodded her acceptance.

"Why should we trust you?" the constable asked, turning back to Zeus.

"What trouble could we cause? We'll be unarmed in the middle of the swamps with your search party. You said it yourself: the next mining platform is half a day away, so we can't escape."

"You can even use us as bait," Fiore said, trying to sweeten the deal.

"Stop talking," Billix muttered. "Just stop talking."

The constable turned to the couple, hugging each other. The man's eyes pleaded while the woman's simmered with anger. The constable then turned to Weelah. She had stopped crying, but could only give a defeated shrug. The constable opened the cell door and waved the strangers out. "Well, boys, congratulations. This has never happened in my history of law enforcement. You just went from criminals to deputies."

Chapter 11

The hovercraft skimmed over the dark waters, leaving swirling eddies in its wake. Although the vehicle didn't ride on the surface of the water itself, an occasional wave slapped the side, causing a chilled spray to drizzle the inhabitants. Zeus' mind was just as turbulent as the water.

The sky was a perpetual shade of twilight, a drab blue as if muted by a screen, and the same murky blue as the water—even the same shade as the indigenous species, such as the constable, steering the hovercraft. Zeus debated if the murky blue leaves sprouting from the murky blue trees of the murky blue forest that grew along the shoreline were actually that color, or if it was a pall created by the murky blue sky. He deduced that it was the former since Hydrynx, on his lap, was still green. Fiore's hair and leather were still a deep black, and his teeth—exposed by his enthusiastic smile—were bright white. A faint white light glowed from Fiore's goggles, a sign that technology aided his view of the environment around him.

Billix was still purple, albeit a paler shade now, one that Zeus attributed to fear as he rambled on with questions like, "What was that? What's in these waters? Did I see teeth? And claws? Are there things with teeth and claws in these waters? What's that over there? Can the things in the water leave the water? Can the things in the water jump on our hovercraft? The things that can jump from the water, do they have teeth? And claws?"

After the constable released Zeus, Fiore, and Billix, he shared that this was the second time that children had been stolen from the rig. When it first happened, two months ago, the constable and rig inhabitants assumed that nature was being feisty, that an unknown animal got bold enough and hungry enough to snatch an innocent morsel. But then the constable received word from the three nearest neighboring rigs that the same thing had happened to them. It had happened to those rigs again today.

Billix had suggested using the science buoys surrounding the rig that monitored both weather and tidal happenings to search for any kind of disruptive patterns. A few unnatural patterns were discovered, giving the search party a rudimentary direction to go. There was still quite a large area to cover. Four hovercrafts filled with armed deputies and capable citizens headed out to four different areas. The one Zeus found himself on included Fiore, Billix, the constable who made it very clear that he wanted to keep an eye on them, Weelah, and Hawanna, the father from the constable's office.

Being the independent owner and operator of a cargo ship, Weelah seemed quite capable of taking care of herself, even if she didn't have the two guns strapped to her waist holster and the four knives in her boots. Zeus speculated that he might see how capable she truly was if Fiore didn't stop staring at her breasts.

Feeling the need to save his partner by distracting him, Zeus slid closer to Fiore, confident that the noise of the hovercraft, as well as Billix's prattling, would keep their conversation private. "We need a plan."

Fiore leaned in and said, "From what the constable said, it's a pretty simple one. We're gonna go to an island that's roughly in between all four of the rigs and—"

"That's not what I meant. I mean to get out of this."

"Get out of…? Zeus, we're looking for missing children."

"I understand that. And I sympathize with the families. I do. But we only have a few more days before the deadline to turn in Dryn Tammeryn."

"We need to help these people."

"Fiore, we don't have time to—"

"Look, we may hunt sentient beings for a living, but ultimately it helps people. We have no friends and only a couple contacts. I understand your need to keep a distance, but we shouldn't forget about what's in here." Fiore pointed to both his and Zeus's chests simultaneously.

Zeus reeled back, his lips peeling away from his teeth. "How are you so sappy? We'll give it a day. If a resolution to this problem doesn't present itself, then we'll have to make one. Deal?"

Fiore heaved a deep sigh. "Fine. But we're not going to talk about it until we have to. So, we should go back to trying to figure out why Sivka Corp sent those men after us."

"If it was truly Sivka Corp who sent those men."

"You don't think so?"

Zeus had been pondering that hypothesis ever since he heard it. "It doesn't make sense, but it could be possible. I'm more worried about how to get Tammeryn back."

Fiore stroked his chin, contemplating. He then nodded and said, "Agreed. Let's try to figure that out."

Zeus smiled, happy that his partner was finally focusing on the right things. His good feelings were dashed pretty quickly, however, when Fiore continued with, "And maybe try to figure out how I could get a date with Weelah."

"I'm pretty sure if you find her daughter, Weelah will throw herself at you. Now, about Tammeryn—"

"Yeah? You think so?" Fiore asked, smiling. Even though Fiore's goggles hid his eyes, Zeus knew they were focused on Weelah.

"Of course. But her daughter is currently missing and in danger, so I'm sure that she's not thinking about any sort of romantic interlude right now. Back to Tammeryn, we need to—"

"Well, I know that. Afterwards, I mean… after we find her daughter, you think she'd go out with me?"

"Fiore, seriously, we need to focus on our bounty."

Fiore sighed. "We should go back to step one and try to find out more about him. His personal information."

"We already tried hacking into his personal information, remember? I'm sure every other bounty hunter in the galaxy tried that as well."

"That was before we had Billix," Fiore said, nodding to the young man. Billix sat huddled in a nearby seat, knees pulled to his chest, arms wrapped around his shins. A rogue wave splashed the side of the hovercraft and he jumped. "Thing with teeth! Thing with teeth!" The constable yelled at him to sit back down and shut up.

"Him?" Zeus asked, almost laughing.

Fiore held up his left arm and pointed to his computerized sheath. "He hacked into this thing faster than I could turn it on. When I got my surgeries, they told me that the computer system in here was nearly impossible to hack into."

Zeus squinted and smirked. "Surgeries? More than one? What else have you had done?"

Reeling back as if he saw a thing with teeth in the waves, Fiore stammered, "I… uhh… I… umm… had… a nose job."

"What?"

"Oh yeah. Totally. You should have seen that thing. It was larger than your head. And hooked. With a bump. And sideways. Oh, look! We're coming up on an island!" Fiore jumped from his seat and moved to the front of the hovercraft.

Zeus knew relatively little about Fiore. He was okay with that, since Fiore knew very little about Zeus. What Zeus did know was that he could trust Fiore. Even though he wanted to ply his trade as a bounty hunter, Fiore honestly believed he was helping people, almost as if it were a form of law enforcement. Zeus extended that courtesy to Fiore, always having his back and never lying to him, except the occasional, harmless white lie to get Fiore back on the proper course. The fact that Fiore had far more secrets than Zeus originally suspected was intriguing. That would have to wait, though. Even though Fiore abruptly changed the subject and ran away, he was right—they were approaching the island.

The constable guided the hovercraft onto the land, but thick brush prevented him from bringing it too far inland. Needing to settle in a small clearing by a copse of trees, he stopped.

"All right, crew, we're goin' to head toward the center of the island. Once we get an understanding of the environment, then we'll formulate a new plan," the constable said as he handed a gun to Hawanna and then checked his own firearms.

Weelah drew a gun with one hand and a knife in the other. "Got it."

"Good. Let's go."

The six moved through the trees and brush. Despite being in perpetual twilight, there was enough light to make artificial illumination unnecessary. They moved with ease through the forest; the trees and brush were spaced far enough apart to offer little hindrance. The constable nodded toward Fiore and Billix. "You two got anythin' useful in them fancy eye pieces?"

"I set my goggles to register heat signatures," Fiore said, slowly turning his head from left to right and then back again, scanning everything in front of him.

Billix tapped away at his robotic arm, scanning the area around him as well. "I'm flipping through a variety of different spectra as well as wave harmonics."

"Excuse me?" the constable asked.

"Well, I'm using different filters for the noises around us and transferring them to a visual representation. I'm 'seeing' noise. Then I'm trying to compartmentalize the noises around us. So, I can 'see' voices and 'see' mechanical noises, like metal against metal."

The constable looked at Zeus. All Zeus could do was shrug his shoulders. Without so much as a rejoinder, the constable hastened his step just enough to get away from Fiore and Billix. No sooner did he make it to the front of the party than Billix announced that he had found something. "Fiore, I'm seeing some unusual noise to the northwest. Do you see any heat signatures?"

Fiore looked to the right. "No. Nothing."

"Look to the left!"

"Oh. Sorry. Umm, yeah. I see something. Nothing definite, but I see something."

"All right, everyone," the constable said. "We're gonna head northwest—but quietly. Fiore and I will take point. Zeus and Billix next. Hawanna and Weelah take the rear. Move slowly, quietly, and be careful."

"Why am I with you?" Fiore asked as they began their journey.

"If there's any shootin', then I'm hidin' behind you."

The closer they crept to the anomaly, the more in focus it became for Fiore. The small blob of glowing yellow turned into a larger blob, and then separate blobs. When they became clear enough for him to see the blobs moving around, he shifted his goggles back to regular viewing. Once they crept within fifty feet, the constable signaled everyone to stop behind a small group of trees, the last line of foliage before the forest gave way to a clearing bustling with activity.

Figures milled about the outside of a cargo ship, about the size of four large buildings from the mining rig. Its running engines hummed and it had two open hatches—a large one to the cargo bay itself in the back of the ship, and a smaller one toward the front, for the crew.

Four men with guns paced nearby, guarding a group of five sobbing children sitting close together on the ground. Weelah gasped, covering her mouth with her hands. One of the girls looked like a smaller version of her mother. Trembling, tears rolled down her face. She turned to Fiore and buried her face in the crux of his neck and shoulder. Stunned and uncertain what to do, he put his arm around her as gently as if she were made of eggshell. The moment was brief, and Weelah turned back to the scene before them. Wiping her tears away, she readied her gun and knife and whispered, "Let's go."

Fiore shifted his weight as well, ready to rush in without a plan. He looked at the rest of the group, and they all prepared themselves to attack… until they heard a noise coming from the other side of the clearing. A small hovering skiff rustled through the brush and glided into the clearing. Smaller and more maneuverable that the constable's hover car, it rode twice as high off the ground. Three of the kidnappers strode over to it as the skiff lowered to the ground; the fourth stood guard by the stolen children.

Once the skiff landed, two more thugs jumped out, and then they unloaded three more crying children. As if handling baggage, five kidnappers corralled the three newcomers with the group already on the ground. Laughing, the criminals ballyhooed and congratulated each other on their impending payday. Anger building deep within, Fiore watched as the six formed a tight circle with each other, only giving curt glances over to their captives. Noticing that their holstered guns seemed small, he came up with an idea.

As quietly as possible, Fiore procured three ingredients from his bandoleer pouches. Without so much as a click, he inserted the cartridges into the empty slots on his forearm device. He opted for accelerated healing, since it had certainly proved its effectiveness on Jajlava. Feeling experimental, he also included ingredients designed to temporarily add a few layers to his epidermis, effectively thickening his skin. Before he started the process, he reached into another pocket to get one of his special energy bars.

Fiore was so focused on his plan, eyeing and visualizing what he was getting ready to do, that he didn't notice that all of his allies stared at him with looks of abject confusion upon their faces. After his last gulp of his energy bar, he pressed the button to start the process.

The chemicals and nutrients flowed through him, rushing through his blood stream and activating all the proper internal mechanisms. Twitching and fidgeting, his skin itched and felt heavier.

Shifting out from the tree he was hiding behind, he had no obstacles between him and the six men. He could do this! Preparing himself mentally, his breathing mutated into heavy grunting. He ignored Zeus's warning of, "This looks like a really bad idea," and sprinted forward.

Bursting from the tree line, Fiore roared like a caged beast set free and drew the attention of the kidnappers. Fiore stayed focused, aiming for the two men farthest from the children, even as the others started shooting. As he had hoped, their guns released low-level energy bursts; large enough to do damage if they connected with the right body part, but small enough not to bore holes into or blow limbs off a charging madman. Shielding his head with his arms, Fiore continued on his path with a trail of, "Ow! Ow! Ow! Ow! Ow! Ow!"

At the last second, Fiore dropped his shoulder and plowed into the two thugs he was aiming for, bowling them over. He immediately dropped to the ground and curled up into the fetal position. As he had hoped, the energy blasts stopped, parts of his skin smoking and sizzling from the fresh burns. It hurt, but if his plan worked, the pain would be worth it. Then he realized that he had forgotten to communicate any of this to his friends. As he lay there, he hoped that they were smart enough to figure out he'd used himself as a distraction so they could sneak up on the criminals from behind. Luckily for him, they were.

"Drop your weapons and nobody will get hurt!" the constable shouted from behind the lowlifes gathering around the fallen Fiore. They turned to see a woman and two native men holding guns, a green, winged cat with fire in its mouth perched on a young man's shoulder, and a purple cyborg pointing his robotic arm at them.

Looks of hatred and anger washed across the criminals' faces as they pensively looked back and forth to each other. Scowling, they lowered their weapons and bent over to put them on the ground. But before they relinquished them, they all smiled and stood back up, guns still drawn and pointing at the intruders threatening to take their ill-gotten gains from them.

The constable and his posse looked behind themselves to see why....

Chapter 12

Zeus often wondered how he found himself in these situations. All he wanted to do was make himself and Fiore the greatest bounty hunters in the galaxy. He wanted to dethrone The Legend, stripping him of that title. He knew it would be hard work, knew he had to use his brains and Fiore's muscle in the most effective way possible. He also knew that the profession was frought with many pitfalls and dangers. But he always assumed those pitfalls and dangers would come directly from hunting bounties, not trying to be helpful to yellow women with big breasts!

Although, Zeus couldn't blame Fiore for *all* of the bad decisions that had been made since losing Dryn Tammeryn to The Legend. The only reason they followed his suggestions in the first place was because Zeus provided none better. Due to his lack of good ideas, armed kidnappers with guns now surrounded him.

Zeus looked down at the unmoving and smoldering form of his partner, curled up on the ground. He wasn't sure if Fiore was conscious, but he was breathing. Zeus noticed that the burn circles pock-marking Fiore's body decreased in diameter, so at least his advanced healing "mixture" was working. As much as he hated to admit it, Fiore had had a good idea. A bit too altruistic for Zeus's taste with way too much pain, and it would have been better served if Fiore had actually *shared* his idea with everyone else before he executed it. And it certainly wasn't Fiore's fault that no one in their group had the foresight to logically deduce that there was still one more "hunting" party to come back to the rendezvous point.

The constable and his ersatz deputies had the kidnappers surrounded, almost had them unarmed. But the humming engines of their cargo ship drowned out the arrival of the fourth skiff, the one commanded by the kidnapper's leader, Koorza. The same race as Weelah, Koorza's yellow skin had distorted and misshapen ovals of brown, islands in an ocean of yellow. Thick cords of brown hair sprouted from his large head and grew unevenly past his shoulders. He wore mismatched pieces of body armor from different armies of different civilizations: an oval shell on his right forearm, rectangular metal plate on his left, a chest plate of black layered shells, strips of thick hide ringing around his black pants. A necklace of bones clacked against the shell over his chest. The scaly, bone-like ridges protruding from his forehead, along the upper perimeter of his eyes and peaking over his nose added to his already nefarious look of a mass of muscle.

"Koorza?" Weelah asked, her voice holding a familiarity beyond just knowing his name. His only response was a glare, one filled with hatred and anger and insanity. She stepped closer, despite the number of guns targeting her as she did so. "You? You're kidnapping these children? You kidnapped *our daughter*?"

"He's her daughter's father?" Billix whispered to Zeus. "I thought my uncle crossed the line trying to collect the bounty on me. That's just cold. Really cold."

Koorza's face twisted, obviously confused by her statement. He jumped from the skiff and strode over to the small group of children, walking to the little girl with the same skin tone and facial ridges as his.

Growling, he looked at his thugs and barked, "Who took her?"

The two that had kidnapped her and Hawanna's son pointed to each other. Before they could utter a word in their defense or call the other one a liar, Koorza shot them both, blowing a large hole in each of them. They each lived long enough to look at the freshly cauterized circles where their chests had been before collapsing lifelessly to the ground. The children whimpered or cried, all hugging each other as they huddled closer together in their small group.

If Fiore was conscious, Zeus hoped that he saw that!

Koorza eyed the small group of infiltrators, particularly Weelah. As he turned to them, he stumbled over Fiore's foot. Growling, he looked down at the body and asked, "What is this?"

"Some crazy guy who charged us," one of his thugs said. Pointing in the direction of their new captives, he continued, "Probably one of theirs."

"Charged you?" Koorza asked, examining the body. "What'd you do?"

"Shot him!" the thug said with pride.

More to himself, Koorza leaned closer to Fiore and said, "Now why would they send one of their own, unarmed, charging into a camp of criminals?"

"Well, he did distract us. That's how they got the jump on us."

Koorza glanced at his new captives. "They don't seem like they're cold-hearted enough to send one of their own on a suicide mission. Especially if Weelah's with them."

Attempting to further the subterfuge, the constable said, "A couple of hours ago he was a prisoner. He figured better to die for somethin' than rot in a jail cell."

Zeus tried to think of something to say to help, but nothing came to mind. He simply stared at Fiore, hoping he would wake up soon.

"Don't believe that," Koorza chuckled about the constable's comment. His scowl returned as he went back to viewing Fiore. Curious, he couched next to the body. He grunted to his thug, "You said you shot him, right?"

"Yeah. We all hit him. Repeatedly."

"I see the holes in his clothes… but no burn marks? How did—?"

Koorza's line of questioning was cut short when Fiore delivered a perfectly executed upper cut, hard enough to knock the gun from Koorza.

Zeus stood frozen, utterly shocked that Fiore—Fiore!—finally connected a punch. The erupting chaos snapped him out of his short-lived spell. Shouts rang out and energy blasts blazed through the air. The constable yelled unheeded commands while Hawanna and Weelah yelled to the children to curl up into balls and cover their heads with their hands. Billix just hollered for no reason, emerald energy beams flashing from his cybernetic fingertip. The thugs yelled random profanities and orders at each other.

The moist ground making it difficult, Zeus ran as best he could toward the nearest thug, a red-skinned creature much taller than he. But he was quite lanky, and Zeus used that to his advantage. A punch to the armpit and a kick to the knee dropped the criminal. As he writhed on the ground, Hydrynx belched a plume of flame, leaving the man even redder than he originally was, and no longer willing to fight.

Billix ran in circles, shooting at anything that resembled a thug. He missed. Every time. His energy blasts either hit the damp ground with a sizzling hiss, or blasted the bark off a tree in the forest surrounding the clearing.

The constable, Hawanna, and Weelah fared a little better. Covering each other, they moved from tree to tree, staying behind protection while getting closer to the children. The constable even managed to shoot one of the thugs.

Zeus ran to Billix, trying to rein in his enthusiasm by guiding him through the madness. Ushering him to behind a fallen tree, Zeus helped Billix aim. Even though Billix still missed everything he aimed at, he created enough of a distraction for Weelah to shoot another thug. Realizing that Billix had better aim when Fiore shook him by the scruff of his shirt, Zeus looked for his partner.

Despite delivering one good punch to the unsuspecting Koorza, Fiore found himself in trouble. Blood trickled from the left corner of Koorza's mouth, a smear of orange from his wicked smile to the bottom of his chin. The two circled each other, sizing one another up and down. Fiore swung first, a right jab easily parried; Koorza retaliated with three punches to Fiore's exposed ribs.

Even with the benefit of the temporary skin thickness, Fiore grimaced and spun, trying to back away from Koorza. Frustrated, he rushed Koorza, lowering his head and charging. Again, he missed. This time, Koorza drove his elbow into the center of Fiore's back, sending him face first to the mucky ground. Wasting no time, Fiore scrabbled to his feet and rushed his opponent. Even though he missed again, he shortened the distance. Trying to take advantage, Fiore turned and swung. Missed. Koorza offered a flurry of punches to Fiore's face. Doing what he usually did in these situations, Fiore fell forward, grasping for any part of his opponent. Wrapping his arms around Koorza's waist, Fiore pulled him to the ground, both men landing in an explosion of mud. Fiore tightened his grip, leaving Koorza few options other than to drag himself toward his gun.

Zeus' attention bounced from watching his partner's pitiful performance at fisticuffs to the children huddled on the ground to the remaining two thugs shooting at his allies who were pinned down behind trees. He looked at Billix and said, "We're going to do what Fiore did."

Even though part of Billix's face was covered with machine parts, and the rest of it had no discernable features, Zeus could tell that it held a look of disgust. "What? Are you crazy? No! That's stupid. We need a better idea."

"There is no better idea. We run right at the remaining two kidnappers, you shooting your laser finger, to distract them. Simple math: the constable, Hawanna, and Weelah have more guns than the kidnappers."

"You and Fiore have been partners for too long if this is the best idea you can come up with. It's stupid. I'm not gonna do it!"

Zeus frowned. "First of all, you haven't shot anyone yet, even with the advanced targeting system that you claim to have. Second, what better idea do you have?"

Billix paused and frowned as well. "You're confident that this will work?"

"I'm running out there with you, and I'm unarmed."

As Zeus hoped, his plan worked. Billix ran from their cover first, green bolts of energy zipping from his cybernetic fingertip, still missing what he aimed at. Zeus followed, albeit farther behind Billix than he implied. Their actions were enough to draw the attention of the gunmen, each firing once before Weelah and the constable took them down. The battle, however, was far from over.

Fiore struggled to contain Koorza, the criminal leader crawling across the ground. Fiore tugged and twisted, trying to stop Koorza without letting go. Koorza dug his hands into the dirt and pulled himself and Fiore along, getting closer to the gun with every effort. Fiore kicked and squirmed, even trying to dig his feet into the moist dirt, to no avail.

As Koorza inched his way closer to his weapon, the captive children witnessed the fall of the final criminal. Once he hit the ground, they jumped up and ran to their saviors, Weelah's daughter leading the way. But her path led right in front of Koorza. With one final lurch, Koorza grabbed both his daughter and his gun.

Gun pointed at his daughter, Koorza said to Fiore, "Time to let go."

Fiore did as instructed.

The rest of the children huddled behind the constable, Hawanna, and Weelah, as the trio tentatively pointed their guns at Koorza. Tears streamed down Weelah's face as she begged, "Koorza, please. Not my baby. Not my baby."

"Sorry," he growled with a smile. Getting a better grip on the crying little girl, he stood and backed toward the lower ramp of his cargo ship. "But she's my ticket out of here."

Fiore looked to Weelah, pointing her gun at Koorza but unable to shoot, and then to Koorza getting closer to escaping with his daughter. From where he lay on the ground, Fiore saw Koorza's side and back as the criminal kept moving closer to the ramp. Lumbering to his feet, Fiore looked around for anything he could use. Then he found it: Billix!

Facing those who wielded guns, Koorza ignored Fiore sprinting toward Billix. Before Billix could voice his dissent, Fiore tackled him and did a lopsided somersault. With his left arm wrapped around his purple friend, Fiore used his right arm to aim Billix's right arm. Just as Billix found his voice to tell Fiore to stop, Fiore squeezed, causing Billix to release a wheezing squeak and a bolt of green energy from his index finger.

The energy blast caught Koorza's left hip. The force knocked him over, dropping both his gun and his hostage. Taking advantage of the situation, the constable and Hawanna shot at Koorza while Weelah rushed to rescue her daughter. Close enough to the entrance to his ship; Koorza scrambled up the ramp to make his escape. In seconds, the cargo ship lifted from the ground and made a hasty retreat.

Kneeling and crying, Weelah hugged her daughter while the two exchanged blubbering, "I love you"s. Hawanna and his son did the same. The constable tried to keep from falling over as the rest of the children rushed to hug him, bustling past each other to cling to his legs. Billix flailed and kicked until Fiore released him. Completely frustrated, Billix reached down to scoop up a glob of mucky dirt and threw it at Fiore, and then berated him, but the speed at which his words flew from his mouth made them incomprehensible. Zeus watched and shook his head. He couldn't help but smirk as he turned to Hydrynx, on his shoulder, and said, "Not too bad, huh?" Hydrynx replied with a clipped mewl and two clouds of smoke puffing from its nostrils.

Zeus felt good about this part of the mission; he couldn't deny it. He also felt good that it took very little time. He had to confess, Fiore did well by negotiating a free trip off this planet. Now the question was, where did they need to go?

Chapter 13

Fiore munched away on a piece of fish. He couldn't remember what the constable had called it, just that it was a hearty local species. He shoveled scoopfuls of eggs into his mouth, from an indigenous bird, but, again, Fiore forgot the name. He didn't care too much about the names. They were certainly tasty enough, and he was grateful for the free meal, but his memory simply didn't deem animal names important enough to retain. However, what he did know and intensely enjoy was the large container of Thuthil whale milk. Sipping slowly, he savored the creamy succor and the faint aroma of happiness. Once emptied, he placed the container on the table and slid it to the constable. "More, please."

Even though Fiore knew that he lacked the skill to read people, he certainly understood the constable's wan expression. Glaring, the constable poured more milk from his private reserve into the recently emptied container. Three of the six worm-like hairs of his mustache twitched. Fiore decided that this would be his last glass of milk, recognizing that the constable was losing patience with him. "Thank you."

Sitting across the table from Fiore, the constable offered only an exasperated stare as response. Starting to feel uncomfortable, Fiore added, "I don't just mean for the Thuthil whale milk. I mean for breakfast. And a place to sleep."

The constable heaved a deep sigh, ruffling his mustache worms. "You and your... friends... really helped yesterday, this I can't deny. But I have my doubts about your motivations."

Genuinely confused, Fiore stopped drinking the milk, a row of droplets gliding across stray hairs of his mustache. "What... what do you mean?"

The constable crossed his arms and leaned back in his chair, judging. "I don't know how I feel about you. Even though you displayed a considerable amount of bravery yesterday, you only did so to get Weelah to give you a ride off this planet."

"We exchanged favors."

"You extorted her."

"What other option did we have?"

"You could have asked nicely."

"Asking nicely costs money."

Frowning, the constable leaned forward, placing his elbows on the table and folding his fingers together. Feeling uncomfortable, Fiore leaned back in his chair and crossed his arms over his chest, trying to hide his heart and soul from the constable's prying eyes. "There it is, Fiore. Money. That is why I doubt your motivation."

"But… money motivates everybody."

"I know who you are, Fiore."

"What… what do you mean?"

"I mean, I know you and Zeus are bounty hunters, you told me as much. I mean, I know there's a ten billion cred bounty on Billix. I mean that it would have been beyond easy to keep all three of you locked up until it came time to collect the bounty."

Surprised, Fiore's arms dropped, as did his jaw. "You… you… knew?"

"Even though this is literally a back-water planet, we still have modern amenities. As official law enforcement, I have access to even more. Not to mention, you three were using Billix's personal car. I can't say I agree with the concept of bounty hunting, but I can't say I disagree with it neither. I *must say* that I cannot fathom what that twitchy, purple kid did to be worth ten billion creds."

Face twisting, Fiore tried to comprehend. "Why didn't you…?"

"Because you and Zeus *did* help us. You and Zeus helped rescue kidnapped *children*. Two of whom I know personally. *That* is worth more than money, Fiore. There are two types of people in this galaxy—those who can't put a price on that, and those who can. I can't, and I know Zeus *can*. I'm just trying to figure out which type of person *you* are."

Fiore frowned and looked out the window of the constable's office, to the activity on the street outside. Weelah and a few of the locals helped Zeus and Billix get Billix's broken hovercar into a cargo container. Weelah had even agreed to bring the hovercar along. Fiore watched as everyone hastily shoved the hovercar into the rectangular pod per Zeus' command. Taking offense at the careless treatment of his personal property, Billix expressed his opinion. They bickered, ending when

Hydrynx sided with its master by offering a quick flare of fire from its nostrils. Billix stormed away, swearing.

Not turning back to the constable, Fiore said, "I trust Zeus."

"Should you?"

Fiore stood and walked toward the door. "Yes."

Just as the container door slammed shut, Fiore joined the commotion. And caught the wrath of Billix, "About time you showed up! It's not like you could have helped, being the largest sentient being on the planet. With the added ability to make yourself even stronger with the push of a button."

"I was eating breakfast," Fiore replied, even though he knew that Billix knew that.

"Breakfast? I thought you had a bandoleer full of chemicals and energy bars. Anyway, you could have helped. Maybe my hovercar wouldn't have gotten another dent."

"How does that even matter?" Zeus yelled. "It's already a mess!"

"I still have to get it fixed, and each dent costs extra!"

"Where do you take your vehicles that they charge you by the dent?"

"It's not like I have an overflowing list of contacts, like you guys. A veritable bevy that I can pull from, like you guys."

Fiore frowned. "We're working on it."

As the locals who helped wandered off, Weelah approached the bickering trio. Addressing Fiore and Zeus, she said, "I can't believe you two are bounty hunters. And you," she turned to Billix, "what could you have possibly done to be worth ten billion creds?"

Being shorter than her, Billix and Zeus could only look up and stare, clearly confused as to how she knew so much about them. Fiore leaned down behind them and whispered, "I'll explain later."

Laughing, Weelah gestured for them to follow her as she walked toward an open-topped skiff. "C'mon. Let's get moving."

As they followed, Billix mumbled to himself, "I'm in so much trouble. I'm in so much trouble. I'm in so much trouble...."

Zeus scowled at Fiore. "You knew she knew? How does she know? I don't like this. I don't like this at all."

Fiore stopped his partner and looked directly in his eyes. "Zeus, trust me on this. Yeah, I know I've had a bad idea here and there, but this isn't one of them. We helped her get her daughter back. Her daughter. We can *trust* her."

Zeus stared hard at Fiore and examined his unflinching expression. He nodded. "Okay. Okay, Fiore. I trust you."

They boarded the skiff and as it lifted them to the cargo ship hovering above the town's streets, Fiore looked back to see the constable leaning against his door. With his arms crossed, the constable offered a knowing smile and a slight wave goodbye. With the breakfast conversation still fresh in his mind, Fiore could only muster a nod of recognition.

Once aboard the transport, Weelah went right to work dropping the grappling lines to the cargo unit on the ground. It took seconds to connect and minutes to reel the container with Billix's car into the cargo hold. Once the container was secured in the holding bay, she turned to the men and asked, "So, where to, gentlemen?"

Three faces twisted from the question, none holding the answer.

"Well," Fiore started. "We can't go back to our headquarters. Sivka Corp. probably has it under surveillance, waiting for us to come back."

Zeus frowned as he glanced from Fiore to Weelah. Fiore knew that Zeus was uncomfortable with his openness with information, but viewed this as a test to see how much Zeus trusted him. Zeus said, "We can't go to Billix's, either. Every bounty hunter in the galaxy has probably been there."

"Yeah, thanks for that, guys," Billix moaned. He crossed his arms over his chest and slouched in his seat. "All kinds of strangers in my place. Touching my stuff. Half of it's probably broken by now. And I have some really awesome stuff!"

"Sorry. I just didn't think it would take this long for The Legend to hunt you down," Zeus replied.

"After seeing what you two are capable of, I'm relatively certain *that* is not a bad thing."

"We can handle him. We almost beat him the last time."

"Almost," Billix huffed. "Speaking of *my place* getting trashed, why don't we go to Dryn Tammeryn's?"

"What do you think we'll really find? His place has probably been ransacked and picked over more than yours."

Billix winced at that comment. "It's still a place to start. Maybe there's something that everyone else missed?"

Brows knitting, Zeus pondered the question, absentmindedly petting Hydrynx, asleep and purring on his lap. "I guess we have no other real option, do we?"

Fiore felt helpless and desperate. He had felt that way last night, when he could only watch as the kidnappers wrangled the newly stolen children. That was why he had rushed forth with no regards to his own safety. That plan was the type of thing Zeus criticized him about—acting without thinking. High risk, no contingency. But it had worked, and that fact Fiore couldn't let go of. "Actually, why *don't* we go back to our headquarters?"

"Umm, didn't you *just* say that it might be crawling with goons from Sivka Corp.?" Billix asked.

"Well, yeah, but that's another mystery we need to solve. Why are they after us? We know they'll be there and we'll be prepared. Maybe we even let them capture us…?"

"They're after you two, not me."

"With a ten billion cred bounty on your head, *everyone* is after you," Zeus said, a bit of mirth in his voice. "But he's right, Fiore. Since there's a time limit to Tammeryn, we should focus on him."

"So, we're back to Tammeryn's?" Fiore asked.

"Why don't you guys go to the person who put the bounty on Dryn Tammeryn?" Weelah asked.

Billix crossed his arms and offered a wan expression to Fiore and Zeus, wordlessly admonishing them for not having such foresight. Zeus offered his own wan expression, crossing his arms to mock. "Because it was posted on the wire anonymously. Exactly the same way we posted the bounty on Billix."

"Shouldn't there be a source, though?" Weelah asked. "The wire is on the universal web, right? To access it, you still need some form of computer. Can't you guys find a way to track which computer in the galaxy was used to list the bounty?"

Zeus cocked his head. "That… that isn't a bad idea, but it's not as easy as it sounds. The wire is set up for anonymity, except if the person posting the bounty doesn't pay. There's no way the average person could go to the wire and just find where the bounty was posted. Even an expert might not be able to do it. I could probably do it, but I'd need my system back in our headquarters and a few hours. I think I'd be able to.…"

"Got it," Billix said, tapping away at his robotic arm. "Not the specific computer, but the building where it's located. Here, I just gave it to Fiore."

Forearm sheath beeping, Fiore accessed the information Billix had just sent. "Wow! He's *good*!"

2">

in to the wire's system. How did you *bypass* the security?"

"It's a gift, I guess."

Giving an exasperated sigh, Zeus turned back to Fiore and asked, "So, where does Billix think the listing came from?"

Fiore tapped away. "Planet Genture. City Fedrah. The building appears to be... a library?"

Zeus laughed, causing Hydrynx to wake up and scowl at its master. The dragon-cat offered a low growl before shifting and returning its head to rest on its paws. Going back to stroking his pet, Zeus chuckled, "I guess your tracking system must be off. There's no way a ten billion cred bounty was listed on the wire at a library."

"Actually," Weelah said, "it makes perfect sense. If you truly want to remain anonymous when posting to the universal web, do it on a public computer."

Billix smirked while Zeus glowered. Feeling uncomfortable looking back and forth between the two of them, Fiore asked, "So... we're... going... to... Genture...?"

Still scowling, Zeus mumbled, "Fine." But as Billix started to smirk, Zeus added, "Don't blame me if this is a dead-end!"

Weelah looked upward as if in prayer and muttered, "Men. Such stupid creatures," as they continued to bicker.

She guided her cargo ship to the nearest orbital jump-port. It took less than five minutes for her to set the coordinates and the jump-port to come to life. As the ship slipped through, Weelah yelled at everyone to stop arguing....

Chapter 14

Zeus admired the city of Fedrah from the library window. Being one of the taller buildings in the city, the library offered an amazing view. Coupled with the fact that most of the land on the planet Genture was flat, Zeus could see a great deal of the city.

The buildings flowed nicely with the well-manicured landscape, few structures and no trees reaching taller than two stories. Patches of the green grass, naturally tinted red at the tips, along with bushes of purple-hued flowers flowed aesthetically beside the clean streets. The buildings, designed more for form over function, each were the perfect mix of stone, glass, and metals. The indigenous populace respected the environment, and it showed. Zeus knew this from the *History of Genture* book, old-fashioned bound paper, in his hands.

After they arrived at the library, they quickly figured out what they had to do to get the information they needed. To be less conspicuous, they decided to split up, Zeus opting for reference material about the planet's history. Fiore followed Weelah around, attempting to converse with her while she scanned the shelves of bound paper books. However, she bent over and Fiore lost focus. He tripped over his own feet, landing face first onto a small shelf.

Books scattered and Fiore cursed. Zeus rolled his eyes and Weelah watched with mouth agape, oblivious to the reason why he tripped. Billix slouched in his seat as if that would hide him as the librarian scuttled past on her six tentacle legs. By the time she got to the fracas, Fiore stood blushing with an armful of books. Without so much as a word, but under heavy glare from the librarian, Fiore handed the books to her one at a time as she returned them to their rightful places on the shelf. Once they completed the task, the librarian returned to her post, and had been scowling at Fiore ever since.

After reading a few more interesting paragraphs, Zeus took a moment to look back at Billix sitting at the row of public use computers. A dozen monitors were located on two long tables in front of a dozen chairs. When accessed, a holographic keyboard glowed on the tabletop according to user preference. Since Billix was half computer himself, all he needed to do was plug a small cord from his robotic arm into a port along the side of the monitor. However, it took five minutes to sift through the data records to determine if the computer was the one used to post the bounty for Dryn Tammeryn, so Zeus used this time to learn more about the planet Genture.

Turning back to the window, Zeus continued to admire the daily flow of the city. One of his favorite things about bounty hunting was the travel, and the ability to learn about new planets and species and cultures. He thought of changing his profession to one in which he had access to this kind of knowledge, like professor or museum curator or librarian. That thought quickly faded from his mind as he looked over at the librarian behind the main desk. A native of Genture, the librarian had a stout body and inky purple skin. Two tentacles sprouted from her shoulders and four smaller tentacles from the ends of each of the larger ones. The librarian sat behind the main desk, her bulbous head rested on her tentacled hand, the eyes at the end of two stalks displayed her blend of boredom and frustration as she stared dubiously at Fiore.

Sitting at a table, looking nervous because he was trying to be inconspicuous, he read a book that he had downloaded to his forearm computer. Zeus hoped it was a guide to better himself at either bounty hunting or playing Terrellian poker. Zeus chuckled—again Fiore provided a beneficial distraction, keeping the lone sentry occupied so she didn't notice Billix's suspicious activities.

The library was like many municipally run libraries—a mix of different media available to the public. This one boasted a fine collection of bound paper books as well as a third of the area dedicated to books and other material on thin electronic tablets. Along one wall were a dozen floor-to-ceiling monitors, solely for the purpose of borrowing books digitally.

Two dozen other library guests milled about. Some roamed among the shelves looking for something to read while others sat at one of the many tables reading what they had procured from the shelves. Most were native Genturians, just as squat and purple and tentacled as the librarian. Other species were present as well, but Zeus deemed none of them suspicious or threatening. Other than reacting to Fiore's disruption, they all kept to themselves and never gave a second glance to anything else.

Two Genturians entered the library, whispering between themselves. Even though they appeared to be young, Zeus followed them anyway, taking care to appear casual by glancing from his book to the window. Sure enough, they were students working on a school project.

On his way back to his original vantage point, he passed by Weelah and whispered, "Did you find anything interesting?"

She whispered back, "Billix needs to hurry."

"Other than Fiore getting ousted from the place by a disgruntled librarian, what's the risk?"

"The cameras. This is a public institution, so security isn't the best. I doubt it would take much to hack into the system to see what the cameras are looking at. Run a simple profile recognition program, and anyone in the galaxy can find Billix."

"That's only if someone is looking for him. I doubt anyone would think to look in a library."

"He's worth ten billion creds. *Everyone* is looking for him. Someone might be desperate enough to randomly scan public places on well-populated planets. It's a long-shot, but for ten billion creds and no other leads?"

Zeus frowned. She was right, and it frustrated him that he hadn't thought of it first. However, that gave him an idea. He looked at the librarian. Even though she kept one eye stalk focused on Fiore, the other now lolled about, glancing from one library guest to the next, including Billix. He wasn't sure how astute she was. Did she notice that the four of them all came in together? He didn't want to take any chances, especially since Fiore had created such a ruckus.

Zeus turned to Weelah and whispered, "Okay, I'll distract the librarian. While I'm doing that, you go tell Fiore to send a message to Billix. Tell him that once he discovers which computer was used to place the bounty, he needs to find out when, and then hack into the library's security system...."

"...And download the footage from the security cameras," Weelah said, more enthusiasm in her voice than Zeus would have liked. "So we can also *see* the person who posted the bounty. Got it."

Grousing to himself, Zeus made his way to the librarian while watching Weelah inch her way toward Fiore. He didn't like the way Weelah threw around the word "we," and he certainly didn't like the way she interrupted him. Needing to stay focused, he pushed his consternation aside and approached the front desk. If there was one trait Zeus was jealous about Fiore possessing, it was his easy going personality when talking to people. Sure, Fiore was a bumbling fool around any attractive woman, but he had zero issues starting a conversation with any species of sentient creature, and the mental acuity of who or what he talked to was low priority. Fiore could talk to a rock. That notion made Zeus smile. That was it! Fiore always led every introduction with a smile. Presenting the most beaming smile possible, Zeus asked with sugar-coated words, "Hello. I was wondering if you could assist me?"

One eyestalk snapped right to him, the other slowly turned to him as well, as if pained by turning away from Fiore. Once both eyes looked at Zeus, the librarian asked, "Yes?"

Keeping the librarian's attention away from Fiore while maintaining a clear line of sight of his partner, Zeus leaned against the desk and slid the Genture history book to the librarian and said, "The history of this planet is fascinating. Do you happen to have any other books about Genture?"

The librarian grunted. "Do you want paper, digital tablet, or download?"

Zeus fought hard to keep the profanities in his head from flying out of his mouth as Fiore's eyes crossed in ecstasy while Weelah whispered in his ear. Not entirely sure that Fiore was going to retain anything he heard, Zeus regretted this plan, but charged forth anyway. "I'm just visiting for a while, so paper books are good."

The librarian sighed and mumbled in monotone, "Then the books you're looking for would be found *right next to* the book you already found."

Blushing, Zeus maintained his smile and stood straight. "Well, yes. I guess that does make sense. Thank you for your time."

By the time the librarian's left eyestalk curled back to watch Fiore, Weelah was gone. Fiore pecked away at his computer screen, and Billix received the message seconds later. Billix looked up and shot a confused look at Zeus. Trying to be as nonchalant as possible, Zeus gestured to Billix to hurry. Billix gestured back with one finger and then looked around. Cautiously, he pulled another wire from his mechanical arm and plugged it into the nearest computer. Once he synchronized with the security system, he contorted his face and pointed to the computer, implying the question, "Happy now?"

Zeus was satisfied. If the bounty had indeed been uploaded to the bounty wire from this library, then Billix only had three more computers to try. Zeus knew in his gut it would be the last one. Everything seemed to be under control; all was going according to plan.

Satisfied that neither he nor Billix commanded any attention from the librarian, other than the obligatory cursory glance, and that none of the other library attendees were other bounty hunters, Zeus decided to find Weelah.

Offering the occasional glance to make sure Fiore remained seated and not breaking anything, Zeus moved from his vantage point to the area of the library consisting of long, floor-to-ceiling shelves. Strolling down the aisle, he looked left then right, down the book-lined alleyways, offshoots from the main aisle. On occasion, a library guest would be there, but they would simply glance at Zeus and then languidly go back to perusing the shelves. He made mental notes whenever a title or topic caught his interest, but he resisted his desire to take a moment to explore, histories and sciences begging for his attention. Then a yellow hand reached from around the corner of an upcoming opening between shelves, grabbed his shirt, and yanked him from the aisle.

Standing eye to chin with Weelah, Zeus froze, not entirely sure about the motivations behind her abrupt action. However, being this close to her, he understood why she turned Fiore's mind to mush. But why did she grab him? Was this her idea of flirting? Hinting at more lascivious intentions? Before Zeus could travel further down the path of questions, he realized that she was afraid. She trembled as she whispered, "Look."

Zeus followed her gaze, and immediately became embarrassed by thinking such ludicrous thoughts about her motivation for grabbing him. He quickly felt the same fear she did when he saw what had caught her eye. Standing at the entrance, looking around the library with a scowl on his face, was Koorza....

Chapter 15

"What do we do?" Weelah asked.

Zeus watched the massive Koorza stride into the library. He aimed for the center, where the librarian sat as an omnipresent sentry at her desk. From his vantage point, Zeus saw Billix unsuccessfully finish sifting through the data on the third-to-last computer and move to the next one. Two computers left, and Zeus knew very well that Fate would not allow such fortune as Billix finding the necessary information on this one, especially since all Koorza had to do was walk another twenty feet and look to his left to see Billix.

"There's only one thing we can do," Zeus sighed. He stepped out from his hiding spot.

"Are you crazy?" Weelah whispered from behind him. "He'll see you."

"I know. That's the point."

"You're using us as bait?"

"Do you have a better idea? If he sees Billix, it's all over. Plus, Fiore does this kind of thing all the time, and it seems to work out... usually."

Weelah cursed, and then eased herself from their hiding spot.

Muscles twitching as if they were ready to rebel and jump right out of his skin, Zeus readied himself for anything as Koorza strolled further into the library. With every step, the large, yellow-skinned beast scanned the room. One of the librarian's eyestalks shifted half of her gaze to Koorza, undoubtedly preparing herself to ask him if he needed any assistance. Before he made it that far, Koorza looked right at Zeus and Weelah. With audible gasps, they both pulled back into their hiding spot.

"He's coming this way," Zeus whispered to Weelah. "Do you have your gun with you?"

Indignant, she snorted, "No! It's a library! I left it back on the ship."

"Your knives?"

"They're on the ship as well."

"Doesn't do us any good there."

"Yeah, genius? Isn't your fire-breathing cat-lizard-thing in the same place for the same reason?"

Zeus had no meaningful rejoinder, so he changed the topic. "You go that way, I'll go this way."

They ran to the end of the book-lined aisle between the shelves that led to another book-lined aisle. At the end of it, Weelah went left and Zeus went right. However, Weelah found herself in a dead-end. She turned just as Koorza made his way down the same aisle. The tight enclosure added to the tone of his ominous voice. "You know, Weelah, I was a bit surprised to see you on Ruuka."

"How'd you find me here?" Weelah growled.

"Simple," he said, as he pulled out a knife from the sheath strapped to his leg. "I got to my ship and just waited for you to leave the planet. I followed you right through the jump-port to here."

"Why?"

Predator to prey, he sauntered to her and scraped the tip of his knife along the shelf, leaving a jagged gouge along the way. "Well, when I told my boss about how you ruined my score, he and his associates weren't too happy with me. That makes me not too happy with *you*."

"You're kidnapping children. You almost took our daughter."

Koorza smiled, now standing inches from Weelah. "Eh. It's a living."

Weelah spat on him, her hatred dripping from his cheek. "You disgust me."

Koorza smiled, the wicked points of his sharp teeth looking more dangerous than the knife in his hand. "Heh. You ain't no angel yourself, Weelah. A few years back, my criminal friends were your criminal friends. Remember that?"

"I do," Weelah said, standing firm as Koorza brought the tip of the blade to the underside of her jaw. "Then I remembered we had a daughter, and I grew up."

Koorza's smile turned into a sneer as he leaned in. However, he stopped after a book ricocheted off his head. Snarling, he turned just as Zeus threw another book; it bounced off his shoulder.

Even though she was smaller than Koorza, Weelah still had sufficient bulk to take advantage of the distraction and shove Koorza into the shelves. She caught him in the side, where the burn mark from Fiore's shot was still fresh, and then leapt over him as he fell. Growling, he groped for Weelah as she escaped, but missed.

Weelah followed Zeus down another aisle of books. They turned the corner to see two younger patrons conversing about a book they held open. Weelah and Zeus turned the other corner to lead Koorza away, his growls echoing behind them.

"I'm gonna find you two!" Koorza shouted.

"Quiet, please!" the librarian shouted back.

Zeus and Weelah scurried along a larger main aisle, but when they came to a crossroads, Weelah went right while Zeus bolted to the left. He knew he didn't have much time to double back, but he wanted to check on Billix's progress. One computer left!

Zeus sprinted back the way he came, hoping to catch up to Weelah. Maybe they could find an exit in this section of the library, and lead Koorza away, possibly even lose him. Crossing over the main aisle, he ran down the way Weelah went. Unfortunately, Weelah came running back; the opposite direction lead to a dead end.

The collision rattled Zeus to his bones, starbursts popping into his vision. He didn't even remember landing on the floor, just that he sat there now, stunned. Even though she was closer to Fiore's size, the jolt was enough to topple her as well. They both moaned and shifted to get back to their feet, but they were too late. Seated on the ground, they could only look up at Koorza, blocking their escape.

A vengeful deity ready to smite, Koorza glowered over the fallen. "I was debating about taking you to Myzzer. Explain to him why he wasn't getting his shipment of kids and then have him do with you whatever he needed to. But now… now I think I'm going to finish you myself."

Stepping forward, he blocked out the overhead light and became a morbid silhouette. He cast a foreboding shadow upon Zeus and Weelah, the glint of his blade and the white of his pointed teeth the only brightness. Then a second shadow appeared.

From behind Koorza, Fiore chopped at the hand holding the knife. He connected, and the force caused Koorza to wince in pain and drop the weapon.

Surprised, Zeus wondered if Fiore knew what to do next. He did not, and demonstrated his lack of skill by simply wrapping his arms around Koorza. Taking advantage of Fiore's ineffective tactic, Koorza thrust himself backward and slammed Fiore into the nearest shelf. Fiore's grip loosened, and he took an elbow to the gut, knuckles to the face, and a heel to his shin before Koorza even turned around. With a sadistic smile, Koorza licked his fanged teeth, then charged the dazed and wobbling Fiore.

Driving his shoulder into Fiore's sternum, Koorza connected with a meaty smack. Struggling to stay on his feet, Fiore churned his legs in an awkward backward run. Coordination never being his strong point, he eventually tripped over his feet. Careening off the book-filled walls of the shelves, the two men knocked about and tumbled into the open room, crashing into tables and desks. Getting to their feet, Zeus and Weelah chased after.

As the two mounds of muscle grappled—Fiore trying to maintain some form of balance while Koorza knocked him around with ease—they slammed against shelves and broke every piece of furniture they came in contact with. The library visitors dropped what they were doing and fled for the nearest exit, some screaming as they ran.

Both Zeus and Weelah danced around the scuffle, looking for any opportunity to help Fiore. Zeus primed himself to attack as Koorza slammed Fiore to the floor, but stopped himself as Fiore got back to his feet and found his way into a headlock. Fiore escaped the headlock by being tossed into a nearby desk, reducing it to splinters. Weelah tensed to pounce, but Fiore blocked her opportunity by standing up again. Koorza jumped behind Fiore and wrapped his arms around the taller man's shoulders, pinning his arms behind his own neck. Zeus readied himself again, but was cut short as he was jumped from behind.

"Not in my library!" the librarian screamed as she threw herself onto Zeus' back.

With purple tentacles wrapping around his forehead and chest, Zeus stumbled forward from the extra weight. He grabbed a hold of the tentacle squirming about his face and pulled as he screamed, "What are you doing? Get off of me!"

"You're wrecking my beautiful library!"

Zeus managed to pry her arm from around his head, each of her suckers yanking his skin with an audible pop. "Oww! I am not! The psycho with the yellow skin is. Go jump on him!"

"You brought him here!"

Zeus lost his grip, her four finger tentacles suctioned to his cheek, mouth, and neck. "Did you see him walk in with us?"

"That doesn't matter. He was after you and you came here. So, *you* brought him here!"

Zeus couldn't argue; her tentacles squirmed over his mouth. Using both hands to struggle with the tentacles, he twisted and turned his whole body. That only aided in his loss of balance, sending them both crashing into shelves and desks. As the librarian's grip tightened around Zeus' head, he started to get tunnel vision and see stars. Luckily, Weelah intervened.

With one pull, Weelah lifted Zeus to his feet by using the latched-on librarian and guided him to the main entrance. Both eyestalks swiveled around to look at Weelah as the librarian unleashed a tirade, "You're next, girlie. When I'm done with this one, I'm gonna suction your pretty face right off your head!"

Ignoring the threats, Zeus and Weelah worked together to extricate the overzealous librarian. Zeus focused on simply walking while supporting the excess weight. Weelah held onto the librarian with one hand and smacked away tentacles with her other hand while pushing toward the door.

Another crash from behind him and Zeus assumed Koorza had thrown Fiore into more shelving. He hoped that Fiore could keep Koorza distracted. Once at the exit, Zeus grabbed onto the doorway while Weelah pulled. If not for the tentacle over his mouth, he would have screamed from the pain—the librarian's suction cups pinched and pulled his skin, refusing to let go.

"You're gonna have to rip his skin off to get rid of me!" the librarian screeched. "Unless you get out of my library, I'm not letting go."

Weelah yanked the purple-skinned woman again. Zeus almost blacked out from the pain. Thoughts of giving in to her demands raced through his head just as an emerald beam flashed by.

The librarian shrieked and relinquished Zeus. She dropped to the floor and brought both hands to a burn mark on her posterior. Taking advantage of the opportunity, Weelah grabbed the librarian and dragged her outside. After rushing back inside, she shut and locked the doors.

"I'll kill you!" the librarian screamed, pounding her tentacled fists against the door. "Whatever you do to my library, I'm going to do to you!"

Sitting on the floor, Zeus gasped for air and massaged the sorest parts of his face. He looked up to see Billix leaning over him. "Are you okay? I didn't realize what was happening. I saw the librarian beating on you, so I shot her with a low-level energy beam. Gave her a mean burn, but nothing major...."

"*You* shot her? You can't hit anything. If you aimed for the ceiling right now, I'd bet that you'd miss." Zeus barked through raspy breath.

Weelah ran over to help Zeus to his feet. "Quit goofing around. We need to help Fiore."

"Hey!" Billix yelled at Zeus. "I can shoot! If I have time to aim and you're not yelling at me. And Fiore's not throwing me around."

"Yeah?" Zeus yelled, pointing at Koorza. "Shoot him, then."

"Fine!" Billix yelled back. He pointed at Koorza with his cybernetic hand and used to his other one to stabilize his arm. Closing his left eye, his right one glowed red. As soon as Koorza threw Fiore to the ground, Billix fired. And missed.

But he did garner Koorza's attention.

Billix fired again, and missed again.

Smiling a wicked grin of sharp teeth, Koorza approached, sauntering as if he knew nothing could harm him.

"Seriously?" Zeus asked.

"Don't pressure me!" Billix yelled as the green beam from his fingertip flashed three feet above Koorza's head.

"He's right in front of you, coming right at us, so in theory, he should be getting easier to hit."

"This isn't very easy, you know!"

"Even with a cybernetic targeting system build right into your head?"

"What part of, 'don't pressure me,' aren't you understanding?"

Continuing to make his way closer, Koorza laughed, as another beam flickered nowhere near him.

Zeus clenched his fists and crouched, readying himself to strike the larger man's knees when he got close enough. "Would you like Weelah to pick you up and shake you? You seem to aim better when someone is shaking you."

Fiore stood up from the splintered remains of what used to be a desk. Even though he had a wobble in his step, he rushed toward Koorza. Zeus smiled, knowing that the impact would surely do some damage to

Koorza—if not for Billix. He shot again and missed Koorza. The beam hit Fiore in the shoulder and dropped him back to the floor.

Weelah poised herself for attack. "Again, how are you guys bounty hunters?"

"I'm not a bounty hunter, remember? I'm a pawnshop owner! Still here against my will!" Billix shouted as he fired three more times, resulting in three more misses.

Zeus jumped behind Billix and grabbed him by the shoulders. Shaking the purple cyborg as hard as he could, he yelled, "He's five feet away! How can you keep missing?"

An energy beam struck Koorza in the center of his chest, knocking him to the floor. But it didn't come from Billix....

Chapter 16

Stunned, Fiore stared at Koorza, dead on the ground, wisps of gray smoke corkscrewing upward from the smoldering burn wound in the center of his chest. Fiore was certainly happy that he was no longer getting thrown around the library by the yellow-skinned thug, but anxiety skittered through him once he realized that it wasn't Billix who had shot him. Reflex and self-preservation dictated that he find cover.

All at the same time, he and his friends ran to the librarian's circular desk in the middle of the library. They ducked behind it as they huddled together.

"Who did that?" Billix whispered. "I didn't do that. Where'd that come from? What's happening?"

"Whoever it is, I'd like to thank them," Weelah whispered back.

Zeus poked his head over the top of the desk and looked in the direction of where the energy bolt came from. He quickly crouched back down and looked at Fiore. "I think it's Sivka."

"Sivka?"

"I saw brief flashes of black clothing moving behind the shelves along the perimeter. I think the blast that took down Koorza was meant for us."

"Sivka," Weelah moaned. "You two are just a bundle of awesome."

"What are they doing now? Are they getting closer? They're coming this way, aren't they?" Billix said.

"I don't know," Zeus replied. "I didn't get a good look. Fiore, use your goggles. See where they're going."

"I was just about to do that," Fiore lied. The goggles had been on his head for so long that he forgot they were there. Sliding them down over his eyes, he adjusted the different views. He settled for heat vision.

Slowly turning his head, Fiore found them. Two figures were creeping along the back wall. Before he could say anything, Billix said, "Found them. They're moving along the back wall."

Fiore also forgot that Billix could see different spectra through his cybernetic eye. Trying not to feel like a disappointment, he pointed and said, "They're heading that way."

"Look at the ceiling in the far corner," Zeus said. "The grate for the climate control system has been removed. That's probably how they came in."

"Then why are they moving back to that?"

"To leave," Billix said.

"But why would they leave?" Fiore asked. "They're after us, but didn't get us yet."

"Who cares?" Billix replied. "Maybe they're aborting the mission because they missed you two? Maybe they need to regroup? Maybe they're calling it a failure because they accidentally killed a civilian."

"Koorza's no civilian," Weelah snorted.

"*We* know that. *They* don't," Billix argued. "If they wanna leave, then let's not stop them."

"I'm gonna stop them," Fiore said, moving his goggles back to the top of his head. He positioned himself at the edge of the desk, ready to sprint.

"What?" the other three behind the desk whispered in unison.

Crouched like a runner at the starting line of a race, Fiore turned his head to look back at his partner. "Zeus, they invaded our home. They're hunting us. They just accidentally killed someone that could have been us. We still have no idea why. In short: we have questions, they have answers. I'm not letting them get away."

As Fiore turned and rushed out from behind the desk, he heard Weelah moan, "I hate it when someone with too much testosterone makes sense."

Other than a slight stumble leaping up the few steps that separated the lobby area from the labyrinth of bookshelves, Fiore took the most direct route to the corner of the library. Mentally preparing himself for a fight, which consisted of the lone thought, *I hope I don't have to fight with them*, Fiore ran down the last aisle of shelves and jumped around the final corner to startle the two figures. "Ha!"

They looked exactly like the men who ambushed Zeus and Fiore in their headquarters—humanoid and clad from head to toe in black. Even though they each carried a gun and were very close to the opening of the climate control ductwork, the two turned and ran the opposite direction. Without thinking, Fiore gave chase.

With noiseless grace, the two Sivka operatives sprinted through the bookshelf aisles and leapt to the foyer area. Fiore pursued, his churning arms knocking books from shelves as he passed. In a flurry of paper, he burst from the book area screaming, "They're coming! Get them! Get them!"

The gunmen sprinted past the desk, and no one attempted to stop them. Fiore paused at the desk and yelled at Zeus, "What part of this plan didn't you understand?"

"The part where you forgot to tell me the plan!" Zeus yelled back.

"Do I really need to tell you everything? We've worked together long enough that I shouldn't have to tell you every detail."

Weelah and Billix turned to Zeus with quizzical expressions. Defensively, Zeus said, "We've known each other for less than a year."

"Well, we've got them on the run now, so let's get them," Fiore said as he followed his prey toward the other side of the library, where the aisles of shelves were lined with electronic readers.

Finally understanding the plan, the others joined Fiore in the chase. Quickly noticing that there were four aisles that opened up the back wall, each went down a different one. Cornered, with their backs to the wall, the two figures in black aimed their guns at the four approaching.

"There is a way we can all get out of this," Zeus said to the gunmen, hands held palm out and shoulder high. Billix aimed the glowing fingertip of his mechanical hand at the captives. Chest puffed out and fists clenched, Fiore stood next to Zeus. Weelah stood with fists ready as well, but in a much more combat-competent stance than Fiore.

The figures said nothing. Standing shoulder to shoulder, they stood firm while pointing their guns at Zeus.

"We just want to know why you're after us," Zeus continued.

The two men glanced at each other, then back to the four closing in on them. Silence still their answer.

"Come on," Fiore barked. "Why is Sivka Corp chasing us?"

The two men lowered their weapons, bodies going limp. Without a single word uttered between them, they changed gun cartridges, and then pointed their weapons at each other. Trying to intervene, Fiore and Zeus shouted at them not to pull the triggers. Fiore assumed that since they changed cartridges, the result would be more devastating than what had happened to Koorza. However, the gunmen did lower their weapons, but not because of anything that was being shouted at them.

Both gunmen brought their right hands to their helmets. Then, both turned to Fiore and Zeus. Quickly, they changed cartridges again and aimed, one at Zeus, one at Fiore. One of them said, "Orders confirmed. Targets acquired."

Fiore and friends turned and ran, each retreating down a different aisle. Fiore heard the familiar ring of tranq darts as they bounced off of the surrounding shelves. As he ran, he grabbed a handful of electronic readers from the shelves and tossed them over his head. The sounds of projectiles were replaced with the sounds of handheld electronics bouncing off his pursuer or being crunched under his boots.

Fiore burst from the aisle at the same time as everyone else in his cadre. They all leapt down the steps to the lower level of the lobby area, aiming once again for the librarian's desk. All four scuttled behind it as Zeus yelled to Billix, "Shoot them! Shoot them!"

Between popping up to shoot and ducking back down behind the desk, Billix replied, "I'm so glad you're yelling at me again! Because it worked so well last time. You yelling at me. Helps me with my aim."

Even though Billix's emerald energy beams only blasted small wooden desks and chairs into splinters or reduced electronics to chunks of melted plastic and charred glass, they were frequent enough to hold the Sivka Corp gunmen at bay. In separate aisles, each operative crouched at the base of the shelves for protection, and returned fire in between Billix's suppressive, albeit inaccurate, energy beams.

Fiore knew that once the gunmen realized that Billix had terrible aim, they would rush the desk. And they seemed to have plenty of darts to tranq everyone behind it. He looked around and found a full cart of paper books near the desk—just out of reach.

Trying to time it just right, he jumped out, grabbed the cart, and pulled it back behind the desk with him. Feeling clever, he smiled. Until his saw the worried expression on Weelah's face as she looked at his shoulder. There was a dart in it.

Nonchalantly, he removed it and tossed it aside.

Confused, Weelah asked, "So… there's nothing in the darts?"

"They're tranq darts. I can take one or two with no effect," Fiore replied. He tapped his forearm mechanics as he continued, "Maybe four or five more if I amp up."

Weelah shook her head. "You're a freak."

Prideful, Fiore smiled. Fighting a losing battle with his eyes, his gaze then slowly slid from her face to her cleavage.

Weelah snatched a book from the cart and smacked Fiore over the head with it. "It wasn't a compliment or a flirtation. Idiot."

Blushing and feeling stupid, Fiore quickly shifted his attention to the cart, taking books and throwing them at the gunmen. Weelah followed his lead and hurled books as well. Zeus and Billix continued to yell at each other while Billix's aim worsened. Weelah was the only one with any accuracy, her books hitting their target with every throw.

Fiore didn't fully comprehend the intricacies of the term "stalemate," but he was pretty confident that he was in one right now. As the standoff continued, he realized that neither his group nor their adversaries would gain any form of competitive advantage unless someone took drastic action. As usual, he deemed himself to be the one to do so.

In between tossing a book, and woefully missing his target, Fiore looked around to see what he could use as a shield. He debated amping up and rushing them, but figured they could still shoot him with enough darts to take him down. Maybe use Billix? After all, every time Fiore shook Billix, he aimed better. He decided against it; one tranq dart and Billix would be useless. The book cart maybe? He examined its size and dimensions, but a commotion from outside the library interrupted him.

"This is the Fedrah policing unit number one two eight," an electronically amplified male voice announced from outside.

The fighting on the inside stopped as all participants looked at the nearest window. Escorted by the sounds of sirens, yellow and orange flashing lights approached from both the ground and the air. The sirens stopped once the vehicles did, uniformed Genturians emptying out.

The voice continued, "We have secured the perimeter of the building. Surrender peacefully and immediately, or we will be forced to—ma'am! Stop! What are you…?"

After his voice fell away, the familiar voice of the librarian filled the air. "Get out of my library! If the members of the policing unit don't kill you, then you can be sure that I will! I know you're in there breaking my books! I'm gonna re-bind them with your skin!"

"Ma'am, please, *let go!*" the man's voice returned. The Sivka Corp gunmen didn't wait any longer, sprinting out from between the shelves and leaping over the librarian's desk with ease.

Stunned, Fiore and friends looked at each other. Simultaneously, they all jumped up and followed the two men in black. By the time they caught up with the Sivka Corp gunmen, Fiore saw the last set of boot-clad feet disappear into the ductwork above.

Coming to a halt, Fiore and friends stood under the opening and looked up. Concerned, Fiore said, "I don't think I'm gonna fit."

"Me neither," Weelah moaned.

The policing unit officer's voice echoed through the air again, "I repeat—if you do not exit the building and surrender yourselves peacefully, we will use any means necessary to remove you ourselves."

Fiore didn't like the phrase "any means necessary," and thought about what ingredients to pull from his bandoleer to survive a skirmish with the local policing unit. However, Zeus started to run away and said, "Follow me. I have an idea."

Fiore and the others chased after Zeus to the lavatory.

"I read about their refuse systems. Underground, but close to the surface. And large. Large enough to fit Fiore and Weelah. Fiore, shoot the floor here," Zeus said, pointing at the base of the far wall.

Fiore lifted Billix and shook him. Cursing and swearing, Billix's limbs flailed about, his finger beam discharging four times in the exact same spot, creating a crater in the floor that dropped right into the refuse system.

"Oh, this is a bad idea," Weelah said, crinkling her nose from the noxious odors emanating from the hole. "I'd rather face the policing units. I think I can handle them."

Zeus pulled the top of his shirt up over his nose and said, "I think you could too. But can you handle the librarian?"

Weelah sighed. "Okay. Let's get moving.

Zeus hopped into the hole first, landing with a shallow splash. Billix followed and Weelah jumped down after him. Fiore jumped in as well, but not before taking advantage of his perspective to look down Weelah's shirt one more time....

Chapter 17

"We're back!" Fiore announced as he and Weelah walked through the door. Zeus grimaced, wondering why his partner felt the need to state the obvious, and state it loudly enough for the whole building to hear. He wondered if he should sit down with Fiore and explain to him the finer points of "laying low," such as paying cash for a room in a motel building located in the slums of a slum-infested planet.

Fiore strode over to the small, round table in the center of the motel room and deposited the goods that he carried—four containers of four different types of milk. Weelah followed suit by placing plastic containers of food on the table, but wore an expression of confusion while watching Fiore's exuberance. Zeus understood—after first arriving in the room and showering a few hours ago, the four decided to send Fiore and Weelah for something to eat and drink. This area of the city was treacherous, but they decided that the sheer size of both of them should keep any would-be dangers at bay. For added measure, they armed them with a small arsenal. Undoubtedly, Weelah couldn't figure out how Fiore could view such a dangerous assignment as a fun adventure. But they returned without suffering any ordeals along the way.

Smiling, Fiore distributed the goods. "You know, for such a downtrodden area, we were able to find an impressive selection of milks. Great deals, too! Here, Zeus, I found some Puzal Grouse leg for you. I'm sure it won't be as good as the place you like on Estrassus, but I saw it and figured you'd like that over anything else that was available."

Surprised that Fiore knew his favorite food, Zeus opened the container. Still warm, it actually smelled better that what he usually got on Estrassus. Trying to maintain a certain image of aloofness, Zeus masked how much he truly appreciated the gesture with a simple, "Thanks."

However, it was much easier to hide his sentimentality when Fiore offered the milk containers he'd found. He placed a container of gray liquid on the table and said, "Here's some Vigill Rock Mouse milk." Zeus couldn't help but think to himself, *it's the color of fester*!

"Heffill Cow milk." Dull green. *Maybe it's regurgitated moss?*

"Nebbrute Duck milk." Yellowish pink. *There's a bird in this galaxy that produces milk?*

"Merris Gob Weasel milk." Creamy orange with flecks of deep red. *The color of a popped pustule.*

Knowing that Fiore had purchased the milk from the ghettos outside compounded the lack of appeal Zeus had for the beverages. Shifting in his seat uncomfortably, Zeus mumbled, "I think I'll take my chances with whatever kind of water comes from the sink."

"Me too," Billix said, opening the container of food in front of him, but unable to stop looking at the Nebbrute Duck milk. "Duck milk? Really? There's a bird in this galaxy that produces milk? What is *wrong* with the planet Nebbrute if the ducks feel the need to evolve into milk-producing creatures?"

Fiore looked at Weelah and gestured to the milk, offering her first pick. Flattened brow and pursed lips, she moaned, "No, thank you."

Wasting no time, Fiore sat down and opened his container of food. He washed the first parts of his meal down with the Vigill Rock Mouse milk.

Trying not to watch Fiore gulp down the thick gray liquid, Zeus focused on his dinner. Surprisingly, he found it to be quite tasty and enjoyed it. With every bite of the delicious meat, his mind drifted further and further away. However, Weelah brought it right back. "So, while we were gone, was Billix able to look through the data he downloaded from the library computers?"

Zeus tensed from her comment. He didn't like the fact that Weelah asked questions like she was a part of the team. There was no team—only Zeus and Fiore! It only made Zeus stew more when Billix answered, "I was. After taking two showers—two! Because I needed two showers from our little sewer traipse—I did look at the data. Sifted through it. Every bit of it from that day. I got a name. I didn't get a chance to look at the security camera footage yet, but…"

"Wait," Weelah interrupted. "You got a name? Who is it? Who put the bounty out on Dryn Tammeryn?"

Again, Zeus was not happy with her asking the questions.

Billix huffed, agitated that he'd been interrupted, but he answered anyway, "A single name. Myzzer. I don't know anything about the name. I haven't cross referenced it yet, but…" Billix stopped when Zeus and Weelah exchanged surprised glances. "What?"

Attempting to wrest some power from Weelah's influence, Zeus said, "That was who Koorza said was his boss."

"So, what would a thug boss want with Tammeryn?" Fiore asked, finishing his meal and opening the container of Heffill Cow milk. "And how could he have ten billion creds to use as a bounty?"

"He's… a bit more than just a thug boss," Weelah said her voice trailing off as she spoke.

The men at the table looked at her, wordlessly asking for her to continue. Pushing her container of food to Fiore, she slouched and sighed. "He's a criminal overlord."

Both Fiore and Billix accessed their computers, searching for evidence to support Weelah's statement. Zeus glared at her and asked, "How big of a criminal overlord are we talking about?"

"Big," both Fiore and Billix said at the same time.

Confused, Zeus asked, "If he's so big, how come we haven't heard of him before?"

Billix shot Zeus an incredulous look and snapped, "Because up until two days ago, I was a legitimate small business owner. An upstanding tax-paying citizen. I never associated with such an element, nor had any aspirations to. Then you two came along and…"

Waving his hand dismissively at Billix, Zeus turned to Fiore and said, "Okay, so if he's so big, how come *you and I* haven't heard of him?"

Still reading the information from the screen of his forearm sheath, Fiore answered, "He's mentioned as pure speculation in these news articles. He's a ghost. He's an urban legend that only urban legends talk about."

"Trust me, he's very real," Weelah mumbled.

"Is he real enough to have ten billion creds lying around for a bounty?" Fiore asked.

Weelah frowned, mulling over his question. She looked up at the men around the table and said, "I can't imagine that. He is into a lot of illegal activity, including child abduction, as we've recently learned. But… I just can't believe he has that kind of wealth."

Crossing his arms over his chest, Zeus leaned back in his chair. Brows furrowed as he pondered the new information. "Something just doesn't seem right about this."

"It's the only lead we have for finding Tammeryn," Fiore said as he started to eat from Weelah's container of food. "And we still have nothing more on why Sivka Corp is after us."

Zeus prided himself on being the brains of the operation, but it did make him feel good anytime Fiore was able to keep up. Of course, those good feelings disappeared as he watched Fiore chug from the container of Nebbrute Duck milk, sickly pink liquid oozing along both sides of his mustache. "You're right. Clearly, we need to learn more about Myzzer and why he wants Tammeryn. Especially since it doesn't seem like he can pay ten billion creds."

"You guys can't pay ten billion creds either," Billix said, absently poking at his food while blatantly staring at the Nebbrute Duck milk dripping from Fiore's face. "But that certainly didn't stop you from posting a bounty for me. Against my will. Seriously, do Nebbrute ducks lay eggs? Are they really birds? Do they have teats? How does one even begin to milk a duck?"

"Our bounty on you is a calculated risk," Zeus said. "As long as we don't lose sight of you, we don't have to worry about paying anyone. But Myzzer... if it gets out that he posted a bounty and didn't pay, the blow to his reputation would be irrecoverable, no matter how powerful he is."

"Who would know?" Fiore asked. "Maybe he just assumes that he'll get Tammeryn and kill whoever delivers him?"

"That just doesn't sit well. Someone like Myzzer knows that information would get out, no matter how clandestine the bounty-money exchange is. We need to find Myzzer. Find out what he wants with Dryn Tammeryn. Weelah? What do you know about Myzzer? Have you ever been in contact with him?"

Weelah intertwined her fingers and placed them behind her head as she lounged back in her chair. "Speaking of paying... I think I should get a cut of the bounty for helping you two beyond this point."

"What?" Zeus asked. "You said you'd transport us to where we needed to go."

"And I did that. You rescued my daughter, and I'll never forget that. But the deal was I would take you someplace off Ruuka. I did that. In fact, the only reason why I transported you to here was because I needed to clean up as well from our lovely journey through the sewer systems of

Fedrah. So, my debt has been paid and I'm going to go now. Unless we discuss a fee for future transport."

"Okay," Fiore said.

"No," Zeus said, sitting to attention in his chair. "We can use public transportation. The nearest jump-port in this city can't be that far away. We can pay someone from there."

"Okay," Weelah said. Giving credence to her unspoken threat, she stood and angled her body toward the door. "Have it your way. I can't really say it's been nice, but...."

"Zeus," Fiore said, panic in his voice. "Public transportation? That will slow us down, and near impossible to use while trying to keep a low profile with Billix."

"Then we'll use less-than-scrupulous methods of transport."

"You mean like smugglers? First of all, we don't know any. The only contacts we have are in this room right now. Second of all, that hardly sounds efficient. And, most importantly, once a smuggler finds out who Billix is, then we're going to have trouble."

"Speaking of both Billix and fees," Billix said. "I want a cut of the action, too."

"What?" Zeus yelled. "You were the one who came up with the idea!"

"I didn't have all the facts!"

Weelah nodded at Billix. "Come on, little purple guy. You only need to stay hidden for two days. We can do that at Ruuka."

"Sounds good to me," Billix stood from his chair and strolled to Weelah.

"Fine!" Zeus yelled, slapping his hand on the table. "One percent each."

"Four," Weelah said.

"Two," Zeus fired back.

"Three," Billix jumped in.

"Seven!" Fiore barked.

"Total!" Zeus shouted. Jumping from his seat, he slapped his hands on the table. "Seven percent to be split between the two of you, however you see fit."

Weelah and Billix looked at each other and shrugged their shoulders. Weelah said, "That sounds good to me."

"Me, too. Shall we spilt it fifty-fifty?" Billix asked Weelah.

"Yes. Let's."

Billix turned to Fiore and Zeus, but pointed at Weelah. "See? She's nice, smart, and kind. You two are not. Her, good. You, bad."

Fiore smiled and went back to finishing his dinner. Zeus fumed and asked through gritted teeth, "Now that you are working for us, is there anything you can tell us about Myzzer?"

Both Weelah and Billix returned to their seats. Smirking just enough to show hints of her fangs, Weelah said, "Now that I'm working *with* you, I'd be more than happy to share."

Showing that he didn't like this situation at all, Zeus glared. He stewed in the silence of the room until the only noises were Fiore's exaggerated, wet gulps of Merris Gob Weasel milk. When he could no longer tolerate the sounds of his partner enjoying his drink, Zeus growled, "Please, continue then."

Weelah's smirk faded as she settled in to discuss business. "Koorza and I met him only a few times. I never liked him, so Koorza usually did all the talking to set up the deals. But, there are a couple things that I do know. He loves underground fights."

"Underground fights?" Billix asked.

"Yes, the more brutal, the better. He loves them so much that he *hosts* fights at one of his clubs every few days. Rumor has it that this club also serves as his main office."

"Excellent!" Fiore said. "We go to one of his fights and break into his office."

"Not quite that easy," Weelah said. "Obviously, since they're held so close to home, he won't let just anyone in. It's invitation only."

"Okay," Zeus said. "We find him, we get invited."

"If it were only that easy," Billix said. "How do we find him? If we do, how do we get invited? There needs to be more to this plan."

"There is," Zeus replied. "Weelah, even though it's been a long while since you and Koorza were… involved with such indiscretions… do you think you'd be able to track Myzzer down?"

"I'll try. I'm sure I can still find a few contacts willing to help me."

Fiore elbowed Zeus and smirked. "Contacts. She has contacts. She's a good contact to have because she has contacts."

Zeus responded with a tone that he'd use on a child, "Yes, I understand. Contacts are good."

"Let's say we actually find him. What then? How are we going to get invited to the fights?" Weelah asked.

"Simple. Fiore and I will just use our status as bounty hunters."

Weelah and Billix just stared at him blankly.

Offended, Zeus snapped, "What? It will work!"

With a sigh of frustration, Weelah said, "Okay. Sure. So... are we ready to leave this slime bucket of a motel?"

"Yes..." Zeus said as he turned to Hydrynx. Lying in the corner, Hydrynx twitched its nostrils from the smell. Expressing dissatisfaction with a growling cough, it expelled two puffs of smoke from its nostrils. Sighing, Zeus said, "...after I take another shower."

Chapter 18

Zeus walked through the casino with Fiore and Billix. Being one prone to logic, he had never understood the appeal of such a place. Sentient creatures of all shapes and sizes huddled around all kinds of randomization machines. The machines flashed lights and made noises. Some even vibrated a bit. But all they *truly* did was devour money. At times, they spewed out a flow of creds to a lucky few patrons, causing even *more* lights and noises and vibrations, but as a whole, the machines took more than they gave. Zeus knew this, and found zero appeal.

There were other games of chance that disguised themselves as game of skill. Players used cards or chips or dice or other variously shaped objects in an attempt to beat the casino. Again, most were destined to fail. The only skilled players were the ones who knew the odds, and if they *truly* knew the odds, then, like Zeus, they simply wouldn't play.

This casino had whole rooms dedicated to wagering on events. Mostly sporting events from all over the galaxy, but there were more than a few rooms that offered betting on everything from the outcome of judicial trials to how high a specific tree would grow in a predetermined amount of time. These were true games of chance, wagering on an outcome with no control over it. A chill skittered down Zeus's spine as he drew a correlation between what he was about to attempt and what was happening in those rooms. Were they truly so different?

Yes, Zeus thought to himself. Even though there were many variables involved in this plan, he knew he and his partner could control their fate. He turned to Fiore. His confidence waned.

Walking in a gape-mouthed stupor, Fiore took in all the sights and sounds. Not paying attention to where he walked, the lumbering giant jostled other patrons and bumped into various pieces of décor. Sighing, Zeus scolded, "Fiore! Pay attention. You're acting like you've never been in a casino before."

Snapping his gaze from the nearest set of flashing lights, Fiore looked at his partner and blushed. "I… umm… actually, I haven't.…"

Zeus didn't even know how to reply to that unveiling of knowledge. He knew very well he shouldn't assume certain things about his partner, and he didn't want to pry too deeply into his personal life. Fiore was a seven-foot tall, four hundred pound human being so scary looking that Zeus wondered how he didn't break mirrors. Humans were hardly a large species, compared to all the other sentient ones inhabiting the galaxy, but Fiore was large, and scary looking, for any species! Zeus sometimes had a difficult time comprehending the incongruities between what he assumed about Fiore and what Fiore did to shatter those assumptions. Of course, one assumption Zeus made was about Fiore's age. Easily a decade or two older—maybe even more thanks to potential medical procedures as well as that chemical infuser Fiore had on his forearm. Yet, Fiore was physically uncoordinated and, as he had just demonstrated, relatively inexperienced in many aspects of life. "You've never been to a casino before? How is that possible? You're all but addicted to Terrellian poker."

Fiore stammered, "I've… uhh… I've never… I… wait. Do you mean there's Terrellian poker here?"

"Yeah," Billix said, sounding just as confused as Zeus. He pointed to an overhead sign designating a poker area. "It's right over there."

Without another word, Fiore aimed right for it, leaving a slack-jawed Zeus in his wake. Billix turned to Zeus and started, "Are you sure you two are bounty hunters? Where did you find him?"

Zeus cut him short by placing his hand in the air, palm toward Billix's face. "Stop. Just… stop. Tap into the security cameras to locate Myzzer."

Billix grumbled something that Zeus couldn't hear over the crowd noise and machine chimes. While Billix hacked into the security system, Zeus watched as Fiore sat down at a table, refused free alcohol, blatantly gawked at a woman's cleavage, and promptly lost the first hand of Terrellian poker. Zeus decided that when this bounty was over, he wanted to find out more about his accidentally enigmatic partner. He turned back to Billix. "Any luck?"

"Nice pun," Billix said. "Found him. V.I.P. section, right over there."

In an alcove edged by two pillars with elaborate swirls etched into them, sat a man surrounded by four women on a plush couch. In front of them was a drink-infested table. His expensive suit, long sleeved layers of copper and bronze, did little to hide his bulk. Neither as tall as Fiore nor as wide, still the man's immensity wasn't to be trifled with. Snow white fur sprouted from his sleeve openings and lined the parts of his chest exposed from the "V" shape of his shirt. His fingers and face looked skeletal, bone white and appearing just as hard. His head formed a triangle, top wide, chin pointed. Thick ridges sprouted from his cheeks and forehead and ran upward along his face and jutted out from the top of his head, giving him an even more sinister look. He had no lips or nose, only gouges for a mouth and nostrils. When he laughed, he exposed jagged teeth and made the sound of bone scraping bone.

"Are you sure that's him?" Zeus asked, even though his gut feeling told him that it was.

"Am I sure? Yes, I'm sure. Weelah said that Myzzer was a Tarzian. The security system shows that he is the only Tarzian in the casino. So, it's him," Billix replied. "So, what's the plan, genius?"

As they made their way to the V.I.P section, Zeus growled, "Just let me do the talking."

Billix snorted in contempt. "Yeah, because you have social skills. You and your overwhelming power of persuasion. This ought to be good. I should just go to that room over there and place a wager that I'm not going to make it out of here alive."

"Shut up," Zeus hissed as he approached the table.

Myzzer coughed out the tail end of a laugh; the surrounding women all tittered, in a cooing manner. As Zeus stood in front of the table, Billix behind him peeking around his shoulder, the laughter stopped. The women looked confused and turned to Myzzer, now smirking as if Zeus was the next joke. "Do I know you?"

"Not yet," Zeus replied.

"Do I want to know you?"

Zeus nonchalantly looked over his shoulder, as if offended by the question.

"So, why would I want to know you?"

"Business."

Zeus tried to keep his responses short. Short answers didn't give away information. If he didn't give away information, Myzzer would keep asking questions. If Myzzer was interested enough to ask questions, that meant he was interested enough in Zeus, meaning Zeus had value. That was what Zeus thought until Myzzer squinted and said, "You've interrupted my fun. Now you're boring me. You should leave."

Damn it! Despite Billix's growing unease becoming palpable from behind him, Zeus held his ground and said, "It's about one of your less... savory... business dealings."

Smirk disappearing, Myzzer's face went stone cold. His glare remained impassive, yet held a hint of curiosity. Keeping his stare on Zeus, Myzzer said, "Ladies."

Recognizing the command, all four women quickly left the couch with the alacrity of fleeing a demilitarized zone. Once alone on the couch, Myzzer leaned forward, the sharp edges of his face menacing. "Exactly what business dealings are we talking about?"

Feeling good about where the conversation was going, Zeus said, "The fights."

Myzzer's bone-like face softened a bit. Zeus assumed that the fights were low on Myzzer's list of unsavory business. "What about them?"

"I want to attend."

Myzzer laughed and frowned at the same time. "No one ever asks to be invited. Are you two Galactic Police? Or local?"

Zeus snorted and smirked. "My name is Zeus. We're bounty hunters."

"I'm not a bounty hunter. I'm—" Billix blurted from behind Zeus. Snapping his head around, Zeus cut him off with a snarl almost as feral as Myzzer's.

Zeus turned back to the crime lord, now leaning back and sinking into the plushness of the couch. "No."

Frowning, angry at Billix for ruining the conversation, Zeus said, "No?"

"Limited seating. All filled. Now leave before I..."

"We want to compete," Zeus quickly said, hoping he didn't sound too desperate. From behind him, Billix made a squeaking noise akin to a fearful gasp. Zeus hoped that Myzzer didn't hear that.

Myzzer cocked his head, his expression both angry and curious. "You two? Compete?"

"Not us," Zeus replied, trying to ignore Billix's exhalation of relief. He pointed at Fiore at the Terrellian poker table. "Him." Billix made the squeaking gasp noise again.

Myzzer shifted in the couch to get a better look. Despite the bony features of his face, Zeus could tell that he was impressed. Impressed was good. "Human?"

"Yes."

Frowning, Fiore slapped the table, obviously losing again. Making his next wager, he blatantly stared at a green-skinned woman in a low cut dress as she walked by. Of course, he then lost the next hand.

Zeus mentally sighed, and immediately started thinking of contingency plans.

"Okay," Myzzer said.

Trying not to express any form of confusion, he turned to Myzzer and said, "What?"

Still watching Fiore, Myzzer leaned back. "I like him. He's a monster of a human. I can't wait to see him in the ring."

"So… we're in?"

Myzzer nodded, his expression still showing that he was impressed. He stood to adjust his suit, shooing away potential wrinkles. Reaching into his pocket, he procured a card and handed it to Zeus as he walked out from the alcove. "This is your invite for tomorrow. Be there, Zeus the bounty hunter, or else you'll be the one with a bounty on your head."

As Myzzer strode away, Billix mumbled from behind Zeus, "I know what it's like to have a bounty on my head. I have one on me now. It's not a good feeling. Not at all."

"Quite whining. You're getting paid to be a bounty now," Zeus said as he looked at the card. Pitch black with a red hologram of a Tarzian skull. Either a skull or a face, Zeus couldn't tell the difference.

"That's only if I live through this! Half the galaxy is looking for me, and you drag me along to tell a criminal overlord that we're handlers for a fighter to participate in an illegal fight. Not to mention you represented your best friend without his knowledge as the fighter to fight in the aforementioned illegal fight."

In the brief time that Zeus had known Billix, he learned how to ignore him. He simply put the card in his pocket and gesturing for Billix to follow as he started toward Fiore. "He'll understand."

"So, you're gonna tell him now?"

"No. When we get back onboard Weelah's ship."

"Wow. You're a piece of work, you know?"

"This is hardly the place to tell Fiore the plan. Trust me, he'll love it. I just want to get out of this place without incident."

Glancing around nervously with every step, Billix moaned, "I couldn't agree more about getting out of here. I feel so exposed. Too exposed."

Zeus walked up to Fiore and said, "We talked to Myzzer. We're in. Let's get back to Weelah's ship."

"Great," Fiore said, his voice lacking any kind of conviction. "After this hand."

Fiore immediately lost.

"Too bad," Zeus said, his sympathetic words not holding any conviction either. "Let's go."

"One more hand," Fiore said. "I'm going to win this one."

"Have you won a hand yet?"

"No."

"The entire time Billix and I were talking to Myzzer, you haven't won a single hand?"

When Zeus mentioned Billix's name, he looked over at the purple cyborg, verifying his location. Standing close to a throughway, they both had to endure the occasional jostle. A drunk creature came stumbling through. Creatures whooping in revelry pushed past. Disgruntled losers shouldered by. Wait-staff scuttled around.

"That's why I'm confident that I'm going to win this hand," Fiore replied, anteing up.

He lost.

No sooner than the dealer pulled the chips away from Fiore, Fiore set more out and said, "One more hand."

Zeus noticed that Billix drifted farther away from him as the crowd thickened. Bigger creatures took little interest in hampering their movements for the sake of others as they plowed through the sea of bodies, causing ripples and eddies. Scowling, Zeus gestured to Billix to return to his side. Billix gestured and mouthed that he was trying with no success. Zeus scowled deeper and gestured with more flair. Billix offered a one finger gesture, then tried to make his way back to the Terrellian poker table. Fuming, Zeus looked back to Fiore just in time to see him lose and say, "One more hand."

"No! Fiore, we have to go!" Zeus yelled.

"Billix is right, you yell a lot, and that makes it hard to concentrate."

"Well, you two can commiserate about it back on Weelah's ship. Now let's—" Zeus cut himself short as he looked back to see how Billix was doing. Billix was gone....

Chapter 19

Fiore didn't understand why Zeus was getting so mad. They'd gotten what they came for with no fuss, so why couldn't they afford a few minutes to enjoy themselves? And Fiore needed to win back all the money he had lost at the Terrellian poker table. Through a series of bad losses, he felt confident that he had cracked the codes of a few of the other players—the yellow creature with the four eye stalks liked to bluff, the other player who looked like a mound of gray mush wrapped in scarves bet high when he had a good hand, and the green woman with the low cut dress exposing her great expanse of cleavage… cleavage… cleavage…

"Damn it!" Fiore barked when he lost again. He scolded himself for falling into what was clearly her strategy. Focusing, he commanded himself to look up at her face, away from her bountiful trap. However, her face looked like two light bulbs bobbling atop a greasy funnel. The longer he looked, the more his stomach twisted. Sweating, his throat tightened. He glanced around at the other players, but his eyes inevitably found solace in her cleavage.…

"Fiore!" Zeus yelled. Frustrated from losing again, Fiore turned; ready to yell back that they should stay a little longer. Then he remembered why they shouldn't. Billix had just disappeared.

"Come on!" Zeus waved as he rushed into the crowd.

Fiore looked ahead to see the sprigs of green hair atop Billix's purple head bobbing along. Someone carried him with ease, and he didn't look conscious. Fiore looked back to the table to collect his remaining chips, but with one glance remembered that he no longer had any. Leaping up from his chair, he chased after Zeus.

Being bigger than most, Fiore pressed through the crowd and caught up to his partner with ease. However, being bigger than only "most" meant there was always someone bigger than he—and that individual did not appreciate it when Fiore ran into him.

Fiore tried to apologize, but the larger creature shoved him, slamming him into a wall. His attacker was humanoid shaped with skin shimmering gray, a pluming fin ran from the top of its head all the way down its back. Face devoid of any features other than black marble eyes, a sleeve of skin dangled from its chin. It rippled as a deep, gurgling voice said to Fiore, "You spilled my drink. You're gonna pay for that."

"Okay," Fiore said, reaching into his pocket. "How much did it cost?"

"Quit messing around!" Zeus yelled at Fiore as he continued to pursue Billix. "We don't have time for this."

The fin-headed creature shoved Fiore again and said, "Not what I meant."

Tightening his right hand into a fist, Fiore concentrated on the creature's face. With unblinking focus, Fiore reeled back and swung. He connected! However, he quickly realized that the creature's skeletal system wasn't made from bone as his punch ended with an ineffectual slap into rubbery skin.

"My turn," the creature said, reeling back. Fiore dropped to the floor, avoiding a punch so forceful that it cracked the wall.

While on the ground, Fiore decided to take advantage of the thick crowd. Staying on his hands and knees, he crawled in the direction of Zeus, toward a set of stairs.

After a minute of scuttling among legs of varying thickness and knocking people over, Fiore finally got to his feet and bounded up the stairs. At the top, he took a moment to catch his breath. The second floor had a promenade that lined all four walls, leaving the center open for the luxury tables. Floating about the open air, on the same level as the second floor, were platforms holding private gaming tables and seats for players willing to pay a premium for the seclusion. The smaller ones accommodated only the game and two seats while the larger ones could fit eight players.

All along the promenade were more gaming tables and machines and rooms with lights flashing and patrons cheering and noises sounding. Zeus ran along the near wall, ready to make the turn from the corner of one concourse to its perpendicular. Looking ahead, Fiore saw Billix, still unconscious. The hooded figure carrying Fiore's purple friend was large, but nimble enough to veer around people.

Was it The Legend? Fiore had only seen The Legend once, but it was from the unflattering position of lying on the trash-covered street of an alleyway. Looking upward, he remembered The Legend being immense, godlike. Logically, he knew he was probably bigger than The Legend, but the veteran bounty hunter could certainly be big enough to carry an unconscious Billix with ease, like the individual Zeus pursued.

Knowing he wouldn't be able to catch the cloaked figure, not even if he injected himself with a concoction to build muscle and set his nerves aflame, he quickly came up with an idea. No concoctions this time, just his natural grace. Getting a running start, he leapt over the banister and jumped onto the closest hovering platform.

The platform dropped and wobbled, but the gyros reacted accordingly, bringing it back to proper height and orientation. More surprised than upset, the patrons simply watched as Fiore jumped to the next platform. Other than a few jostled stacks of chips and spilled drinks, Fiore repeated his actions all the way to the other side of the promenade with no damage, to himself or others.

Upon safely landing, he sprinted toward Billix's captor. A pang of regret skipped through his chest—Zeus didn't see him execute his stunning feat, and he certainly wouldn't believe Fiore if he told him.

Running straight ahead, Fiore rushed to intercept the individual who had stolen Billix. The cloaked figure turned down a hallway. Fiore followed, and Zeus caught up with him.

The bounty hunters pulled up when they saw that the only egress from the hallway was a locked service door. The cloaked figure was trapped. As they approached, Fiore pulled a few cartridges from his bandoleer and loaded them into his forearm unit. Muscle builders. Sensory enhancers. Painkillers. Striding alongside Zeus, Fiore said, "I think it's The Legend. I'm gonna be more prepared this time."

The hooded figure turned, shoulders slumped, and gently placed Billix on the ground. Fiore's finger hovered over the button to start the infusion process, waiting for The Legend to attack. However, he wouldn't need the boost; Billix's captor dropped his hood and it wasn't The Legend.

It was Huva. "Settle down, boys. I'm not The Legend."

"Huva?" Zeus snapped.

Despite hoping to prove himself against The Legend, Fiore wasn't entirely disappointed to see her. The cloak hid her upper body, but he didn't need to see it to remember how magnificent it was. The cloak didn't hide how muscular she was. Her mohawk of pinks and whites and reds flowed to one side of her face and over her chest. Fiore liked that. He liked the shade of her skin, a soft fuchsia. He smiled.

"Yes, me," Huva snapped back. With ease, she snatched Billix from the ground and hefted him over her other shoulder. "Now, if you two don't mind, get out of my way. I have a bounty to collect."

Zeus shifted his body a bit to stand in her way. "We can't let you do that."

Huva scowled.

In an effort of solidarity, Fiore moved behind Zeus and said, "We can't let you take our friend."

Zeus turned to give Fiore a look that let him know he had said something stupid. Fiore couldn't fathom what it could have possibly been. Before he could ask, though, a commotion from behind him commanded his attention.

Yelps of shock and fear rippled through many of the patrons on the promenade, along the main walkway. Plowing through them, the gray individual that Fiore had offended earlier stormed toward him. Fists clenched, he aimed right for Fiore, making a gurgling trumpeting noise, rippling the skin sleeve dangling from its chin. When the creature saw Fiore, he charged.

Frozen, Fiore was too shocked to push the button to infuse the ingredients into his body, his finger still hovering over it. The disgruntled casino patron raised both of his fists over his head, ready to pulverize. It was going to hurt, Fiore registered, but still too shocked to move, to drop his finger the minute distance to the one option that would give him a chance in the upcoming fight. But when the gray monstrosity got close enough to spray Fiore with spittle from its undulating skin sleeve, he suddenly halted. Then convulsed. Knees buckling, he dropped to the floor in a disheveled pile of gray muscle.

Standing there holding a two-pronged device, arcs of crackling electricity dancing between them, Valla looked down at the unconscious creature and smiled. "I was hoping this would work."

Zeus frowned, "So, you put our lives at risk with an item that you didn't know would work or not?"

Valla's tilted her head and regarded Zeus with confusion. She flicked open her brown cloak to slide the device into an empty hoop of her belt, other odd-looking devices dangling from it. She said, "No. You two put your lives at risk by provoking this individual into attacking you. I stopped him with an untested device, thus saving you."

With Billix slung over her shoulder, Huva strode toward the hallway opening and said, "And you two are currently putting your lives at risk if you don't get out of my way."

Moaning, Billix shifted. Arms and legs still as limp, he raised his head, his non-cybernetic eye only half open. "Unngh. What's going on? Where am I? Am I flying?"

"Friends of ours are trying to kidnap you," Fiore answered. "But we'll get you out of this."

As Fiore suspected, Zeus glared at him with the "you said something stupid" look. Fiore frowned and mouthed the word, "What?" in response.

"See?" Billix mumbled. "I told you someone would think I'm a real bounty. Now look at me. I'm flying and I don't know how."

Scowling, Huva looked back at Billix and said, "You're not flying. You're over my shoulder. What do you mean that you're not a real bounty."

Through his half-shut eye, Billix looked at Huva and said, "I gave these idiots the idea to post a fake bounty to get a real bounty. Wow. You're pretty."

With a disgusted grunt, Huva dropped Billix and walked closer to Zeus and Fiore. One fist clenched, she used her hand to waggle her index finger. "What is he talking about?"

"It's a long story," Fiore said.

"It's none of your business," Zeus said.

"Again, you are incorrect," Valla pointed out. "Since our business is bounty hunting, and he is a bounty, that makes him our business."

"He's not a real bounty," Fiore said.

"He's our bounty," Zeus said.

Huva looked at Billix, now sitting on the floor slowly flapping his arms in an attempt to fly again. Frustrated, she closed her eyes and shook her head. "You two aren't making any sense. What's going on?"

"And why is there a dart sticking out of your shoulder," Valla asked Fiore.

Fiore plucked it out and sighed, "Not again."

"Down!" Zeus yelled, wrapping his arms around Valla and diving to the ground. A barrage of tranq darts clattered against the wall where they had been standing.

Fiore grabbed Billix's right arm, Huva grabbed his left, and the both sprinted onto the promenade. Huva yelled, "What is going on?"

"Long story," Fiore yelled back. "We have to get out of here!"

"Whee!" said Billix.

Thanks to the commotion Zeus and Fiore had caused earlier, the casino security guards had come to investigate. Fiore and Huva started to run, but stopped when they saw the dozen incoming guards. They changed direction as security gave pursuit, unwittingly using them as shields— tranq darts dropped half of the guards. Confused, the remaining guards split between chasing Fiore and Huva and attempting to find out where the tranq darts were coming from. They called for more security as the small crowds on the promenade turned into one screaming mass of chaos.

With Billix in tow, Fiore and Huva joined Zeus and Valla behind a bank of gaming machines and leaned Billix against the nearby wall. Crouched low, they used the swarming mass of casino patrons running about as cover. Billix giggled uncontrollably.

"Would someone please tell me what's happening?" Huva asked.

"Sivka Corp. The rumors of them having a goon squad are all true, and they're after us," Zeus replied.

"What reason would Sivka Corp have for pursuing a couple of no-name bounty hunters?" Valla asked.

"Hey!" Zeus snapped indignantly.

Watching the commotion, Fiore said, "We'll tell you all about it later."

"No, we won't," Zeus replied.

With an earnest look in his eye, Fiore turned to his partner and said, "Zeus, seriously. They can help us. We have at least two long-term situations we need help with, as well as this current one."

"We're progressing well enough on our own without their help. And we *already* have to give a cut of our bounty to Weelah and Billix."

"We've progressed *because* of Weelah and Billix."

"Whee!" Billix squealed, as he juggled three tranq darts that he had pulled from the wall they crouched against. He dropped them and laughed, then pointed to behind Fiore and said, "Oh, hey. Look."

Everyone looked to see the gray creature with muscle and fin standing behind Fiore. With his fists raised over his head, the creature let out a gurgling roar. He faced the same results as the last time he attacked Fiore; Valla zapped him with her electricity deployment device. The creature convulsed and crumbled into an unconscious mass of muscle.

Fiore gestured to Valla while addressing Zeus. "See?"

Zeus glowered as two tranq darts and a red energy beam flashed over his head. "Fine! Follow us to our transport ship and we'll explain everything. Okay?"

Huva nodded, while Valla asked, "You have a transport ship?"

"It belongs to a friend of ours," Fiore explained. "It's a big one, so we took a skiff to get here. The skiff is docked in the regular docking bays, on the first floor."

"You use the word 'friend' way too liberally," Zeus muttered.

The group looked around, trying to figure out the best course of action. Hundreds of patrons still ran about in a panic, all trying to flee down the stairs and lift tubes. Furniture and gaming tables had been overturned and broken, debris scattered about the promenade floor. Casino security ran around confused, concerned about the safety of their patrons while trying to ascertain the locations of the mysterious tranq dart shooters and attempting to close in on the hooligans crouched against the wall who were responsible for starting this whole mess. Unfortunately for Fiore and his friends, a small contingent of security crept closer to them on either side while another handful laid down suppressive fire of red energy beams toward the general direction of where the tranq darts were coming from. Then Fiore had an idea.

Looking at his friends, he smiled and said, "I have a plan. Follow me."

"So, what's the plan?" Huva asked, as Fiore readied himself to sprint.

Fiore glanced back, confused. "I said to follow me."

"That's your plan? It looks like you're getting ready to run into the middle of... everything!"

"That's usually his plan," Zeus moaned. "I'm actually surprised he told us this much of his plan."

Laughing and slightly slurring, Billix added, "I love his plans. He has the best plans. He usually gets shot. His plans are the best."

Fiore frowned, but continued with his plan anyway. Slinging the still limp Billix over his shoulder, he said, "We all have to go together. Now!"

As expected, Fiore's plan involved running straight through the middle of the chaos. Billix kicked his feet and squealed, "Whee!"

The others kept pace with Fiore, shoving stray patrons out of the way, dodging tranq darts, hoping the red energy beams from security would continue to miss. Fiore slowed his pace by a step just as he got to the promenade's railing, allowing the others to catch up. As one, they all went over the railing, landing on the closest hovering gaming platform. Their combined weight caused the platform to drop precipitously, but before it crashed, the propulsion units kicked in. When the bottom of the platform finally touched the ground of the first floor, it was as gentle as a lover's kiss. Before the propulsion unit forced the platform back to its original position hovering along the second floor, Fiore and friends leapt safely from it.

Even though the panicked need for exodus had reached the patrons of the first floor, there were no Sivka Corp. gunmen shooting at them, and the small contingent of casino security stayed too busy attempting to keep the evacuation orderly.

Fiore and Huva led the way through the crowds to the docking bays. Billix continued to enjoy the ride, "Whee!"

Chapter 20

This was not going well. Zeus did not like how the events at the casino had turned out. He was thankful and a bit surprised that they made it out with no injury, but he was thoroughly displeased with the price he and Fiore had to pay—two more people they might have to share their bounty with.

As soon as everyone boarded Weelah's cargo ship, a whirlwind of voices reverberated along the metal walls of the hull.

"Who are these two?" Weelah asked as Huva and Valla followed Zeus, Fiore, and Billix.

Rubbing the non-cybernetic parts of his head with his non-cybernetic hand, Billix asked, "What did you use to knock me out? My head is killing me. Is my brain going to explode? Why was I giggling when I woke up? Why did I think I was flying?"

Even though she pointed at Billix, Huva ignored his words and asked Zeus and Fiore, "I wanna know what you two meant when you said he's not a real bounty."

Valla addressed the pair as well by asking, "I am more than curious as to why Sivka Corp. is after you."

"You never told me how the meeting with Myzzer went. Are we invited to the fights?" Fiore asked. Zeus wondered if his partner was a master of ignoring the maelstrom swirling around him, or if he simply didn't know it existed.

"Stop!" Zeus shouted. Crossed arms and glaring stares waited for him to continue. He looked at Weelah first. "These two are Huva and Valla. Sisters. Rival bounty hunters."

"You know, Zeus," Valla started, "*You* are the only one who views us as rivals."

"Don't be so sure of that," Huva grumbled.

"Well, I certainly think the four us would make a good team. I'm pretty certain Fiore thinks we would—"

Zeus lobbed a heaving sigh at Valla to interrupt her. She caught the hint and rolled her eyes. "Fine. We're 'rival' bounty hunters. But we're rival bounty hunters wondering what you meant by Sivka Corp. being after you? The rumors of them having their own black ops squad are true?"

"Very," Zeus answered. "They raided our headquarters. What is particularly interesting is that every time we've encountered them, they've used tranq darts."

"Except with Koorza," Fiore interjected. "They blew a hole through his chest."

"Who's Koorza?" Huva asked.

"An ex-boyfriend," Weelah said dryly.

"Not a good one, I assume."

"Hardly. He was a man, after all."

"I understand. Men are disgusting."

"Vile."

"Rancid."

The two women stopped their commiserating to share a look of disdain aimed right at Fiore. Sweat percolated along his brow as he withered from the heat of their blazing glares. "So… yeah… Sivka Corp. After us. Don't know why."

Squinting, Valla leaned closer to Fiore and said, "Are you sure it's Sivka Corp?"

Fiore reeled back and said, "Absolutely! We took a gun that they left behind, the first time they attacked us, to Billix's uncle. He used to be a bounty hunter, but is now a king of a primitive tribe."

Valla shook her head and frowned. "Wow. That… that sure is the proof that I needed. How could I not trust the word of a crazy ex-bounty hunter, leader of a primitive tribe?"

"Especially since he tried to collect the bounty on my head," Billix moaned. "Me. His own nephew. His sister's son. Me."

"Speaking of," Huva turned to Zeus while pointing at Billix. "What did you mean when you said he's not a real bounty?"

Not liking her accusatory tone, Zeus frowned and crossed his arms. "It was an idea we had to lure The Legend out. We posted a bounty on Billix. Since we posted it and we have him, then we don't have to worry about anyone trying to collect."

Huva ground the heels of her palms into her closed eyes and grumbled, "Of all the stupid…"

"Well, what have you done?" Zeus spat. "You're looking for The Legend too, so what was your big plan to find him?"

"He's right, Huva," Valla said. "That wasn't that bad of an idea."

Billix perked up, smile on his face. "Yeah? That was my idea. I came up with it. Well, not for *me* to be the bounty. But the idea in general."

Valla looked at Billix and offered him a warm smile, conveying that she was truly impressed. Zeus glowered at this.

"Oh!" Valla squeaked, startled. She looked down at her feet to see what caused the surprise. Hydrynx rubbed her ankles in figure eights. "What is that?"

"That's Hydrynx," Zeus answered. "I made it."

"This is fantastic!" Valla exclaimed. Using both hands, she snatched Hydrynx from the floor and scrutinized it like an archaeologist discovering an artifact. Hydrynx wore a flat expression across its feline face while Valla turned it in her hands, flipped it, and lifted it over her head. "Simply phenomenal."

Torn between wanting to bask in the glory of his accomplishment with a potential peer and wanting to rid himself of a known rival, Zeus gave a guarded, "Thank you."

Valla held Hydrynx straight out from her, examining it. Smiling, she brought the creature in close enough to rub its furry face against hers and coo, "You're such a cutie, too. Aren't you? Yes, you are. Yes, you are."

Hydrynx purred.

"My sister, the galaxy's most feared and reviled bounty hunter," Huva moaned, the sarcasm in her voice obvious.

"You don't listen to her," Valla said to Hydrynx as she sat down, placing the hybrid on her lap. Its expression shifted from mild displeasure to pure ecstasy as Valla's lithe fingers ran through its soft green fur. Its purring grew louder as wisps of smoke curled from its nostrils. Exuberance on her face, Valla looked up at Zeus, "Is that smoke? Can it breathe fire?"

The lapping waves of approval eroded the sandy bunkers he tried to build around his heart. With a bit more pride in his voice than he hoped to share, Zeus said, "Of course. I did splice cat genes with a dragon's."

Valla gasped with awe while Huva twisted her face and groaned in disgust. Both sisters said in a tone befitting their feelings, "Where did you even find dragon genes?"

"I know, right?" Billix asked, the heel of his skin and bone hand pressed against the non-metallic part of his forehead. "I'm not the only one who thinks that's absolutely insane, right? Seriously, dragon genes. Where? That's crazy, right?"

"I agree with the little purple guy," Huva added, putting her hand on Billix's shoulder.

Billix smiled, but it quickly faded when he looked up at Huva. Exaggerating the rubbing motion of his head, he asked again, "What was it you used on me to render me unconscious? The headache will go away, right? Are there any side-effects? Will I have permanent damage?"

Huva removed her hand and crossed her arms over her chest with a huff. "It's a simple Tylruvian dioxin. One quick spray and out you went."

"Tylruvian dioxin! Do you have *any idea* what Tylruvian dioxin does to my species?" Billix shrieked.

Concerned, Valla looked up from petting Hydrynx. "No. What does it do?"

"I don't know! That's why I was asking! Do *you* know what it does? I sure would like to know!" Billix asked, panting.

Snidely, Zeus tapped the metallic shell of Billix's head and said, "Why don't you use your super computer brain to find out?"

Even more panicked, Billix said, "Why didn't I think of that? Is that part of the side effects? Cognitive degeneration? Okay. Okay, I gotta calm down. Accessing the universal web now."

"Is he always like this?" Huva asked Weelah.

Weelah sighed. "As far as I know. I only met these fine examples of men a couple days ago. The only reason why I'm still with them is because they saved my daughter's life and they let me in on a cut of the Dryn Tammeryn bounty."

"What?" Huva barked. Clenching her fists, she turned to Zeus and growled, "You said you didn't want partners. You said you two work alone. The only team that you need."

"I agree with my sister," Valla said. "We offered to help and split the bounty, but you said no."

"That was before Sivka turned our headquarters into a hot zone," Zeus said. "After Billix wrecked his hover car, we had no transportation. We had no choice but to hire Weelah."

Huva turned to Weelah and said, "Equal share in the bounty if you help us out instead."

"Deal."

"Hey!" Zeus shouted.

Billix looked at the women, then back at the other men and said, "Sorry, guys. But I feel safer with them than you."

"They drugged you and kidnapped you!"

"They operated as effectively as they could within the parameters of information they had at the time. Especially since I learned that there are no lasting side effects of Tylruvian dioxin to my species."

Weelah looked at Zeus and Fiore. "I'll take you back planetside. I'll even drop you near a jump port."

"Sorry, but I think you're leaving soon, sweetie," Valla said, kissing Hydrynx between its ears. Gently placing it on the floor, she stood and walked over to her sister, now standing in solidarity with Weelah and Billix. Holding its tail high and flicking it in rebellion toward its creator, Hydrynx padded over to Valla's feet.

Arms crossed and frowning, Zeus turned to Fiore and said, "So, are you going to join them, too? Make your own little band of bounty hunters team?"

Eyebrows rounding to display how truly sad he felt, Fiore said, "Zeus, you know that I would never do that. I'm sticking with you. But if we all work together and split the bounty evenly, we'll get one third. I may not know a lot, but I know that one third of the bounty is better than no thirds of the bounty. Plus, we're running out of time, and we still have no idea what Sivka wants with us."

Zeus eased a little on the inside. It never ceased to amaze him the lengths Fiore would go to maintain the partnership. A strategist? No. A fighter? Hardly. Intuitive? Up for debate. But loyalty? That was where Fiore excelled. With loyalty came trust, and that was one thing that Zeus was self-aware enough to know he was lacking. How could he not trust Fiore? Zeus knew that he needed to trust more, so why not let Fiore be his guide? Fiore trusted these people, so Zeus decided he would try to trust them as well, albeit in a much more guarded way. Zeus made a noise akin to a grunt, "Fine."

"Everyone gets an equal share?" Huva asked, her tone stern.

Zeus grumbled throatily, "Yes."

The air in the cargo ship shifted. Tension vaporized into levity, frowns into smiles. Except for Zeus, of course, who quickly added, "But I'm the one who makes the decisions!"

Huva pursed her lips while a wan expression washed over Weelah's face. Billix and Valla simply shrugged. Fiore remained ever faithful, and looked upon Zeus, awaiting his next order.

"Okay, genius," Weelah said. "So what's the next course of action? Are we going to Myzzer's fights?"

Huva and Valla looked at each other, then back at the others. Huva asked, "Myzzer? *The* Myzzer? Most dangerous crime lord in the galaxy, Myzzer?"

Valla followed up with, "How is he involved?"

"Yes, *that* Myzzer," Zeus answered, incredulous even though he himself had never heard of the man until yesterday. "He's the one who put the bounty out on Dryn Tammeryn."

The sisters reeled back, their faces showed nothing but surprise. Draped in smugness, Zeus continued, "We decided to take a different approach to finding Tammeryn. We decided that if we found out who posted the bounty, then maybe we could find out why they wanted him and why they wanted him delivered to a specific location on a specific time and date."

Valla said, "That's very impressive. How did you do that?"

"I have my secrets."

Billix wasted no time sharing those secrets. "We hacked into the wire and discovered that the posting was made from a library on Genture, so we went there and found the computer that was used, and I examined the user directory to find that it was Myzzer. Then we were attacked by Sivka Corp. Again."

Ignoring Zeus' icy glare at Billix, Huva asked, "There is never a dull moment with you guys, is there? So, now we're going to track down Myzzer?"

"Myzzer hosts illegal underground interspecies fights. We entered Fiore into them. While he's fighting, we'll have an opportunity to break into Myzzer's main office and see if we can find some information as to why he wants Tammeryn."

"Wait! What?" Fiore snapped. "When did we enter me into the fights?"

"While you were losing at Terrellian poker!"

"I told you he wasn't going to be happy with this," Billix muttered. "Why would he be? You entered him into a death fight without him even knowing. He sucks at fighting. Have you seen him fight? He's not very good at it."

"Death fight?" Fiore shrieked; Zeus actually flinched from the disturbingly high pitch. "I agree with Billix! I'm not very good at death fighting!"

Huva couldn't help but chuckle until her sister elbowed her. "What?" Huva asked, still wearing a wide smile. "This is pretty funny."

"Glad you think so, because you're coming with me!" Fiore shouted.

"Oh, come on—" Huva started.

Zeus cut her off with, "Actually, that's what I was thinking, too. Weelah and Billix will stay in the cargo ship—"

"About time," Billix blurted. "I finally get a chance to rest. And not get shot at. And not get drugged. And not get kidnapped. And not—"

Stopping the rant before it could gain any more momentum, Zeus continued, "They'll tap into whatever security and cameras they can find, and let the four of us know what's going on as we go planetside. Once we get to the fights, Huva will be Fiore's trainer. Valla and I will find and break into Myzzer's office."

"That's all great, Zeus," Fiore said, looking worried. "But what about me and all the fighting to the death?"

"You won't need to do that," Zeus said. "All we need is enough time to sneak into Myzzer's office. With a little bit of luck, we'll find what we need quickly, and you won't even have to fight."

Huva elbowed Fiore and then lazily tapped his forearm cybernetics. "Don't forget, you have this, you big sissy. With the touch of a button, you can gain muscle and endurance. Of course, when you get your ass kicked, all you need to do is use a different set of ingredients and you're all healed up."

Fiore grimaced at Huva. Huva laughed and punched him in the shoulder. "You better rest up. You've got a big day tomorrow."

Weelah tried not to laugh, but couldn't stop a smirk from tugging at her lips. She led Huva and Valla out of the cargo hull. "Follow me. I have a few sleeping quarters that I don't use. I'm sure I can find enough provisions to make for a comfortable night's sleep."

Prancing with its tail in the air, Hydrynx followed Valla, dangerously close to her ankles.

Billix looked at Fiore, now a slouching hunk of misery, and said, "Well, I'm going to turn in as well. Get some good sleep for tomorrow. Big day."

After Billix left, Zeus showed as much affection as he could muster in the form of a pat on Fiore's shoulder. He actually began to feel bad for his lummox of a partner. Fiore usually ran into trouble shoulder first and head down, so Zeus assumed that his partner would have been good to go with this idea. Assumptions were a part of all relationships, every partnership, and he wondered if he was too presumptuous offering up Fiore's name for the illegal fights. "We both knew bounty hunting wouldn't be easy. I can't imagine these fights are to the death. You've lost fights before… a lot of fights… so, you should be okay."

Fiore sighed. "I need a milk."

"Okay. Let's see if Weelah has any on this ship." Zeus knew Fiore's anxiety must be running deep—not once during the last conversation did he look at Weelah's or Huva's cleavage.…

Chapter 21

Fiore was nervous. Standing next to Zeus, Fiore leaned over and said, "I'm nervous." Even though he spoke at regular volume, the crowd noise muffled it to a whisper.

"Now is not the time for that," Zeus replied, frowning. He didn't look at Fiore, scanning the room instead. The flashing colors and dancing patrons of the frenetic club made it nearly impossible to see further than a few feet.

But now, standing in the club, wasn't when Fiore started to feel this way. The bad feelings had begun long before now. Flutters had tickled his belly yesterday when he first heard that he had been signed up for an illegal interspecies underground fight run by the biggest crime lord in the galaxy—with the potential of death. The flutters had mutated into roiling squirms this morning when everyone on Weelah's cargo ship teased him about getting his ass kicked. He couldn't even eat breakfast, simply forcing himself to chew down a nutrition bar. When the time came to go planetside, to the club, with Zeus and the sisters, wriggling fingers squeezed everything within his chest.

As they approached the club—a flashy building in an overcrowded, flashy city on an overcrowded, flashy planet—they bickered about accidentally coordinating. Zeus and Valla both wore their cloaks; Zeus in his drab green while the red of Vallas's cloak matched the color of her sister's hair. Fiore and Huva both wore black pants and boots, however Huva's pants were much tighter on her shapely legs. As always, Fiore wore his stylish black vest and bandoleer of chemical cases; Huva's vest was black as well and, like her pants, form-fitting.

"Well at least they'll know we're on the same team," Fiore rationalized.

"Shut up, Fiore," the other three said in unison.

The doormen were impeccably dressed in the latest fashion of high-end professional wear, but their immense muscles tested the integrity of every stitch. Faces like mismatched knuckles and skin like burled wood, their intimidating stares threatened to rip unwelcome guests to shreds. Even though Fiore stood eye to eye with them, he knew that if he did anything stupid, it would be a fight he would lose. *Another* fight he would lose.

"We're here for the fights," Zeus said, holding the invitation that Myzzer had given him.

The doormen didn't move, not even a glance downward to Zeus.

Frowning, Zeus jabbed the air in front of him with the invitation. "I said we're here for the fights. We're participants. This invite is from Myzzer himself."

Wordlessly, one doorman grabbed Zeus by the wrist and looked at the card in his hand. The other tapped a cybernetic node in his ear, and mumbled a number. No one moved, breathed, or even blinked for seconds. The doorman who had spoken turned to his associate and nodded. The other simply released Zeus and stepped to the side. With a voice like an exploding artillery shell, the doorman said, "Door at the back of the club. Show your card there."

The foursome entered the club. Fiore expressed his feelings of anxiety, but Zeus ignored them while scanning the club. Fiore tried again, "I'm not getting nervous *now*. I've *been* nervous."

"Uh-huh," Zeus replied. He then turned to his companions and pointed. "There. I think I see the door over there." Zeus led the way into the crowd, and the rest followed.

Music thumped and lights flashed. One color filled the room, then disappeared to allow the chromatic piping that edged the bar and furniture to glow brightly, only to be replaced by another color. All kinds of creatures danced—on the floor, on floating platforms, on pedestals jutting from the walls. The scene hypnotized Fiore as he and his friends made their way through the club. Until he remembered why they were there.

His heart sank, wondering if he'd survive to ever come back and enjoy this club, or any club like this one. He had never been to a club like this, and it saddened him that he couldn't enjoy the experience. Then he saw scantily clad women dancing in cages dangling from the ceiling. His soul smiled.

But he took another step closer to the door at the back of the room, and his heart re-sank.

Then the cage dancer closest to him bent over.

He remembered why he was there.

How did the dancer keep her breasts from popping out?

He was heading to a fight to the death.

Wait, did that other dancer have six breasts?

"Come on, you Felluvian dung pig," Huva barked as she elbowed him. It didn't help, as Fiore responded to her jab by turning to look at her cleavage.

The four finally made their way through the crowd to the door at the back of the club, Fiore having endured seventeen more distinct crises of faith broken up by an equal number of lustful pangs by the time they got there. Two more massive doormen greeted them in the same stolid manner as the ones guarding the club entrance, and the exchange with them happened similarly to the first. This time, however, the door opened to a hallway; the noise of the club muffled to nil as the door closed behind Fiore and his friends.

"Now what?" Fiore asked, hoping that this meant the plan failed and they could try something else that didn't *directly* put his life in jeopardy.

"We follow the hallway," Zeus replied, glancing up at the cameras embedded in the ceiling. He quickly put his head down, using his hood to conceal his face, and led the way. Valla did the same. Huva didn't seem to notice or care, and Fiore couldn't stop looking at each one as he walked past them. The hallway sloped downward, then made a sharp turn, leading them back the way they had come, but deeper underground. Another door awaited them, but this one was open, with noise coming from it.

The hallway led to a massive room. Two stories from ground to ceiling, the room boasted tinted windows around the top perimeter. Zeus said something about it looking like a vast warehouse converted to meet the current needs, but his words didn't register with Fiore. He couldn't stop looking at the crowd.

Everyone in the audience was well dressed. Expensive fashions and flashy jewelry adorned every attendee. They all seemed even wealthier than those who had been floating on the exclusive high-end tables at the casino yesterday. Success and fortune emanated from every soul in the stands. Fiore knew that Zeus yearned for that level of luxury and extravagance. Actually, Fiore only *assumed* that was the level of luxury and extravagance Zeus wanted. A stray thought floated through Fiore's head: he had no idea *what* Zeus' goals were. He knew nothing of Zeus's past or his motivations; just that he liked Puzal grouse legs and he wanted to be a successful bounty hunter. Through the raging screams of anxiety in his head, Fiore heard the little whisper of his conscience making him feel guilty for not really knowing anything about his best friend.

Fiore wanted to say something to Zeus, but he had no idea what. Even if he could articulate any of the feelings swirling within him, he no longer had the chance. An insectoid approached, yelling, "Hey, hey, hey! Who are you and where do you think you're going?"

The angry creature stood on two legs, but had four arms, tiny hairs covering the shimmering black exoskeleton. It was shorter than either Zeus or Valla and wore clothing that resembled strips of thin cloth sewn together in vertical patterns, making a fringe effect every time it moved. Head like an ant, its skin and large black eyes moved enough to show expression. Its snarling frown showed that it was very unhappy.

Offering a similar expression, Zeus held out the card one more time. "Here. This is our invite. We're participating."

The insectoid snatched the card from Zeus and looked it over. "Last minute addition. How am I supposed to run a successful fight with all kinds of last minute changes?"

Fiore tried to think of an answer, but realized the question was rhetorical after Zeus snapped, "Just tell us where to go and when we're on."

The creature sighed and squinted its eyes; they shined like polished obsidian. It pulled out a handheld computer and tapped on the screen. All business, it asked a series of questions and tapped away at the screen as Zeus answered. "Fighter's name?"

"Fiore Dentellare."

"Species?"

"Human."

"Weight class?"

"I don't know. He's four hundred pounds."

"Heavyweight. Small, but he's still heavyweight. Home?"

"Parts unknown."

The insectoid paused to give an exasperated huff. "Occupation?"

"Bounty Hunter."

Face still angled toward the screen, the insectoid shifted only its eyes to Zeus. With a wan look and flat words, the creature said, "Look, if you're not going to take this seriously—"

"I'm serious! We're bounty hunters." Zeus snapped.

The insectoid sighed and went back to tapping away at the screen. "I'm just saying that the crowd might not buy into it. The girls? I could believe that those two are bounty hunters. You and your pal? Not so much."

"What? Why not? We're dressed exactly alike!"

The insectoid finished up and returned the computer to an unseen pocket among the cloth strips. Expression shifting to boredom, it said, "I don't know. Something about your demeanor. Like you two are too innocent. Like you're virgins...."

The girls erupted with laughter, even though Valla tried to hide hers. Zeus went red with fury, while Fiore went red from embarrassment. Again, he struggled to find a good response. He didn't need one, though. The insectoid pointed to the arena and said, "You're up next. Don't get killed before you get the chance to be deflowered."

Nervousness gripped Fiore by the throat as he tried to swallow the dry lump that formed when he suddenly realized the enormity of the situation. He followed the others closer to the arena. Circular and bigger than their apartment headquarters, the arena floor—packed dirt pockmarked with random gouges and streaked with blood splatters of many different colors —was lower than the warehouse floor by two feet. A solid wall, four feet high, surrounded the perimeter of the arena. Dents and missing chunks warned spectators to keep their distance, but didn't stop them as nary an empty spot around the ring could be found.

As the current match wound to an end, the cheers of the crowd ebbed and flowed like the waves of a malicious ocean. The seating area wrapped around three-fourths of the arena, and angled so that the spectators in the stands could see past the spectators crowding the central wall. The only gap in the stands was for a large throne, where Myzzer sat, close enough that Fiore could see the rapt fascination in his hungry eyes. Two gorgeous women—with ample cleavage—sat in Myzzer's throne, one either side of him, their legs draped over his. One had her head resting on his shoulder, while the other sat more attentively, watching the fight, but drawing lazy circles on his chest with her fingers. All three in the throne cheered along with the crowd. Fiore couldn't make out who they cheered for or against. He just knew *what* they were cheering for: blood.

And they got it.

By the time Fiore and his friends made their way through the narrow path between the front of the stands and the people lining the wall to the ramp leading down to the pit, the match had ended. A yellow-skinned biped—the same species as Weelah and Koorza, and roughly the same size as Fiore—stood victorious. Fists raised over his head, he absorbed the adulation of the raucous crowd. The loser was dragged away by two thugs in Myzzer's employ, leaving a trail of blood across the arena floor. This made Fiore feel a little better—the loser was noticeably smaller than the victor. Fiore immediately felt guilty for being happy that the loser was smaller, but he clutched at the glimmer of hope that his opponent might be smaller as well.

"I can do this," he said, mustering all the bravado he could find.

"Good attitude," Zeus replied, not looking at him. Instead, he continually glanced around, searching. "Found it. Over there."

"I see it. I agree. It's very likely that's what we want," Valla replied.

"Okay," Zeus finally addressed Fiore, "Valla and I are going to sneak through that door over there. With all the activity going on, it should be pretty easy. Good luck!"

"You're not gonna watch my fight?" Fiore asked, disappointed.

Zeus tilted his head, confused, "I can't. Valla and I are going to try to find Myzzer's office, to see if we can find any reason why he'd want Tammeryn. The whole reason why we're here, remember?"

Fiore did know the plan, but he had hoped the sisters could go do that while Zeus stayed behind to support him. Instead, Zeus followed Valla into the crowd. Before he could collect his thoughts, his body was jolted to one side, and he twisted to keep from falling over.

Strutting past him, but not before hitting Fiore's shoulder with his own, the fighter who won the last match barked a laugh and said, "Your turn, Tiny."

Huva pushed Fiore, still a bit disoriented, toward the ramp that led down into the pit. Rounds of hand slaps on his back and shoulders accompanied him along the way. In a daze, he walked, wondering if the cheers and screams were for him or against him. He stopped when he got to the center of the arena and looked around. The faces, even the ones rimming the wall around the arena, blurred together, a swirling amalgam of colors. The crowd noise buzzed through his brain, lowering only when the announcer's voice warbled through the room, "Ladies and gentlemen, please give a warm welcome to our next set of fighters. First, weighing in at four hundred pounds and hailing from parts unknown, is one of the meanest, craziest bounty hunters in the galaxy, celebrated for cracking skulls and breaking bones to bring in the most dastardly of outlaws—the human known as Fiore Dentellare!"

Absolutely loving his introduction, Fiore raised his fist in the air.

The crowd erupted.

Fiore had no doubt that they cheered *for* him.

Huva slapped her forehead and slid her hand down her face.

Fiore raised his other fist in the air, and the crowd replied with thunderous ovation. He slowly turned full circle, to make sure that he wordlessly addressed everyone in attendance, including the host. Myzzer simply smiled, as if he knew the punch line of a joke before the fruition.

"Aaaaaaand now for his opponents," the announcer said, barely audible over the crowd's adulation for Fiore.

Fiore stopped turning. Did the announcer just say *opponents*?

"Hometown favorites," the announcer continued. Fiore strained to hear what the announcer was saying and wondering why he kept using plural words. "Undefeated for over an entire year. You know them! You love them! The Beast Brothers!"

All of Fiore's good feelings disappeared.

The crowd cheered louder....

Chapter 22

"You're just going to leave him?" Valla asked from behind Zeus.

Focused on the door, Zeus continued to jostle through the gauntlet of elbows and shoulders. "He'll be fine."

Struggling to keep pace, Valla continued, "He won't be fine. You know that and I know that."

"He has your sister to help out."

"Not in this situation. She's not going to be in the arena with him, you know."

"He's gotten out of worse situations than this."

"Has he? Really? He got out of worse situations by using his superior fighting skills? Is that it?"

Ten paces from the door, but still within a crowd of people, Zeus stopped and turned to face Valla. She stopped as well and crossed her arms over her chest, souring her face into an angry frown. Trying desperately to ignore how her pouty bottom lip made her far cuter than she intended, Zeus said, "Look, he and I are bounty hunters. We both know the risks, and we each have our jobs to do. He has to do what he has to do so I can do what I have to do, which is just as dangerous, by the way. And *you* are the one putting him in more jeopardy by delaying me from doing my job."

"*Our* job," Valla huffed as she stormed past him. "You're a terrible friend."

Angry that she not only engaged him in this meaningless conversation, but now she took the lead, Zeus hastened his pace to pull even with her. "We're not friends. We're business partners. There's a—"

Valla halted and extended her arm. "Stop!"

Zeus stopped walking and said, "Hey, you started it. I was just trying to explain to you what—"

"No. Not that. It's clear what your feelings are. About everything. I meant, 'stop before we walk through that door'."

"What? Why?"

Valla pulled a handheld computer from her cloak and started tapping away at its screen. "This is the first door that we encountered with no guards. We should assume there are security precautions behind it."

Zeus grunted, upset at himself for not coming to the same conclusion as quickly, but the feeling of inadequacy passed, since one of his specialties was infiltrating computer systems. Overriding the security of a criminal overlord should be easy. Excited to get started, he retrieved his own handheld computer, but as soon as he did, Valla said, "I'm in. Mostly cameras, which should be easy enough to override and show a continuous loop of nothing special, aaaand done. I found a rudimentary schematic. I'm overlaying it with the bio-signatures I'm picking up, and I think I know where we need to go."

A weird mixture of admiration and anger swirled through Zeus' entire body. He tried to think of ways to ask her about the technology she used without seeming weak. All he could come up with was, "Are you ready now?"

"Almost," she replied, excited. From her cloak, she retrieved a small canister with a simple trigger mechanism. "Okay, now I'm ready." She opened the door.

Even though she seemed to trump him with her technology, Zeus knew enough to make sure that they weren't being observed. He looked over his shoulder. No guards. No patrons looking their way. Myzzer's attention remained on the arena. Zeus felt smug, knowing that he thought of something that Valla didn't. Or did she? Maybe she knew that no one noticed them. Maybe she had the *entire* situation under control. Zeus's thoughts evaporated into steam when Valla stepped through the door and looked back to say, "Are you coming or not?"

Zeus stormed into the hallway and shut the door behind him. "So, what are you holding? Perfume?"

Valla turned just enough to shoot Zeus a look letting him know that she wasn't upset, instead confused as to why he would ask such a stupid question. Holding the canister with her finger poised on the trigger, she replied, "No. Why would you even think that?"

Within ten feet, the hallway made a sharp right turn. Zeus snorted at her question. "So, what is it?"

As they turned the corner, she said, "I'll show you on the two guards we're about to run into, if you haven't already alerted them with all your talking."

Valla was right about the guards being there. Tall, frightfully large, well dressed. But they showed no signs of being forewarned about their presence. By the time the guards noticed the interlopers, Valla had depressed the trigger mechanism twice. Two tiny pink clouds puffed from the nozzle, and rendered the guards unconscious within the span of one inhale. Once they slumped to the floor, Zeus and Valla moved on.

Unable to think of anything pithy to say, Zeus settled for, "That spray is very impressive."

"Thank you," Valla replied, keeping her full attention to the hallway, attempting to ferret out any further danger. "I made it myself."

"That must have taken quite a while."

Valla jerked to a complete halt and regarded Zeus with a blend of curiosity and indignation. "Why would you think that?"

Flustered by her reaction, Zeus stopped in his tracks as well. Stammering, he said, "The speed... of it. The speed of how fast it works. And... and the way it seems to work on different species with the same effectiveness."

Valla wrinkled her nose and shook her head. "It's simple biochemistry. Most living things bigger than the size of your hand have quite a few chemical compositions in common. All I did was isolate the pertinent items and develop a neurotoxin to disrupt a few of them. I estimate that my spray is effective on more than ninety percent of the galaxy's known sentient species. Now, come on."

As Valla continued down the hallway, Zeus followed, fuming. Never before had he felt so stupid. That infuriated him. Especially from a woman probably his age. One of the few he could view as a peer. A young woman who was quite attractive. Zeus froze when he realized that he could see the curve of her hips beneath her cloak as she walked. And admired them.

Lowering his hood, he ran his hand through his hair and whispered to himself, "I'm turning into Fiore."

Valla glanced over her shoulder, "Did you say something? Are you okay? You're sweating."

"No. I'm fine," he replied; flipping his hood back over his head and walking past her, resolve in his step.

Valla hastened her pace to keep up. "Are you sure? Why are you walking so fast all of a sudden?"

As soon as Zeus turned the corner, a gun barrel greeted him. Holding the gun was another guard, enormous and dressed nicely like the others. He growled, "Yeah. Why are you walking so fast?"

Zeus interrupted the guard's statement by punching his throat, funneling his recent frustrations through his fist. Eyes bulging, the guard was powerless to stop Zeus from disarming him. A kick to the knee dropped the guard to the floor, and a chop to the back of his head rendered him unconscious. Zeus was satisfied at how well that went. He also felt a little less angry.

Zeus looked up to see that the thug had been guarding a lone door. "Is this Myzzer's office?"

"I think so," Valla replied, taking the guard's gun.

"Let's have a look at this lock." Lock picking was his expertise. He thought back to his youth, about the ennui he had suffered, and the aggressive ways he tried to break out of it. Science and technology had called to him, and he had answered, creating machines and writing programs that had application value. But he had so desperately wanted to escape from the ever tightening yoke of his parents. They wanted him to use his talents to go to school and then get a job, preferably at a large and reputable company like Sivka Corp. Trying many ways to rebel, to express himself, to discover who he really was, he started with locks. At the time he felt similar to a locked door, the answer to what was behind it being so close, yet unattainable without the proper key. He didn't like that, so he learned how to get through the door without a key, how to move past locks and override security mechanisms.

Crouching, Zeus examined the door. Just a simple metal plate with a single slide-latch. Curious. He expected more. Maybe the complexity lay within the perceived simplicity. Was the metal plate a scanner of some sort? Palm reader? DNA tester? Zeus had even heard of ones that needed to be breathed on, but had never seen one. Was this one?

Leaning closer, Zeus looked for wires that might be peeking out from where the plate met the door, or from around the latch. What kinds of sensors were there? What could the consequences be? A litany of dire outcomes ran through Zeus' mind as he scrutinized the area, trying to discover any evidence leading to or away from any of those scenarios.

Valla pushed on the door.

It opened with ease.

Fighting hard to keep his voice at a low volume, Zeus jumped to his feet and whisper-yelled, "Are you *crazy*?"

"No," Valla answered as she peeked inside the room. "Just logical."

More stunned than if he had discovered up was down, Zeus stammered, "What... how... in what way... *possible*... could that have been a logical move?"

Valla regarded Zeus with a squint that made his manhood shrivel. "Seriously? Myzzer is one of the most powerful criminal overlords in the galaxy. Agreed?"

"He is."

"And this is a secret office in a secret back room of a secret underground warehouse in a night club that blends in with all the other nightclubs in the galaxy."

"True."

"And we needed to show an invitation every step of the way to large guards with weapons."

"Yes."

Valla turned and continued into the office as she said, "So, why would he need to lock *this* door? Who would be stupid enough to try to break into *this* office?"

Shaking his head, Zeus followed. "Apparently, us."

"Exactly. Now, let's start looking for any connection between him and Dryn Tammeryn. I'll start with the computer. You go look over there," Valla said, shooing him to the other side of the room with a flick of her hand.

Zeus thought about arguing, but decided against it and simply followed her suggestion. Myzzer's secret office looked like many other offices—two rows of file cabinets, luxurious chairs for guests, elegant yet practical furniture, commercialized artwork of questionable quality adorning the walls. There was even a potted plant in the corner, a spiral of orange and purple leaves tall enough to tickle the ceiling. The floor to ceiling windows that overlooked the arena at the other end made Zeus feel exposed, but he assumed that everyone he could see couldn't see him because either they were focused on the fights or the windows were one way.

The cabinet drawers were mostly empty. Zeus thumbed through whatever folders were available. A slight chuckle passed over his lips when he deduced that the files were employment records, finding a folder that contained papers and images of one the guards that he had encountered. He had to admit that he was more than a little impressed with the organization and level of detail Myzzer exhibited.

In between looking for Tammeryn's name or image in the files, he glanced up at Valla, sitting at Myzzer's desk. Deftly, she accessed his computer. Part of the desktop broke free, sliding up and tilting to give the user better access to the touch screen it had become. Her lithe fingers danced across the screen, opening and exploring various files. She mumbled to herself, "There is quite a bit to go through."

Finding nothing of interest in the file cabinets, Zeus shut the drawers and joined Valla at the desk. Giving his hand-held computer to her, he said, "Here. Download what he has onto here. We can have Billix scan through it when we get back to the ship."

Without saying a word, Valla retrieved her own handheld from her cloak and interfaced it with Myzzer's computer.

Zeus frowned. Frustrated, and with nothing else to do, he decided to open the drawers of Myzzer's desk. He stopped after the first one. "What. Is. This?"

As the data flowed from Myzzer's computer to Valla's, she looked over as Zeus pulled a badge out of the drawer.

An I. D. badge.

For Sivka Corp.

"Is that what I think it is?" Valla asked.

Zeus tilted his hand to view the three-dimensional image of Myzzer's face. "It certainly seems that one of the most feared and dangerous criminal overlords is an employee of Sivka Corp. named Rigel Ryktir."

"Fascinating."

Zeus slipped the badge into a cloak pocket and looked at the computer, anything to avoid looking at Valla. Being this close to her and uncertain how he felt about her, he didn't want to look into her endlessly blue starburst eyes and accidently tap into any more feelings that might be lurking inside of him. "Anything interesting?"

"I don't know. I wasn't looking for anything interesting. You told me to copy the files and we'll have Billix look for anything interesting. Remember saying that?"

Zeus sighed. This was why he preferred to work alone. Sure, Fiore talked too much once in a while, but he certainly wasn't antagonistic like this. He debated if he should try to give a rejoinder, or if he should change the topic, or if he should even talk at all. However, the three guards bursting into the office made the decision for him.

"How about you both step away from the desk before I turn you to ash," one guard said. His thick-skinned face was covered with dozens of small horns, extending over his hairless head.

Confusion etched across her face, Valla stepped forward and asked, "Before you fail at doing what you think you're about to do, might I ask what exactly alerted you to our presence? Was it an alarm? Did we miss a camera or two?"

Zeus's eyes almost popped from his head, astounded that Valla didn't seem to understand the gravity of the situation.

So taken aback by the question, the guards couldn't even react. The one simply said, "The guards you took out were supposed to check in with us every ten minutes. They didn't, so we came lookin' for them."

"Ugh!" Valla said, tossing her head back and throwing her hands to the sky. With a disappointed look on her face, she walked back to where she had been standing and said to Zeus, "Well, there you go. We'll just have to remember that for next time."

As if completely oblivious to the large men with guns at the other end of the room, Valla grabbed her computer and tucked it in her cloak. She then fished around and removed two gloves, wires of every color snaking in and out of the material, all connecting to a round node embedded in each palm. Casually tossing one to Zeus, she said, "Here, put this on. When I tell you to, press the button and face your palm to the floor."

Zeus felt just as dumb as Fiore usually acted as he slipped the glove onto his hand. Obviously Valla had a plan, but he couldn't begin to fathom what it could possibly be. The guards didn't appreciate her attitude, all three tensing up and tightening their grips on their guns. The horned one barked, "Hey! We told you to stop."

Still ignoring the large men with guns, Valla turned to Zeus, "Ready?"

"For what?" Zeus yelled, his voice squeaking more than he had hoped.

"Duck!" she yelled, grabbing the gun she had taken from the guard Zeus had rendered unconscious, and shooting blindly at the trio of thugs. Zeus ducked as the guards returned fire.

The energy bolts missed Valla and Zeus, but shattered the windows behind them. Taking advantage of the commotion, Valla grabbed Zeus' ungloved hand with hers, and jumped out the window.

Chapter 23

Fiore knew he was not a smart human being. He also knew that was an area of his life he needed to improve—as well as his tactical thinking and hand-to-hand combat. Any of those qualities he'd love to have right now.

The crowd had cheered for him mere seconds ago. This he knew and felt in his bones. Then his opponents entered the arena, and the crowd's exuberance increased tenfold.

The Beast Brothers.

And they looked it.

Each of the three brothers was a full foot taller than Fiore and easily outweighed him by a hundred pounds. Their muscles were so striated that their veins rippled under their smooth yellow skin. All three wore leather straps crisscrossing over their chests, allowing Fiore to see every rippling muscle at their disposal to rend him limb from limb. Thick, ugly faces rested atop squat necks, nappy hair sprouting from their heads and chins. Except the one brother, though—the bottom half of his face had been removed at some point in his life and replaced with dull metal jaws, jagged teeth barely fitting together when he closed his mouth.

The other brothers had distinguishing features as well. The left hand of one had been lost, presumably in a past fight, and replaced by a solid metal mace, many of the spiked points dulled or bent. The third of the trio was accessorized by a six-inch rusted spike protruding from the top of his skull, to the right of center. Fiore assumed that the spike was the reason why this brother's right eye crossed inward. However, their deformities certainly didn't detract from their menace. In fact, the additions only added to their ferocity… and to the crowd's zeal.

Still pre-fight time, the brothers circled Fiore—now in the center of the arena—either shouting threats at him or absorbing the crowd's adulation. As he removed cartridges from his bandoleer and inserted them into his forearm mechanism, he thought, *what would Zeus do?*

Fiore knew that Zeus would use his mind to calculate the weak points of his opponents, then use his skills to render them immobile. Well, Fiore didn't have that kind of skill, and he knew it, thus his need to add ingredients to his infusion device, ones to bulk him up, give him strength, dull the impending pain, and aid in healing. He needed more than that, though. He needed to think, to come up with a plan. He didn't have brains like Zeus, but he *did* have brains and he could think his way out of this. He *knew* he could!

Heavy with bloodlust, the voices of the crowd merged into one malicious drone. Trying not to panic, Fiore looked around, praying for options. His prayers answered, he found potential in the form of a drunkard, half passed out and drooling, his arms dangling over the arena wall. Fiore smiled.

The intoxicated attendee was a Yebleveen. A greasy sheen of fresh sweat coated the thick wrinkles around the pug snout, watery mucus dripping from his cavernous nostrils. Two pockmarked tusks curled upward from thick lips too numbed to close, ropes of drool hung like glistening webs. Four thick sausage fingers on each hand, all just as wet as his face, barely held onto empty mugs, drained of whatever alcohol had been used to assist this man into his current condition. Fiore didn't know anything about the planet Yeblevee or its culture, like Zeus probably did, but he saw that this guy was the only Yebleveen in the audience.

"Wait!" Fiore shouted so loud that the effort burned the inside his chest. "I want to enact the Yebleveen Rule of Odds!"

As if his words gave an individual slap to their faces, every attendee stopped cheering and silently turned to their host. Frowning, Myzzer leaned forward in his throne. "You wish to enact... what?"

"The Yebleveen Rule of Odds," Fiore repeated. *Talk like Zeus, talk like Zeus, talk like Zeus,* he chanted to himself as he continued, "It states that in a sanctioned interspecies fight in which one team of species is outnumbered by another team of differing species, the outnumbered team is allowed to increase their ranks by using differing species of their choice to equal the other team of differing species."

Murmurs rippled through the crowd, excited by the new twist. Even though Fiore didn't know what the word "palpable" meant, he certainly felt it in the air.

Myzzer glanced around, aware of what the crowd wanted. Like a demanding king, he pointed to the lone Yebleveen in the crowd and bellowed, "You! From the planet Yeblevee!"

The drunkard perked up and jerked around, wondering who was talking to him. Resting his hip against the arena wall to steady his swaying, he followed the gestures from the crowd to the host of the event. After a belch, he garbled, "Yeah?"

"Is it true? Is what our fighter in the arena is proclaiming true?"

Through crossed-eyes, the Yebleveen looked around at all the faces staring at him. He hiccupped and said, "Yeah?"

The crowd erupted. Caught up with the excitement, the Yebleveen raised both arms and whooped along. Until he wobbled, stumbled, and went toppling over the edge of the barrier, landing with a thud on the arena floor.

Snickers and giggles lowered the volume of the crowd, just long enough for Myzzer to say to Fiore, "Well, there's your first 'teammate.' Who are you going to name as your second?"

Without hesitation or words, Fiore pointed to Huva.

Huva screamed.

The crowd cheered.

Despite her resistance, a mix of Myzzer's guards and crowd members close enough escorted her to the arena entrance. With one collective shove, she stumbled down the ramp and stopped next to Fiore.

The cheers died down enough for Myzzer to be heard. "So, are there any other requests or suspect rules that I should know about? Or may I begin my fight?"

"Nope. We're good," Fiore replied. He turned to Huva and gave her a wink.

So angry that she couldn't change her facial expression to anything other than a snarl, she punched him in the shoulder. "Idiot! Weapons! Ask for weapons!"

"Oh, yeah! Good idea." By the time he turned to address Myzzer, the pseudo-king had lounged back in his throne, partially pinned down by beautiful women, and the crowd noise exceeded that of a starship's engines. He shouted back at Huva, "I think it's too late!"

She punched his shoulder again. "Idiot!"

"Ow! Stop hitting me. Hit them!" Fiore rubbed his shoulder and nodded to the brothers. Ignoring the drunkard, the brothers started to circle Huva and Fiore.

Watching all three, Fiore grabbed a nutrient bar from his pouch and chomped away as he finished adding cartridges to his infuser. Once he swallowed, he started the process, his body vibrating for a few seconds.

Glancing at his machine, then back at the brothers, Huva asked, "So, what'd you do?"

"I infused myself with a chemical mixture to dull pain and increase healing."

Huva snorted derisively. "You have any ingredients to make you huge and strong?"

"Yes, but I don't think that would do any good in this situation," Fiore said, hoping he didn't need to give voice to the notion that he didn't have the skills necessary to harness the burst of size and strength effectively. However, the look of utter disgust and confusion Huva gave him made him realize that he did. He tried, "What I mean is—"

Fiore was cut off as the brother with the unnatural hand charged. Right before contact, Huva shoved Fiore, simultaneously pushing him out of the way and creating enough backward momentum for herself to avoid the rampaging Beast Brother. Stumbling, Fiore slammed into the brother with the spike in his head, inadvertently knocking him backward. The brother windmilled his arms, trying to find his footing, but instead he tripped over the drunken Yebleveen crawling around on the arena floor.

The crowd cheered.

Fiore smiled and waved to the crowd.

The brother with the metal jaws punched Fiore hard enough to send him tumbling and rolling along the arena floor.

The crowd cheered louder.

Keeping his head down, the Yebleveen crawled along the perimeter of the arena, aiming for the ramp. With short, jerky movements, he tried to scurry around the skirmish between Huva and the brother with the spiked mace for a hand.

The Beast Brother smiled, saliva flowing over thick lips and matting his beard. "I'm gonna have fun with you, girl. I can't wait to get between your legs."

"Between my legs, huh?" Huva mumbled to herself. She smirked and sprinted toward her opponent.

Feet shoulder width apart, the brother's smile grew as he braced for impact. There was none. At the last second, Huva dropped and slid on her hip, feet first between his legs. Once behind him, she popped up to her feet and kicked him in the back of the head. He stumbled forward, but didn't fall. Pivoting around, he raised his weapon. Looking down, she saw the Yebleveen crawling along the dirt floor. Using the back of his shirt, she picked up the drunkard and tossed him at her opponent. The collision was enough to knock the mace-wielding Beast Brother to the ground.

Even though Fiore lay on the dirt floor, he saw what Huva had done and smiled. Unfortunately, so did the brother with the metal jaws.

The tossed Yebleveen landed by the metal-mouthed brother. Despite the bottom half of his face being angled chunks of metal, the brother smiled; Fiore could see it in his eyes. With one arm, the brother snatched the Yebleveen off the ground and threw him at Fiore. Feeling a bit proud of himself for using tactical logic to guess what his enemy was going to do, Fiore jumped to his feet and caught the living projectile. Holding him with one hand, he then shook him as if he were Billix.

"What are you doing?" the Yebleveen yelled, voice warbling. "I'm gonna puke!"

Fiore stopped. "Sorry. I'm used to holding someone else."

Before Fiore could return the Yebleveen to the ground, he saw the metal-jawed brother charge. More so out of reflex, Fiore threw what he was holding. As soon as the Yebleveen left his hands, Fiore hollered, "Sorry!"

Fiore cringed as he watched the collision. He had little time to do much more than that; the brother with the spike through his head tackled Fiore. Luckily, his most recent chemical infusion deadened the pain. Being smaller, Fiore knew he should be quicker, should be able to squirm out of his opponent's grip. But he couldn't. He writhed and wriggled, hoping that his battle partner would soon have an opportunity to help. While getting his face ground into the dirt, he tried to call for her help, but was rewarded with awful tastes instead.

Displaying fantastic skill in hand-to-hand combat, Huva engaged the brother with the mace hand. He landed one punch to her waist, but the rest of the fight consisted of her punching or kicking his face. Unfortunately, he shifted his tactics, using his size advantage to push forward and grab her by her throat. Raising his built-in weapon over his head, he readied it for a crushing blow, but paused when he saw his metal-jawed brother get to his feet. Laughing, he bellowed to his teammate, "Look, brother, I have a snack for you!"

The crowd laughed and cheered as metal jaws opened to expose the dripping shaft of an eager gullet. Cheers filled the air as he lunged for Huva. Digging her heels into the dirt, she used every muscle to pull. She yanked the arm holding her just enough as the jagged teeth clamped shut. The brother no longer held her; his severed hand fell to the arena floor. He flopped to the ground as well, cradling the stump of his wrist under his other armpit, howling in pain.

Whoops of shock and surprise rippled through the crowd as Huva escaped certain death. Backing away, she made her way to her struggling partner. Even though Fiore was thankful for that, he couldn't articulate his gratitude with a hand grinding his face against the arena floor and a knee on his back pinning him down.

The metal-jawed brother wasted no time for sympathy on his newly handless sibling. He turned to Huva, roared, and charged. In one fluid motion, Huva ripped the spike from the head of the opponent pinning Fiore and jammed it into the right eye of his stampeding brother.

Fiore fell in love.

An arena-shaking roar of pain erupted from the metal-jawed brother as he grabbed at his face and stumbled backward. He tripped over the crawling Yebleveen and landed next to his wounded brother. As they writhed in tandem, Huva turned to the last brother, crowd cheers echoing through the room.

Jumping off Fiore, the last brother, eye no longer crossed, held his hands in front of him to halt Huva's advance. "Whoa, whoa, whoa! I'm done!"

Fists clenched, Huva waited for Fiore to get to his feet before she growled to her opponent, "What do you mean?"

With a broad smile, he said, "I mean for the first time in a decade, I feel great! I can't thank you enough for removing that damn spike. I'm done fighting. I'm retiring."

"What about your brothers?"

"Are you kidding me? They're the ones who put the spike in my head!"

"How do we know that this isn't some kind of trick?"

"Easy. I'll show you. Bye!" He left the arena, all but skipping the whole way.

Silence. Stunned silence enveloped the whole room. Even the newly maimed fighters stopped their bellowing to watch their brother leave.

The Yebleveen stood up and started to dust himself off. He stopped when he noticed that the attendees in the stands watched him in silence. With still blurred gaze, he looked at his fight partners and asked, "Did we win?"

The crowd answered with an eruption of exuberance so loud that Fiore thought he might go deaf. Smiling, he waved to the attendees, then flexed his arms, then struck a different pose, then wondered why Huva glared at him.

The celebration was short-lived, though. Energy beams blasted through the glass windows from the office above, followed by Valla and Zeus jumping through....

Chapter 24

Time froze for Zeus. Everything just stopped.

In the past few days, he had found the adventure that he'd sought in his life. Not quite in the ways he had imagined, but adventure hardly ever came as one might expect. But he never expected to be jumping out of a window, willingly inviting a two-story plummet, hand-in-hand with a rival bounty hunter. This moment was one he would never forget, assuming he survived any longer than the few seconds of descent.

He didn't breathe; couldn't. His heart didn't offer a single beat. Neither sweat nor chill could be measured. He heard nothing. Just one frozen image of being almost thirty feet over the packed stands of a small arena.

Within a fraction of a second, the catharsis of the moment shattered; the sensation of falling punching him in the chest. The shrill screaming of Valla next to him pulled him back into the moment. "Push the button! Palm down! Push the button!"

Instinctively he already had his hand out in front of him, as if it would cushion his imminent impact. Having already pushed the button on her glove, Valla needed Zeus to push his to active them in tandem. He finally did as they threatened to crumple the tops of attendees' heads. He almost wished he hadn't pushed the button.

With an audible whoosh, his momentum reversed, as if bouncing off an invisible air bag. Even though he doubted he could have survived a collision with the ground, he wondered if it would have felt better than having every bone in his body smash against his insides from the sudden stop in descent, and being flung back upward.

The push up into the air was nowhere near as grand as the shattering pain led him to believe. Out of reflex, he released Valla's hand and waved his arms for balance. He was indeed going to hit the floor.

Regaining enough of his wits, he twisted his body and bent his knees. As soon as his feet made contact with the ground, he moved with the backward momentum, taking the brunt of the fall with his posterior.

Sliding to a halt, he felt a bit of pride for surviving such an ordeal. Of course, just like every other good feeling on this mission, it was short-lived when he noticed that Valla had landed on her feet with the grace and poise of a gymnast dismounting a simple apparatus.

They were in the center of a cleared-out section in the stands, the strewn bodies of the attendees who had been there now forming the perimeter of the circle. Zeus jumped to his feet and ran to Valla. Ripping the glove from his hand, he shoved it at her. "What in the name of all the gods on all the planets are these?"

"Gravity manipulation gloves," Valla said, her tone implying that she was surprised by his lack of knowledge.

Zeus regarded the frightened attendees, wriggling and shoving each other to get to their feet after being knocked away by the shockwave of the gloves. "So, when we pushed the buttons, it was like detonating an anti-gravity bomb?"

"The gloves are more like sophisticated magnets that interact with the planet's electromagnetic field. When I realized that we had to jump from a two-story window, I calibrated them to deliver a pulse that would create a sort of magnetic cushion for us. But if you need to think of that as an 'anti-gravity bomb,' then you go ahead. Look! There are Fiore and my sister."

As Valla bounded through the agitated crowd, Zeus could only seethe, the tone she took with him becoming irksome. He was just as smart as she! He had invented interesting and complex gadgets, to, and he could think through different scenarios if he had the time. However, he said nothing and simply followed her.

Climbing out of the arena, Huva asked her sister, "Did you get what we came for?"

"We think so. We'll have to sort through a lot of data, but we definitely found something of interest. Why were you in the arena?"

Huva nodded toward Fiore as he made his way out as well and said, "Because of this genius."

"Hey!" Fiore snapped back. "What are you upset about? We won!"

"Woo!" came from the Yebleveen stumbling around the arena. Every time he raised his arms to celebrate, he started to wobble, causing him to drop his hands to regain his balance. Once steadied, he'd raise his arms in victory again, starting the cycle of fighting gravity over again.

"See?" Zeus said to Valla. "I told you he'd be fine."

Valla ignored his comment and scanned the room as it was quickly deteriorating into pandemonium. Not wanting to be outdone yet again, Zeus tried to find the exit before she did amidst the madness, and opted to swallow the follow-up snarky comments brewing in the back of his mouth.

Most of the attendees were affluent, leading lives of spoiled excess where servants tended to their every need. A trip to an underground gladiatorial arena gave them the sense of being dangerous without actually experiencing real danger—until now.

Once Zeus and Valla burst from the office windows above their heads and came crashing down right into their laps, the attendees wanted to leave—now! The fastest way possible. Even if that meant clambering over each other. Friends stepped on friends; lovers left one another behind. Clothing and jewelry that had been the objects of bragging mere minutes ago were now torn and discarded, their usefulness crushed in the avalanche of panic. Zeus felt a blend of mirth and disgust.

Zeus shoved aside his desire to be introspective and analyze what this scene said about society in general; four of Myzzer's guards shouldered their way through the screaming crowd. They approached with guns raised, intent on taking no prisoners.

Without hesitation, Valla threw her gloves at two of the guards. Out of reflex, they each caught one. Then shot straight into the air. Again out of reflex, they released the gloves before they realized how high in the air they were. Flailing, they kicked and screamed on the way back down, each landing on one of the other guards. As if planned, Huva used the confusion to render the guards unconscious.

Zeus sneered at Valla. "Nice going. However, your gloves are now stuck on the ceiling."

Valla extended her left hand, palm up and used her right to pull her computer from her cloak. With one push of a button, both gloves fell directly into her outstretched hand.

Zeus wanted to tell her that he hated her, if only he didn't like her so damn much.

"Can we finally go now?" Valla asked.

Grunting his affirmation, Zeus resigned himself to following her out, but his ego made it a priority to regain control of the situation once aboard

Weelah's ship. Fiore followed along behind him, mumbling, "We won. I can't believe we won. That was amazing. Huva and I won."

Before Zeus could get too far, the blurred movement of a massive hand flashed through his peripheral vision an instant before connecting with him. Sprawling, he toppled into the first row of seats in the stands. Dazed, he looked up to see a monstrous being standing before him: taller than Fiore, the yellow-skinned creature had brutal metal jaws and a freshly gaping wound where his right eye should be. Outstretched fingers maliciously curled, the metal-jawed creature advanced. Unable to even comprehend what was happening, let alone react to it, Zeus tried to scrabble away, but failed to get to his feet. With one last effort, he raised his hands to shield his face, but with the sloshing crunch of metal being driven through a skull, the threat was no longer imminent.

Moving his hands aside, Zeus watched his attacker's left eye cross and tongue flop from his mouth over his jagged bottom jaw. With a spike in his head, he dropped to his knees, then ultimately to the floor. Standing behind him was another yellow-skinned mammoth of a creature of similar build. Looking down at Zeus, he winked and said, "He deserved it."

Fiore ran to Zeus as the yellow creature turned to leave. Looking up at his partner, Zeus barked, "What was that all about?"

Pointing to the lump of yellow on the floor, Fiore said, "He was one of the opponents we beat." His gaze was lost in the distance as he muttered, "And we just beat him again. Yes!" He punctuated his conclusion with a fist pump.

"For such a simple creature, you are ridiculously complex," Zeus mumbled as he got to his feet. "Now, let's go."

Following the last members of the fleeing mob, the four bounty hunters made their way to the exit. Peeking over his shoulder, Zeus looked at Myzzer, still sitting in his throne. The crime lord simply sat there, immobile like the bone his face resembled. Expressionless, with his two female companions long gone, Myzzer didn't move, didn't flinch, only watched as those who had invaded his secret office and ruined his illegal fights escaped.

Zeus ran from the arena, but he couldn't run from Myzzer's haunting glare....

Chapter 25

Zeus stewed. He did that when things didn't go his way, and he found himself doing that a lot lately. Temples actually hurting from frowning, his soured face constricted tightly, brows crushing together over the bridge of his nose. The plan had worked, and this should make him happy. They'd gathered information, potentially about their bounty. He was also right about Fiore surviving the death match. So why did Zeus feel such anger?

Heaving a deep sigh, he leaned back in his chair and forced his brows to unfurrow, using his thumb to aid the effort. A pang of jealousy skittered through him as he watched Fiore retell the tale. Zeus so wished that he could feel and express such exuberance.

Weelah's cargo ship was considered small when compared to most other cargo ships. It had certain amenities like sleeping quarters and hygienic showers. But it didn't have meeting rooms, so the small bridge had to be used as such when circumstances dictated a necessity for one. It had a table and two workstations to fit Weelah's five passengers. Luckily, it had just enough room for Fiore to jump around as he reenacted the victory in the underground fighting arena.

"And then she delivered a devastating uppercut!" Fiore boasted as he delivered an uppercut through the air. "And then she threw him into a headlock!" He mimicked putting an invisible person in a headlock, twisting his torso about.

Swiveled around in the pilot's chair, Weelah laughed as she watched Fiore reenact the fight. Sitting at a workstation, Billix watched with open-mouthed awe. Standing with her arms crossed, Huva hardly seemed amused as Fiore continued to expound about her exploits, "And then she picked him up, slammed him down, and jumped on him! Boom!" To add flair to his story, Fiore jumped and pounded his feet on the metal floor, sending a thudding echo through the entire bridge. Zeus swore he felt the ship lurch out of orbit.

With an expression of confusion, Huva said, "Even though your story is rather flattering, it happened nothing like that."

"Well, that's how I saw it," Fiore replied.

"That's because you were on the ground with one of our opponents standing on your head."

Billix coughed. "Wait. You had someone standing on your head? His foot was stepping on your face? You let him do that to you?"

"I didn't really mean to let him do that to me. In heat of the battle, things happen. But my teammate helped me out."

Shaking her head and frowning, Huva moaned, "Again, I need to remind you that I was only your teammate because you dragged me into that mess."

Holding his arms out, Fiore flexed, the veins in his biceps wriggling like snakes. Despite his facial hair being a bit thicker than usual, it didn't stop his beaming smile. "Right! I did! It was my great decision that helped us win."

Huva turned and threw her arms into the air. Weelah laughed again. Even Billix chuckled.

Glaring at the green-haired, purple-skinned companion, Huva growled, "What are you laughing at? Don't you have a database to hack into?"

Visibly quaking in fear, Billix spun in his chair and went back to tapping away on the computer in front of him. "Nothing. Laughing at nothing. In fact, not laughing at all. No laughing here."

"Now, sister," Valla said, voice smooth and even-tempered. "Don't get mad at him for not being able to do something that I'm having difficulty with."

That notion flicked a spark of happiness deep inside Zeus. It shouldn't have, since if she and Billix failed, that meant a new plan. But just this once, he was glad to see that Valla didn't have the upper hand.

Zeus sat at the same table as Valla. Trying not to appear too smug, he peeked over at her as she pecked away at her computer screen. "Can't get in?"

A worried frown slowly formed on her young face. "No. It's very disconcerting."

"Really?" Zeus asked, savoring her defeat.

"Yes. I've been able to sneak into government databases all over the galaxy. Yet, I can't get anywhere with this."

"Well, don't forget, Sivka is a corporation, concerned about money and profit, which is far more important than citizens to any government."

Valla stopped and looked up at Zeus. Expression softening, she smiled. "Thank you. I appreciate your kind words." Retaining her smile, she returned her focus to the computer screen.

Kind words? Zeus replayed his statement in his mind. The sarcasm was there, he knew it was. How did she misinterpret that? He recalled his words, his tone, his sentiment. His words were softer than he'd intended. Clearly, that made it seem like he was commiserating with her about a shared problem. Mind swirling, upset that he was no longer enjoying her failure, he only muttered, "Well, you know."

She glanced back up at Zeus and said, "See? I knew you could be a good friend."

Flustered from having no idea how to interpret this exchange with Valla, Zeus straightened himself in his chair and looked away from her. To distract himself, he pulled out his handheld computer and synced up with Valla's handheld, tapping into the data they had downloaded from Myzzer's computer. Instead of sitting around moping, he decided to help. The faster they found the information, the faster they could collect the bounty, and it didn't really matter who found the information first. Zeus glanced up to look at Valla. She noticed, and looked up as well. Offering a big, bright smile, Valla almost giggled, then went back to data mining. Zeus smiled as well. And then realized he was smiling.

What the hell is wrong with me? he wondered. *I'm a bounty hunter! I'm sitting here with my competition, acting like a smitten school child! I'm acting like Fiore!* With that thought, Zeus looked at his partner, just in time to see him attempt a round-house kick. He failed miserably, and shook the hull as he fell to the metal floor. Everyone winced, except Billix.

Zeus noticed that Billix didn't notice, and decided to go see what he was working on.

Crossing her arms over her chest, Huva looked down at Fiore, still on the floor. Nodding toward Billix, she said, "Idiot. You're so stupid that you've made the kid who can't shut up flabbergasted."

"Zeus?" Billix asked, jerking his head as if Huva mentioning his name snapped him out of a trance.

Looking over Billix's shoulder, Zeus replied, "Yes?"

"Do you remember in the library, when we copied the data from the computer Myzzer used, to find out that he was the one who posted the bounty?"

Not sure about the seriousness of the question, Zeus offered a guarded, "Yes."

"Remember how I said I was also able to hack into their security system, and I downloaded the video footage of that day, and I'd look at it later?"

"Yes."

"Well, I looked at it just now. And I'm still looking at it."

Perplexed. Zeus felt his patience waning. "So? We know it was Myzzer who listed the bounty."

"Well, it's not Myzzer sitting at the computer typing in the bounty specifics."

"What? It has to be."

"It's not. I think it's Dryn Tammeryn."

Complete silence fell over the deck; even Fiore stopped flailing about, re-enacting his battle. Zeus almost knocked Billix out of his chair to get a close look at the monitor. Sure enough, Zeus watched an unassuming humanoid with green skin devoid of any hair sitting at the very computer where the bounty was placed. "It can't be."

"Maybe that's the real Myzzer, and the Myzzer we saw was a fake?" Fiore asked, as he slowly made his way closer, peeking over shoulders to look at the monitor as well.

"It's not," Weelah said with certainty. "I've met Myzzer face to face more times than I care to remember, and he's a Tarzian, just like you described."

"Maybe it's a coincidence, that Tammeryn and Myzzer were at the same library on the same day?" Fiore asked.

"No," Billix answered. "The time stamp on the video is the exact time that the bounty was placed. The time stamp is right there. It's time stamped."

Zeus stepped away from the monitor and walked back to the table where Valla still sat. Flopping down in the chair, he tried to think of logical reasons for what he saw, but he was used to achieving deep contemplation only in solitude. Even if Fiore was around, Zeus could distract him with something shiny, or send him on a menial task. There was too much noise, too many distractions, too many people in too cramped a space. He couldn't think. "There has to be a logical explanation."

"I think it's fairly obvious that Tammeryn is trying to set up Myzzer," Valla said.

"But why use himself as bait?" Weelah asked.

"Especially for ten billion creds?" Billix added. "Ten billion's a lot! There's not a soul in the galaxy who wouldn't hunt someone for ten billion creds. He would have known everyone under the thousands of suns would be after him. I should know. I'm worth ten billion. My own family tried to collect."

"The purple kid's right," Huva said. "It makes no sense that he'd put ten billion creds on his own head. Even to frame Myzzer."

It didn't make sense to Zeus. None of it did. Klaxons and swirling red lights should have gone off the very second Zeus found out about this bounty. Ten billion creds. No one puts a bounty on anyone for ten billion creds. That didn't make sense; now nothing made sense. Every answer only yielded more questions; every path he followed led him farther from his goal. And he still couldn't think.

Frowning, Valla turned to the group. "Another part that makes no sense is that he listed it anonymously. It took Billix's genius to ferret out Myzzer's name."

"Genius?" Billix said, grinning wide. He turned to Fiore and whispered, "You hear that? Genius. She called me a genius. Well, not me, specifically, I guess. More like my data mining skills. But she used my name and genius in the same sentence."

Fiore huffed, and turned back to the conversation. "Wait. Myzzer has a Sivka employee badge. Sivka's special secret ninja army patrol is after Zeus and me. Could there be a connection there?"

"There could be, but nothing obvious right now," Huva replied. "Myzzer had no idea who Zeus was when they met, or who you were at the fights, or else he would have done more to detain you. Or kill you."

Fiore smoothed the bristles of his beard, contemplating. "How about Dryn Tammeryn? Do we know where he works yet?"

"No," Huva said. "We looked, but couldn't find anything."

"This is true," Valla confirmed.

"We looked, too," Billix said. "Remember? Right about the time you hijacked me into this plan, I had asked you where he worked, and you said you didn't know, and I said I could look it up for you, and you said okay, and I did, but I couldn't find anything."

Weelah looked confused. "So, there's a ten billion cred bounty on a ghost?"

Every time Zeus threaded together a logical series of ideas, it quickly unraveled when someone talked. Strands of thoughts swirled in his mind like a million ribbons in a tornado. Every time he tried to follow an idea, it was gone by the time he reached for it. His brain was churning, yet he felt mired. He was trapped in a small ship surrounded by constant stimuli and an impossible puzzle to solve. Just as he was about to give up, simply give into the lunacy around him, Hydrynx leapt onto his lap.

The feline genes within Hydrynx came to the forefront as it showed blatant disregard for what was happening around it. It took a few seconds to knead Zeus' pants and then curl up on his lap. A small cloud of smoke puffed from its mouth as it looked up at Zeus and meowed, demanding that its master scratch that special spot behind its ears. Something clicked within Zeus.

Not entirely sure how his demanding pet had triggered some kind of unknown mnemonic device, Zeus just went with it. It certainly wasn't a direct solution to the problem at hand, but it couldn't lead the group any further away from it. It had been brought up early on, before a lot of this chaos ensued, but it had been rejected. Well, it certainly seemed like a good idea now. A smile slid across his face as he swiveled his chair to face the group. While he scratched that special spot behind Hyrdynx's ears, Zeus said, "We're going to Dryn Tammeryn's apartment."

Chapter 26

The sun shone brightly on the city of Fulson, planet Tarsim. The buildings of the immaculately clean city had such an aesthetic flow that Fiore thought it might have been designed by an artist as opposed to stodgy old city-planners. The last time he was here, Zeus had been rambling on about it, the history, or beauty, or both. Fiore made a mental note to ask him about this city when they had some down time. Maybe he could use it as a bonding moment? Fiore wanted to learn more about his partner, but had a hard time breaking through Zeus' standoffish exterior. Maybe taking an interest in Zeus' love of learning about the cities and planets they visited on missions would help? But now was not the time for sightseeing; it was time for work.

Fiore adjusted the light-dampening settings of his goggles to compensate for the sun's glare off the various buildings in the city of Fulson. He then adjusted the magnification, trying to peek into the windows of Dryn Tammeryn's apartment to no avail. The darkness settings of the windows were set on high, and Fiore couldn't see through them. Just as he was about to change the spectrum of his vision, the skiff he was on floated around the corner of the building.

Weelah's skiff held the four passengers comfortably; it had no roof and was designed to seat two and hold an ample amount of cargo. Since she was current on all her galactic cargo and shipping permits, she had permission to hover the skiff above the three-story mark that other non-commercial craft had to stay below. Languidly circling the building around the twenty-story mark, Fiore and the three women watched Tammeryn's apartment. They watched for rival bounty hunters while trying to catch a glimpse of Zeus and Billix on the inside. They remained vigilant for anything that looked out of the ordinary. Fiore hadn't seen anything amiss, and now could no longer see Tammeryn's apartment window. What he did see, though, were the three prostitutes loitering along the sidewalk outside of a bar on a neighboring block.

Adjusting the magnification of his goggles, Fiore continually compensated for the skiff's movement through the air. One green, one blue, and one yellow with non-uniform red spots across her body, all three prostitutes had long hair that shimmered in the sunshine, wisps flirting with the soft breeze. As did their short skirts, doing a tiny dance every time a gust whooshed by. Their legs were smooth and glistened as well, although the blue one had three legs, causing Fiore to wonder about the rest of her anatomy. He followed the flowing curves of their bodies up to their chests, so much cleavage he didn't know where to look first. Wait! Did the green one have six breasts?

"Fiore!" Huva yelled, causing him to jolt and rock the skiff. Weelah stabilized the vehicle as Huva continued her tirade. "Seriously? You're in a vehicle with *three* women and you're blatantly looking at street trash."

"I was looking at the apartment," he blurted as he turned his attention to the three sets of hateful eyes.

Her normally pink skin shifting to vermilion in anger, Huva pointed to the left, at the building, and said, "*That* is where his apartment is. This," she then pointed to the right, down to the street, right at the trio of prostitutes and continued, "is where you were looking."

Blushing, Fiore shrugged. "Well, the skiff moved. I couldn't see the apartment anymore."

So incensed that even her Mohawk bristled back at an angry angle, Huva scowled. "The skiff moved? Because of that you decide to be a Felluvian dung pig and gawk at prostitutes? I guess you finally got bored at gawking at us."

"First of all, you and Weelah usually hit me when I gawk… stare at… *admire*… you. And I don't gawk at Valla."

Now it was Valla's turn to allow her emotions to darken her skin as she crossed her arms and furrowed her brows. "You don't gawk at me? Why not? Don't you think I'm worthy of your lechery?"

"No! I mean yes! I mean, of course you deserve my lechery!"

"Eeeew!" Valla sneered as she turned in her seat, away from Fiore.

"Wow. What a way with women you have," Weelah said. Fiore felt parched from the dryness of her words. "Do these antics of yours actually work on women?"

"Uhhhh…" was the only response he could muster.

"Again, eloquent as always. How long have you been doing this for? Your lechery? How long have you been using lechery to impress women?"

"Ummm…" he had hoped for a different vowel and more consonants.

"You're human, right? With your mess of hair and unkempt beard, you look like you're thirty? Forty?"

Genuinely offended, Fiore found his voice, "Hey! I've been on the run for three days! No good chance to groom, you know. Forty. I'm not that old!"

"But you're certainly old enough to know that women are more than just cleavage and legs."

Fiore looked over the edge of the skiff and contemplated jumping to escape this verbal bludgeoning. Again, he wished he had Zeus' gift of words to get him out of this no-win situation. As he tried to calculate the ingredients he'd need to infuse into his body to survive a five-story fall from the skiff to the roof of a neighboring building, something caught his eye. Something not good! Pointing, he yelled, "Zaurn! Zaurn!"

Weelah winced and looked at Huva. "Is he having a seizure?"

"I'm afraid not," Huva answered, and she and her sister both looked to where Fiore pointed. Weelah leaned over as well.

A few stories below, floating on an open-topped vehicle much like Weelah's skiff, Zyf and Bahb aimed for the window of Tammeryn's apartment. Hovering next to them was Zossa on his cycle.

"Okay, who are they?" Weelah asked.

"Rival bounty hunters," the other three said in unison.

Fiore tapped the computer screen of his forearm mechanism and spoke into it, "Zeus, hurry. The Zaurns just showed up."

Within a second, Zeus replied with an agitated whisper, "We need more time."

"Why are they here?" Huva mumbled.

"Obviously, the same reason we are," Valla replied. "Maybe Zeus and Billix tripped a warning device?"

"Well, whatever the reason, we have to get rid of them," Huva said as she retrieved her gun, as long as an arm and designed for long-distance targeting.

Uncomfortable with the idea of cold-blooded murder, even if those in question had shot at him before, and unwilling to try his debating skills any further, Fiore acted upon his first instinct. He grabbed the skiff controls, causing it to lurch just as Huva squeezed the trigger. The thin red energy beam discharged and missed its target; the usual buzz of the weapon was lost among the shouting.

"What are you doing?" Weelah yelled, fighting to regain the controls from Fiore.

The skiff dove forward, then straight up, followed by a lurch to the right and left. The sudden bustle slammed Huva into the side, driving her ribs into the top of the door. She dropped her gun over the side. Bracing herself with one hand against the vehicle, she grabbed a fistful of Fiore's hair. "Stop it!"

"No!"

As the aircraft wobbled and pitched, Valla used her arms and legs to brace herself from the commotion. "What are you doing?"

"I can't let you kill them in cold blood! We're bounty hunters, not assassins!"

"I know!" Huva screamed, still holding onto Fiore's hair. "I was aiming at their vehicle! I just wanted to incapacitate them!"

Immediately relinquishing the skiff's controls, Fiore sat back. "Oh. Why didn't you say so?"

Veins of crimson webbed across her skin as she seethed through gritted teeth, "Why? Didn't? I? Say? So?"

"Huva!" Valla yelled, pointing over the side as she situated herself in her seat.

Everyone looked. The Zaurn Brothers noticed that they had been shot at. And they didn't appear too happy about it. Both of the saurian vehicles angled toward Weelah's skiff.

"Okay. *Now* you can shoot them," Fiore said to Huva.

"Thanks to you, I *dropped* my gun. Idiot."

"I have a small one in there," Weelah said, pointing to a compartment close to Huva.

Scowling, Huva fetched the gun and glanced at her sister. "Did you bring one?"

"Two," Valla said, producing them from her cloak as if by magic.

Glaring at Fiore, Huva growled, "You?"

"Umm, no. These are the only guns I need." Fiore flexed both of his biceps.

"Stop talking."

"Them and my brain." Fiore pointed to his own head to clarify his statement. "It's very useful."

"No! Do not use that. Do *not* use that."

Blue and green beams of crackling energy flashed by the skiff. The three Zaurn brothers did indeed take exception to being shot at, and replied it in kind. Weelah angled her skiff away and retreated. "Hold on. Even though it might be a good idea to get above them and push Fiore out and onto them, I'm gonna try to get us out of here."

"Be careful," Fiore said as he braced himself.

"Well, you should have thought of that before you put us in this situation."

"No. I meant be careful of the other brother. There are four of them."

Looking over her shoulder to gauge the actions of her pursuers, Weelah took a moment to address the sisters. "Is he right? Is there another one?"

Reacting to the new realization, the sisters looked above and over the sides of the skiff. Huva replied, "He is. And the missing brother is the craziest of the four."

As if on cue, Zarn appeared. Directly in front of the skiff. On a heavily fortified hovercycle, he aimed a gun as big as his arm.

Jerking back on the controls, Weelah avoided colliding with the newest obstacle, her skiff scraping the left side of the hovercycle. She over-compensated as the glob of crackling orange energy from Zarn's gun narrowly missed her and the other passengers. The bottom of the skiff scraped the top edge of the nearest building as she brought it over. While the vehicle skidded across the rooftop, Fiore lost his balance and toppled over the side.

Rolling and bouncing along the roof, Fiore thought of the ingredients necessary to mend each scrape and bruise. The skiff finally skidded to a stop, as did Fiore. From hitting his head so many times along the way, his vision had blurred, but quickly came into focus when he saw Zarn approach the roof from above. Coming in fast, Zarn leapt from his hovercycle before it came to a complete stop. Fiore tried to get to his feet, but Zarn slammed into him just as his sliding hovercycle slammed into a row of containers.

Rolling along the roof again, Fiore struggled with Zarn. The berserk saurian scratched and bit Fiore, piercing his skin on occasion. Managing to wrangle it free, Fiore shoved his forearm against Zarn's neck, holding back a snout full of snapping teeth. Insanity raged behind bulbous eyes, blood-shot with rage. Saliva sprayed from his forked tongue as it wriggled about, slapping Fiore's face.

Fiore struggled with the saurian's squirming body, failing at every attempt to gain leverage. Wincing with every claw swipe, Fiore growled, "What is *wrong* with you?"

"Kill! Chomp! Yum!" Zarn replied.

"This is why none of the other bounty hunters like you!"

A yellow beam flashed behind Zarn, a fraction of a second before he relinquished his grip and leapt away. Skittering across the rooftop back to his hovercycle, smoke swirled from his right hindquarter. Valla smiled and holstered her discharged gun.

Before Fiore could express any kind of gratitude, though, Zarn's brothers arrived on the rooftop to shoot back.

The roof served as a loading area for a warehouse. This much Fiore surmised from the number of containers and crates stacked high and neatly, making great cover for the women and him to hide behind. Since there didn't seem to be any bystanders, Fiore also assumed that the area was seldom used, and they didn't have to worry about interference from the authorities—at least for a while. A glimmer of pride tickled inside his chest, proud of himself for using deductive reasoning. He couldn't wait to tell Zeus. If he survived.

Hiding behind a wall of rectangular crates and cylindrical containers, Fiore jerked every time an energy blast struck and created a new scorch mark. He attempted to calculate how long they could remain behind the wall before it lost structural integrity. He stopped trying as his head hurt; some forms of thinking and logic were better suited for Zeus.

"So, Fiore," Zossa called out in between shots. "I see you decided to team up with Huva and Valla after you turned down our help. I can't tell you how much that hurts our feelings."

To punctuate his statement, he fired twice at the wall.

"It's because of Zarn! He's psycho!" Fiore yelled back. All three women now looked at him with incredulous expressions. Confused as to why they were looking at him like that, he mouthed the word, "What?"

The women shook their heads in unison.

"That's not a very nice thing to say. He's still my brother, after all," Zossa laughed.

Fiore peeked through a gap in the containers. Zossa stood by his hovercycle while Zarn paced in circles around him, bubbling froth dripping from his mouth, tongue draping to the side. Zyf and Bahb stood by their vehicle as well, both using their guns to take random shots at Fiore and the women. Fiore mumbled, "I *really* don't like these guys."

"Why are you here, Zossa?" Valla called out.

"I should be asking you the same thing," Zossa replied. "No one's been to Tammeryn's place since The Legend took him."

Ambling closer to his brother, Zyf said, "One can only assume that there must be something of perceived value for Zeus and Fiore to team up with Huva and Valla."

Zossa shot three times, hitting a spot near Fiore, sending burnt splinters flying through the air. "Is that true, Fiore? Do the four of you think there's something of value in there?"

Zyf shot as well, but stopped and looked contemplative. He craned his neck to the left, then right, as if that helped peer around the blockades. Looking over at Weelah's skiff, he said, "Zossa, I feel the need to point out that Zeus does not appear to be with them. Nor do I see the purple fellow who is, to the best of my knowledge, still worth ten billion creds."

Zossa paused in his shooting and growled. "You're right. They must be in the apartment. Zyf. Bahb. Cover us. Zarn, let's go."

Zossa holstered his weapon and jumped on his vehicle. Zarn—laughing like a lunatic—retrieved his hovercycle from the pile of containers where it had crashed. Fiore and the women looked at each other, expressions of worry and anger passed among them. Knowing that they needed to stop the Zaurn brothers, all four rushed from their hiding spots. Huva shot at Zyf and Bahb. Weelah threw small machine parts that had been spilled from the broken crates at Zarn. As Zossa's hovercycle started to float from the rooftop, Valla retrieved a small cylinder from her cloak and aimed. Direct hit, the grappling device embedded itself into the back end of the hovercycle. As the cord's slack between the hovercycle and the handle diminished, Valla tossed it to Fiore. Out of reflex, Fiore caught it and gripped it with both hands. Zossa accelerated before Fiore could brace himself, but he didn't let go.

With a bone-jarring yank, Fiore left his feet. However, his weight was enough to stop Zossa from zooming away. Falling face first, Fiore slammed against the rooftop. Hands cramping, shoulders numb from pain, Fiore refused to let go, even though he was being dragged. His chest and thighs burned as he scraped along the rough surface, finally coming to a devastating halt against the raised edge. Despite his head getting crushed and ground into the cold stone, he held tight. The cord went slack again, allowing him to peel his face from the barrier. Rubbing his jaw, he sat up and watched Zossa swing his hovercycle around, landing once again on the rooftop. A tiny sense of satisfaction skittered through him. However, the two massive hands crashing down on his shoulders crushed it.

Bahb tossed Fiore across the rooftop, which lead to more toppling and tumbling and rolling and skidding. More bruises and cuts and scrapes. Fiore added another bang to his head as he slammed to a halt against the roof's access door.

Propping himself up with one hand, Fiore attempted to get his bearings. Fists clenched, Bahb lumbered toward him and growled, "This is gonna hurt."

This, Fiore had no doubt, was going to be a true and accurate statement.

Chapter 27

Billix wrinkled the parts of his face not covered by cybernetics. It was an expression that Zeus assumed to be frustration. Billix sighed: a long, defeated, and exasperated huff. "What are we looking for again?"

"Anything that will tie Dryn Tammeryn to Myzzer or Sivka, or both," Zeus replied.

"Well good luck with that. There's no way we're going to find anything in this place. It's a mess!"

Zeus feared that Billix wasn't wrong. Tammeryn's apartment was a disaster area.

The main living area was a spacious room that had an offshoot kitchen and a hall that led to three other rooms. A bomb detonation would have been less destructive. Barely any patches of the floor were visible. Chairs and tables and shelving units had been overturned and broken into chunky pieces. Decorations smashed. Wall hangings strewn about. Broken personal affects filled in the gaps.

As they moved further into the residence, Zeus winced at the smells emanating from the kitchen. Doors had been ripped off the empty and broken cabinets, everything they once contained speckled the disaster area like a garnish. Plates pulverized to pebble-sized bits. Utensils bent into unnatural shapes. Even the food refrigeration unit had been pulled from the wall and smashed open, its contents now smeared about the floor and walls and counters: the cause of the offensive smells. Zeus doubted that Tammeryn would have kept anything of value in the kitchen, so he opted not to waste time sifting through the odoriferous trash.

Billix chuckled at Zeus' disgust and said, "Not going to check in there? Could be hiding something. Perfect hiding place. No one would look there."

Zeus offered a quick scowl and tried not to step on any detritus as he made his way toward the hall. "Do *you* have anything of great value hidden in your kitchen?"

"No. Of course not. But, then again, I'm not a target of dubious nature."

"Dubious or not, you're still a target. Ten billion creds on your head, remember?"

Billix sighed again. "I'm not. I'm not going to get into *this* argument again. I'm just not."

Zeus smirked as Billix followed him into Tammeryn's bedroom.

Just like the rest of the apartment, the bedroom was trashed. Strips of foam hanging from large gashes, the gutted bed would have looked more in place at an abattoir. Empty closets appeared to have vomited clothing. Furniture was flattened.

Billix made a noise of sympathetic pity. "Shame. Looks like he lived alone."

Crouching in front of a pile of wood and metal that used to be a desk, Zeus poked through the wreckage. "Why do you say that?"

Shuffling around the perimeter of the room, Billix replied, "Well, even though everything is everywhere, I haven't seen any pictures or images or holograms. No family. No kids. No spouse or significant other."

Zeus grunted. "For the better."

"Really? Is that what you really think?"

Snorting derisively, Zeus replied, "Yes. Yes, I do."

"So... there's nothing between you and Valla?"

Zeus froze; the mere mention of her name made his insides both hot and cold, impossibly at the same time. He went back to sifting through debris, and hoped that his reaction went unnoticed. "No."

"Nothing? Really? Nothing at all?"

"Nothing."

"Seriously? You two have a lot in common. A lot."

"Nothing. Is. Going. On. Between. Us."

"Okay, okay. I believe you."

Now seething, Zeus tried to put Valla out of his mind by grabbing a handful of electronics and hoping they were salvageable parts of a computer. They weren't. Billix continued, "After all of this is over, I'm going to ask her out. Assuming I survive. Or any of us survives. But I'm going to ask her out."

Zeus contorted his face to form a mix of disgust and confusion so powerful that pain ripped across his forehead and through his cheeks. "What?"

"A date. I'm going to ask her on a date. Surely she dates. Maybe something traditional, like doing dinner."

Zeus stood, if for no other reason than to stretch out his clenched muscles. "She's a bounty hunter, like me. We're feared. Respected. Sometimes reviled. We don't do dinner!"

"What do you mean you don't do dinner? You don't eat? I've seen you eat. I've seen *her* eat!"

"That's for sustenance, not socialization."

"She and I've socialized while we've eaten already! Ooh, maybe we've already been on a date. I wonder if she'd see it that way?"

Zeus' head hurt. He thought it simply couldn't get any worse. Until his earpiece crackled to life and Fiore yelled directly into his brain, "Zeus, hurry! The Zaurns just showed up."

Agitated, Zeus hissed back, "We need more time."

Turning to Billix, he said, "The others have company. Put away your silly fantasies and focus. We need to hurry."

Throwing his hands in the air, Billix yelled, "Focus? Hurry? Focus on what? Hurry to find what?"

Zeus kicked a pile of debris. "I don't know! You're the one with a cybernetic eye that can see all kinds of spectrums. How about you start using that?"

"Huh," Billix said. "I didn't think of that. That's a good idea."

Knowing that any words he could utter would only lead to arguments and worsen the situation, Zeus simply crossed his arms over his chest and watched Billix slowly turn in circles. On the fourth rotation, he stopped. Pointing to the floor by the far wall, he said with surprise in his voice, "I think there's... something... under the floor?"

Zeus made his way through the debris to the spot where Billix pointed. He bent down and cleared away the wreckage to find nothing but the floor. "There's nothing here."

"Under the floor. Under it. There's something there. A small piece of electronics."

Standing straight, Zeus looked at Billix and said, "I think you're either reading something wrong, or you're looking at building infrastructure. It's the floor."

"Look again. Obviously, it's a hidden compartment. Look for an access panel."

"There's nothing here!" Zeus shouted. To emphasize his point, he stomped a few times on the spot Billix insisted something existed. Zeus triggered a mechanism that commanded the access panel to slide away and reveal a hidden compartment. Even though Billix had few facial features, and half of them had been replaced by cybernetics, Zeus easily read his expression to mean contempt. Choosing not to acknowledge it, Zeus crouched down and looked into the newly opened compartment.

His emotions bifurcated when he retrieved the contents—he was certainly satisfied that they had found something, but frustrated that it caused more questions than answers. He showed the item to Billix.

Mouth going slack, Billix said, "Is that a Sivka Corp. I.D. badge? Dryn Tammeryn is an employee of Sivka Corp.?"

"It certainly looks that way," Zeus replied, turning the badge in his hand, looking at the three-dimensional holographic image of his bounty. He noticed something wrong. "This isn't his name."

"What do you mean?"

"I mean, look. The name on the badge is Torrell Loren. But the image on it is clearly Dryn Tammeryn."

"And why would he keep his employee badge hidden in a floor safe?"

"That is a very good question."

"What is going on, Zeus?"

Zeus sighed and placed the badge in his pocket. "I don't know. But we should really get out of here."

"Yeah," Billix whispered, obviously still trying to process the implications of finding the badge.

Shuffling through the ankle-deep mess on the floor, Zeus stepped into the hallway. As soon as he did so, Billix grabbed his cloak and yanked him back into the room. For a fraction of a second, Zeus thought Billix had gone completely insane from being exposed to Fiore too long, until he saw and heard projectiles whistle past his face. Darts. The same tranq darts that the Sivka Corp. secret police used.

Unable to regain his balance, Zeus fell backward into the room, landing hard on his posterior. Panicked, Billix slammed the door and braced himself against it. "That was Sivka Corp., wasn't it? Was it Sivka Corp.? As I was switching my vision back, I saw figures in the main room, and assumed they weren't friendly, and I was right. They're Sivka Corp.!"

Zeus leapt to his feet and looked around the room for options. He had a small gun, but he doubted it would be enough to shoot their way out. He certainly didn't trust the energy blasts from Billix's finger, unless Fiore was shaking him. "How many are there?"

Still flattened against the door, Billix said, "Five. There are five of them. Two still in the main room, three moving down the hallway. This way. Coming toward us."

Looking along the perimeter of the ceiling, Zeus asked, "Can you access a schematic of the building's infrastructure? A vent system of any kind up there?"

"How about the window?" Billix asked, pointing. He quickly slapped his arm against the door, as if the extra reinforcement would be enough to stop the approaching menace.

Zeus ran to the window and drew back the light-dampening covers. Profanity spewed from his mouth. Quickly releasing them, he ran away from the window, toward Billix. "Not a good idea!"

As soon as Zeus crossed the room, the window and parts of the surrounding wall exploded inward. Zarn and his large hovercycle burst through, skidding along the floor, creating a wave of trash. Before the hovercycle smacked into the far wall, Zarn leapt from it, landing in the center of the room.

Zarn's forked tongue, as long as an arm, whipped about the air as if it were no longer content living inside of a mouth. Bubbling saliva flowed over broken and jagged teeth as he smiled a lunatic's grin. Ribbons of blood trickled from various cuts and scrapes, a few pieces of glass and wood and plastic jutted from his skin. Poised to strike, he swayed back and forth, hissing, "Kill. Flesh. Yum."

Quivering behind Zeus, Billix whispered, "That guy is psycho."

"He is," Zeus replied. That gave him an idea. Louder, he continued, "You're right, Billix, he is a psycho."

Frowning, Billix whispered angrily, "You know there's a reason why I'm whispering. So the psycho doesn't hear me. Sometimes you're as dense as Fiore."

Zeus pondered the validity of Billix's statement, realizing that this plan would be one Fiore would have come up with. That was an introspection that would have to wait until later; he needed to focus. "What? You don't want him to know you think he's psycho? Trust me. He *knows* that he's psycho. *He has to be.*"

Zarn stopped swaying and straightened his posture. Even though his blood-shot eyes remained feral, they now held small amounts of confusion. Zeus had gotten his attention.

"What. Are. You. Doing?" Billix whispered a panicked huff for each word.

"Yes," Zeus said, steeling his gaze, looking right at Zarn. "You have to be the crazy one, right? Comparatively, Zyf is smarter."

Zarn reeled back, Zeus' words more harmful than a blast from his gun.

"Bahb is stronger."

Zarn snarled and curled his clawed fingers.

"And Zossa is…" Zeus paused, savoring Zarn's reaction. The saurian tensed his legs and tightened his arms, tongue twitching spastically. Right when he thought Zarn's anger was ready to burst through his skin, Zeus finished his thought, "…prettier."

Anger radiating from him, Zarn howled and charged Zeus. In one fluid motion, Zeus pushed Billix out of the way and opened the door. For a brief flash before he closed it again, Zeus saw a flurry of scales crash into two of the black uniformed Sivka Corp. guards. Pausing for a moment against the closed door, Zeus heard the familiar sounds of the guns rapidly discharging darts, as well as screams and swearing.

Satisfied that his plan had worked, Zeus rushed to Zarn's hovercycle. Hopping on, he yelled at Billix, now picking himself off the floor, "Come on!"

Running as best he could through the debris, Billix yelled back, "Nice plan! I'm really happy it worked, but you could have told me about it."

Starting the hovercycle and angling toward the newly formed hole in the wall where a window used to be, Zeus said, "I couldn't tell you the plan. Zarn was standing right there."

As Billix got on the hovercycle behind Zeus, he snapped back, "You could have warned me! Told me to brace myself. Or go limp. You communicate your plans as well as Fiore does."

Again, Zeus noted that Billix's statement was not inaccurate. Again, something to ponder at a later time. Lacking any form of intelligible retort, Zeus simply yelled back, "Shut up, and hold on!"

Zeus and Billix zoomed away from Dryn Tammeryn's trashed apartment….

Chapter 28

Fiore bounced, then rolled along the rooftop, eventually coming to a complete stop on his back. A nice breeze kicked up and cooled his sweat-filmed arms and face. It felt nice. It also felt nice not to think about his current situation. He just wanted to lie there, let his mind go, let his body enjoy the nice day. However, Bahb had other plans.

With ease, Bahb grabbed two fistfuls of Fiore's vest and hoisted him to his feet. Within half a second, Fiore found himself bouncing and rolling across the rooftop again. This time when he stopped, it was due to slamming against the stone ledge of the rooftop, smacking the back of his head. Hard. After the starbursts dissipated, the blurred vision remained.

Bahb sauntered to Fiore, taking time with every step. As Fiore's vision cleared, he sat up, muscles arguing against his decision to move. How could he be having such a difficult time with Bahb? Bahb was fat! Just earlier today Fiore stood victorious in a small arena of a death match against three adversaries—three monstrous adversaries. Now he was getting tossed about like a toy by a lone humanoid lizard. A fat one, too! But, in the arena, he had had a partner.

Bursts of pain exploded in every joint as he stood and looked over at his arena partner. She was assisting her sister and Weelah in a shootout against Zossa and Zyf. The saurians had his companions pinned down. Or did they? Upon further investigation, Fiore saw an easy escape route for any one of them to take to come help him. On the verge of realization that he could take the same winding path among the crates and containers to go to them, Bahb interrupted Fiore. Again.

Standing eye-to-eye with him, Bahb grabbed Fiore's vest. Arms too sore and numb to move, Fiore acted boneless as Bahb held him. With his right eye swelling shut, Fiore said clumsily over a swollen lip, "Why are you so mad at me?"

Bahb growled. "That's a stupid question. We're rivals!"

"No, not like this."

"What?"

"I mean, when Zeus and I cross paths with you and your brothers, we fight, we insult each other. One team wins, one team loses, then we go our separate ways. That's part of our profession. This... this seems way more... personal."

"You wanna know why I'm mad at you?" Covered in green scales, Bahb brought his wide, flat face closer to Fiore's. Nostril slits flaring, Bahb peeled his lips back to expose rows of tiny teeth, dripping with saliva. Rage twisted inside of him like a trapped animal. Then as if flipping a switch, Bahb's face went slack and he loosened his grip. His voice barely a whisper, he said, "It's because of Geholla."

Fiore winced with confusion, "Who?"

Bahb then winced with confusion. "What do you mean, 'who'?"

"I mean, I don't know who you're talking about."

Frowning, Bahb tightened his grip, "You don't even know her name?"

"Her? Her who?"

"Geholla! The beautiful orange goddess you were so disrespectfully ogling the last time we were in this city, when you took Dryn Tammeryn from us and let him slip from your grasp to The Legend."

Fiore had to think. He certainly remembered the moment of losing Tammeryn to The Legend, the lowest point of his life. But an orange goddess? His eyes shifted back and forth, as if his memories were laid out before him, scrutinizing every detail. Then he remembered the orange-skinned girl and her saurian friend. "Do you mean the prostitute with the tentacles?"

Growling, Bahb slammed Fiore against the nearest piece of loading equipment. "Yes, she is a Retukian, but how dare you insult her like that."

Fiore groaned and rubbed his head. "I didn't insult her. I mean, she's really a prostitute. Didn't you know that?"

"No!" Bahb barked, his eyes blood-shot.

"Seriously? Haven't you ever talked to her?"

Bahb's face went slack, defeated. Shoulders slumping, Bahb completely released Fiore. Turing away, Bahb offered a slight sniffle. "No. I've... I've just... admired her from afar."

Taking advantage of the pause in fighting, Fiore popped specific cartridges from his bandoleer and inserted them into his wrist device. He knew that if Zeus were in the same situation, he'd exploit Bahb's weakness. Fiore just couldn't do that. Bahb looked to be in real pain. "So... why not?"

Still with his back to Fiore, Bahb mumbled, "You've seen her. She's perfect. She's flawless. I'm just a big, fat lizard who still lives with his brothers."

Fiore jittered as his device infused the chemicals into his system. The cuts and bruises healed as the aches and pains dissipated. He could see out of both eyes now that the swelling went down. "Well, you could meet her, for the right price."

Fists clenched, Bahb snapped around, face tensing from anger. "What did you say?"

Putting his hands up in front of himself, Fiore backed away. "I meant to introduce yourself! Just to say hi. To finally talk to her. Use it as an opportunity to get to know her, to see why she's a prosti... to see why she does what she does. Who knows? Maybe she's looking for someone to rescue her."

Bahb's expression softened again. "Do you really think so?"

Fiore nodded. "Sure. Why not?"

Bahb smiled. But it quickly faded into a frown as a thought struck him. "Have you ever... 'talked'... to her?"

"What?" Fiore blushed, thankful that his beard hid most of it. "No! No, no, no, no."

Bahb's frown deepened, fists clenching again. "Why not? Isn't she pretty enough for you?"

Wondering how he found himself in trouble so quickly after getting out of it, Fiore stammered, "No... yes, I do... no... I mean, I've never... talked... to a prosti... a woman like her...."

Before Bahb could respond, Fiore saw something in his peripheral. He turned just in time to see Zeus driving a hovercycle with Billix sitting behind him and yelling. As they came in for a landing, they zoomed close to Zossa, forcing him to dive out of the way. But Zeus lost control as they touched down on the roof. Both he and Billix—still yelling—jumped and rolled as the hovercycle skidded into a stack of containers. The collision halted the hovercycle, but sent the containers tumbling toward Bahb. He tried to dive out of the way, but his considerable girth did not lend itself to maneuverability. One of the containers struck him in the back and knocked him to the ground, landing with an audible slap.

Getting to his feet, Billix yelled at Zeus, "What was that? That was a terrible landing! Terrible. When we first got on, you said you could operate one of those. Clearly you had a minimal knowledge of that machine. Minimal!"

Zeus got to his feet just in time for Fiore to run to him and yell, "Why'd you do that? Bahb and I were having a nice moment."

Running both hands through the mussed curls of his hair, Zeus yelled at Billix, "First of all, you ingrate, I rescued you from Sivka Corp *and* Zarn! Second of all, I do know how to operate a hovercycle, but usually not with someone *screaming* in my ear the whole time I'm doing it. And you—" Zeus turned to Fiore and continued, "you need to remember that we have a lot of competition, and Bahb is one of the worst. We aren't partners with the Zaurn brothers, we aren't friends with them, and there is no way in this reality that we have 'moments' with *any* of them."

Fiore stood devoid of any expression, merely blinking. Once Zeus finished his tirade, Fiore said, "Did you say Sivka Corp?"

Zeus squeezed his eyes shut and slapped his palm against his forehead.

Zyf and Zossa stopped shooting, as did Weelah and the sisters. Tentatively, they moved out from behind their ersatz palisades. All five furtively glanced at each other as they made their way toward Zeus and Billix. Still unable to talk from frustration, Zeus looked at Billix. The purple cyborg caught the hint and said, "Yes. Yes, he did say Sivka Corp. We were in Dryn's apartment, and Sivka Corp. came in. A lot of them."

"Sivka Corp?" Zyf asked.

"Yes. Yes, Sivka Corp," Billix replied. "They have a secret security force that's been hunting us. Constantly. Everywhere we go."

Zyf chuckled. "I have heard that they have such a security force. I also heard that they were tenacious and dangerous. If you three have been escaping them, then I have my doubts...."

His sentiment fell short as he fell forward, unconscious from the three tranq darts sticking out of his back. All eyes looked to the sky behind them to see two hovercycles carrying three humanoids clad in all black, each holding a gun. A third hovercycle came up behind the first two; this one carrying a Sivka Corp. security guard and Zarn. The crazed saurian used his claws to hold onto the hovercycle while using his teeth to gnaw on it. The Sivka Corp. guard swatted and kicked at the angry lizard.

"Move!" Zeus and Zossa yelled in unison.

Everyone on the roof scattered from everyone above the roof, returning to the security of crates and containers. Whoever had guns used them, forcing the Sivka Corp. guards to land their hovercycles on the rooftop.

The three operatives on the two hovercycle made controlled landings and set up defensive positions behind stacks of crates. The fourth operative tried to join them, but after contending with the snapping jaws of Zarn, he opted for leaping from the hovercycle before crashing it into a machine designed to move the various crates and containers. Nimble as well as insane, Zarn escaped harm from the collision, and furiously scrabbled to Zossa.

Tranq darts dinged off the metal containers protecting Fiore. Zeus crouched next to him, as did Billix, wincing after each ping. The three were unable to shift position, pinned down from the constant barrage of projectiles. Fiore hoped for help from the women, but saw that the Sivka Corp. guards had found a perfect spot to hide—untouchable by the energy blasts from the women's guns, but able to keep the women pinned down if they tried to seek a better vantage point.

Fiore looked at the Zaurn brothers, hoping to enact some form of unspoken code to come to the aid of a fellow bounty hunter in the face of a common threat. Apparently, no such code existed, or the Zaurn brothers didn't care about codes, spoken or otherwise. The Sivka guards completely ignored the saurians, allowing Zossa to try to reign in Zarn's insanity so he could help rouse the unconscious Zyf and Bahb. Fiore frowned and mumbled, "Pinned down with no guns."

Looking around to assess the situation as well, Zeus said, "Well, either you infuse yourself with the necessary ingredients to bulk up into your berserker mode and take about fifty darts to the face as you rush them, or you grab Billix and shake him."

"Come here, Billix," Fiore said without hesitation.

"No!" Billix shouted. In an attempt to prove that he didn't need to be shaken to be effective, he poked his finger through a gap in the containers and discharged three energy blasts. One beam charred the ground two feet in front of him, one beam blasted a bird from the sky, reducing it to a puff of feathers, and the final beam struck the hovercycle he and Zeus had ridden, causing it to burst into flames. "I'm shooting! I'm shooting! See? Look! I'm shooting! No need to shake me!"

"You can't aim!" Zeus shouted back. "Fiore! Shake him."

Careful to keep his body shielded by the makeshift barricade, Fiore started to crawl toward Billix. Some of the feathers from the unfortunate target floated down, a few tickled as they landed on Fiore's nose. He stopped crawling when he noticed something from above casting a circular shadow on part of the roof, not too far from him. The shadow grew. Rapidly.

Just as Fiore raised his head to see the source, a shockwave from an invisible blast slammed into him. He had hoped that after making peace with Bahb that he would be done tumbling around the rooftop, but the force threw him against a nearby piece of equipment. He saw stars again as he hit and bounced off, rolling to a painful stop. Through a film of tears, he was able to deduce by the pattern of debris that he had started near the center of the event that caused the mess.

Fighting through the burning pain of reluctant muscles, he rolled over and pushed himself to one knee. Wobbling, he paused to steady himself before he tried to stand any further, but halted his efforts as two large black boots slammed against the rooftop in front of him. Despite the pulled muscles in his neck, he lifted his head and followed the boots to long, sturdy legs in black pants. They kept going up to a thick torso, draped in a long black coat that flapped in the breeze. Fiore didn't need to look any further to know who it was, but he did anyway, stopping at a familiar face.

The Legend.

Chapter 29

Zeus rubbed his hands against his temples, but it did very little to stop the throbbing. He had been thrown. This much he knew. He opened his eyes and became disoriented, upside down on a disheveled pile of containers.

Before he tried to right himself, he wiggled his fingers and toes. Satisfied that nothing was broken or missing, he flipped his feet forward hard enough to pull himself out of the pile, landing right side up. He wobbled a bit, pain jabbing him from so many different places that he couldn't tell which parts of his body were the angriest.

Glancing around, he tried to assess what had happened and locate his companions. Billix sat up in the same pile of containers. Using his flesh hand to rub the non-mechanical parts of his head, Billix moaned, "What was that?"

"I don't know," Zeus replied. It felt like being hit by a shockwave, but there had been no explosion. It reminded him of the magnetic field manipulation device Valla had used in Myzzer's underground arena. Similarly, the debris was scattered evenly in a circle. Zeus looked to where he thought the women would be. All three were alive, and trying to free themselves from similar piles of crates and containers. Zeus found Fiore as well; his partner very near the center of the invisible, silent explosion. Then his heart almost seized.

The Legend.

In the middle of the debris-free zone stood The Legend.

And he was looking right at Billix.

As if by magic, The Legend raised his arm, pointing at Billix. A canister with a cord shot out from the sleeve of his jacket. As soon as the projectile struck Billix, a net burst forth and wrapped around him. The trailing cord tightened the net.

"Fiore!" Zeus shouted. He pointed at The Legend. "Detain him!"

Zeus knew very well he would have a better chance teaching physics to an ant than Fiore completing the requested task, but he hoped that he could serve as a distraction long enough to free Billix. Zeus ran to Billix, who squirmed like a worm while yelling, "Get me out! Get me out! Is that The Legend? He got me! The Legend has captured me! I'm so dead! I'm gonna die! Get me out!"

"Calm down!" Zeus yelled. "I can't get you out if you don't stop squirming."

Billix did as instructed. "Okay. Okay. I stopped. Can you get me out? How bad is it? Don't let The Legend get me!"

"I won't allow him to take you," Zeus said, his words lacking sentiment.

Grabbing different parts of the cord and netting, he looked for a starting point to unwind the tether. He yanked and pulled, but nothing gave way. Then from behind him, he heard, "Here, let me try."

Before Zeus could protest, Valla pulled a small tube from her cloak and crouched next to him. One end of the tube glowed blue, and when she touched it against the net, the strands severed. Without looking at him, she said to Zeus, "Why don't you just use your cutter?"

"I don't have one," Zeus growled through gritted teeth.

"Well, you really should think about carrying one from now on."

"I'll take that under advisement," Zeus mumbled, as he stood to check on Fiore. As he suspected, his partner was not faring well. Fiore clung to The Legend's right leg, but the more experienced bounty hunter simply dragged the extra baggage along as he advanced toward Billix.

Worried about the Sivka Corp. operatives, Zeus looked over to the last place he'd seen them. Gone. The only evidence of them ever having been there was the smoldering hovercycle that Billix had accidentally shot. At least he didn't have to worry about them—just one seemingly unstoppable adversary making his way closer. Curious about other problems, he looked at the Zaurn brothers. Zossa and Zarn had their unconscious brothers secured in the vehicles as they prepared to escape.

"Hey! Where are you going?" Zeus yelled.

"Away from this insanity!" Zossa yelled back.

"What about the shared moment between Bahb and Fiore?"

"We're your competition, remember? We don't share moments."

Desperate for them to stay and become a diversion, or at least fodder, Zeus remembered something Fiore had mentioned. "What about the unwritten bounty hunter code about helping each other out in the face of a common threat?"

Zossa contorted his reptilian face in confusion so emphatically that his scales seemed ready to pop off. "What? There's no unwritten rule like that. And the threat isn't a 'common' one. He's all yours."

"He has Dryn Tammeryn, remember?"

Zossa froze. Squinting, his expression grew grim, pernicious. He turned to his brothers. Zarn had roused Zyf and Bahb. Even though they were less than alert and oriented, they shared similar expressions of cold-hearted focus and determination. Zarn's face continued to twist further into monomaniacal seething, tongue dripping with saliva and insanity. In one fluid motion, all four brothers pointed their guns at the shared threat.

But The Legend was faster.

He pointed a handheld mechanism at the brothers and squeezed the trigger. A pulse rippled through the air. Everyone looked around at each other, confused and curious as to why The Legend's attack yielded no damage. Shrugging their shoulders, the Zaurn brothers fired their guns. Nothing happened.

Zossa frowned and continued to pull the trigger again and again with the same impotent results. Zyf holstered his gun while Bahb slapped his a few times and tried again. Nothing. Zarn put his gun in his mouth and chewed on it.

Zeus looked over at Weelah and Huva to see if their guns were just as useless. They were. Huva gestured to Weelah to get the skiff ready for impending use. Weelah protested at first, but quickly acquiesced and ran to the vehicle. Huva cracked her knuckles, joining the Zaurn brothers in readying herself to engage with The Legend.

Still wrapped around The Legend's leg, Fiore looked around and saw that his arena partner was ready to fight. He relinquished his grip and jumped to his feet, joining Huva.

"You need to hurry," Zeus said to Valla, but kept watching the situation with The Legend unfold.

Halfway finished, Valla hissed back, "I'm cutting as fast as I can."

"Cut faster."

"She's cutting as fast as she can!" Billix yelled. "I don't see *you* helping. You didn't even bring a cutter. For someone who claims to be so smart, you always seem to be woefully unprepared."

"I'm keeping an eye on the situation," Zeus mumbled.

The Legend slowly turned in a circle, watching the six figures surround him. With a minimal flick of the wrist, the mechanism in his hand transformed. Pieces shifted, parts moved and turned, and it reassembled itself into a gun with three barrels. He squeezed the trigger.

Three spheres of crackling yellow energy shot from his gun, striking the rooftop in front of the Zaurn brothers. Zossa and Zyf fell backward while Bahb wobbled, but didn't fall. Zarn charged The Legend like a rabid animal. With a simple swat, The Legend smacked the feral saurian away as easily as if he were a lame moth.

Huva charged from The Legend's right side when she saw that Bahb came in from the left. Fiore ran at him head on. The Legend used his massive hands to stop two-thirds of the attack; his right grabbing a fistful of Huva's shirt, his left blanketing Bahb's face, stopping the bulbous lizard in his tracks. Fiore drove his shoulder into The Legend's chest. Wrapping his arms around The Legend, Fiore continued to churn his legs, knocking his opponent off balance. Twisting, The Legend pushed down on Bahb, the lizard's head hitting the rooftop hard. Using the residual momentum, he released his grip on Huva, effectively tossing her through the air. She landed on the rooftop, not as hard as Bahb, but it left her just as dazed.

"Hurry!" Zeus yelled again at Valla.

"Stop yelling at her!" Billix yelled back. "She's moving as fast as she can. She's almost done. Every time you yell, you're distracting her. Stop it!"

Zeus whipped around to Billix, arms now free, and pointed to the skirmish only fifty feet away. "The Legend just disposed of the Zaurn brothers and Huva with ease, Weelah doesn't have the skiff operational yet, and Fiore is the only thing really standing between you and the greatest bounty hunter in the galaxy, who thinks you're worth ten billion creds."

Billix's non-cybernetic eye widened. In a panic, he began tugging at the cords and net wrapped around his legs. "Hurry, Valla! Hurry! The Legend is coming! We have to hurry!"

Zeus looked back at Fiore. He still had his arms wrapped around The Legend, still keeping him off balance. The Legend pounded his fists against Fiore's back, but to no avail. Fiore pushed and twisted, keeping his arms wrapped around his adversary. The Legend squeezed his right hand between his body and Fiore, and used it as a lever. With great effort, he began prying Fiore away from him. Left hand popping free, Fiore flailed, trying to grasp anything. With one quick grab, Fiore caught the open edge of The Legend's coat, and... stopped struggling. Holding it open, Fiore stared at the right side of The Legend's ribcage. That distraction was all The Legend needed to drive his fist into Fiore's gut. Air forcibly removed from his lungs, Fiore collapsed.

What was that about? Zeus asked himself. Fiore had been doing well—"fantastic" on a sliding scale of "one" to "Fiore"—and then he stopped. Did he see something? Trigger some form of paralyzing defense? Something that mildly hypnotized him? Zeus would have to push those questions aside. With no more obstacles, The Legend strode toward Billix.

Zeus turned to warn Billix and Valla, but they snapped away the last cord. Grabbing his hand, Valla helped Billix to his feet. Staying tightly bunched together, the trio ran away from The Legend, but tried to weave their way among the containers and machinery as they aimed for Weelah's skiff. The Legend cut them off, jumping out from behind a set of containers as his prey rounded the corner.

Valla pulled a canister from her cloak and sprayed The Legend's face. Zeus recognized the spray, the same one she had used in Myzzer's underground offices. However, it had zero effect, harmlessly wicked away by a ventilator in the cybernetics covering the lower half of his face. But her distraction was just enough to slip past his outreached hands.

The Legend continued his pursuit. Then Zeus saw something he never thought he'd see—Fiore jumped out from behind a piece of machinery with his fist cocked back. He swung and connected perfectly with The Legend's face. Fiore followed with a devastating uppercut, hitting so hard that it lifted The Legend off his feet, landing him in a pile of toppled containers.

Stunned silence consumed everyone. Zeus assumed that, like he, everyone needed a pause for their brains to register what they had just witnessed. Fiore broke the spell as he made his way to Weelah's skiff. "Let's go."

Having shaken off the effects of fighting The Legend, Huva joined her sister and allies as they piled into the vehicle. After a few curses under her breath about the vehicle's temperament, Weelah started the ignition. It started, albeit chugging louder than before. Zeus felt thankful as they hovered off the rooftop, especially once he saw that the local law enforcement had finally noticed their shenanigans, their representatives starting to close in.

The Zaurn brothers opted not to try for a second attempt at either The Legend or Billix. They simply got on their vehicles and sped away. Zeus took a moment to relax, his thoughts returning to what Billix and he had found in Dryn Tammeryn's apartment. Until he noticed the shadow creep across the skiff.

Before he could look up to see what had caused the shadow, a thick cable dropped from the sky, the end of it zooming past the ascending skiff. No sooner had it zipped by, then the cable drew taut and pulled the other way. In a blink, The Legend shot upward, passing by the skiff just long enough to snatch Billix.

Again displaying uncustomary skill, Fiore lunged and grabbed Billix's robotic leg. Having a hold of Billix's robotic arm, The Legend jolted to a stop.

Being in the middle of a tug-of-war, Billix screamed, begging for Fiore not to let go. The sisters yelled orders to Weelah on the best way to maneuver her skiff. Zeus wrapped his arms around Fiore's waist, hoping the added weight would tip the scales. The Legend's ship slowly flew away, making the cord that The Legend rode even tighter, the tension against Billix growing harder. Small parts snapped off or sprung from Billix's robotic limbs, until one finally gave way, breaking free in a burst of sparks.

The Legend rode the cable back into his ship and flew away, gone before the entrance hatch had even closed.

The sudden release caused Fiore to fall backward.

All he held was Billix's leg.

Chapter 30

Fiore sat on the grated floor; the cold from the metal wall seeped past his thick hair and chilled his head. He didn't care. Even though his goggles were over his eyes, shaded black, he saw the sideways glances, the looks of concern from the others. He didn't care. Knees bent enough to rest his forearms on, he held onto Billix's robotic leg, broken off at the knee. That, he cared about.

Twice. Twice he'd lost to The Legend. Twice he'd lost a bounty to The Legend. Twice he had had *physical possession* of a bounty, and The Legend had taken it from him.

Fiore shifted Billix's leg from one hand to the other and sighed. Huva walked by and gave a casual glance down at him, one filled with pity. She took a seat in the copilot chair, next to Weelah in the pilot's chair. Even though she whispered, Fiore could still hear Huva say, "I never thought I'd ever think this, let alone say it, but I feel a little sorry for him."

Weelah replied, "Yeah. I know what you mean. Despite the fact that he's an idiot, he does try."

Try. That was the key word. Try. Not succeed, but try. A softer way to say, "Failure." Try. A broken piece of robot leg was what trying was worth.

He sighed again.

At the small table, he heard Zeus and Valla sharing whispers. She said, "Aren't you going to talk to him?"

"Why?" Zeus asked.

"Because he lost Billix—to The Legend. He's lost to The Legend twice now. It's obvious that it's eating him up inside."

"Well, if you know so much about what his feelings need, then why don't you go talk to him?"

"Because he's your friend."

"First of all, we're partners. Second of all, this is Fiore we're talking about. Give him a gourmet milk and he'll be back to normal. And third of all, I'm busy working on getting us into Sivka Corp.'s main office." Zeus gestured to the two I.D. badges hooked up to his computer.

Valla frowned and spat out a snide, "Really?"

"What?"

"Look me in the eye and tell me that you don't regard Fiore as your friend."

Stone faced, Zeus paused from his work and looked at Valla. Fiore wasn't sure what Zeus had planned on saying, but his expression softened, and he whispered, "Fine. Yes. Yes, I do consider him my friend."

"Then talk to him."

"I... I don't know what to say."

Valla shook her head and stood. "Men," she huffed, as she walked over to her sister.

For the first time—as far as Fiore knew—Zeus had referred to him as a friend. He just wished it could have come a different time, a time when he could feel good about it, instead of now, when life sucked.

Hydrynx strolled over to Fiore and sat on its haunches, glaring. Fiore looked down at the cat-dragon creature and grunted. He went back to staring ahead, feeling sorry for himself. Hydrynx growled and mewed a small burst of fire. The flame rippled along Fiore's leg, but quickly dissipated. Fiore sighed and shifted two feet to his left, allowing Hydrynx to take his spot. Hydrynx curled up and closed its eyes, purring.

Physically overpowered by a cat-like creature. This was what his life had been reduced to. He so wanted adventure, wanted to see the galaxy, wanted to be *respected*. To escape the life he once had. When he first set out to be a bounty hunter, he had realized very quickly that he lacked a few skills—skills that Zeus possessed. That was why Fiore thought they would make such good partners, good friends. Clearly not good enough, though, if Zeus admitted to Valla that he didn't know how to talk to Fiore, and that all of his problems could be solved with milk. Although Fiore had to admit that he certainly had a craving for some Thetheurvian desert-goat milk right now.

Fiore sighed some more. Despite the fact that Zeus knew little about him, he, in turn, knew little about Zeus. He admitted that he only had himself to blame. Zeus had never been forthcoming with personal information. Fiore respected that, and had never pushed too hard for it. Did Zeus see it that way? Maybe Zeus viewed it as a lack of interest; that Fiore didn't care enough to ask? Not only that, but Fiore also withheld information from Zeus, such as who he really was and his other source of income. He wanted to wait to share that with a friend—a real friend—not just a partner. Would they ever reach that level of comfort? Would they have nothing more than an arms-length friendship?

Fiore wondered if Zeus thought that friends were as interchangeable as this robotic leg in his hands. But... it wasn't that easily interchangeable. "Zeus?" Fiore asked, voice raspy from disuse. "Could you put this leg on me?"

The already silent cockpit of Weelah's cargo ship became even more so as everyone looked at Fiore, all visibly confused. *Those* were the looks he was used to, not the ones of pity they had been giving him.

"Umm, you have two perfectly good legs," Zeus replied.

"If I didn't. If I were missing one, could you... or someone more qualified... attach this *specific* leg to me?"

Zeus turned to Fiore, giving him his full attention. "Not without quite a bit of work first."

"Why not?"

"Well, when cybernetics are implanted, especially complicated ones like Billix's leg, they're made specifically for that individual. Basically, that leg was built for Billix, and all the internal programming was created specifically for him. To attach it to you would take a considerable amount of time to reprogram...."

Fiore cut Zeus off by leaping to his feet, causing everyone else to flinch with surprise. Excitement in his voice growing, he walked over to Zeus, holding the leg with the reverence of making an offer to a deity. "So, you're saying all his robotic parts are... are... talking to or communicating with him?"

"That's a great oversimplification of the process, but... yes."

"So, this leg is still communicating—or trying to communicate with him—right now?"

Zeus' face went slack, but his eyes lit up, finally joining Fiore on this path of logic. "Yes!"

"So, we can use his leg to track him? To find him?"

"Yes! Fiore... that's a *really* good idea."

Fiore chose to ignore the utter surprise in Zeus' voice. Instead, he clapped his hands and then pumped his fists in the air.

"Valla?" Huva asked. "Can you go help Zeus figure out how to do whatever it is he needs to do? It disturbs me that at this moment, Fiore is the smartest one on the ship, and that has to stop."

"I couldn't agree more," Valla mumbled, as she walked back over to the table, making an effort to avoid Fiore's gyrations and flailing arms. Fiore continued to celebrate until he disturbed Hydrynx's nap; the cat-dragon belched a small fireball toward Fiore's feet. Fiore knew that was simply a warning, with more to come if he didn't settle down.

As Valla sat down next to Zeus, Fiore wandered over to Huva and Weelah. He smiled, and they both rolled their eyes. As Fiore opened his mouth, Weelah cut him short with a waggling finger usually reserved for scolding a child and said, "You have this moment. Don't ruin it by talking."

Fiore frowned as both women turned their backs on him.

Sulking, Fiore returned to where he had been sitting, careful not to disturb Hydrynx again. Content enough that he had come up with a good idea, he decided to celebrate by himself in his own mind, fantasizing about taking down The Legend and stealing both bounties from him. Fiore then imagined what he would do with twenty billion creds. Then remembered that ten billion of that didn't actually exist, and he'd have to split half of the other ten billion with Zeus. Then he remembered the deal with Weelah and Huva and Valla. And, of course, Billix. How much would he have left after taxes? Would he even have to pay taxes? He made a mental note to ask Zeus about bounty hunting tax laws. Once he took care of that, then he'd....

"Got it," Valla said. "I think I found Billix."

"*We*," Zeus emphasized. "We found Billix."

"Well then. Will one of you send the coordinates to my nav system?" Weelah asked.

Once she received them, a large overhead monitor lit up, displaying star maps. Zeus tapped away at his computer. Three areas slowly flashed red. Tiny specks of glowing blue near the red highlighted areas flashed as well.

Zeus stood and walked over to the map, pointing to one of the red areas as he spoke. "This is Kreeva, where the corporate headquarters of Sivka Corp. are located." He pointed to the second red area, significantly smaller than the other two. "This is where Billix is. Since it's close to a planet, but nowhere as big as a moon, I'm assuming it's The Legend's ship or satellite." Finally, he pointed to the third red area. "This is where Dryn Tammeryn is to be dropped off for bounty delivery and collection. The blue lights represent jump ports."

Everyone examined the map, accompanied by the occasional sigh or grunt. Huva finally said, "So, where should we start? Can we even do both?"

"We need to start with Sivka Corp., to find out why they've been after us," Fiore said.

"No," Zeus said. "We can deal with them later. We need to get Tammeryn and Billix from The Legend."

"If we go to Sivka Corp., we can access their mainframe and figure out why Myzzer and Tammeryn have employee badges," Valla countered.

"That would make sense, if we didn't know where the bounties are," Zeus replied.

Weelah cleared her throat to garner everyone's attention. Looking less than proud, she avoided eye contact and said, "We can go to both. This cargo ship has a few escape pods that have been modified for deep space travel."

Fiore at first felt bad for Weelah, being on the receiving end of confused stares; he knew how that felt. Running her hands through her thick hair, Weelah explained, "This was the ship Koorza and I used when we were... together. Obviously, most of our cargo wasn't legal. So, we always thought that we might need to abandon and blow the ship."

Worried, Fiore immediately started looking around, wondering where the explosives were. Noticing what he was doing, Weelah said, "I have long since removed all self-destruct mechanisms, Fiore. But I did keep the shuttles. They can easily make the trip to both Sivka Corp. and The Legend. In the meantime, I can take my ship to the drop site to recon it. The shuttles have jump-port clearances, so you can meet me at the drop site."

"Wonderful!" Valla said. "So, who should go where?"

Nodding toward Zeus and Fiore, Huva answered, "You and I should go pay a visit to The Legend, and allow these two to go find out why Sivka's after them."

"Oh, no!" Zeus shouted, jumping to his feet. "No. No. There is no way Fiore and I are going to let you two go face The Legend by yourselves."

Huva moaned, "How chivalrous."

"We'd be crazy to trust our competitors to get a bounty worth ten billion creds and then bring him back to us."

"Crazy to trust? Are you serious? We've been in firefights together. I saved Fiore's life."

"That's exactly the argument someone who's ready to betray their partners would use."

Huva threw her hands to the ceiling and turned her back on the argument. "You're as exasperating as Fiore. No wonder you two are friends."

"It's okay, Huva," Valla said. "Boys will be boys. So, I'll go with Fiore and you go with Zeus."

"Why can't you and I go together?" Zeus asked, frowning.

"Because Huva and Fiore are too big to fit in one shuttle together," Weelah answered. Zeus' cheeks turned pink from her heavy glare.

"So, it's Huva and Zeus, Fiore and me. Who wants to go where?"

"I want to find Billix," Fiore said.

"Are you sure you want to face The Legend again?" Zeus asked.

Just the mere mention of The Legend's name transported Fiore back to their scuffle on the rooftop. Fiore had surprised everyone, even himself, when he had kept The Legend from advancing on Billix. Fiore had lasted in the fight against The Legend longer than Huva or the Zaurn brothers, all who had more experience than him. He couldn't recall a specific strategy he had employed; he'd just wrapped his arms around The Legend and tried to keep him off balance. Of course, The Legend was able to break free, but Fiore had grabbed his jacket. He remembered trying to think of ways to use "grab his jacket" as a form of tactical advantage, but as he pulled the jacket away from The Legend's body, Fiore saw it: a chemical infusion unit.

Embedded along his ribcage, just below his chest, The Legend had a chemical infusion unit identical to the one Fiore had on his forearm. It had surprised Fiore, giving him pause long enough for The Legend to take advantage of the situation and punch him in the gut.

Since getting back to Weelah's ship, Fiore hadn't had time to reflect about what he had seen, too busy feeling sorry for himself and wanting Thetheurvian desert-goat milk. Had The Legend started the same way as Fiore? Did this mean that Fiore had the same potential as The Legend? Could Fiore become *the best*?

Fiore had thought about sharing the information with the group, but decided to wait. He was certain it was the exact same unit. It had to be—it had taken Fiore a long time and a substantial sum of money to get his. And that was after all his other surgeries. He didn't want to bring any more attention to himself or his past by letting the others know that the greatest bounty hunter in the galaxy had the exact same piece of equipment... tool... weapon... as he. Fiore was quite thankful that an alternate solution to finding The Legend yielded positive results. Then he felt bad for being mad at Zeus for withholding information, when he realized that he had just done the exact same thing again. "Yes. I want to face The Legend again."

Everyone seemed shocked by the seriousness of Fiore's tone, a few glances exchanged. Maybe that was what Fiore needed. Maybe he needed a role model. There was no better way to study his potential role model than by infiltrating his compound....

Chapter 31

"Stop fidgeting," Zeus hissed.

"I can't help it!" Huva snapped back. "This outfit is not comfortable."

Zeus couldn't blame her; their outfits were dreadfully uncomfortable. The one-piece repair-tech overalls were made from a gratingly thick material, made worse by the fact that neither set of overalls fit their current wearers. Zeus had programmed the Sivka Corp. I.D. badges to show that Huva and he were repair-techs. He knew that would be the best way to gain access to all parts of Sivka's corporate headquarters.

The headquarters were located in a complex consisting of five different buildings, including a manicured park with pond, as well as plenty of places for their employees to relax and socialize when necessary. Getting through the outer perimeter of the complex proved no challenge. So, all they had to do was wait for a couple of repair-techs to wander too close to their hiding spot. At first, Zeus thought it was fortunate that they were able to appropriate the uniforms from a male and a female, until he realized that Huva needed to wear the male's. Much to Zeus' dismay, the uniform Huva wore was way too tight, while his was a little too big. Huva had been complaining ever since.

Scratching at her collar, pulling it away from the back of her neck, Huva griped, "It itches."

Since she couldn't button the shirt all the way, it looked as if Huva's cleavage was fighting to escape, and her fussing with the collar caused her breasts to bounce and ripple. Feeling like Fiore, Zeus couldn't help but take the occasional peek. "If you keep acting like this, others will suspect that we aren't truly repair-techs."

Huffing, she wrapped both of her hands around the straps of the standard issue rucksack full of tools draped over her shoulder. "There are so many employees milling about so absorbed in themselves that we could stroll into the building naked and no one would notice."

"First of all, this centralized park is designed to encourage milling. When we get inside, there will be less meandering. Second of all, if you keep shifting your overalls, you'll be very close to being naked."

Huva's frown said more than words as she shifted her breasts to more modest levels of display while she and Zeus entered the office building.

As soon as they stepped foot inside, Huva's jaw dropped. Zeus barely glanced around the main foyer, aiming directly for the maintenance lifts. Huva struggled to keep up, slowing down to gawk at the surroundings, then hustling to catch Zeus when he got too far ahead of her.

The main lobby was four stories tall, transparent floors and walls staggered throughout. Spheres of all sizes floated about, displaying three-dimensional images of various Sivka Corp. products when not being used by visitors to access the company directory. Stairs and lifts transported species of all shapes and colors from the ground floor to the various waiting areas and foyers of any of the three floors above. For those visitors who liked a more personal touch, or needed specialized help, dozens of physically alluring specimens from a variety of planets offered their smiling-faced assistance.

Zeus didn't care. He had seen it all before.

Huva continued to look over her shoulder as they entered a hallway at the far end of the lobby. "This is amazing. It's almost as busy as a jump-port. Like a jump-port for bodies instead of vehicles."

Zeus grunted as they walked down the hallway, transparent tubes with subtle lights lining the edges of the floor. Flora of all hues grew on the outside for aesthetic purposes.

"Nothing?" Huva asked in disbelief. "This place is amazing… awe inspiring… for a soulless corporation, and your reaction is a grunt?"

"We're on a mission," Zeus mumbled. The hallway ended with a set of doors.

"Time to see if your alterations to the badges work," Huva said, producing the I.D. badge with her picture on it.

Zeus did the same, and said, "They'll work."

The badges worked, and the doors opened up to another spacious room, but nowhere near as large as the lobby, or as visually stunning. Various species dressed in the same types of overalls that Huva and Zeus wore milled about—checking equipment for their next assignments, discussing the workday, making plans for post-quitting time activities. In teams of two or three, the repair-techs would get on a lift and ascend through the skeletal structure of the building, areas unseen by any eyes other than their own.

Zeus and Huva walked over to a lift that was away from the concentration of the more social repair-techs. Other than the occasional leer at Huva's chest, she and Zeus moved unnoticed. As she made a feeble attempt to contain her cleavage, Huva asked, "How did you know the way to the maintenance lifts?"

"I studied the building schematics before we left Weelah's ship," Zeus lied.

"Good memory," she said, as they got on the lift.

Zeus typed in the destination on the touch screen, the one hundred seventieth floor. "I'm the smartest person I know."

"Must not know a lot of people."

As the lift started its ascent, Zeus looked up at Huva and scowled. Huva shrugged and said, "My sister is smart. I'd say even smarter than you."

Plenty of insults came to the forefront of Zeus' mind, but they would not help the mission, so instead of giving voice to any of them, he glowered in silence for the rest of the ride.

Once at the proper floor, they exited through the "repair techs only" door, and entered one of the building's many office areas. Zeus used the handheld workstation locator he'd procured from the repair-tech whose jumpsuit he now wore to guide him. Keeping their heads down, they walked through the expansive room full of workstations. Each cluster was framed out by five-foot tall walls to form six hexagonal workstations surrounding a common space reserved for meetings.

They found Dryn Tammeryn's cluster; the name "Torrell Loren" was displayed as a glowing yellow light on the wall of his workstation. As they approached, Zeus noticed a Genturian in the neighboring workstation. Three of his eyestalks focused on the work scattered about his desk, the fourth watched as Huva and Zeus approached. Remembering his last encounter with a Genturian, the bloodthirsty librarian, Zeus scowled directly at him. Showing as much fear as an eyestalk could display, it quickly minded its own business and joined the other three.

Huva and Zeus entered Dryn Tammeryn's workstation and crouched down. Removing her work satchel and poking around the tools on the inside, she whispered to Zeus, "What are we looking for?"

"Anything," Zeus said as he opened the nearest desk drawer and looked through it. "Anything that explains why there's a bounty of ten billion creds on him. Anything that connects him to Myzzer. Anything that explains why Sivka's mythical hit squad is after Fiore and me. Anything that connects *anything* to *anything*."

Huva grunted, and looked through the desk drawer closest to her. Finding nothing more than standard office supplies and loose papers with no relevant information, Huva crawled under the desk while Zeus powered on Dryn Tammeryn's workstation computer. While waiting, he noticed an eyestalk peering around the corner. Through gritted teeth, Zeus growled, "Move it or lose it, buddy." The eyestalk disappeared.

"Zeus," Huva whispered from under the desk. "I found something. A secret compartment. Hold on… there's something in it.…"

Crawling out from under the desk, Huva handed Zeus an I.D. badge. This one had no employee picture, and was a different color. She asked, "Why do you think it's different than the others?"

"I don't know," Zeus replied, genuinely unsure and a little surprised that he had never seen one like this before. "I'm going to look through his data files, to see if we can figure that out. After that, we'll head over to Myzzer's—or Rigel Ryktir, or whatever his real name might be—work area."

Before Zeus could get too comfortable with his plan, he heard from the Genturian's workstation, "Hello, Mr. Ryktir."

Zeus and Huva froze, staring at each other. Zeus heard a deep voice, Myzzer's voice, reply, "Hello, Grunk. Any word from Torrell Loren?"

As quickly and quietly as he could, Zeus turned off Dryn's computer. He crawled to the centralized common area formed by the six hexagonal workstations. Huva followed.

"No, sir. It's been three days and still nothing," Grunk said. "I'm assuming corporate has taken notice, because of the repair-techs."

"Repair-techs?"

"Yes, sir. Two of them just entered Torrell's workstation."

Zeus scampered from the common area to an adjoining workstation that he guessed to be empty. He guessed right, hiding behind the wall that connected it to the common area. He cringed as he realized that Huva wasn't going to make it out of the common area fast enough, and watched as she slid under one of the desks. He heard Myzzer moan curiously as he entered Dryn Tammeryn's workstation. Shortly after, Zeus heard Myzzer's heavy footsteps get closer.

From his vantage point, Zeus watched Myzzer enter the common area and look around. Zeus' mind reeled, thinking about how just recently the massive crime lord had hosted an illegal fight to the death, and now he wandered around the offices of a multi-planet corporation. Zeus' mind all but froze when he saw Myzzer lean over to look under the nearest desk.

There were three desks in the common area. It would only be a matter of seconds until he found Huva. Zeus looked at her: she had her fists clenched, ready to strike.

Myzzer looked under the second desk. Zeus tried to calculate the best possible chance for survival. He decided that he would run once Myzzer found Huva hiding under the desk. He *wanted* to run. Running would be the best option, especially since he knew the most efficient way out. But spending too much time with Fiore had affected him, knowing very well that his simpleton partner would not leave Huva behind. Now that he decided not to run, Zeus had no idea what his options were.

Putting his hand on the desktop, Myzzer looked around the common area again as he braced himself to lean over. Huva's muscles tensed, ready to strike. Zeus held his breath, still not certain what to do. Myzzer started to lean over.

"They were here just a second ago," Grunk interrupted, standing in Dryn's workstation and looking into the common area.

Myzzer stood and growled. Grunk turned and scampered back to his desk. Myzzer strode out of the cluster and mumbled, "Repair-techs, indeed."

As soon as Myzzer left, Zeus hurried to Huva and helped her out from under the desk, wondering how she fit her massive frame under it in the first place. He whispered, "Come on. Hurry. We need to follow him."

"Seriously?"

"Yes. Now, come on."

"Why do you have a death wish? What did your parents do to you to make you like this?"

"You have no idea," Zeus mumbled, as they stood and watched where Myzzer went.

Confident they were far enough away that Myzzer wouldn't feel like he was being followed, but close enough not to lose him, Huva and Zeus left the workstation cluster. As they walked past Grunk's area they paused just long enough for Zeus to say, "We were never here," while Huva displayed her fists in a menacing fashion. Zeus was confident that Grunk would not take any of his four eyes off his work for the rest of the day.

Despite Myzzer's size, once he left the room and traversed the hallways and corridors with the various other employees, he moved along without garnering any form of attention. Huva and Zeus walked the hallways just as freely, just two maintenance workers on the way to fix something important, not two bounty hunters in pursuit of an intergalactic crime lord. There was plenty of body traffic to keep Myzzer from being suspicious. After a hike across one of the many bridges between the buildings, the journey ended with Myzzer turning down one final hallway. When Huva and Zeus arrived, he was gone.

More of an alcove, the hallway terminated at a locked door. Both Huva and Zeus tried their badges with no success. Confused, Zeus said, "I don't understand. As repair-techs, we should have access to every room of every building in this complex."

"Do you think security caught on that our badges have been altered? If Myzzer's here, then he surely must have noticed that his badge as Rigel Ryktir has gone missing."

"Security would simply issue him a new one. Despite him having a high status in the company, he wasn't *that* high. However, I know a way past this."

Utilizing the touch screen next to the door, Zeus flipped through various menu options, until the screen displayed a request for an access code. Zeus entered ten digits and waited. Access was still denied. Flabbergasted, Zeus could only stare at the display, muttering, "That should have worked. That should have worked."

"What was that?" Huva asked.

"It was universal code. I... I... stumbled upon it while hacking into Sivka's computer systems."

"Well, smartest guy you know, let's try this." Huva used the I.D. she'd found at Dryn Tammeryn's desk.

It worked.

As quiet as a conspirator's whisper, the door slid open....

Chapter 32

Fiore fidgeted. Valla said, "Could you please stop fidgeting? When you do that, you jostle the whole shuttle. It makes maneuvering quite difficult."

"Sorry." Fiore didn't know what else to say. He didn't know what to say for the entire trip from Weelah's cargo ship as he and Valla aimed for Billix, presumably being held in a stronghold of some sort by The Legend. Fiore fidgeted when he was uncomfortable, and he was very uncomfortable being alone with Valla. She was a stunning young woman, and despite the fact that she sometimes talked like Zeus, Fiore found that he was attracted to her. However, it was the fact that her intelligence obviously surpassed his own that made him uncomfortable to the point where he could barely muster enough words to form sentences beyond, "Umm...."

After another stretch of deafening silence, Valla said, "What's your name?"

"Fiore," Fiore answered.

"No, your real name."

"Fiore," he said, becoming suspicious.

"I know what that word really means, and I have a hard time believing that parents, no matter what cultural norms dictate or support, named a male child that. What's your real name?"

Cheeks warming from fluster, Fiore said, "I need to keep it a secret."

"Why?"

"I'm a bounty hunter! This is a dangerous profession, and I don't think it would be in my best interest to use my real name. I bet Valla isn't your real name."

Valla winced from confusion. "It is."

"It is?"

"Yes. And Huva is my sister's birth name."

"Really?" A hint of pride rippled through him, thinking he had a great rebuttal. "You're not worried about your enemies finding you?"

"No," Valla answered without hesitation. "First of all, the only enemies we make are the ones we hunt and capture. Those we hunt and capture either end up incarcerated or dead, so there is nothing to fear from them. Second of all, if there are ancillary reasons to fear them, such as a disgruntled friend or relative of someone we've hunted and captured, then Huva and I are quite capable of keeping ourselves safe and controlling the situation."

Fiore paused and pondered his predicament, knowing he didn't have the mental fortitude to maneuver his way out of the current conversation. Instead, he relied on a favorite of his. "Oh, look over there."

However, this time, there was actually something over there to look at: a satellite as large as a five-story building. The hangar bays almost made it seem inviting, but the dozens of weapons clearly showed that no unannounced visitors would be welcome. Valla aimed right for the satellite.

"Umm, what are you doing?" Fiore asked.

Valla glanced over her shoulder to look at Fiore. "Exactly what we said we were going to do: get Billix and Tammeryn."

Fiore's number one go-to plan had always been to rush straight ahead as fast and as hard as he could, but he knew this was begging for suicide. The satellite had more weapons than a small army. "Yeah... but... we're aiming right for The Legend's stronghold. The one with all the guns and lasers and missiles and who knows what else he has ready to kill us."

Valla sighed, clearly exasperated from always having to explain herself. "Fiore, what would it take to defeat The Legend?"

"Umm, an army?"

"Exactly. He knows that too. Look at his satellite, Fiore. It's designed to stop an army. It's *prepared* for an army. We are too small for him. His sensors would see us as space debris, if they could even see us at all. He won't see us coming, because he *can't* see us coming."

"Okay. How are we getting in? I'm sure there are at least sensors or some kind of security system at all of the hanger bays."

"We're going in through the backdoor."

"Excuse me?"

Valla sighed again. "The refuse expulsion area, Fiore. No one feels the need to put a security system where they throw out their trash."

Having heard her argument, his smitten feelings for her intensified. Guilt offered a slight twist to sensitive spots within his chest, making him feel like he was betraying Zeus in some way. Was he, though? Fiore made an assumption that Zeus had feelings for Valla, but was it an accurate one? Now Fiore felt guilty for once again knowing too little about his friend and business partner. He tried to come up with a plan for how to learn more about Zeus, but it fell to pieces as he was interrupted by the sudden jolt of landing and Valla saying, "We're in."

As if waking from a dream, Fiore blinked rapidly and looked around. "How'd we get through the doors?"

"I overrode the system."

"And the airlock? Is this room pressurized? Does it have oxygen?"

As Valla opened the shuttle hatch, Fiore inhaled deeply and held his breath, his cheeks puffing out.

"Fiore. You sat with me the whole time. You were here every step of the way. Weren't you paying attention?"

Lungs burning from holding his breath for so long, Fiore let loose a roaring exhale. After a few cleansing gulps of air, he replied, "Of course I was paying attention. I just wanted more detail, that's all."

"You're lying. Make sure you pay attention this time. This is clearly a life or death situation."

"I know!"

"For some reason, I doubt that. Now pay attention."

"I am!"

"After what you've *just* shown me, I can't be too sure any more," she said, as she reached into her cloak and pulled out her handheld. After a few quick screen taps, her handheld projected a hologram of red vector lines in the shape of the satellite. Five green pinpoints of light flashed in the three-dimensional map floating above Valla's handheld. "This is the satellite we're in."

"Got it."

"The five flashing lights are life forms. We're these two lights. Understand so far?"

"Yes!"

"Okay. We can assume these two are Billix and Dryn Tammeryn since they're very close together, which means this one all the way over here is The Legend. Now, his security system is too sophisticated to control and override globally, so like what I did with the refuse doors to get in, I'm going to have to do localized overrides as we make our way to our targets."

Fiore wasn't sure now if he liked her less or liked her more. He certainly liked that she challenged him, making him want to be a better bounty hunter. He did really like the way she accentuated the fullness of her bottom lip when she became frustrated. But he certainly didn't like that some of her comments demeaned him. Much like some of Zeus' comments to him. Fiore now wondered if those demeaning comments that Zeus would sometimes make were an attempt to be helpful. Maybe constructive criticisms? The next time they were alone together, Fiore was going to talk to him about his communication skills and…

"Fiore!"

"What? I'm listening!"

"No, you're not. Your eyes glazed over."

"You started to talk too technical! I couldn't keep up!"

"You were probably thinking about cleavage."

"Was not!"

"Again, I doubt the validity of your words. Now *listen*. I'm going to say this as simply as possible. Do not go rushing into any corridor or alcove or room unless I say it's okay. Do. You. Understand?"

"You don't need to be so mean about it."

"With you? Sometimes it's necessary." Valla drew her gun and walked to the door out of the refuse room. "Once we exit this room, we're going to be in a corridor. We're going to follow it to the right. When we get to the end, we're going to stop so I can recalibrate my security override parameters—or, as you probably think of it, my computer magic. Now, get your gun ready, and do as I say."

"Umm… I don't have a gun."

Valla's face went slack, all expression falling away. "Seriously, no gun? You willingly walk into the stronghold of the greatest and most feared bounty hunter in the galaxy with no gun?"

Fiore raised his arms and flexed his biceps, veins bulging under his skin. "These are the only guns I need."

Valla frowned so hard that it looked to Fiore like it might hurt. Her normally fuchsia-hued skin darkened to a burgundy as her starburst blue eyes went blood-shot. Fiore now saw the family resemblance to her sister.

Reaching up to point her index finger at his face, Valla marched up to Fiore and growled, "I don't know how you managed to survive the fifty—or however many—years you've been alive with that attitude, but it's not going to work on this mission. If I die on this mission, I will make sure to find a way to take you with me! You say that you're a bounty hunter? Well, now is the time to prove it. So, eyes up, mouth shut, and follow my orders."

Valla stormed back to the door, and used her handheld to override its security system. She opened it and stepped through. After looking up and down the corridor, she gestured to Fiore. "Come on."

He was going to tell her that he wasn't that old, but decided against it. In fact, he decided just to keep his mouth shut and follow her through the door.

Chapter 33

Zeus and Huva entered the secret room and looked at each other, compatriots in confusion. Before them was a lone metal catwalk leading to another door, fifty feet away. A few steps forward, and they could see that they were in a warehouse, one designed for supply acceptance and distribution.

Cautiously, they moved along the catwalk, attempting to determine what exactly was being supplied and distributed. Four stories tall, the large warehouse had the usual equipment about. Large claws and magnets hung from the ceiling, ready to move inventory. Lifts large enough to fit a standard house moved up and down from one floor to another. Vehicles designed to carry goods zipped along the ground or hovered between the floors. Huva and Zeus saw a set of bay doors open on the floor level, but couldn't see what the warehouse vehicles were unloading. Machine motors whirred and chugged. An occasional voice shouted over the equipment's activities.

Then Zeus heard a noise that chilled him to the bone.

Children crying.

Unsettled, Zeus' heart pounded against his ribs as he quickened his pace along the catwalk. Crouching to hide behind the suspension cables, he and Huva got a better view of the unloading area. They saw the cargo: children. Over two dozen children of all races were being herded out of the cargo ship and into the warehouse. Brutish looking men sprayed mists at the children's faces, calming them, making them more docile.

Myzzer stood at the forefront, barking commands. "These seven are meaty enough to send to the labor division, I think. Those three are pretty enough to resell. The rest are off to research. Let's see if anything new comes out of these experiments. And move it! We got another shipment right behind this one."

The men buzzed around like agitated insects, obeying Myzzer's commands. A small cargo vehicle drove up and stopped. The seven children designated for labor were loaded into the box shaped container like compliant chattel. A vehicle carrying pods backed up; the men placed a limp child designated for research into each pod. The remaining three children were placed in an open-bed vehicle, lined with soft packing material for more fragile cargo.

"This… this is what would have happened to Weelah's daughter?" Huva whispered.

"Most likely," Zeus replied.

"We need to go down there and stop this."

"The two of us against two dozen criminals? Even if we do get lucky and manage to find a way to overpower them, I find it inconceivable that we could do it before they sound an alarm or alert others."

"Then we… we need to… to… I don't know. Report this."

"We need to get closer."

"What? I thought you said you didn't want to confront them."

"I don't." Zeus pulled out his handheld computer from his work satchel. "I can record what's going on here, but this isn't a good vantage point. We need to get closer. You heard Myzzer. There's another shipment coming."

"Closer. Okay, let's do this."

As if any noise could be heard over the whining equipment and shouting men below, Huva and Zeus crept along the rest of the catwalk and down the stairs as quietly as possible.

Zeus pondered the situation. Was Tammeryn involved with this? He almost had to be, considering Zeus had used his secret badge to get into this clandestine warehouse. And Myzzer had come to his workstation just minutes ago looking for him. What level of involvement, though? Why would Myzzer look for Tammeryn at his workstation if he put a bounty on him? Zeus also knew enough about Sivka to wonder why this was happening in the first place. Sivka Corp. was the largest and most profitable company in the galaxy. Clearly, no one of importance in the Sivka organization knew of these transgressions. But, if they didn't, then why had Sivka's secret guards been activated? None of this still answered why they kept coming after him and Fiore?

The heavy smells of machine oils and vehicle exhaust assaulted Zeus as he and Huva reached floor level. Pushing them out the forefront of his mind, he and Huva snuck from the stairs to behind a stack of containers. Crouching, he prepared his handheld to record the arrival of the newest shipment.

Just as before, the bay doors opened to reveal the back end of a cargo ship. Those doors of the cargo ship opened to reveal two dozen more frightened children. Immediately, a few men jumped aboard the cargo ship and used the same spray they used on the other children. The results were identical: sluggish little drones trundled out from the cargo ship. Myzzer barked commands, directing where the children would go. The men followed his orders.

"I hate just sitting here. Watching. Not doing anything," Huva whispered from behind Zeus, her muscles tense, ready to strike.

"We're not 'doing nothing.' We're collecting evidence that will help these children far more than whatever plan you wish to enact," Zeus whispered back. He then pointed to a stack of crates ten feet away. "Now, we need to sneak over there so I can get a clean shot of Sivka Corp.'s logo."

Staying as low as possible, they maneuvered their way to the new vantage point. Being aware of the whereabouts of Myzzer's men at all times, Zeus captured the images of the children being whisked away, the Sivka Corp. logo on the back wall looking like the eye of a demanding god. Satisfied with what he had recorded, Zeus slid his computer back into one of his pockets. When he looked at Huva crouched next to him, Zeus gave a nod. Then he realized something was missing. "Where's Myzzer?"

"Right behind you," a deep voice growled.

Out of reflex, Zeus jerked to the right, but he wasn't fast enough. In one motion, Myzzer knocked Huva to the ground and grabbed Zeus by the back of his collar. Zeus was thankful that Huva remained conscious and retaliated with a kick and a punch, keeping Myzzer occupied. He had very little time; the other men took notice of the scuffle and made their way over to join in.

Zeus reached into the repair-tech satchel and yanked out the first thing he grabbed: a small laser cutter. He tore off the safety mechanism and turned it on. The thin red beam burned a hole deep into Myzzer's forearm.

Roaring like an animal, Myzzer reeled back and grabbed his injured arm, thick gray smoke puffing from between his fingers. Zeus kicked Myzzer in the knee, but due to his lack of comparative mass, did little more than stagger his opponent. Standing about the same height as Myzzer, Huva's roundhouse punch connected to his jaw with an audible crunch. A second punch dropped him to the ground. The two bounty hunters leapt from their hiding place and were greeted by two dozen angry Sivka workers. Armed with a laser cutter and Huva, Zeus knew that wouldn't be enough against a wall of thugs using various tools as weapons.

Being more nimble than his closest assailant, Zeus avoided the attacker's strike and counterattacked with a punch to the throat. Huva made short work of the thug closest to her, simply overpowering him with a barrage of devastating knuckles-to-nose punches. Eyes bulging and muscles primed for a fight, Huva roared. Zeus couldn't help but notice the parallels between her and Fiore. Wondering if she was coherent enough to tell the difference between friend and foe, he grabbed her arm and said, "Huva! There are too many. This way. Follow me."

To his surprise, she wasn't too consumed by berserker rage to eschew reason, and followed him as he ran to the open back doors of the recently arrived cargo ship. She made short and bloodied work of the ship's captain and two crewmembers. Zeus jumped into the pilot's chair while Huva tossed the recently bloodied bodies from the ship.

"Hurry!" Huva shouted, as Myzzer's goons ran to the ship.

"Got it!" Zeus shouted back. Guessing at the controls, he shut the cargo bay doors, sealing the ship and readying it for space travel. He soon figured out how to fire up the engines and send commands to open the outer doors of the warehouse. Fumbling with the controls, Zeus shot out from the hangar the moment the doors had opened wide enough.

Huva sat next to him, accessing the ship's computers. "I'll find the nearest law enforcement station on the planet."

Zeus aimed the ship straight up. "We're sticking with the original plan."

"What?" Huva snapped. "We have proof that the largest corporation in the galaxy is involved with trafficking children. Children, Zeus! Even you can't be so cold-hearted that you'd put a bounty before the well-being of children!"

"I'm not," Zeus said, even though he wasn't entirely sure if he meant it or not. "However, the closest station is in the city. I'm flying a cargo ship that I have zero experience with in an unfamiliar city, where maneuvering would be of the utmost importance. Look at the sensors, Huva."

She did. The display showed a dozen ships departing from the very location they'd just fled. Zeus continued, "Even if we did manage to get there, don't you think that the local law enforcement might be on Sivka's payroll?"

"I didn't think of that," she mumbled.

"We can't outrun them, but we can make it to one of the off-planet jump-gates and get to the collection point."

"But what good would that do?"

"You know where the meeting place is, but they don't. Once they find out where jumping to, they might turn away. If not, maybe we can use it to our advantage."

Huva inhaled, her jaw muscles flexing from clenched teeth. "Are you sure this will work?"

"Absolutely," Zeus said, again not entirely sure if he meant it or not.

Chapter 34

Conflicted. Fiore felt conflicted. Skulking along the corridors of The Legend's secret headquarters had certainly given him a thrill, the kind he had hoped for when he became a bounty hunter. It was an extra-added bonus thrill that it was his idea that helped his friends find the secret headquarters. But part of him wanted to find The Legend.

When he had first decided to become a bounty hunter, he had wanted to be the best. He went through painful surgeries, including the addition of the infusion device, to achieve that goal. The Legend was the best, and Fiore knew that if he could win against The Legend, even just once, it would help his credibility. He also knew that it was far more important to steal Dryn Tammeryn and rescue Billix. Collecting the largest bounty in history? *That* would go a long way toward making him the best—not to mention, he wanted Valla to like him.

Fiore didn't know how this adventure was going to turn out, but he had met three attractive women along the way. He was not willing to part ways with them without asking at least one of them on a date! Sure, he knew very well that none of them thought he was very intelligent, but he was a specimen of physical human perfection with large, rippley muscles. He oozed masculinity! Women liked that! Well, he was fairly confident that women liked that. Watching Valla's feminine curves flow under her cloak as she walked, he decided that she was going to be the one he'd ask on a date first.

As she did at the end of every corridor, she stopped, and held up her hand to signal that Fiore should do the same. Just as she had done so before, she pecked away at her handheld; confusing the localized security systems into thinking everything was fine. It took four explanations for Fiore to understand that much of what she was doing, so he accepted it and stopped asking.

"This is the last corridor," Valla said, tapping away. She nodded down the hallway, other corridors branching off from it. "Right over there is where Billix and Tammeryn are. I'm guessing that those hallways lead to holding cells, Billix down one way, Tammeryn down the other."

"What about The Legend?" Fiore asked.

Valla tapped her handheld a few times to produce the three-dimensional hologram of the space station. Three of the five flashing dots were in the same position as when they had first arrived. "He hasn't moved since we got here. That's a very good sign."

"Yeah," Fiore responded, still feeling conflicted. But he waited patiently as she finished the process of fooling the area's security sensors, then followed her when she advanced.

Valla had assumed correctly; the hallway they went down housed six holding cells, three on either side. However, the transparent walls showed that the cells looked more like furnished apartments. Fiore made a mental note that, when it was time to install holding cells in his secret headquarters, it would be an act of class to keep the detainees comfortable. Large bed, soft couch, refrigerated food storage unit, lighting that the prisoners could control. The lavatory was exposed, but other than that, the captive couldn't complain. Well, other than about being a captive.

In the center cell sat Dryn Tammeryn, lounging on the couch with a book. When he saw Fiore and Valla approach, he jolted to his feet and dropped his book, surprise etched across his face. "Who are you? What are you doing?"

Still tapping away on her handheld, Valla answered, "I'm Valla, and this is Fiore. We are bounty hunters, here to collect you."

"The Legend already caught me," Tammeryn said, a worried look rippling across his featureless, green face.

"Right," Valla said. "We're stealing you from him."

"I don't want to go with you."

The cell door opened, and Valla pointed at Fiore. "That doesn't matter. If you don't come willingly, my associate here will simply sling you over his shoulder. You are a bounty and we have less than an hour to get you to the prearranged meeting location. Why you chose the location that you did is beyond me."

Fiore entered the room, and Tammeryn pressed himself against the corner of the walls, as if even the slightest crack could offer escape. Then his body relaxed, his face displaying a quizzical expression. "Wait. Did you... did you say that... I... chose the location?"

Halting halfway into the room, Fiore said, "Yes, she did."

"Why? Why would she say that?"

"Well, we saw you."

"Saw me? Saw me doing what?"

Fiore took in a deep breath and let it out slowly, in a therapeutic way, becoming exasperated with this conversation. He wondered if this was how people felt when they talked to him. "We saw you post a bounty for yourself at the Genturian library, but you didn't use your name. You used Myzzer's, but I'm not sure why."

Tammeryn's expression went from confused to surprised. "So… you *know* that I posted the bounty? *And* I used Myzzer's name?"

"Yes," Fiore and Valla said in unison.

Tammeryn straightened his posture. "I will come with you willingly, under one condition: I will not answer any questions until the aforementioned drop-off time. Agreed?"

Valla and Fiore exchanged glances, then answered in unison, "Agreed."

"Good. Okay, let's go."

Tammeryn exited the room and headed down the hallway as if leading the way. Valla and Fiore followed him into the corridor. Before he could get too far, Valla stopped him. "Wait. We need to collect another bounty."

Tammeryn stopped and said, "Ah, yes. The purple cyborg who babbles. Curious that he, too, is worth ten billion creds."

"Long story," Fiore said, as he ran to the other hallway. "We'll explain when all this is over. I see Billix! He's…"

"No!" Valla and Tammeryn yelled.

Alarms sounded. Lights flashed. Valla and Tammeryn cursed.

"Fiore set off the alarms, didn't he?" Billix asked over the claxons.

"Yes," Valla said, as she ran to Billix's holding cell while furiously tapping away at her handheld.

"I thought it was all clear, since we got Tammeryn!" Fiore explained.

"I *told* you that I had to do one area at a time."

"Right! And we entered the holdings *area*."

The alarms went silent and the lighting returned to normal. "The holdings area consists of two different hallways. It didn't occur to you that they were two distinct zones?"

"Oh… no." Feeling stupid, Fiore stepped away from Billix's cell as Valla finished the final sequence of overrides. The door slid open, and Billix walked out, a slight hitch in his step from the ill-fitting prosthetic replacing part of his missing leg. Even though mechanics covered half of Billix's face, and the other half was smooth and all but featureless, Fiore knew Billix was glaring at him.

Looking at Tammeryn, Billix grimaced. "Him? This is the guy worth ten billion creds? He certainly doesn't seem like he's worth ten billion creds."

"Neither do you," Tammeryn replied.

"I'm not! Zeus and Fiore… oh, never mind. How are we going to get out of here?"

Valla referenced the hologram of the space station while walking down the corridor. The glowing light she had tagged as The Legend was now moving, as were dozens of other new globs of color. "Judging from these new energy signatures, we can assume that these are robots or vehicles of the security system that Fiore triggered on their way here to blast us to tiny pieces. We need to get to the hangar. Fiore, you take lead —go that way."

Taking point, Fiore ran the way Valla indicated, away from the robots and vehicles that he had awoken. Confused, he asked, "Why are we going to the hangar?"

"The shuttle barely held the two of us. Where did you think we were going to put our bounties?"

"Still not a bounty!" Billix yelled, while limping as fast as he could behind everyone else.

"Oh," Fiore mumbled. "Then what about Weelah's shuttle? Are we just going to leave it?"

"You can buy her a new one with your share of the ten billion. Turn down the next hallway."

Running full sprint, Fiore did as he was told. Excitement tickled behind his chest as he saw a clear path to the hangar—until a hatch in the ceiling slid open, and The Legend dropped through.

There he stood, tall and ominous, the dark king of bounty hunters. Even his shadow exuded regality, instilling dread in those who saw it. Except for Fiore—not this time.

Standing tall, he puffed out his chest and said to Valla, "Give me your gun."

"Does he mean me?" Billix cried. "He means me. He means me, doesn't he? I'm his gun. He thinks I'm his gun."

"What are you talking about?" Tammeryn asked. He then turned to Valla and put his hand on her shoulder. "What is he talking abou—Never mind. We need to get out of here. We need to run!"

Valla handed her gun over to Fiore and asked, "Are you sure about this?"

"Yes," Fiore said, taking her gun and sliding half of it into the front pocket of his pants, handle grip sticking out.

"Are you sure?" Valla asked again. "Everyone knows you're not very good with a gun. Are you sure you don't want to use Billix?"

"No!" Billix screamed. "No using Billix! No using Billix!"

"What are you three talking about? Why are you even letting him do this if he's not good with a gun?" Tammeryn asked.

The Legend laughed, so deep and rumbling that it echoed, threatening to bend and warp the metal walls of the corridor. All talking ceased. The Legend flicked the right side of his long coat back to expose a holstered gun.

Without a word, Valla, Billix, and Tammeryn backed away from Fiore and crouched down, huddling against the far wall.

Fiore cracked his knuckles, trying to steady his shaking hands. His stomach flopped over, as he doubted the wisdom of his decision. His throat tightened. Sweat flowed over the back of his neck.

The Legend pulled two cartridges from his belt and placed them in the bio-accelerator. It hummed, and he was ready.

Fiore kept his left hand ready to draw, while the fingers of his right hand glided over the cartridges of his bandoleer. Which ones should he choose? For certain, he would get shot, so he started to think of the chemicals needed to accelerate the healing process, and maybe numb the pain. Would enhanced muscle help? Probably not, he decided. Better reflexes. They would certainly help, especially since it became rather apparent that was what The Legend did. Even from this distance, Fiore could see The Legend's eyes widen, his hands trembling in anticipation. Fiore reached for the cartridges that would yield the same results.

Then he changed his mind.

Grabbing only one cartridge, one he thought he'd never use, he inserted it into his bio-accelerator on his forearm and pressed the button to start the process. The infused chemicals interacted with his system immediately. A sense of calm washed over him. His hands stopped shaking, his stomach untied itself from the various knots it had been in. He was thoroughly relaxed.

With a new sense of serenity, Fiore noticed that The Legend was getting impatient, body jerking and hand twitching, clearly not wanting to besmirch his reputation by drawing on a show-down opponent who wasn't ready. Fiore didn't want to keep him waiting any longer.

Hand unflinching, it hovered over the gun tucked in his pocket. With steely focus, Fiore watched The Legend's right hand, looking like a coiled serpent ready to strike at the first sign of movement. His right hand. Fiore had an idea.

Jerking to the right and twisting to pull his left shoulder out of the way, Fiore made an assumption—and he was correct. As soon as he flinched, The Legend shot. A crackling bolt of energy buzzed by Fiore, right where his left shoulder had been a fraction of a second ago. Before The Legend could fire a second time, Fiore drew his gun.

He pulled the trigger.

A yellow flash of light struck The Legend in the center of his chest.

With a look of utter disbelief on the exposed parts of his face, the monstrous humanoid dropped to his knees and fell on his side.

The realization of what he had just done led to an excitement that nullified the chemical-induced relaxation he had been feeling. With child-like exuberance, Fiore ran to The Legend. Standing over the fallen body, Fiore smiled. "Did you see that? Did you see what I did?"

"Nice shooting," Valla said, as she walked by.

"I can't believe you hit him," Billix said, as he followed Valla. "I really can't believe it. Seriously. Pure disbelief."

Tammeryn said nothing as he followed the others into the hangar.

"Come on, Fiore, we need to hurry," Valla called to him.

Smiling so broadly that it started to hurt, Fiore said, "I just want to really absorb this moment. Really soak it in."

"Well, don't soak too long, because we have a deadline to meet," Valla said. "And the energy blast from the gun is barely strong enough to stun someone his size."

"Oh. Really?"

Answering his question, The Legend flung his arm out and grabbed Fiore's ankle.

Jumping back, Fiore freed himself from The Legend's grip. Running backward into the hangar, he shot at The Legend. And missed. Repeatedly. By the time he joined the others, Fiore had made two dozen minor energy burns along the walls, floor, and ceiling of the corridor; not a single mark on his target, now unsteadily making his way to his feet.

By the time Fiore made it to Valla, she had overridden the doors with her handheld and closed them. He tried to ignore the looks of derision coming from Valla and Billix. Even though he had no discernable lips, Tammeryn worked his mouth into a snarl of disgust and said, "You're a bounty hunter? With shooting skills like that?"

"I was moving," Fiore mumbled, cheeks burning with embarrassment.

Valla examined the three ships in the large hangar, and chose the one that looked to be the fastest. With a few pokes of her handheld's screen, she overrode the controls and made the ship her own. "Come on. We have maybe a two-minute head start. Let's make the most of it."

Without hesitation, Fiore boarded the ship. He wanted to get this over with so he could hire an instructor for shooting lessons.

Chapter 35

Zeus guided the ship through the jump-port with ease. Being a Sivka Corp. cargo ship, it had a license to pass freely through any jump-port. But so did every one of the dozen ships in pursuit. He was just far enough ahead of his pursuers to get his bearings once he came out of the other side, just above the atmosphere of the planet Herrysh.

As he put the coordinates of the drop point into the nav system, Zeus recalled what he knew about the planet. One of the oldest in the galaxy, it no longer had any inhabitants. In the early years of jump-port travel, the planet served as a travel hub, causing a population explosion never to be seen again. Entire cities were erected and populated during any given year. Buildings grew in number and size to accommodate the influx of hundreds of millions of citizens and businesses. Once it became as easy as pressing a few buttons and guiding a vehicle through a glorified hoop, the population disappeared just as quickly. As the cities started to die, the Federated Galactic Government bought the whole planet. Now it was used as military training grounds.

Dropping from the atmosphere to the surface, the remains of one of the megalopolises grew closer. What started as a smudge on the surface of the planet grew into thousands of dirty fingers reaching from the grave. Close enough to zoom among the decayed and broken buildings, Zeus felt like an interloper observing an arcane ritual involving the secrets of time and death. However, a flash of yellow energy passing by the ship reminded Zeus that he could easily join these rust-stained skeletons in their tomb.

Without so much as a word, Huva found and activated the weapons systems. Fortunately, this cargo ship was armed with a few energy weapons; small, but if used properly, they could be effective. Unfortunately, so were the ships chasing them. Zeus was thankful that they, too, were cargo ships, the only vessels available to Myzzer and his men at the time of escape.

"Zeus!" Huva yelled, as more yellow energy beams flashed outside the ship's windows. "A few of those almost hit us!"

"Their weapons are small yield, so they don't take up space on the ship or drain too much energy. They're designed to fend off pirates. We can take a few hits."

"A few! There are twelve ships chasing us. We can't live through that."

"Well, if you'd shoot some of them, then we wouldn't have to worry about it."

"I am! Small energy beams, not much damage, remember?"

"We're almost to the drop point."

"Hurry!"

"I said we're almost there! You listen as well as Fiore."

Even though Zeus focused on flying the ship, he felt her glare burn into the back of his head hotter than the energy blasts he fought so hard to avoid. He flew along a main artery in a valley of buildings, leading them out of the city. The buildings that formed the channel diminished in size as they sped past. Within seconds, Zeus flew above buildings no taller than five stories, charred and decimated from past explosions.

No longer protected by the city's structures, Huva looked through every window she could. "I don't see anyone else, Zeus! You said every bounty hunter in the galaxy would be here!"

The buildings became even smaller, two stories at most, while the streets narrowed. Zeus aimed for the center of the small town they flew over. He struggled with the controls as energy blasts pelted the craft. "I said 'most'! Most bounty hunters! I'm assuming they didn't want to risk getting caught on a government-restricted planet. The Federated Government monitors this planet closely, and is known for quick and immediate response."

"Yeah?" Huva asked, head swiveling to look from one window to another. "Then why don't I see them either?"

Zeus had no answer, and quickly pushed the question from his mind, trying to figure out how to land safely. Or at least crash so he and Huva could survive. Suddenly, a ship zipped by in front of him, from port to starboard. A second ship soon followed.

Trying to maintain his course, Zeus snatched occasional glances at what was happening outside the windows. Two black fighters, sleek and speedy, loaded with weapons, looped around Zeus and aimed for the group of cargo ships behind him.

The lead fighter released an arsenal of smoke-tailed missiles, red beams, yellow bolts of energy, and jagged blue streaks of electric arcs. Every aspect of the attack missed all of the ships, and only half even hit the nearby buildings. The second fighter crippled the small fleet with alacrity, needing only twelve shots to maim the twelve ships, each sparking and smoking as they dropped from the sky. Crashing in various places, Zeus surmised that if the pilots were capable enough, they could have survived. However, he found himself in a similar situation.

Being hit a few too many times, the ship was going down. Struggling with the controls, Zeus strained to keep from descending too quickly. Huva reached over and helped with the controls, pulling the nose of the ship up just enough to avoid smashing into the ground upon initial impact. Skidding along the main street, both Zeus and Huva yelled as green and yellow flora splattered against the cockpit window, until they came to a jarring stop.

Panting and dripping with sweat, Zeus and Huva looked at each other for a full minute. Getting their breathing under control, they offered each other faint smiles before exiting the ship.

"Excellent landing," Huva said, stepping out.

"Thanks," Zeus grunted, following her. He looked around, tickled with pride; he'd landed on the exact spot of the predetermined bounty collection point. Once the center of a town, crossroads formed a circle around the base of a statue long gone. Nature made its intent to reclaim known, as weeds and trees and brush forced their way through cracks and crevices, rending streets and obscuring single-story buildings. Now all he needed was the bounty. Anger began to percolate in him, as there were mere minutes left, and Fiore was nowhere to be found.

"Look!" Huva said, pointing to the sky.

Zeus looked up, just in time to see the second fighter shoot the first fighter's wing. The first fighter wobbled, but the descent was controlled enough to crash land with no further damage. One hundred yards beyond the small town's buildings, in a field of shoulder-tall yellow and green grasses, the wounded fighter skidded to a stop. The second fighter landed gently behind the first one. Hatches opened simultaneously on both ships.

Jumping out of the first ship came Fiore, then Tammeryn, Valla, and Billix. Only Fiore could be seen over the grasses, but Zeus saw swaths being cut through the grasses as everyone ran toward the meeting place. The Legend jumped out of the second ship, and followed in hot pursuit.

Knowing there was little they could do, Zeus and Huva started screaming, "Run! He's right behind you! Don't look back, just run!"

Zeus's chest tightened as Fiore began to pull away. Then he stopped, looked back, and reached into the weeds. Lifting him high enough for everyone to see, Fiore held Tammeryn. And ran.

Every step Fiore took, Zeus's heart pounded louder and harder. By the time Fiore burst from the field of grasses, Zeus felt his pulse threaten to burst through his fingertips. With seconds to spare, Fiore ran between buildings and covered the short distance to Zeus. "Did it!"

Even with his mouth drier than the dust coating the dead town, Zeus shoved his handheld computer at Tammeryn, and said, "I have our account information all set up. We know it was you who placed the bounty. Fiore and I got you to the drop point by the prescribed time. Make the transfer."

Laughing and tapping away, Tammeryn said, "You did. Well done, you two."

Fiore tapped away at the screen on his forearm mechanics. He stopped. His hands shook. His eyes sparkled like stars. Smile wide enough to split his face in half, he looked at Zeus and said, "The money's in our account. We did it. We did it!"

Zeus smiled, and then laughed. "Yes! I knew it! I knew we could do it!"

Whooping like a lunatic, Fiore ran to Zeus and lifted him over his head. Both men howling with overwhelming joy, Fiore started jumping up and down. Until the sisters, now standing next to each other, yelled in unison, "*Guys!*"

Fiore stopped jumping and returned Zeus to the ground. Zeus looked around to see two dozen armed Federated Government agents emerge from the surrounding building ruins. Teeth gnashing, Zeus spat, "This was a legal bounty! We have every legal right to—"

Tammeryn cut Zeus short by putting a hand on his shoulder. "Zeus. It's okay. You're right. The bounty was legal. They're with me."

"Wait. What?"

Looking at the agents, Tammeryn gestured to them and said, "Twelve ships went down, including one with Myzzer. Round up the survivors. I'll take care of this."

"What… what's happening? Who are you?"

"I'll get to that, but I think you have a more pressing matter," Tammeryn said, pointing toward the field he had come from. The Legend stood there, the grasses stopping just below his shoulders. Unmoving, he waited like a statue dedicated to his own greatness. When he had everyone's attention, he lifted his arm out from the grasses. The Legend held out Billix.

"*Noooo!*" Zeus roared, a conflagration igniting within his chest and burning his heart to ash. "No! No! No! No!"

"Billix!" Fiore called out. "Are you okay?"

Dangling by the back of his shirt, Billix moaned, "Yeah."

"How?" Zeus yelled at Billix. Pacing around, his arms flailed as he continued his tirade. "How could you? How could you let him catch you?"

"What?" Billix yelled back, swinging as he kicked his feet. "You really expected me to outrun the greatest bounty hunter in the galaxy? While wearing a cheap leg prosthetic? I'm just happy to be alive after all of this! And let me remind you that I didn't volunteer for this! *I never wanted to be a part of this*!"

"No!" Voice going hoarse, Zeus continued to yell. "No! We're not paying!"

"We have to," Fiore said. "If we don't, our reputations will be tarnished. And it'd be illegal not to pay. Don't forget, there are Federated Government agents all around us."

"No," Zeus mumbled, tears streaking down his cheeks. "No. No. No. No."

With seriousness in his tone that Zeus had never heard before, Fiore said, "Zeus. It's okay. We captured Dryn Tammeryn. *We* did. The biggest bounty in history, and *we did it*."

"I can't, Fiore," Zeus whispered, choking on sobs. "I can't do it."

"It's okay. I'll do it." Fiore turned and walked to The Legend, tapping away on his bio-infuser's screen.

The tears stopped, and Zeus could only seethe as he watched Fiore buy Billix from The Legend for ten billion creds. The Legend dropped the purple cyborg, and Billix ambled his way to where everyone else stood. The Legend said something to Fiore, then turned and walked away. Fiore walked back with a smirk. Something The Legend said to Fiore made him smirk. Zeus didn't care what it was, he just wanted to strangle Fiore for smirking right after losing ten billion creds.

As soon as Fiore joined the group, Tammeryn smirked as well, and said, "So, would anyone care to know what's going on?"

Five angry countenances answered. Tammeryn laughed and continued, "I'll take that as a yes. I'm a Federated Government agent. I had an undercover assignment to pose as a Sivka Corp. employee."

"I think we all figured that out. But why?" Valla asked.

"Because Sivka is involved in trafficking children," Huva answered.

"Exactly!" Tammeryn said, too gleefully. "When we heard the rumors, we needed to investigate. However, when you investigate the largest and most powerful corporation in the galaxy, you need to be careful and very, very prepared."

"So, you went undercover and collected evidence," Huva said. "Then why did you place a bounty on yourself?"

"Because the undercover assignment was for three years. *Exactly* three years. After all the paperwork had been signed, I had to show up at this exact extraction point at this exact time. I couldn't be extracted before, or else the lawyers would say that the operation, and all the evidence collected, would have been invalid. Myzzer started to piece things together, so I needed to ensure my safety for these last three days." Tammeryn drew close to the group and lowered his voice. "So, I embezzled eleven billion creds, and used ten billion to put on my own head, with a clause stating that I had to be delivered here alive. That served a double purpose: I knew whoever found me would ensure my safety, and it also made Sivka Corp. use their secret goon squad. They're already down eleven billion creds, and with a ten billion cred price tag on my head, they would have had to spend *another* ten billion or more to hire someone to get me. Instead, they used their own secret police, and they got quite sloppy, which only adds to the Federated Government's case against them."

"Why did you use Myzzer's name when posting the bounty?" Fiore asked.

With a tone that clearly let everyone know that he was proud of himself, Tammeryn said, "I certainly wasn't going to use *my* name! I figured if anyone was savvy enough to hack into the wire, they'd see Myzzer's name and hunt him down. The bounty on me was too high for him to pay off anyone who hunted him, so it would flush him out and cause him to get sloppy as well. Which… well, we know how that turned out." Tammeryn nodded to the agents coming back from their searches. Nine of those who pursued Zeus and Huva were in custody, including Myzzer—bruised, bloodied, and burned, but aware enough to glare at Tammeryn as two agents escorted him to one of their ships.

Watching the agents take Myzzer away with his hands bound behind his back, Tammeryn mumbled to himself with a hint of glee in his voice, "Yeah, he looks none too happy, does he?" He turned back to the group of five weary souls and said, "I can't thank you enough for all your help. Well, I guess I'll be seeing you."

"Wait!" Zeus snapped. "You said you embezzled eleven billion creds, but only put out ten billion for the bounty. What about the other billion?"

The other four had enough energy left to look at Tammeryn with want in their eyes. A wry smile slid across his green face as he strode over to Fiore. Taking hold of Fiore's wrist, Tammeryn tapped away on the screen of the bio-infuser and said, "Took you long enough to ask. I guess Zeus is the smart one, huh? After going head-to-head against the galaxy's most dangerous criminal overlord, and collecting evidence against the largest corporation in the galaxy, I figured this would be a good time to retire. The pension from the Federated Government isn't enough to change my looks and identity and disappear. So, I decided to make my own pension plan."

Tammeryn released Fiore's arm and said, "But you helped, so here's a little thank you. However, it seems you might need to split it with the others, Zeus."

As Tammeryn turned and headed toward the other agents and their ships, Fiore continued to stare at his computer screen.

"Well?" Huva asked.

"One million one," Fiore replied, smiling. "This is one cred more than the biggest bounty before today!"

The sisters gasped and hugged each other, laughing. Even Billix smiled and said, "Then, after Tammeryn, this is the second largest bounty in history, right? You two officially received the second largest bounty in history!"

"Third largest," Zeus said, voice cracking as if he hadn't used it for years. "Since you let The Legend capture you, you became an official bounty, making you the second largest."

"Really? You're still stuck on that? You just had a million handed to you, and you're upset, *blaming me* for losing ten billion. Ten billion that *you* wagered on this gambit, by the way. Meanwhile, my hovercar was totaled, my life was in nonstop peril, and *who knows* what happened to my apartment or store. And all I'm getting is one sixth."

"Don't forget about two of Weelah's shuttles," Huva added.

"And *our* third," Valla said.

"They're right, Zeus," Fiore said, taking their side. "If you're worried about money, we now have money. If you're worried about status, we got both the first and third highest bounties in history, all on the same day."

Fiore was wrong. Zeus wasn't worried about the money. He wanted the prestige, the respect of being the best. How could he be the best if no one else knew he was? Sure, Fiore was right about them receiving the third highest bounty. But it was given out of pity! *And* he was going to have to *split it*. On top of that, they captured and collected the largest bounty ever, but had to give the whole thing away to pay for the *other* largest bounty ever. Who would ever call to mind Zeus and Fiore as being the best when The Legend was involved? They would be relegated to numbers two and three, meaning they were the first two names ignored after The Legend. In Zeus' mind, none of this met his goals, so he was going to have to work harder. Starting with Fiore.

Zeus looked up at Fiore, looked at the potential within his clumsy partner. Now that this bounty was taken care of and Sivka Corp. would no longer be hunting him, Zeus could now spend time on his new project—making Fiore better. First, though, he needed to find out who Fiore really was.

"Zeus?" Fiore asked. "Why are you looking at me like that?"

Smirking and shaking his head, Zeus lied, "Just thinking about how we're going to spend our money."

Chapter 36

"What is this?" Zeus asked.

Billix walked past Zeus and snatched the ball with dozens of thin, multi-colored wires spiraling from it out of his hands. Gently, he placed it on a shelf next to similar looking items. "Treat this with respect. This is a Tanggoarian hexel-unit processor. Very valuable."

"It's over fifty years old."

"I know! That's why you should treat this with respect, and why it's so valuable. It's very rare."

"Value and rarity are mutually exclusive."

"I know! It's valuable because it's in such high demand!"

"If they were in such high demand, you wouldn't have four of them on your shelf."

"You know what? When you showed that weird moment of generosity by helping me get my store back in order, I thought there might be a decent human under that green cloak of yours. But, no! Still mouthy. Still irascible." Billix punctuated his statement by turning and walking to a different part of his pawnshop.

"I'm only helping so I can get a better look at your inventory!" Zeus yelled, and walked to the other side of the shop.

Fiore chuckled to himself as Huva helped him return a toppled shelving unit to its original, upright position. Billix was right, though, about Zeus' unusual moment of generosity—he forfeited his time to help the others. Naturally, Fiore helped as well. He wanted to forge lasting relationships, and he felt badly for disrupting Billix's life.

Upon returning to Weelah's cargo ship after watching Tammeryn and the other Federated Government agents haul away Myzzer and his crew, they all decided to assess the damage done to Billix's apartment and pawnshop.

Offers were made and remade to help Zeus and Fiore with their headquarters, but Zeus refused any and all help. More concerned about his shop, Billix forwent visiting his apartment. When they entered, he cried a little from his non-robotic eye.

Even though to Fiore it looked very similar to the first time he had visited the shop, Billix assured him that other bounty hunters looking for him had indeed ransacked it. His spirits slowly lifted as he noticed that nothing had been stolen, and that the damage was minimal.

Shelving units had been pushed over onto each other, partially stacked like toppled dominos. Weelah, Huva, and Fiore helped with those, lifting one unit at a time, while Zeus and Valla assisted in returning the fallen items back to the shelves.

After Fiore and Huva got the last shelving unit standing, Billix hurried over to look at the knee-deep mess on the floor. "Oh, good! Nothing's broken."

"How can you tell?" Fiore asked.

Billix twisted his face in disgust and shook his fists at the sky. He walked away mumbling, "He's just like Zeus."

Shaking her head, Huva said, "Your sensitivity is overwhelming."

Now was the time. He had helped Billix return his shop back to normal, and Fiore thought there was nothing left to do except to make his move. "Then why don't you teach me?"

As if watching Fiore's head turn inside out, Huva's face twisted into a horrified expression. "What? What are you talking about?"

This was it! Fiore knew he would never get a better chance, so he went for it. "I choose you."

"Choose me?" Huva's shriek belied her size. "Choose me for what?"

Fiore tried to wiggle his eyebrows, but the act simply made the goggles resting on his forehead wobble. "A date. Maybe more."

Silence. No one breathed, nor even blinked. The only noise was the clang of the tool that Zeus dropped. Huva reeled back, even her face tried to retreat from her skull. So heavy with anguish her words almost fell to the floor as she said, "A date?"

"Yes."

"Why?"

"Don't answer," Zeus whispered. "Please don't answer. Just stop talking."

Fiore tried to look coy, but instead looked constipated. "Well, the six of us have been working very closely together in tight environments. Obviously, some romantic entanglements are bound to happen. Despite the fact that all three of you women are spectacular and amazing in your own ways, I choose you."

Finally allowing the shock to penetrate the terror, Huva's face went slack, jaw dangling. After a minute of awkward silence, she uttered, "Me? You choose me… to date?"

"Yes."

"No."

"Why not?"

"Wow," Billix said to Zeus, who was now digging the heels of both hands into his eyes. "He didn't notice? Your partner is really dumb. He really didn't notice? How could he not have noticed?"

"Notice what?" Fiore asked Billix.

Answering the question, Huva turned to Weelah. Weelah had just enough time to smile as Huva embraced her. Then they kissed, long and deep.

"Oh," Fiore said, Billix's words stinging his brain like angry hornets.

"What was he thinking?" Valla whispered rhetorically.

Zeus stopped rubbing his eyes and turned to Valla. "Well, he does have a point about when sentient beings of relatable species work closely together for an extended period of time."

"No!" Valla snapped. "No. I respect your intellect and your drive to succeed, and maybe if I didn't know you, I'd entertain the thought. But you're arrogant, self-centered, belligerent, and just all around mean."

"What? You just said you respected my drive to succeed. All those other qualities you listed are good qualities to have when trying to succeed."

"But they're not qualities I find endearing in a potential mate."

"You women are crazy, no matter what species you are. So, tell me, what qualities do you find endearing?"

"A nice guy! Sensitive. Kind and helpful. Kind of like…" Valla's words trailed off as she turned to Billix. In a huff, she stormed over to him. Placing both hands on his face, she kissed him.

Zeus frowned and cursed.

Billix wobbled after Valla disengaged from him. The red light of his cybernetic eye flickered while he gasped for air. He then smiled and said, "She kissed me! Did you see that? Came over and kissed me. Wait… did she also say something about a potential mate?"

"Stop talking, Billix," Valla said, as she crossed her arms over her chest and glared at Zeus.

Zeus simmered, holding her gaze with a glare of his own. Finally, he gave up. Snorting his contempt, he turned and walked to the exit. "Come on, Fiore. There's nothing more for us here."

Hating to part on such bad terms, but not knowing what else to do, Fiore put his head down, turned, and followed Zeus.

Zeus mumbled to himself the whole walk from the pawnshop back to their headquarters, pushing his way through the street crowds with abandon. By the time they walked down the hallway to their door, Fiore thought Zeus looked sad. Then he really looked sad once he opened the headquarters' door.

Their apartment was just as they had left it—table on its side, hole in the wall, refrigeration unit door on the floor, couches askew, walls riddled with tranq darts. Zeus heaved a soul-deflating sigh.

Hydrynx padded over to Zeus and sat down in front of him. The winged cat released a meow lasting half a minute, while fumes rippled the air around its mouth. Zeus sighed again, and went to a nearby cabinet to retrieve food for his pet.

After feeding Hydrynx, Zeus joined Fiore in the center of the room, assessing the damage.

"Well, it's just you and me, partner," Fiore said.

"*That* is the way it should be," Zeus replied.

After the embarrassment at the pawnshop, Fiore was perfectly okay with that....

Epilogue 1

Zeus stroked behind Hydrynx's ears as he watched his computer monitor, the percentage completed meter zooming through the sixties and into the seventies. "Do you think we'll find him this time?"

The dragon-cat hybrid responded with half a mew and a wisp of smoke from its nostrils.

The meter zipped through the eighties and nineties. Zeus tried to dampen his hope, but couldn't stop himself from being disappointed when the meter hit one hundred percent complete and yielded zero matches. "Damn it."

Zeus slouched in his chair, causing Hydrynx to shift on his lap. Hydrynx raised its head and offered Zeus a look of scorn. Zeus frowned at his pet, and resumed scratching behind its ear. With his other hand, Zeus manipulated the image on his monitor. The picture was Fiore without his beard. More accurately, what Zeus thought Fiore would look like without his beard, his goggles, and his wild hair obscuring his face. "That has to be what he looks like under all that brush. Right?"

Hydrynx stretched and yawned.

"You're no help, considering you've burned all of his beard and hair off at least four times. I thought you'd have a good idea of what he looks like."

Hydrynx simply stared at Zeus with a look of aggressive indifference, until its owner started scratching behind the ears again. Zeus frowned. "Next bio genetic hybrid I make will have the ability to communicate with me, so I'm not reduced to being some lonely, crazy person talking to myself all the time."

Hydrynx offered no response.

Zeus sighed. Despite being one of the most gifted abusers of computer networks to ferret out information—and he begrudgingly included Billix and Valla on that list—he still had limits. He needed a better computer system capable of rifling through more databases. There was one person to contact, but first he altered the image of Fiore again. Changing it the only way he could think of, he added a few wrinkles around the eyes and mouth. Zeus didn't like it. It made him look older than Zeus thought he might be under all the hair. Certainly much older that he acted.

Zeus thinned the jaw line a bit more, and started his search again. He needed to know more about Fiore, other than that not being his real name, and that he had an unnatural affinity for gourmet milk. And that he was either too dumb or too gullible when it came to the tattoo on his right shoulder—the Grim Reaper holding a flame thrower standing on a bed of skulls laced together by one pink rose with the calligraphic inscription, *Il Fiore Dentellare*. Fiore had told Zeus that the tattoo artist said it meant "Death Face." Laughing out loud to himself, Zeus remembered the look on Fiore's face when he told him that it was an old Earth language called Italian for "The Pink Flower."

Zeus flipped to a different screen on his computer, and punched in the comm number for the one person who could help in his search. While he waited, he rationalized that Fiore *could* be that old. Zeus's parents had had so many procedures and chemical treatments that he sometimes thought they looked younger than he did. The screen beeped and came alive with the image of his mother. "Zephyr?"

"Yes, Mom. It's me. Is Dad there?"

His mother huffed and threw her hands in the air. "You can't be serious! The first time you call in almost a year, and you ask for your father?"

"Well, I'm looking for a new job, and I wanted to see if he had anything available."

Looking aghast, his mother said, "What is wrong with you, Zephyr? Haven't you been watching the news?"

"About Sivka Corp? I've seen it."

"Your father is the *president* of Sivka Corp! Do you *really* think now is the time?"

"So, you're saying Dad wouldn't hire me back?"

Zeus's mother sucked her teeth and rolled her eyes. "The last time he was generous enough to give you a job, you hacked into the government databases of three different planets for fun, created some kind of winged green cat just to see if you could, and tracked down known criminals because... well, I don't know why!"

"No one caught me, so I don't know why Dad would be mad."

"No one *outside of Sivka Corp.* caught you! Your father is under enough pressure right now and doesn't need your sarcastic, flippant attitude to make things worse. If you want to come home and visit, then—"

"Mom?"

She sighed. "Yes, Son?"

"Is there any truth to the rumors about Sivka Corp. having a covert group of security guards?"

Again with indignation, his mother snapped back, "Because the galactic police found a few crazies dressed in all black with Sivka Corp. tech? Don't be ridiculous!"

"Have the police interrogated them yet?"

"No. Each one of them killed themselves. Crazies, all of them."

Zeus remained quiet as he contemplated this information. His mother mistook his silence and said, "Your father will be fine. He's a smart man. With the help of his fellow corporate officers and the board of directors, he'll get through this."

"I don't doubt it," Zeus replied.

"Would you like to come home?"

"I'm too old to live with my parents."

His mother sighed, frustrated with his games. "That's not what I meant and you know it. We could set you up with a house next to our estate."

"Sorry, Mother, but I like where I'm living now."

"You've been gone for too long."

Zeus chuckled. "It's been two years, Mother."

"Well, that's long enough to have lived out your little adventures, whatever they may be."

Zeus scowled at her demeaning comment. "This is the very reason why I left, Mother."

"Well, then. A visit? Your brother and sister miss you."

"But not Father?"

"I already told you—he's been very busy and—"

Zeus terminated the communication.

Sitting back, yet still stroking Hydrynx, Zeus took a moment to push down the frustrations and feelings of abandonment. He rationalized that many of the galaxy's greatest names throughout history were misunderstood loners. No family or friends, and if they did have any, they were limited, usually just a partnership here and there. Zeus wanted to be one of those great names in history—the best at something. Right now, he wanted to be the best bounty hunter, and he had learned less than a year ago, when he met Fiore, that he'd need a partner to do it.

Sitting up and tapping away at his computer, Zeus pushed the conversation with his mother from his mind, and continued to search for more information about his partner....

Epilogue 2

Fiore stepped out of the bio-cleansing unit, chemical-infused water still dripping from his naked body. He flipped a switch on the wall, causing the anti-pathogen units embedded in his bathroom ceiling to come alive with a low hum. They also aided in the drying process, and the water tickled his skin as it evaporated. He wiped the steam from the wall mirror to evaluate how well he had shaved and cut his hair.

Running his hand over his smooth chin, he turned from side to side. Satisfied that he hadn't missed any spots, he looked at his hair, now cropped short. He did find it amusing that when he grew his hair long and beard thick, everyone guessed him to be over forty years old. Despite the fact that the operation had made his cheeks and jaw line more chiseled, he thought it was obvious that he was only sixteen.

Not liking the style, he reminded himself that all he had to do was insert a few cartridges into his bio-infuser unit, and his long hair and beard would come back in less than a minute. But he needed to cut his hair and be clean-shaven for what he was about to do.

After he exited the bathroom, he double-checked his bedroom door to make sure it was locked. He knew he would have to tell Zeus sooner or later, but for right now, he'd rather it be later. Or at least, when Zeus started sharing more personal information with him.

After taking one last look in a nearby mirror, Fiore sat down and started to prepare for the call. He turned on the camera that was attached to a monitor. Adjusting the camera, he made sure it captured only his face and the plain white wall behind him. Clearing his throat, he then tried to soften his voice a bit. The operation had deepened it, a bit too baritone for a sixteen-year-old, he thought. Even though he couldn't sound like his old self, it was as good as it was going to get. "Call Mom."

The blank screen flickered alive. His mother—make-up perfect, jewelry gleaming—appeared, smile warm and soft. "Milton! It's so wonderful to see you!"

"Hi, Mom."

"Oh, look at you! So handsome! Is everything going well at the Special Intra-Galactic Federated Government Ambassador Institute?"

"Yes, Mom."

"Learning about different cultures?"

"Getting firsthand experience, Mom."

"You're looking very fit!"

"I'm getting lots of exercise, Mom."

"Do you need more money?"

"Not right now, Mom. Thanks."

"Are you still having fun with your new friend, Zeus?"

"Yes, Mom."

"Good, Dear. That's good."

"Mom? Is… is Dad around?"

Fiore's mother frowned, looking dismayed. "Oh, Milton. Don't they allow you to watch the news there?"

"They do. I saw."

"Then you should know that your father is very busy."

"He's always busy," Fiore mumbled.

Face going stern, she said, "Milton! Your father is a board member of Sivka Corp! With that comes a great deal of responsibility. That includes helping the rest of the board, the president, and the executive officers clean up a public relations nightmare caused by some degenerate bounty hunters."

Confused, Fiore asked, "Didn't the news say that an undercover Galactic Federation agent exposed the company for trafficking children?"

"Even if that's true, then it was done by a small group of disgruntled employees, and there is no reason to drag management or the board of directors into this."

"But—"

"Now, Milton, I will not stand for any more talk about this. You have me quite upset."

"Sorry, Mom."

"I must be going now, Milton."

"Okay. Tell Dad I asked about him."

Fiore knew that message would never reach his father's ears, because his mother terminated her side of the conversation half-way through his sentence.

Sighing, he stood and walked over to his bandoleer, draped over a chair, and grabbed the necessary cartridges to make his hair grow back. He shouldn't upset his mother like that. He knew better. She was the only one in the family who showed him any attention. His siblings were all too busy for him as well; too busy making his father proud of them. He... well, he just didn't have the brains necessary to get attention the same way his siblings did. So, he had to pave his own path, find a different way to make his father proud of him. Bounty hunting.

Fiore knew that both of his parents would *highly* disapprove. But the danger involved? That would *have* to merit some form of respect. Especially if he could forge his way to being considered *the best*. After all, how difficult was it to sit behind a desk, tap away at a computer, and look at numbers all day, like his brothers and sisters? So he had the surgical operation done.

Looking at his bio-infuser unit, Fiore remembered that day vividly. The fear. The anticipation. The hope. Just ten months ago, he was six and a half feet tall and over three hundred pounds of pampered-rich-boy fat. After having his epiphany to become a bounty hunter—*the best* bounty hunter—he found a scientist willing to help him. It was dangerous, but worth it. The scientist found that less than one percent of the galactic population had the biology necessary to tolerate the drastic forces of manipulation caused by a bio-infuser. Even fewer could tolerate the major surgeries necessary to make him six inches taller and one hundred pounds heavier, shifting half of his weight from fat to muscle. After the operation, the scientist droned on and on about side-effects and taking over two years to truly get acclimated to his new body, something about genetic coding and muscle memory and inherent balance and other terms Fiore didn't comprehend. Fiore hadn't been interested in what the scientist had to say anyway—he had a new body, and wanted to start bounty hunting immediately!

Sure, it took half a week to learn how to walk again, and he fell over a lot for the next few months. He still fell over, but it was now due to trying an unpracticed fighting move, or when he lost his balance on his motorcycle. But he was getting better!

Looking at the cartridges in his hand, Fiore wondered if this was how The Legend had started out. He must have had a similar origin, since he had a bio-infuser unit as well. Did he go to the same scientist? It was possible. Did he have a similar body-altering operation? Judging from his enormous size, he might have. Fiore's mind drifted to when he had used his recent bounty to purchase Billix from The Legend.

Walking up to the idolized bounty hunter, Fiore didn't know what to say. At first, he tried to be professional, paying the bounty in silence. But there was so much to ask, so many things Fiore wanted to learn. After the transfer of funds was complete, Fiore couldn't resist, and figured he had to say something. "Thanks for shooting down the Sivka ships."

"It's the bounty hunter code. When faced with a mutual threat, you help out," The Legend said, a bit of mirth in his voice. He winked, and turned to walk back to his ship.

Back in his bedroom, Fiore looked at the cartridges in his hand and his bio-infuser unit. He inserted the cartridges. It was time to get back to work....

Brian Koscienski & Chris Pisano skulk the realms of south-central Pennsylvania. Brian developed a love of writing from countless hours of reading comic books and losing himself in the worlds and adventures found within their colorful pages. In tenth grade, Chris was discouraged by his English teacher from reading H.P. Lovecraft, and being a naturally disobedient youth, he has been a fan ever since. They have logged many hours writing novels, stories, articles, comic books, reviews, and the occasional bawdy haiku. During their tenure as a writing duo, they even started Fortress Publishing, Inc., a micro-press publishing company responsible for the Drunken Comic Book Monkeys short story collections and the TV Gods anthologies.

CPSIA information can be obtained
at www.ICGtesting.com
Printed in the USA
BVHW05183525042 2
634746BV00001B/2